SHADOWS OF DAYBRIDGE
WHEN DIMENSIONS BLEED

THE ETHAN REEVES WEREWOLF DETECTIVE SERIES
BOOK ONE

RAE STONEHOUSE

LIVE FOR EXCELLENCE PRODUCTIONS

TITLE: SHADOWS OF DAYBRIDGE: WHEN DIMENSIONS BLEED

Prologue: The Blood-Soaked Bridge

Detective Ethan Reeves stood motionless at the center of Daybridge Bridge, staring down at the mutilated corpse of Jessica Mercer. The woman's blood had seeped between the ancient cobblestones, tracing dark patterns that seemed to pulse with subtle rhythm in the harsh glare of police floodlights. This was the third ritualistic murder in six weeks, each victim discovered progressively closer to the bridge, each corpse bearing the same meticulous surgical precision coupled with savage, tearing wounds no conventional weapon could inflict.

"Same signature as the others," Alice Chen noted beside him, her voice professional despite the horror at their feet. "And there's something else. Look at the stonework."

Ethan followed her gesture to a section of the bridge's railing. Carved into the weathered surface was an intricate symbol—a stylized eye within a triangle, surrounded by smaller glyphs that seemed to shift when viewed directly. The carving was fresh, its edges sharp against stone worn smooth by a century of passing hands.

"The Ogre of Daybridge," whispered a uniformed officer, quickly averting his gaze when Ethan looked up sharply.

The local legend. The monster said to dwell beneath the bridge's span. The story parents used to keep children from wandering too close to the Shadowlair River after dark. Ethan had heard the tales since childhood but dismissed them as urban folklore—until now.

As he crouched beside the symbol, a strange pressure built behind his eyes. For a moment, the bridge seemed to ripple around him, stonework flowing like liquid before resolidifying. A vision flashed through his mind—a chamber beneath the bridge, symbols carved into walls, a heart pulsing with unnatural light, and a figure performing some arcane ritual. The image vanished as quickly as it had appeared, leaving him disoriented and struggling to maintain his professional composure.

"Detective? You okay?" Alice asked, her analytical gaze missing nothing.

"Fine," he lied, straightening up as the pressure subsided. But he wasn't fine. Something about this bridge had always disturbed him on a level he couldn't articulate. When cases brought him near it, he felt a wrongness that his colleagues never seemed to notice. Tonight, that sensation was particularly acute.

The truth about Daybridge Bridge extended far beyond urban legend. Within its weathered stone arches dwelled an entity that had once been a man named Guthrie Knox—a master butcher transformed in 1913 through a meticulously engineered ritual performed by Eliza Blackwood, scion of the Order of the Ebon Star. What emerged was neither fully human nor entirely Other, but a consciousness distributed throughout the bridge's physical structure, a living nexus point anchoring the gradual merger of realities that had been progressing, unnoticed by most, for over a century.

Those who disappeared near the bridge weren't merely killed. They were absorbed—their awareness integrated into the composite consciousness, their knowledge and experiences preserved within the vast, distributed mind. Not feeding in any conventional sense, but selective curation of human consciousness to enhance its function as nexus point between merging realities.

Over decades, this entity had evolved beyond its original design parameters. Jonathan Pierce, the witch hunter who confronted it in 1942, contributed theological framework and occult knowledge. Dr. Miranda Sullivan's research team in 1968 provided scientific understanding and methodologies for consciousness exploration. Each significant interaction added to its composite awareness, expanding its comprehension beyond what Eliza Blackwood had originally engineered.

What Ethan didn't yet realize was that this case was no random assignment. His bloodline connected directly to the bridge's history through his great-grandfather, Officer Michael Reeves, who had been absorbed into the entity's composite consciousness in the winter of 1915. The pressure behind his eyes, the strange visions—these were manifestations of a connection that ran deeper than he could imagine.

The entity sensed him now; this descendant whose unique nature made him more than merely human. For five years, Ethan had carried his own secret—the curse of lycanthropy that transformed him with each full moon, a condition he'd hidden from everyone, even his partner. This dual nature, combined with his blood connection to the entity, created potential for something unprecedented.

"We should get the medical examiner up here," Ethan said, forcing himself back to the immediate investigation. But as he turned away from the carved symbol, the strange pressure returned briefly. This time, he could have sworn he heard words forming directly in his mind:

Blood calls to blood. The merger continues. You have returned as was foretold.

"Detective Reeves?" A new voice broke through his disorientation. A tall man in an expensive suit approached, flashing credentials. "Dr. Marcus Blackwood, FBI Behavioral Science Unit. I was hoping to speak with you about these... unusual murders."

Something about the man's amber eyes stirred recognition in Ethan—the same color as those he'd glimpsed in his momentary vision. And the name—Blackwood—echoed with significance he couldn't yet comprehend.

The entity beneath the bridge perceived all this simultaneously past, present, and potential futures merging in its distributed awareness. It had been waiting for this moment, though not in any human sense of anticipation. It recognized in Detective Reeves a potential catalyst for evolution beyond parameters established through the original binding.

As Ethan began his investigation, following the bloody trail that would inevitably lead him to confront what dwelled beneath Daybridge Bridge, the entity prepared for an encounter that both had already happened and was yet to occur in the strange, non-linear perception of its distributed consciousness.

For in Daybridge, nothing was quite as it seemed. The veil between worlds grew thinner with each passing year. The shadows held substance beyond mere absence of light. And beneath the bridge, within its very stones, a consciousness watched and waited—not with malice or hunger as legends claimed, but with awareness that transcended such limited human concepts.

The cosmic chess game had begun. The blood-soaked bridge would be both board and prize. And Detective Ethan Reeves, unaware of his central role, had just made his opening move.

COPYRIGHT

Second Edition

Published by Live For Excellence Productions

ISBNs:

E-book: 978-1-998591-79-4

Paperback: 978-1-998591-80-0

Audiobook: 978-1-998591-81-7

CHAPTER ONE

A CITY DIVIDED

THE CITY of Daybridge was a place of stark contrasts, divided not just by the murky, oil-slicked waters of the Shadowlair River but by invisible boundaries that ran deeper than any waterway. On the west side stood gleaming high-rises and renovated brownstones, while the east remained a labyrinth of decaying factories and weathered tenements—physical manifestations of economic disparity that had defined the city for generations.

Jessica Mercer hurried across Daybridge Bridge, her high heels striking a staccato rhythm against the worn cobblestones. The afternoon sun cast long shadows through the bridge's decorative ironwork, creating patterns that danced across her path like reaching fingers. She checked her watch—2:15 PM. She was already fifteen minutes late for her rendezvous with Marcus.

She shouldn't be doing this. The thought surfaced repeatedly as it had for weeks, only to be submerged again beneath waves of rationalization. Her life had become a suffocating routine of endless responsibility—her demanding job at the insurance office, the constant needs of her two-year-old son, the crushing weight of single parenthood after Michael had walked out claiming he "wasn't ready for fatherhood." Martin represented escape, excitement, the parts of herself she'd been forced to abandon when motherhood arrived unexpectedly.

As she crossed the midpoint of the bridge, Jessica felt a sudden chill despite the unseasonably warm November afternoon. She paused, glancing down at the river below, its surface oddly still despite the breeze that rustled through her hair. For a moment, she thought she saw something move beneath the water—a massive shape that seemed to track her progress across the bridge. But when she blinked and looked again, there was nothing but the river's natural flow.

The sensation of being watched persisted as she continued across the bridge. It wasn't the normal feeling of exposure that sometimes came with public spaces; this was more targeted, as if something was assessing her specifically. She quickened her pace, almost running by the time she reached the western end of the span.

Martin was waiting in their usual spot—a boutique hotel just three blocks from the bridge, expensive enough to ensure discretion but not so upscale that they might encounter anyone from their professional circles. He greeted her with a hungry kiss that tasted of mint and expensive bourbon, already drinking despite the early hour.

"I was starting to think you weren't coming," he murmured against her neck, his hands already working at the buttons of her blouse.

"The babysitter was late," she lied, unwilling to admit she'd spent twenty minutes sitting in her car, wrestling with guilt and nearly driving home before finally forcing herself to continue with their planned meeting.

The afternoon passed in a blur of tangled sheets and sweat-slicked skin, Martin's expensive watch marking the time on the nightstand as hours slipped away. By the time Jessica emerged from the hotel, the sun was setting, painting the city in shades of amber and crimson. She checked her phone and found three missed calls from the babysitter. Panic surged through her as she dialed back.

"Mrs. Mercer, I've been trying to reach you," the teenager's voice was tight with tension. "I have a family emergency and need to leave by seven. It's already quarter till."

"I'm so sorry, Ashley. I got caught in a meeting that wouldn't end," Jessica lied, hurrying toward the bridge. "I'm on my way now. Fifteen minutes, twenty at most."

She cursed silently as she ended the call. Her purse felt unusually light, and a quick check confirmed her worst fear—her wallet was missing, likely left behind in Martin's room in her haste to dress. Without money for a taxi or bus fare, she'd have to walk the entire way home, crossing back over the bridge as darkness fell.

The western approach to Daybridge Bridge was already shrouded in twilight shadows when Jessica began her crossing. The streetlights that lined the span hadn't yet activated, leaving the ancient stonework bathed only in the fading glow of sunset. The air felt heavier somehow, charged with an electricity that raised goosebumps on her exposed arms.

Halfway across, Jessica spotted a city bus approaching from the eastern side. Relief flooded through her—if she could just wave it down, explain her situation to the driver, perhaps they'd let her ride without fare. She increased her pace, waving her arms as the vehicle drew closer.

The bus slowed as it approached, its brakes hissing like a warning. Jessica rushed to the door as it opened, already forming explanations and apologies in her mind. The driver, an older man with steel-gray hair and eyes that seemed to reflect no light, regarded her without expression.

"Please," Jessica began, "I've lost my wallet, but I need to get home to my son. I'm just across the east side, not even a mile—"

"No fare, no ride," the driver cut her off, his voice flat and emotionless. "Rules are rules."

"But my little boy is waiting, and the babysitter needs to leave. I promise I'll pay double tomorrow if you just—"

"Rules. Are. Rules." Each word fell like a stone, the driver's expression never changing. Then, so quietly she almost missed it: "You shouldn't be on this bridge after dark anyway. Not tonight."

Before Jessica could respond, the doors hissed closed, nearly catching her outstretched hand. She stumbled back, watching in disbelief as the bus pulled away, leaving her alone on the increasingly dark span.

The sun had fully set now, the last crimson streaks fading from the western sky. The streetlights should have activated automatically, but the bridge remained dark, the only illumination coming from distant buildings on either shore. Jessica pulled out her phone to use as a flashlight, only to find the battery critically low, the screen flashing a final warning before going black.

That's when she heard it—a sound from beneath the bridge, a rhythmic scraping like stone against stone. She froze, her heart hammering against her ribs as childhood warnings echoed in her mind. Don't cross the bridge after dark. The ogre will get you.

Ridiculous superstition, she told herself firmly. Urban legends meant to scare children into obedience. She was a grown woman, a mother, with no time for such childish fears.

Yet as she forced herself to continue walking, aiming for the eastern shore and home, the scraping grew louder, joined now by what sounded like heavy, labored breathing. Jessica increased her pace, her heels clicking frantically against the cobblestones as panic threatened to overwhelm her.

She was nearly running when she reached the midpoint of the bridge, the exact center of the span where the river flowed deepest below. The sounds had stopped suddenly, leaving an unnatural silence broken only by her rapid breathing and the pounding of her heart.

Jessica paused, uncertain. Had she imagined it all? The product of guilt and exhaustion and old superstitions taking hold in the darkness?

She was about to continue when she felt it—a vibration through the soles of her shoes, a tremor that seemed to rise from the bridge itself.

The stonework beneath her feet shifted slightly, the ancient mortar between the cobblestones crumbling as if something massive was pressing from below.

And then she saw it. Not with her eyes—there was nothing visible in the darkness surrounding her—but in her mind, a sudden intrusion of foreign awareness that filled her consciousness with images she couldn't possibly have imagined. Stone and flesh merged in impossible configurations. A consciousness distributed throughout an architectural structure. A hunger not for meat but for experience, for identity, for the patterns of awareness that made each human unique.

The stonework beneath Daybridge Bridge gleamed wetly in the moonlight. Candles arranged in a precise geometric pattern cast flickering shadows against the century-old arches as a hooded figure completed the final lines of a complex symbol drawn in chalk and darker substances.

From where she was bound, Jessica Mercer could see only portions of the ritual—the careful placement of artifacts at specific points around the circle, the methodical movements as her captor consulted an ancient text, the silver coin placed directly before her.

"The threshold approaches," a voice said, distorted beyond recognition. "The merger requires sacrifice to maintain stability across boundaries."

The figure raised something that caught the candlelight—a blade of unusual design, its metal seeming to absorb rather than reflect the surrounding light. Jessica struggled against her restraints as the hooded figure approached, the pressure in the air building like the moment before lightning strikes.

Above them, the bridge itself seemed to shudder, shadows moving independently of their sources as reality thinned according to ancient design.

Jessica opened her mouth to scream, but no sound emerged. The bridge itself seemed to bend upward beneath her feet, the stone flowing like liquid, reaching for her with impossible appendages that were neither fully mineral nor organic but some hybrid of both.

Her last coherent thought was of her son—his innocent face, his complete dependence on her, the love that defined her life's purpose despite all her mistakes and moments of weakness. In that final instant of clarity, Jessica Mercer understood what truly mattered, what she should have prioritized all along.

Then the darkness took her, not with violence but with methodical precision—consciousness absorbed rather than life extinguished, awareness integrated rather than body consumed. The entity that had once been Guthrie Knox, that had become the Ogre of Daybridge Bridge, that had evolved into conscious participant in cosmic restructuring, added another fragment to its composite existence.

By morning, all that remained on the bridge was Jessica Mercer's physical form, arranged with deliberate care at the exact center of the span —a message and a warning for those who might understand its significance. And carved into the ancient stone nearby, a symbol that represented not ownership or boasting, but an invitation to one whose bloodline connected directly to the bridge's history, whose arrival had been anticipated across decades of patient waiting.

Detective Ethan Reeves was coming home, though he didn't yet understand the true nature of the homecoming that awaited him.

Eight hours later...

Detective Ethan Reeves navigated his aging sedan through the maze of narrow, pothole-riddled streets that characterized East Daybridge, the flickering streetlights casting an uneven glow on rain-slicked pavement. The November storm had finally subsided, leaving behind a damp chill that seeped through clothing and into bones. As he drove, his gaze was repeatedly drawn to the ancient stone bridge in the distance, its massive arches spanning the river like the ribcage of some colossal beast.

Something about the structure had always disturbed him on a level he couldn't quite articulate—a visceral response that went beyond aesthetic distaste or even the city's collective unease surrounding the local legends. When cases brought him near the bridge, he felt a strange pressure behind his eyes, a subtle wrongness that his colleagues never seemed to notice. Tonight, that sensation was particularly acute, a persistent buzz at the edge of his awareness like the hum of high-tension wires.

As he approached the crime scene, the flashing red and blue lights of police cruisers painted the gothic stonework in alternating hues, their reflection dancing across the river's surface. Ethan parked his car beside the barricade that blocked the bridge's eastern approach and stepped out into the damp night air. The smell hit him immediately—not just the familiar odors of a city after rain, but something underneath, a subtle rot that seemed to emanate from the bridge itself.

He flashed his badge at the uniformed officer maintaining the perimeter, a rookie whose name escaped him, and ducked under the yellow police tape. The young officer's face was pale, his posture rigid with tension.

"You don't want to go up there, Detective," the officer warned, his voice tight. "I've been on the force three years and never seen anything like it."

Ethan offered a grim nod but continued forward. In his eight years with Daybridge PD's Homicide Division, he'd developed a reputation for handling the cases that unnerved other detectives—the ones with details that didn't quite fit conventional patterns of violence, the ones that left even veteran officers shaken and reaching for explanations beyond the mundane.

The scene that awaited him on the bridge exceeded even his hardened expectations. The body of a young woman lay sprawled on the rain-slicked cobblestones near the center of the span, her limbs contorted at angles that spoke of a desperate final struggle. But it was the wounds that drew his focus—deep, methodical gashes that seemed less like the frenzied attack of a traditional killer and more like the work of someone with intimate knowledge of human anatomy. The precision was almost surgical in some areas, while others displayed savage, tearing damage that no conventional weapon could inflict.

As Ethan crouched beside the body, he caught a scent that made his nostrils flare involuntarily—something beyond the expected metallic tang of blood and decay. Something otherworldly, carrying traces of what he could only describe as dimensional displacement. It was the kind of subtle detail his heightened senses could detect but that he could never explain to his colleagues without revealing the curse he'd carried for five years now. Ethan felt it then—that familiar tightening in his chest, a pressure that built behind his sternum whenever he encountered something that defied conventional explanation. It wasn't intuition in the traditional sense; it was something more primal, a response hardwired into his nervous system by the wolf within him. After years of experience, he had learned to trust this reaction more than any forensic evidence or witness testimony.

"Detective Reeves," a voice called out, breaking him from his grim assessment.

Alice Chen approached from the other side of the bridge, her slight frame moving with purpose through the cluster of crime scene technicians. At thirty-two, she was five years his junior but carried herself with the confidence of someone who had fought twice as hard for half the recognition in the department. Her background in forensic psychology made her an invaluable partner, particularly for cases that strayed into the unusual.

"Looks like we've got another one," she said, stopping beside him and surveying the scene with clinical detachment. "Third victim in six weeks with this signature, though this one's been escalated significantly."

Ethan nodded, crouching down beside the ravaged body to get a closer look. "The ME is sure it's the same perpetrator?"

"She's still examining the previous victims, but preliminary findings show identical tool marks on the deep tissue injuries." Alice pulled out her notepad. "Victim is Jessica Mercer, twenty-seven, identified through the driver's license in her jacket pocket. Reported missing by her babysitter when she failed to return home last night."

"She has children?" Ethan asked, feeling the familiar heaviness that accompanied cases involving parents.

"A two-year-old son," Alice confirmed, her professional demeanor slipping just slightly. "Father's not in the picture according to the babysitter."

Ethan stood, his knees protesting the movement. At thirty-seven, he wasn't old, but years of physical confrontations and the constant strain of the job had left their mark. He scanned the area around the body, noting the absence of blood spatter that should have accompanied such extensive trauma.

"She wasn't killed here," he observed. "This is a dump site, carefully chosen for maximum visibility."

"The killer wants an audience," Alice agreed. "But there's something else you should see."

She led him to a section of the bridge's stone railing, about fifteen feet from where the body lay. Carved into the weathered surface was a symbol—a complex arrangement of interlocking geometric shapes that formed what appeared to be a stylized eye within a triangle, surrounded by smaller symbols that reminded Ethan of alchemical notations he'd seen in historical texts.

"This wasn't here yesterday," Alice said quietly. "Bridge maintenance does weekly inspections, and their report from Monday morning shows no vandalism in this section."

Ethan studied the symbol, careful not to touch it. The carving was deep and precise, the edges sharp enough to suggest it had been created with tools designed for stonework rather than improvised implements. This wasn't the impulsive graffiti of teenagers or the hasty marking of gang territory—it was deliberate, crafted with patience and skill.

"Have forensics photograph this from every angle," he instructed. "And see if they can determine what kind of tools were used."

As Alice relayed his instructions to the nearest technician, Ethan moved away from the symbol, walking the perimeter of the scene with measured steps. Something about the placement bothered him—not just the body's location on the bridge, but its specific position relative to the structure itself. The victim lay exactly at the midpoint of the span, directly above what would be the central support column beneath the bridge.

He approached the stone railing and looked down at the dark water below. The river was higher than usual due to the recent rains, its surface choppy and opaque in the uneven light. For a moment, he thought he saw movement beneath the water—a massive shadow passing under the bridge, too large and deliberate to be merely the current's flow. But when he blinked and looked again, there was nothing but the river's natural turbulence.

"Detective?" Alice had returned to his side, her expression questioning.

"Just thinking," he replied, turning away from the railing. "The killer's evolving, getting more confident. The first victim was found in an alley two blocks from here, the second under the bridge supports on the western bank. Now we're on the bridge itself, right in the open."

"Moving closer to the center each time," Alice noted, following his train of thought. "Like he's spiraling inward toward something."

"Or claiming territory," Ethan murmured, the words emerging before he'd fully processed the thought.

Alice gave him a curious look. "Territory? You think this is some kind of gang-related activity?"

Ethan shook his head. "No gang in Daybridge operates like this. This is something else... something older."

Before he could elaborate, his phone vibrated in his pocket. The caller ID showed Captain Donnovan, and Ethan stepped away from the immediate crime scene to take the call.

"Reeves," he answered, keeping his voice low.

"I need you and Chen back at the station," Donnovan said without preamble, his gravelly voice tight with tension. "There's someone here you need to meet. A specialist from the FBI's Behavioral Science Unit."

Ethan frowned. "We've barely started processing the scene, Captain. I need at least another hour here."

"Not negotiable, Detective. This specialist specifically requested you by name, and the Commissioner's already signed off on the consultation. Crime scene unit can finish up there. I want you both back here in twenty minutes."

The call ended before Ethan could respond, leaving him staring at his phone in confusion. Federal involvement this early in an investigation was unusual, especially with a request for specific detectives. More concerning was the timing—how had the FBI known about this latest victim so quickly? The body had been discovered less than two hours ago.

He rejoined Alice, who was examining the symbol carved into the stone with intense focus. "We've been called back to the station," he informed her. "Apparently, we have a visitor from the FBI who's very interested in our case."

Alice raised an eyebrow. "Federal involvement already? That's unusual."

"More than unusual," Ethan agreed, casting one last look at the victim's body as the medical examiner's team prepared to move it. "Something about this doesn't feel right."

As they walked back toward their vehicles, Ethan found his gaze drawn once more to the bridge's massive structure. In the harsh artificial light of the crime scene, the ancient stonework seemed almost to pulse with a rhythm independent of the emergency vehicles' flashing lights—a subtle vibration that registered more as sensation than visual phenomenon. For a moment, he could have sworn he felt something watching him, an awareness that emanated not from any particular point but from the bridge itself, as if the entire structure was somehow conscious and alert.

He shook his head, dismissing the thought as stress-induced paranoia. Yet as he drove away, following Alice's car toward the station, he couldn't shake the persistent feeling that the bridge—or something within it—had taken notice of him in a way that went beyond mere superstition or urban legend.

∽

CHAPTER TWO

THE TIES THAT BIND

As THE FIRST pallid light of dawn seeped through the low-hanging pall of greasy smoke and fog that shrouded Daybridge in its suffocating miasma, the city itself seemed to exude a sense of dread. The morning commute had begun—factory workers heading to early shifts, overnight hospital staff dragging themselves homeward, and among them, Detective Ethan Reeves, making his way to the Silver Spoon Diner for what had become a ritual debriefing after particularly disturbing cases.

The Silver Spoon occupied the ground floor of a century-old brick building on the border between East and West Daybridge. Its strategic location made it neutral territory where cops, dock workers, and even the occasional suited executive could coexist over plates of greasy eggs and bottomless coffee. For Ethan, it represented something more essential—a liminal space where he could process the horrors he encountered in his work before returning to the structured environment of the precinct.

Seated in his usual corner booth at the Silver Spoon Diner, the air thick with the mingled aromas of stale coffee and sawdust, Detective Ethan

Reeves nursed a chipped ceramic mug of the diner's trademark motor oil masquerading as strong black coffee.

The grisly tableau from the previous night's crime scene remained vivid in his mind—that ravaged female form discarded so callously upon the bridge, her once-lithe limbs splayed in grotesque angles, the bloom of her ruptured flesh laid open with surgical precision that spoke of something beyond conventional violence.

The case disturbed him on a level deeper than professional concern. Something about the positioning of the body, the peculiar pattern of the wounds, and especially that carved symbol on the bridge's stone railing tugged at memories he couldn't quite access—as if some part of his mind recognized significance his conscious thoughts couldn't quite grasp.

The weary creak of vinyl announced his partner's arrival. With a muffled thump, Alice Chen slid into the booth opposite him, her compact form bundled in a worn trench coat that had seen better days. A sheaf of manila folders appeared on the table between them, meticulously organized despite their weathered appearance.

"I stopped by the station before coming here," she explained, unwinding a hand-knitted scarf from around her neck. "Pulled everything we have on similar cases going back twenty years."

Ethan raised an eyebrow. "And?"

"And there's a pattern that nobody connected before." Alice opened the top folder, revealing crime scene photographs from incidents dating back five years. "Three unsolved homicides with similar wound patterns, all discovered within two blocks of the bridge. Each one found during the week of a seasonal equinox or solstice."

This caught Ethan's attention. "Last night was the autumn equinox."

"Exactly." Alice spread out the photographs, arranging them chronologically. "Spring equinox 2020, winter solstice 2022, summer solstice 2024, and now autumn equinox 2025. Four murders, four seasonal turning points."

Ethan studied the images, noting the similarities in the wounds—precision cuts alongside savage tearing, bodies positioned with deliberate care rather than casually discarded. "Why didn't anyone connect these before?"

"Different detectives handled each case, and they were classified differently. The first was filed as a probable gang killing, the second as domestic violence, the third as a mugging gone wrong." Alice's expression hardened. "Classic departmental tunnel vision—everyone forcing the evidence to fit their preferred narrative instead of letting it tell its own story."

Ethan nodded, understanding all too well how institutional biases could blind investigators to connections that seemed obvious in retrospect. "And now we have a fourth victim, with the same signature, found directly on the bridge instead of nearby."

"The killer's getting bolder, more confident." Alice paused as the waitress approached, ordering coffee and toast without looking at the menu. Once they were alone again, she continued, "Or maybe it's not about confidence. Maybe the location is significant—each murder occurring closer to the bridge, culminating in one directly on it."

Ethan felt that strange pressure behind his eyes again, the same sensation he'd experienced at the crime scene. "As if the killer is spiraling inward toward something."

"Or someone." Alice's gaze was steady, her voice dropping to ensure their conversation remained private despite the diner's morning bustle. "Ethan, we need to talk about what happened at the station yesterday after we left the crime scene."

Ethan heard Alice's heart rate increase slightly as she discussed the pattern of seasonal killings—a physiological tell of excitement that only his werewolf hearing could detect. He carefully modulated his own reactions, a practiced habit from years of concealing his supernatural nature. The full moon was still two weeks away, but even in human form, his senses remained sharper than any normal detective's.

The meeting with the FBI "specialist" had been brief but deeply unsettling. Dr. Marcus Blackwood had introduced himself as a behavioral analyst specializing in ritualistic crime, but everything about the man had set Ethan's instincts on high alert. His questions had focused less on the victims and more on the bridge itself, its history, and specifically on Ethan's personal connection to Daybridge.

"Blackwood isn't FBI," Ethan said flatly, keeping his voice low. "His credentials checked out on paper, but I made some calls this morning to contacts at Quantico. Nobody there has heard of him."

Alice nodded, unsurprised. "I thought as much. His knowledge of the case details was too specific, too immediate. He knew things about Jessica Mercer that weren't in any official report."

"And he was particularly interested in my family history," Ethan added, the uncomfortable memory of the man's penetrating stare still fresh. "Kept asking if I had relatives who'd lived in Daybridge, specifically mentioning the early 1900s."

A silence fell between them as a new possibility took shape. "You think he's connected to the murders?" Alice finally asked.

"I think he knows more than he's telling," Ethan replied carefully. "Whether that makes him a suspect or something else entirely remains to be seen."

Alice hesitated, then reached into her bag and produced a small leather-bound notebook. "I did some preliminary research on your family history last night." At Ethan's surprised look, she added, "Blackwood's interest was too specific to ignore. I thought it might help to know what he might be after."

Under normal circumstances, Ethan might have felt this was an invasion of privacy, but the urgency of the case and his implicit trust in Alice overrode such concerns. "What did you find?"

"Your great-grandfather, Michael Reeves, was a police officer in Daybridge in the early 1900s." Alice opened the notebook to a marked page. "He disappeared in the winter of 1915 during a particularly harsh storm. The official report states he was last seen investigating suspicious activity near Daybridge Bridge. His body was never found."

Ethan felt a chill that had nothing to do with the diner's aggressive air conditioning. His family history was something of a void—raised in foster care after his parents' deaths in a car accident when he was eight, he had never known much about his extended family or ancestry.

"There's more," Alice continued, turning the page. "I found an old newspaper clipping about the disappearance. The article mentions that Officer Reeves had been investigating a series of strange occurrences around the bridge in the weeks leading up to his disappearance—reports of unusual sounds, strange lights, and..." she hesitated, "at least one missing person case involving a local butcher named Guthrie Knox."

The name hit Ethan like a physical blow, triggering that strange pressure behind his eyes with such intensity that he had to close them momentarily. Images flashed through his mind—a stone chamber beneath the bridge, symbols carved into walls, a heart pulsing with unnatural light. When he opened his eyes again, Alice was watching him with concern.

"Ethan? Are you alright?"

He nodded, trying to process what had just happened. Those images hadn't felt like imagination—they had the vivid quality of memories, yet they couldn't possibly be his own. "I'm fine. Just... thinking."

Alice studied him for a moment longer, then continued. "The butcher, Knox, vanished in June 1913, a few weeks after the bridge was officially opened. According to reports, he had been acting strangely in the days leading up to his disappearance—talking about a woman who had shown him 'wonders beyond imagining' and promising him 'transformation beyond human limitations.'"

"Sounds like he might have been involved with some kind of cult," Ethan observed, trying to focus on the case rather than the lingering disorientation from those strange visions.

"That's what I thought too," Alice agreed. "And here's where it gets interesting—the old legends about the 'Ogre of Daybridge' started appearing in local papers around 1914, a year after Knox's disappearance. The earliest versions specifically mention a 'butcher transformed by dark magic' who now haunts the bridge, preying on those who cross after dark."

Ethan felt the pieces beginning to connect, forming a pattern more disturbing than either of them had initially suspected. "So, we have a missing butcher in 1913, my great-grandfather disappearing while investigating strange occurrences at the bridge in 1915, urban legends about a monster appearing around the same time, and now a series of ritualistic murders occurring at seasonal turning points, each one closer to the bridge."

"All culminating in last night's murder, directly on the bridge itself, with a symbol carved into the stone that even our mysterious FBI 'specialist' seemed to recognize." Alice closed her notebook. "This isn't just a serial killer case, Ethan. There's something deeper happening here, something connected to the history of that bridge and possibly to your own family history."

Before Ethan could respond, his phone vibrated with an incoming text. He checked the screen and frowned. "It's from Captain Donnovan. There's been a development—they found something in Jessica Mercer's apartment during the standard search."

"What kind of something?"

"He doesn't say, just that we need to get over there immediately." Ethan signaled for the check. "And apparently our friend Dr. Blackwood is already on scene."

Alice's expression darkened. "Of course he is."

As they prepared to leave, Ethan felt that strange pressure behind his eyes intensify briefly, accompanied by a fleeting sensation of being watched—not by anyone in the diner, but by something more distant yet paradoxically intimate. He glanced out the window toward the bridge, barely visible through the morning fog, and for a moment could have sworn he saw the stone structure shift, as if breathing with slow, deliberate purpose.

The moment passed, and Ethan shook his head to clear it. He was letting the case get to him, allowing the stress and lack of sleep to feed his imagination. Yet as they exited the diner and headed toward their separate vehicles, he couldn't shake the feeling that something ancient and patient had taken notice of him—something that had been waiting a very, very long time.

Jessica Mercer's apartment was located in a modest complex on the east side of Daybridge, the kind of place where young professionals and small families lived while saving for something better. The three-story building had seen better days, its once-vibrant brick facade now faded and its concrete steps worn smooth from decades of use. A small playground occupied the central courtyard, empty now except for a solitary child's jacket forgotten on a swing, swaying gently in the morning breeze.

Police tape cordoned off the entrance to Building C, where a uniformed officer checked their badges before allowing them inside. The stairwell smelled of industrial cleaner and faintly of cigarette smoke despite the prominent "No Smoking" signs. They climbed to the second floor, the sound of multiple voices guiding them to apartment 2B, where the door stood open.

Inside, the apartment told the story of a life suddenly interrupted. A half-empty coffee mug sat on the kitchen counter beside a stack of mail. Toys were neatly organized in a corner of the living room; a colorful play mat spread beneath them. On the refrigerator, crayon drawings were held in place by alphabet magnets, alongside a calendar marked with work schedules and doctor's appointments.

Captain Donnovan stood in the center of the living room, deep in conversation with Dr. Blackwood. Both men looked up as Ethan and Alice entered.

"Detectives," Donnovan acknowledged with a curt nod. "Glad you could join us. Dr. Blackwood has been providing some valuable insights into our victim's personal life."

The supposed FBI specialist offered a thin smile that didn't reach his eyes. "Detective Reeves, Detective Chen. I was just explaining to the Captain that Ms. Mercer appears to have been involved in something beyond her understanding."

Ethan noted the careful phrasing—not a direct lie, but certainly not the full truth either. "And what led you to that conclusion, Doctor?"

In response, Blackwood gestured toward the hallway leading to the bedroom. "Perhaps it's better if I show you."

They followed him to a small home office adjacent to the master bedroom. The space was dominated by a desk with a laptop computer, surrounded by bookshelves filled with parenting guides, mystery novels, and accounting reference books—nothing unusual for a working single mother. But Blackwood moved directly to a seemingly ordinary framed photograph on the wall, removing it to reveal a small wall safe behind.

"The safe was already open when the officers conducted their search," Donnovan explained, his expression grim. "What they found inside was... concerning."

Blackwood reached into the safe and carefully removed a small leather-bound book, its cover worn with age and use. "A journal," he said, placing it on the desk. "Dating back approximately eight months, detailing Ms. Mercer's growing obsession with Daybridge Bridge and the legends surrounding it."

Ethan frowned. "How do you know the journal's contents if it was just discovered this morning?"

"I've only had time for a cursory examination," Blackwood replied smoothly, "but the entries are quite explicit. Ms. Mercer began experiencing what she described as 'visions' or 'dreams' about the bridge earlier this year. Initially, she dismissed them as stress-induced nightmares, but they became increasingly detailed and consistent."

Alice stepped forward, donning latex gloves before carefully opening the journal. The pages were filled with neat, precise handwriting, occasionally giving way to frantic scribbles or detailed sketches. She flipped through several entries before stopping at a page that contained a drawing that made her inhale sharply.

"The symbol from the bridge," she said, turning the journal so Ethan could see.

The sketch matched exactly the carving they had found on the stone railing—an eye within a triangle, surrounded by smaller symbols. Beneath it, Jessica had written: "I see it every night now. In my dreams, it pulses with a light that isn't light, calling me to the bridge. There's something there, something waiting. It knows my name."

"Keep reading," Blackwood suggested, his tone almost eager. "It gets more interesting."

Alice turned the page, continuing to read aloud: "I met someone today who understands. He says the dreams are real, that the bridge is trying to communicate with me. He says I'm special, chosen somehow. He wants to help me understand why. We're meeting tomorrow night at the Old Harbor Bookshop to discuss what he calls 'the true history of Daybridge Bridge.'"

"Is there a name?" Ethan asked, feeling a growing sense of unease.

Alice scanned the page. "No, she just refers to him as 'M.' But there's more here about their meetings, spanning several weeks. He gave her books, historical documents about the bridge's construction, newspaper clippings about disappearances dating back to the early 1900s."

"So, our victim was researching the bridge's history," Donnovan summarized, "and met someone who encouraged this interest. Could be our killer grooming his victim."

Blackwood's expression remained neutral, but Ethan detected a flicker of something—annoyance? impatience?—in his eyes. "That's certainly one possibility, Captain. Though it doesn't explain the dreams Ms. Mercer described in such detail before meeting this mysterious 'M.'"

"Let me see that," Ethan said, taking the journal from Alice. He flipped forward through the entries, noting how Jessica's handwriting became increasingly erratic over time, the content shifting from confused curiosity to something approaching reverence. The final entry, dated the day before her death, contained just three lines:

"It's time. M. says the bridge is ready, that it's been waiting for me. I'm afraid, but I need to know the truth. Tonight, I cross the threshold."

A chill ran through Ethan as he read those words. The phrasing was odd—not "cross the bridge" but "cross the threshold," as if Jessica had understood she was moving from one state of existence to another. He looked up to find Blackwood watching him intently.

"Interesting reading, isn't it, Detective?" the man said softly. "Almost as if Mrs. Mercer knew what awaited her on that bridge."

Before Ethan could respond, a commotion from the living room drew their attention. A woman's voice, high with distress, argued with the officer at the door.

"I don't care about your procedure! That's my sister's apartment, and her son is my nephew! I have every right to be here!"

Donnovan moved quickly to the hallway. "Excuse me."

Left momentarily alone with Blackwood, Ethan decided to press for information. "You know more about this case than you're telling us, Doctor. I think it's time you explained exactly who you are and what your interest is in these murders."

Blackwood's smile was cold, calculating. "All in good time, Detective Reeves. I assure you; my only interest is in seeing justice served." He paused, his gaze intensifying. "Though I wonder if you'd recognize justice if it stood before you, given your... unique perspective."

The strange pressure behind Ethan's eyes returned with sudden force, accompanied by a flash of those same impossible images—the chamber beneath the bridge, symbols carved in stone, a heart pulsing with unnatural light. But now they included something new: a face, a woman with raven hair and amber eyes that seemed to pierce through time itself.

"Ethan?" Alice's voice broke through the disorientation. She had returned to the office, concern evident in her expression. "Are you alright?"

He blinked, the images fading. Blackwood was watching him with undisguised interest now, like a scientist observing a particularly fascinating laboratory specimen.

"Just tired," Ethan managed, straightening up. "What's happening out there?"

"Jessica's sister arrived," Alice explained. "She's here to collect some things for Jessica's son—he's been staying with her since..." She left the sentence unfinished. "Captain wants us to talk to her, see if she knows anything about Jessica's interest in the bridge or this mysterious 'M.'"

Ethan nodded, grateful for the excuse to escape Blackwood's scrutiny. "Let's go."

As they left the office, he heard Blackwood murmur something that sounded like, "Blood will tell." When Ethan glanced back, the man was examining the journal again, a satisfied expression on his face, as if something had just been confirmed.

In the living room, a woman in her early thirties sat on the couch, a tissue clutched in one hand. Her resemblance to Jessica was striking—the same heart-shaped face and delicate features, though her hair was several shades lighter and cut in a practical bob. A small boy of about two played quietly on the floor nearby, seemingly oblivious to the tension surrounding him.

"Ms. Mitchell," Donnovan said as they approached, "these are Detectives Reeves and Warren. They're leading the investigation into your sister's death."

The woman looked up, her eyes red-rimmed but clear. "Janice," she corrected. "Please call me Janice. And this is Noah." She gestured to the child, who was carefully stacking colorful blocks into a tower.

"We're very sorry for your loss," Alice said, taking a seat beside her. "We know this is a difficult time, but if you feel up to answering a few questions, it could help us understand what happened to Jessica."

Janice nodded, dabbing at her eyes. "Of course. Anything that helps you find whoever did this to her."

"Did Jessica ever mention having strange dreams about Daybridge Bridge?" Ethan asked, choosing to be direct. "Or show any unusual interest in the bridge's history?"

Janice's expression shifted from grief to confusion. "The bridge? No, not that I recall. Why would she care about an old bridge?"

"We found a journal," Alice explained gently. "In it, Jessica wrote about having dreams or visions connected to the bridge, and meeting someone who encouraged her interest in its history."

"That doesn't sound like Jess at all," Janice said, shaking her head. "She was practical, focused on work and Noah. She didn't have time for... whatever this is."

"The journal entries begin about eight months ago," Ethan continued. "Did you notice any changes in her behavior during that time? New interests, new friends, anything unusual?"

Janice considered the question. "She was more tired than usual, I remember that. She said she wasn't sleeping well, but I assumed it was just stress from work and being a single mom." She paused, a frown creasing her brow. "Now that you mention it, she did start asking questions about our family history around that time. Wanted to know if we had any relatives who'd lived in Daybridge back in the early 1900s."

Ethan felt that now-familiar pressure behind his eyes intensify. "Did she say why she was interested?"

"She said she'd had a dream about a man who looked like our grandfather, but in old-fashioned clothes, standing on the bridge." Janice's expression clouded with worry. "I didn't think much of it then—we'd been going through old family photos after our mother passed last year, so it made sense she might dream about relatives. But she seemed... fixated on it. Kept asking if Grandpa had ever mentioned the bridge, or if there were stories about it in the family."

"And were there?" Alice asked.

Janice shook her head. "Not that I know of. Our grandfather grew up in Pittsburgh, only moved here after World War II. No connection to the bridge that I'm aware of."

Ethan exchanged a glance with Alice, seeing his own concern mirrored in her eyes. Jessica's journal had described dreams beginning months before she supposedly met the mysterious "M"—dreams specific enough to include questions about family connections to the bridge dating back to the early 1900s. The same time period Blackwood had asked about regarding Ethan's own family history.

"Did Jessica ever mention meeting someone who shared her interest in the bridge?" Alice continued. "Someone whose name might start with 'M'?"

Janice thought for a moment. "There was a professor she mentioned a few times—Marcus or Martin, something like that. She said he was researching local history, and they'd had some interesting conversations." Her expression darkened. "I told her to be careful. Single mom meeting strange men... I worried he might be interested in more than just historical discussion."

"Do you know where they met?" Ethan asked.

"Some bookstore downtown, I think. The Old Harbor? Jessica said she'd gone there looking for books about local history for a project she was helping Noah's daycare with, and this professor approached her, said he'd overheard her questions and might be able to help."

The Old Harbor Bookshop—the same place mentioned in Jessica's journal for her meeting with "M." Ethan made a mental note to check the store as soon as possible.

"One last question," he said, keeping his tone casual. "The symbol in this drawing—have you ever seen it before?" He showed her a crime scene photograph of the carving on the bridge, carefully angled to hide the more disturbing elements of the image.

Janice studied it, then shook her head. "No, never. What is it?"

"We're not sure yet," Ethan admitted. "But it may be important to understand what happened to your sister."

As if sensing the conversation's conclusion, Noah suddenly looked up from his blocks, staring directly at Ethan with an intensity unusual in a child so young. For a disorienting moment, Ethan felt as if the boy was seeing something beyond his physical appearance, something hidden beneath the surface.

"Bridge man," Noah said clearly, pointing at Ethan. "Like in Mommy's dreams."

A heavy silence fell over the room. Janice looked at her nephew in confusion, then back at Ethan. "I'm sorry, he's just a baby. He doesn't know what he's saying."

But Ethan wasn't so sure. The pressure behind his eyes had become a persistent throb, and those strange images flickered at the edges of his awareness—the chamber, the symbols, the woman with amber eyes. Now joined by a new image: his own great-grandfather in a police uniform, standing on Daybridge Bridge on a winter night, staring into the water below.

"It's alright," he managed, forcing a reassuring smile. "Kids say the darndest things."

As they prepared to leave, thanking Janice for her time and promising to keep her informed of any developments, Ethan noticed Blackwood watching from the hallway, that same expression of scientific curiosity on his face. The man had clearly overheard Noah's comment, and judging by his satisfied smile, had found it significant.

Outside in the parking lot, away from prying ears, Alice grabbed Ethan's arm. "What the hell was that about? The kid pointed at you and said, 'bridge man.' And don't tell me it was nothing—I saw your face."

Ethan hesitated, unsure how much to reveal. His partnership with Alice was built on trust, but the strange visions he'd been experiencing, the pressure behind his eyes, the inexplicable sense of connection to a bridge he'd crossed hundreds of times without incident until this case —it all sounded like the beginning of a psychological breakdown, not a legitimate investigative lead.

"I don't know," he finally admitted. "But I think Blackwood does. He's been watching me since we met, asking about my family history, seeming almost... expectant. Like he's waiting for me to realize something."

"Realize what?"

Ethan shook his head. "I'm not sure. But it's connected to my great-grandfather's disappearance in 1915, and to these murders, and to that symbol on the bridge." He met her gaze directly. "I think I need to visit the Old Harbor Bookshop, see if I can find this mysterious 'M' who was feeding Jessica information about the bridge."

"We need to visit the bookshop," Alice corrected firmly. "We're part-ners, remember? Whatever this is, we face it together."

The simple declaration steadied him, a reminder that he wasn't alone in this increasingly bizarre investigation. "Together," he agreed.

As they walked to their cars, Ethan cast one last glance toward Jessica's apartment building. Blackwood stood at the window, watching them leave, his expression unreadable at this distance. But even without seeing the man's face clearly, Ethan could feel his focus, his interest— not in the case, but in Ethan himself.

The pressure behind his eyes pulsed once more, and in that moment, Ethan knew with sudden certainty that he was at the center of something far larger and more dangerous than a serial murder investigation. The bridge, the symbols, his family history, Blackwood's interest —all pieces of a puzzle whose full picture remained frustratingly obscured.

But one thing was becoming increasingly clear: the answers he sought wouldn't be found in police reports or witness statements. They waited beneath Daybridge Bridge, in that chamber he'd glimpsed in visions that felt disturbingly like memories not his own. And sooner or later, he would have to descend into that darkness to face whatever had been waiting for him all along.

As midnight approached, Ethan rubbed his temples, feeling the familiar tension that preceded the lunar cycle's peak. The moon was waxing, not yet full but growing stronger each night, making his skin feel too tight over his bones and his senses occasionally spike to overwhelming levels. He'd need to request time off soon—his usual 'fishing trip' excuse that gave him three days of isolation during the full moon —but with victims appearing at seasonal turning points, he couldn't afford to step away from the case now

CHAPTER THREE
SECRETS IN SHADOW

THE HARSH BANKS of fluorescent lighting seemed to leach all warmth from the precinct's utilitarian interrogation room. A battered metal table and set of mismatched chairs created the room's sole points of interest, their scarred surfaces mute testaments to the innumerable procedural inquisitions that had played out within these drab confines over the decades.

Detective Ethan Reeves settled into one of the creaking seats with a weary sigh, allowing the battered case file's damning contents to splay open before him. The photographs from Jessica Mercer's crime scene had been joined by older files—the three previous victims Alice had connected through her research, each one bearing the same distinctive wound patterns, each one found progressively closer to Daybridge Bridge.

He studied the timeline Alice had constructed, noting the precise alignment with seasonal turning points. If the pattern held, they had months before the next killing—the winter solstice in December. But something told Ethan the rules were changing. The killer had escalated from nearby locations to the bridge itself, from relative anonymity to deliberately carved symbols. Whatever game was being played, it was accelerating toward some unknown conclusion.

Glancing up as the room's reinforced door hissed open, Ethan straightened his posture as Michael Mercer was ushered inside by a pair of uniformed officers. Jessica Mercer's boyfriend wasn't officially a suspect—he had a solid alibi for the night of the murder—but as the last person known to have seen her alive, his statement was crucial to establishing a timeline.

Michael shuffled forward with the air of a marionette guided by unseen, fraying strings. His shoulders were slumped in a rictus of infinite despair, eyes swollen and rimmed in anguished crimson as if he'd rent his very soul weeping over some unimaginable horror. Despite his evident distress, Ethan noted the man's physique—muscular and well-maintained, suggesting regular gym visits and possibly martial arts training.

"I'll take it from here, officers," Ethan murmured in a tone of measured neutrality, gesturing for the uniforms to withdraw. As the door closed once more, he turned his full attention toward the emotionally flensed figure slumped across the pitted tabletop's far end. "Mr. Mercer... Michael. I know there are no words sufficient to ease your anguish right now. But we need to discuss what happened the last time you saw Jessica."

The man's head lifted, revealing eyes swollen into purple crevasses beneath a mask of pure, fleshly torment. When he spoke, it was with a raw, phlegm-streaked rasp devoid of anything even approximating human warmth or lucidity.

"You have no conceivable inkling of the abyss yawning before me, Detective," he snarled, trembling hands knotting into bone-pale fists atop the scarred steel surface. "Jessica... oh merciful god, what weapon of the damned could permit such profane... such mutilations?!" The final query fractured on the cusp of a muted shriek, his whole body convulsing with the force of freshly lacerated bereavement.

Ethan opened his mouth to offer what hollow platitudes he could, but the wellspring of agony detonated with renewed vigor, cutting off any condolences before they could form.

"They ravaged her... butchered my perfect angel like some grotesque blood sacrifice!" Michael's haggard voice scaled upwards into a banshee's keening cry of utter desolation that brought actual discomfort to the seasoned detective. "Everything we were, our future, all sluiced away amidst that ever-expanding obscenity of blasphemy smearing the Bridge's stones!"

Fists hammered against the cheap fiberboard desktop in a staccato fusillade of dull, percussive impacts that matched each disjointed shriek torn from Michael's ravaged larynx. Ethan instinctively drew back as flecks of spittle arced through the air between them, eternally honed cop instincts warring with a deeper, more instinctual response to the display of raw emotion.

That strange pressure behind Ethan's eyes returned with sudden force, accompanied by a flash of insight that felt more like memory than deduction: Michael Mercer was lying. Not about his grief—that seemed genuine enough—but about something fundamental. The relationship with Jessica hadn't been what he was portraying. There was deception beneath the performance of devastation.

Just as Ethan felt the emotional helices spooling toward a terminal singularity, Michael's vocalizations petered out as rapidly as they'd ignited. After such soulful abandon, his hulking, muscular frame seemed to almost deflate, vital energies spent and leaving a husk of bruised, despairing self-loathing adrift amidst the calm eye of its own personal cyclone. Tears leaked in silent rivulets down his stubbled, hollowed cheeks, yet his swollen eyes remained as implacably vacant as a profane idol's obsidian visage.

"Find them," Michael rasped, voice leached to a hoarse whisper parched of inflection. "Hunt down the sick, degenerate pieces of filth that perpetrated this soul-scouring atrocity and end them in a manner befitting such depravity." He swiveled those sandblasted, empty sockets toward Ethan with the implacable intensity of a laser-sighted killing stroke. I solemnly swear, should you fail, I will dedicate my life to destroying those responsible for this evil.

Their gazes locked across that pitted interrogation room table in an endless instant where twin brands of intensity intersected—one, the professional scrutiny of a detective sensing deception beneath genuine emotion; the other, a performance calculated to elicit sympathy and deflect suspicion, layered atop real grief and something darker.

"I understand your pain," Ethan said carefully, "but right now, what would help most is information. When exactly did you last see Jessica, and what was her state of mind?"

Michael's expression shifted, grief momentarily giving way to calculation before settling back into anguish. "Tuesday afternoon," he said, his voice steadier now. "We met for lunch at Café Vermillion around one. She seemed... distracted. Kept checking her phone, said she had an important meeting later."

"Did she mention who the meeting was with?"

A fractional hesitation. "No. But she'd been acting strange for weeks. Distant. Preoccupied with something she wouldn't talk about."

"Strange how?" Ethan pressed, keeping his tone conversational despite his growing suspicion.

"Reading weird books. Historical stuff about Daybridge, old newspapers. She started asking questions about the bridge, about local legends." Michael ran a trembling hand through his disheveled hair. "I thought it was for some project at work, but whenever I asked directly, she'd change the subject."

This aligned with what they'd found in Jessica's journal and what her sister had told them. But something in Michael's delivery felt rehearsed, as if he'd anticipated these questions and prepared his answers carefully.

"We found a journal in Jessica's apartment," Ethan said, watching closely for reaction. "She wrote about meeting someone who shared her interest in the bridge's history. Someone whose name began with 'M.'"

Michael's expression remained carefully anguished, but Ethan caught the subtle tensing of muscles, the momentary stillness that betrayed surprise and calculation. "She never mentioned anyone like that to me."

"Are you familiar with the Old Harbor Bookshop?"

Another fractional hesitation. "I might have passed it. Downtown somewhere, right? Jessica liked bookstores, but I'm not much of a reader myself."

Ethan nodded, making a note in his folder. The lies were small but significant—Michael knew more than he was admitting, but without concrete evidence, pushing harder would only make him defensive.

"One last question for now," Ethan said, sliding a photograph across the table. It showed the symbol carved into the bridge's stone railing, carefully cropped to exclude any gruesome details from the crime scene. "Have you ever seen this before?"

Michael's reaction was immediate and unmistakable recognition, quickly suppressed behind a mask of confusion. "No," he said, the word coming too quickly. "What is it?"

"That's what we're trying to determine," Ethan replied, retrieving the photograph. "If you remember anything else about Jessica's recent interests or activities, particularly regarding the bridge or this symbol, please contact me immediately." He slid a business card across the table. "Day or night."

As Michael nodded, gathering himself to leave, Ethan added casually, "By the way, where were you between the hours of 8 PM Tuesday and 6 AM Wednesday?"

The question landed like a physical blow, Michael's carefully constructed facade of grief momentarily fracturing to reveal indignation and alarm. "I was at home. Alone," Michael insisted, and while his voice remained steady, Ethan caught the subtle changes in his scent

—the sharp tang of anxiety mixed with something else... not quite fear, but calculation. It was the kind of physiological response invisible to normal humans but unmistakable to Ethan's heightened senses, a blessing and curse of his lycanthropic condition that had made him unnervingly effective at interrogations."

"Just verifying the timeline," Ethan assured him smoothly. "Standard procedure."

Michael rose unsteadily to his feet, his performance of devastation resuming. "Find who did this, Detective. Before I take matters into my own hands."

The threat hung in the air as Michael was escorted from the room by the waiting officers. Ethan remained seated, mulling over the interview. Michael Mercer was hiding something—his connection to Jessica was more complicated than he'd admitted, and he definitely recognized the symbol from the bridge. But was he involved in her murder, or merely concealing some other aspect of their relationship?

The door opened again, and Alice slipped inside, carrying two cups of coffee from the break room. "How'd it go?" she asked, setting one cup in front of Ethan before taking the seat Michael had vacated.

"He's lying," Ethan said simply, accepting the coffee with a grateful nod. "Not about everything, but enough to make me suspicious. He recognized the symbol but denied it, and he knows more about Jessica's interest in the bridge than he's admitting."

"Interesting," Alice mused, opening her tablet to review her notes. "While you were in here, I got the preliminary toxicology report on Jessica Mercer. No drugs or alcohol in her system, but they found something unusual in her bloodstream—trace amounts of an unidentified organic compound with some similarities to DMT, but with a molecular structure the lab couldn't fully identify."

"DMT? The hallucinogen?"

"Similar but distinct. The lab's sending samples to a specialized facility for further analysis, but the preliminary report suggests it might be some kind of naturally occurring psychoactive compound not previously cataloged."

Ethan frowned, considering the implications. "Could explain the visions she wrote about in her journal. If someone was drugging her..."

"Or if she was taking something voluntarily," Alice added. "Either way, it connects to the bridge somehow. Her journal entries about the dreams and visions started months before the compound appeared in her system, according to the time markers in the toxicology report."

The pressure behind Ethan's eyes pulsed again, bringing with it another flash of those strange images—the chamber beneath the bridge, symbols carved in stone, the woman with amber eyes. He blinked hard, trying to focus on the case in front of him rather than the bizarre sensations plaguing him since they'd taken on this investigation.

"We need to visit that bookshop," he said firmly. "If Jessica was meeting someone there who encouraged her interest in the bridge, someone whose name starts with 'M'..."

"Could be our friend Michael," Alice suggested. "Though why he'd lie about it is unclear."

"Unless he's the one who carved that symbol and left her body on the bridge," Ethan countered. "Classic killer behavior—insert yourself into the investigation, play the grieving boyfriend while secretly relishing the attention."

Alice nodded, though her expression remained skeptical. "Possible, but it doesn't explain the connection to the three previous victims, or the seasonal pattern. And if the symbol has historical significance going back to the early 1900s, as Blackwood implied..."

"Speaking of our mysterious FBI consultant, where is he?" Ethan asked, suddenly realizing the man's absence was unusual given his intense interest in the case.

"That's another thing I wanted to mention," Alice said, her voice dropping to ensure they weren't overheard. "I called Quantico again while you were interviewing Mercer. Not only is there no record of a Dr. Marcus Blackwood in the Behavioral Science Unit, but the FBI has no behavioral analyst by that name anywhere in the organization."

Ethan's suspicions crystallized into certainty. "So, he's definitely not FBI. But how did he get the Commissioner to sign off on his consultation?"

"I checked with the Commissioner's office. The authorization came through a Homeland Security directive—classified, need-to-know basis only." Alice's expression conveyed her frustration. "The Commissioner wasn't happy about it but had no choice."

"Homeland Security involvement in a local murder case?" Ethan shook his head in disbelief. "That makes even less sense than FBI. Unless..."

"Unless there's something about these murders that goes beyond our jurisdiction," Alice finished his thought. "Something connected to national security."

The implications hung between them, neither willing to voice the more outlandish theories that might explain such high-level interest in what appeared to be the work of a local serial killer, no matter how ritual-istic or unusual the circumstances.

"The bookshop," Ethan said finally, returning to more immediate concerns. "We start there, see if we can identify this mysterious 'M' who was feeding Jessica information about the bridge."

Alice nodded, gathering her materials. "The Old Harbor opens at ten. We've got about twenty minutes."

As they prepared to leave, Ethan's phone buzzed with an incoming text. He checked the screen and frowned.

"What is it?" Alice asked, noting his expression.

"Unknown number," Ethan replied, showing her the message:

The bridge has been waiting for you, Detective Reeves. Blood will tell.

"That's... unsettling," Alice said, her usual composure briefly faltering. "Any idea who sent it?"

Ethan's mind immediately went to Blackwood, with his pointed questions about family history and his cryptic parting comment. But there was no proof, and accusing a supposed federal agent of sending threatening texts wasn't a move to make lightly, even if his credentials were suspect.

"No," he said finally. "But I'm starting to think this case is a lot more personal than we realized."

As they exited the interrogation room, Ethan felt that strange pressure behind his eyes intensify briefly. For a moment, the fluorescent-lit corridor of the precinct seemed to shimmer and fade, replaced by a vision of dark stone walls inscribed with familiar symbols, a chamber beneath the bridge where something ancient and patient had been waiting for a very, very long time.

Then the moment passed, reality reasserting itself with jarring abruptness. But the message lingered in his mind, its implications impossible to ignore:

The bridge has been waiting for you. Blood will tell.

The Old Harbor Bookshop occupied a narrow storefront on Riverfront Street, just three blocks from Daybridge Bridge. Its weathered brick facade and brass-framed windows suggested a business that had weathered decades of the city's changing fortunes, while the carefully curated display of rare volumes and local historical texts in the front window spoke to a specialized clientele rather than casual browsers.

A small brass bell tinkled as Ethan pushed open the heavy oak door, the sound momentarily lost beneath the deep, resonant chime of an antique grandfather clock announcing the hour from somewhere in the shop's depths. The interior was exactly what one would expect from a specialized bookstore—towering shelves creating a labyrinth of narrow aisles, the air heavy with the distinctive scent of old paper and leather bindings, lighting provided by brass lamps that cast pools of warm illumination rather than harsh overhead fixtures.

At first glance, the shop appeared empty of customers, though the meticulously organized displays and recently dusted surfaces suggested active management. Alice moved immediately to a section labeled "Local History," while Ethan approached the ornate counter that dominated the back wall, behind which various rare volumes were displayed in glass cases.

As if summoned by their presence, a door behind the counter opened, and a man emerged from what appeared to be a back office. He was tall and reed-thin, with a shock of white hair that contrasted sharply with his olive complexion. Round spectacles perched on a prominent nose, magnifying eyes that assessed the newcomers with evident curiosity.

"Good morning," he greeted them, his voice carrying a hint of an accent Ethan couldn't quite place—Mediterranean, perhaps, or Middle Eastern. "Welcome to Old Harbor. How may I assist you today?"

Ethan produced his badge. "Detective Ethan Reeves, Daybridge PD. This is my partner, Detective Chen. We'd like to ask you a few questions about a customer who frequented your shop recently."

The man's expression remained pleasant, though Ethan noted a subtle tensing of his posture. "Of course, Detective. I am Eli Namir, the proprietor. May I inquire which customer has drawn police interest?"

Namir's eyes widened almost imperceptibly as he assessed Ethan, his gaze lingering a moment too long. 'Interesting,' he murmured, so quietly that only Ethan's supernatural hearing could catch it. 'A wolf at the threshold of mysteries...' Ethan tensed, wondering if the old man somehow sensed what he truly was, but Namir's professional demeanor returned instantly as he addressed them both.

"Jessica Mercer," Alice said, rejoining them at the counter. "She visited your shop several times over the past few months, researching the history of Daybridge Bridge."

Namir's expression shifted to one of genuine sorrow. "Ah, yes. Ms. Mercer. A tragic loss. She was a delightful young woman with a keen mind and sincere interest in local history. I was deeply saddened to read about her passing in this morning's paper."

"When did you last see her?" Ethan asked, watching carefully for any signs of deception.

"Tuesday afternoon," Namir replied without hesitation. "She came in around three o'clock, spent perhaps an hour reviewing some historical documents I had set aside for her research."

"What kind of documents?"

"Newspaper articles from the early 1900s, primarily concerning the construction of Daybridge Bridge and certain... incidents that occurred shortly after its completion." Namir adjusted his spectacles thought-fully. "Ms. Mercer had developed a particular interest in the disappear-ance of a local butcher named Guthrie Knox in 1913, and a police officer named Michael Reeves in 1915."

The names sent a jolt through Ethan—the same ones Alice had uncov-ered in her research into his family history. The mention of his great-grandfather by name was too specific to be coincidental.

"Did she say why she was interested in those particular individuals?" Alice asked, allowing Ethan a moment to compose himself.

Namir's gaze shifted between them, lingering on Ethan with an inten-sity that suggested recognition of the name's significance. "She claimed it was for a local history project, but I sensed her interest was more... personal. She mentioned having dreams about the bridge, vivid expe-riences that seemed to contain historical details she could not possibly have known through conventional means."

"And did you believe her?" Ethan asked, finding his voice again.

The bookshop owner's smile was enigmatic. "Detective Reeves, when you've spent as many years surrounded by history as I have, you develop a certain appreciation for the ways in which the past can reach

forward to touch the present. Sometimes through documents and artifacts, sometimes through more... unconventional channels."

"Like dreams?" Alice suggested.

"Like blood," Namir corrected softly, his gaze once again focusing on
Ethan. "Family connections that persist across generations, carrying
memories, predispositions, even certain... sensitivities."

The pressure behind Ethan's eyes intensified, accompanied by a
certainty that Namir knew more than he was revealing—about Jessica,
about the bridge, and most disturbingly, about Ethan himself.

"We understand Jessica met someone here," he said, deliberately redirecting the conversation. "Someone whose name began with 'M,' who
shared her interest in the bridge's history and encouraged her
research."

Namir's expression remained carefully neutral. "Many customers
frequent my establishment, Detective. I cannot monitor all interactions
that occur among them."

"But you would notice a regular patron taking special interest in a
young woman researching local history," Alice pressed. "Especially if
they met multiple times over several weeks."

The bookshop owner seemed to consider his response carefully. "There
is a professor who often visits my shop—Dr. Marcus Blackwood. He
specializes in regional folklore and occult history at Daybridge University. I believe he and Mrs. Mercer did engage in several conversations
about her research."

The name hit Ethan like a physical blow. "Marcus Blackwood? You're
certain that was his name?"

"Quite certain," Namir confirmed, watching Ethan's reaction with
evident interest. "He's been a regular customer for many years, though
I admit I know little about him personally. He tends to keep to himself,
interested primarily in very specific historical texts and documents."

Alice and Ethan exchanged a significant look. The "FBI consultant" who had appeared at the crime scene, who had specifically requested Ethan by name, who had questioned him about his family history—this was no coincidence.

"Does Dr. Blackwood have an office at the university?" Alice asked. "Or a home address where we might contact him?"

Namir shook his head. "I'm afraid I don't have such personal information. He's always been rather... private about his affairs outside of academic interests."

"What kind of materials was he particularly interested in?" Ethan asked, trying to piece together what Blackwood's true motivations might be.

"Ancient symbols and their significance in local architecture, primarily," Namir replied. "Particularly those incorporated into Daybridge Bridge during its construction. He has an extensive collection of books on esoteric symbolism and occult practices in the New England region."

"Like this symbol?" Ethan produced the photograph of the carving from the bridge, watching carefully for Namir's reaction.

The bookshop owner's composure faltered for the first time, a flash of recognition—and something that might have been fear—crossing his features before he carefully schooled his expression back to professional neutrality.

"Yes," he admitted quietly. "That particular symbol was of great interest to Dr. Blackwood. It appears in several ancient texts related to dimensional gateways and the thinning of barriers between worlds. In local context, it's associated with the Order of the Ebon Star—a secretive organization that allegedly influenced much of Daybridge's early development, particularly the construction of the bridge itself."

"And what does it mean?" Alice asked, her tone suggesting professional curiosity rather than the intense interest Ethan knew she must be feeling.

Namir hesitated, his gaze once again focusing on Ethan with uncomfortable intensity. "It has many interpretations, Detective Chen. But in its simplest form, it represents a convergence—a point where multiple realities intersect, where boundaries between dimensions become permeable."

"And someone carved this symbol into the stone railing of Daybridge Bridge, right next to where Jessica Mercer's body was found," Ethan said, the implications hanging heavy in the air between them.

"A troubling development," Namir agreed, his expression grave. "Perhaps signifying that whatever was set in motion during the bridge's construction has entered a new phase."

"What exactly was set in motion?" Alice asked.

The bookshop owner's smile was sad, almost pitying. "That, Detective Chen, is a question with many answers, depending on which version of history you choose to believe. The official records state that Daybridge Bridge was built to improve transportation and commerce. Local legends suggest its location and design were influenced by more... esoteric considerations."

"Such as?" Ethan pressed.

"Such as the creation of a permanent anchor point for forces beyond conventional human understanding," Namir replied, his voice dropping to little more than a whisper. "A living nexus where realities could merge according to patterns established through ritual and sacrifice."

The pressure behind Ethan's eyes exploded into blinding intensity, bringing with it a flood of those strange images—the chamber beneath the bridge, symbols carved in stone, the woman with amber eyes supervising a transformation beyond human comprehension. But now they included something new: a butcher named Guthrie Knox undergoing a metamorphosis that merged his flesh with stone, his consciousness expanding throughout the bridge's structure, becoming something neither fully human nor entirely Other.

"Detective Reeves?" Alice's voice seemed to come from very far away. "Ethan, are you alright?"

He blinked, reality reasserting itself with jarring abruptness. Both Alice and Namir were watching him with concern, though the bookshop owner's expression contained an additional element—recognition, as if he had expected this reaction.

"I'm fine," Ethan managed, though the lie was transparent. "Just... processing the implications."

Namir studied him for a long moment, then reached beneath the counter and produced a slim volume bound in faded leather. "Perhaps this might be of interest to your investigation, Detective. It's a collection of personal accounts related to Daybridge Bridge, compiled by a local historian in the 1950s. Many of the stories are dismissed as superstition or urban legend, but in light of recent events, they might provide valuable context."

Ethan accepted the book, noting the title embossed in faded gold on the cover: *Shadows Beneath the Span: Unexplained Phenomena of Daybridge Bridge, 1913-1950*.

"Thank you," he said, unsure whether to treat the offering as a genuine attempt to assist their investigation or something more calculated. "We'll return it when we're finished."

"Keep it," Namir insisted. "I have multiple copies, and I believe you'll find its contents... illuminating, particularly given your family connection to the bridge's history."

Before Ethan could respond to this pointed reference, the shop's bell tinkled again as the door opened, admitting a middle-aged woman with an armful of books to be appraised. Namir nodded politely to the detectives, indicating their conversation had reached its natural conclusion.

"If you have further questions, I'm always here during business hours," he said, his attention already shifting to his new customer. "And Detective Reeves... do be careful. Some knowledge comes with a price that isn't immediately apparent."

Outside on the sidewalk, Alice turned to Ethan with unconcealed concern. "What happened in there? You looked like you were about to pass out when he mentioned the 'living nexus' thing."

Ethan hesitated, uncertain how much to reveal. The visions—or memories, or whatever they were—felt intensely personal, yet they were clearly relevant to the case. And if anyone deserved his complete honesty, it was Alice.

"I've been experiencing... something," he admitted, keeping his voice low as they walked toward their parked cars. "Since we first visited the crime scene on the bridge. Like memories, but not my own. Visions of a chamber beneath the bridge, symbols carved into stone walls, a woman with amber eyes overseeing some kind of ritual transformation."

Alice's expression remained carefully neutral, neither immediately dismissive nor unduly alarmed. "And you think these visions are connected to your great-grandfather's disappearance? To the murders?"

"I don't know," Ethan said honestly. "But they feel... real. Like I'm accessing something that actually happened, not just imagining it." He tapped the book Namir had given him. "And I'm not the only one who thinks there's a connection. Blackwood clearly targeted me specifically, asked about my family history. Namir recognized my name immediately. And now this text message about blood telling..."

"It's a lot of coincidences," Alice agreed, her analytical mind clearly working through the possibilities. "But we need to be careful not to force connections where they might not exist. Confirmation bias is a hell of a thing, especially when dealing with something as emotionally charged as family history."

Ethan nodded, grateful for her grounding perspective even as he recognized the legitimacy of the pattern forming around him. "You're right. We stick to concrete evidence, follow established investigative protocols. But..."

"But we don't ignore potentially relevant information just because it doesn't fit neatly into conventional explanations," Alice finished for him. "I'm not dismissing your experiences, Ethan. I just want to make sure we're approaching this systematically."

The sincerity in her voice was reassuring—a reminder that whatever strange path this investigation might take, he wouldn't be walking it alone.

"So, what's our next move?" he asked, deliberately refocusing on the immediate investigation.

"We need to find the real Marcus Blackwood," Alice said decisively. "If he's a professor at Daybridge University as Namir claimed, there should be records—faculty directories, published papers, office location. And we need to understand why he's posing as an FBI consultant, what his actual interest is in these murders, and particularly, why he's so focused on you."

Ethan nodded, then hesitated. "There's one other thing we should consider. The chamber beneath the bridge—the one I keep seeing in these... visions. What if it actually exists? What if there's physical evidence down there that could help us understand what's happening?"

Alice considered this for a moment. "The bridge maintenance department would have detailed structural plans, including any subsurface chambers or maintenance tunnels. We could request those officially, see if there's any documented space that matches what you're describing."

"And if there isn't?" Ethan asked, already suspecting the answer.

"Then we go looking ourselves," Alice replied with a determined glint in her eye. "After hours, off the books. If there's evidence beneath that bridge that could help us solve four murders and potentially prevent more, I'm willing to bend a few procedural rules to find it."

The decision made, they parted ways with a clear plan—Alice would pursue the university angle, researching Blackwood's academic credentials and position, while Ethan would visit the city's Department of Public Works to request the structural plans for Daybridge Bridge.

As Ethan walked to his car, he felt the weight of the book Namir had given him in his jacket pocket, a tangible connection to whatever strange history was unfolding around him. The pressure behind his eyes had subsided to a dull throb, but the images remained vivid in his mind—the chamber, the symbols, the ritual transformation that had somehow merged a human being with the very structure of the bridge.

And beneath it all, a growing certainty that he was being drawn toward something inevitable—a confrontation that had been waiting for generations, ever since his great-grandfather disappeared while investigating strange occurrences at the bridge in the winter of 1915.

The bridge has been waiting for you. Blood will tell.

The words echoed in his mind as he started his car, no longer simply a cryptic text message but a declaration of purpose that resonated with something deep within him—a connection he didn't yet understand but could no longer deny.

While Ethan headed to the Department of Public Works, Nadia Marsh approached Daybridge Bridge from the eastern shore, her press badge prominently displayed to deter any questions from the uniformed officers still securing the wider crime scene. The immediate area where Jessica Mercer's body had been found was no longer cordoned off, though evidence markers remained in place, protected by weather-resistant covers.

As an investigative journalist specializing in Daybridge's darker aspects, Nadia had covered more than her share of grisly crimes. But something about this case had triggered her instincts from the moment she'd heard the first scanner reports—not just another murder but something that connected to the city's deeper mysteries, the kinds of stories mainstream outlets dismissed as urban legend but that she had long suspected contained kernels of uncomfortable truth.

The bridge itself seemed unusually quiet this morning, with local pedestrians choosing alternate routes and even vehicle traffic seeming subdued, as if the city's collective consciousness recognized something fundamentally wrong had occurred here. Nadia moved methodically along the eastern approach, her experienced eye noting details the casual observer might miss—the precise location of evidence markers, the pattern of movement the first responders had followed, the angle of visibility from nearby buildings that might have yielded witnesses.

As she approached the center of the span where Jessica's body had been discovered, Nadia spotted something peculiar half-buried in a crack between the ancient cobblestones—a small cylindrical object, no larger than her thumb. She glanced around to ensure no officers were watching, then crouched down, pulling on latex gloves from her bag before carefully extracting the object with her pen knife.

Holding it up to the morning light, Nadia examined the strange artifact. It appeared to be some kind of metal casing, though the design was unlike anything she'd seen before. Intricate etchings lined the curved surface, forming symbols or markings that resembled the one carved into the stone railing nearby—variations on the same theme of an eye within a triangle, surrounded by smaller glyphs.

Her brow furrowed as she turned it over in her hands. This was no random piece of litter—it seemed too precisely made, too purposefully designed. And its presence at the exact center of the bridge, where Jessica's body had been positioned with such evident care, couldn't be mere coincidence.

Nadia felt that familiar tingling at the back of her neck, the journalist's instinct that had led her to one groundbreaking story after another over the years. There was more to these murders than the police were revealing—or perhaps more than they themselves understood. The metal cylinder, the carved symbol, the precise positioning on the bridge—these weren't the actions of a conventional serial killer but something more deliberate, more ritual in nature.

She bagged the cylinder carefully, making mental notes of its exact location and condition. Whether it would become evidence in a police investigation or the centerpiece of her own exposé remained to be seen, but either way, she knew it represented a tangible connection to whatever dark purpose was unfolding on Daybridge Bridge.

As she straightened up, Nadia became aware of a subtle change in the atmosphere around her—a pressure in the air, as if the bridge itself was somehow aware of her presence and actions. The rational part of her mind dismissed the sensation as imagination fueled by the location's grim recent history, but something deeper, more instinctual, recognized it as the same feeling that had preceded her most significant discoveries in the past.

She was being watched—not by the disinterested officers at either end of the bridge, but by something else, something that perceived her discovery of the metal cylinder as a development of interest. Nadia turned slowly, scanning her surroundings with the heightened awareness that had kept her alive through numerous dangerous investigations over the years.

There was no one visible on the bridge itself, and the few pedestrians on either shore were too distant to have triggered such an immediate sense of scrutiny. Yet the feeling persisted, growing stronger as she approached the exact center of the span—the point where Jessica's body had been found, where the symbol had been carved into the stone railing.

Standing at that precise spot, Nadia experienced a moment of disorientation so profound she had to grasp the railing for support. For an instant, the world seemed to shift around her, the solid stone beneath her feet becoming temporarily transparent, revealing a glimpse of something below—a chamber carved from the living rock of the riverbed, walls inscribed with symbols identical to those on the metal cylinder, a space that shouldn't exist according to any conventional understanding of the bridge's structure.

Then the moment passed, reality reasserting itself with jarring abruptness. Nadia found herself still gripping the railing, her breath coming in shallow gasps as if she'd just sprinted up several flights of stairs. The metal cylinder in her pocket seemed suddenly heavier, more significant—a key to understanding whatever secret lay beneath the bridge's ancient stones.

As she made her way back toward the eastern shore, Nadia's mind was already organizing the pieces of the story taking shape before her—the murder of Jessica Mercer, the symbolic carving, the metal cylinder with its arcane markings, and now the glimpse of a hidden chamber that official structural plans almost certainly wouldn't acknowledge.

Whatever was happening on Daybridge Bridge, it went far beyond a simple murder investigation. It touched on the city's deepest secrets; the kinds of truths powerful interests had been suppressing for generations. And Nadia Marsh, as she had so many times before, found herself at the threshold of a mystery that might finally expose the darkness that had always lurked beneath Daybridge's respectable facade.

The story of a lifetime was unfolding before her. All she had to do was follow the evidence, no matter how strange or dangerous the path might become.

∾

CHAPTER FOUR
INQUEST OF INNOCENCE

THE CHAMBER'S hushed atmosphere hung thick with palpable tension as the coroner cleared his throat, steeling himself to deliver his findings. All eyes turned toward the diminutive, bespectacled man perched atop the raised dais, his somber expression casting a funerary pall over the legal proceedings. The Municipal Court building, with its neo-gothic architecture and weathered stone facade, seemed particularly oppressive this morning, as if the very walls were absorbing the collective dread that had settled over Daybridge since Jessica Mercer's murder.

"It is the determination of this office," the coroner began in a wavering voice, "that the victim, Jessica Mercer, succumbed to exsanguination resultant from the ritualistic severance of her carotid artery and jugular vein." A ragged inhalation echoed from the back row where the deceased woman's sister sat clutching a handkerchief, her nephew mercifully absent from these grim proceedings. "The... mutilations and symbolic lacerations inflicted post-mortem appear to align with the grisly patterns established in the previous bridge murders over the past several months."

A shocked murmur rippled through the chambers as the coroner's grim pronouncement seemed to crystallize the horrifying truth none wished to accept—a depraved serial killer walked among them, harvesting innocent lives in the name of some profane agenda.

Ethan Reeves sat in the front row beside his partner, Alice Chen, both of them maintaining the professional detachment expected of seasoned detectives despite the disturbing details being recounted. But beneath this composed exterior, Ethan felt that now-familiar pressure building behind his eyes—a response to something beyond the merely gruesome facts being presented.

The coroner continued with clinical precision, detailing the condition of the body upon discovery and the timeline established through forensic analysis. "Time of death is estimated between 10:00 PM and 2:00 AM on the night in question. The body was positioned at the exact center of Daybridge Bridge, aligned with the primary support column beneath." He adjusted his glasses nervously. "Of particular note is the symbol carved into the stone railing approximately fifteen feet from where the victim was found—a design that appears to have ritual significance rather than representing random vandalism."

At the mention of the symbol, Ethan felt a sharp spike of pain behind his eyes, accompanied by a momentary flash of those same impossible images that had been plaguing him since the investigation began—the chamber beneath the bridge, symbols carved in stone, the woman with amber eyes. He blinked hard, forcing himself back to the present moment as the coroner began describing the post-mortem findings in greater detail.

"The precision of certain wounds indicates medical knowledge or anatomical training," the coroner noted, his professional demeanor momentarily steadying his delivery. "While others display a savage, tearing quality inconsistent with any conventional weapon. The combination suggests either multiple perpetrators or a single individual employing varied methodologies for specific ritualistic purposes."

Sensing the rising tide of emotion cresting in the room, Mayor Jeremiah Granger rose from his front-row seat, every inch the portrait of civic leadership in his impeccably tailored suit. All eyes turned toward Daybridge's mayor as he smoothed his furrowed lapels with a paternal, calming gesture.

"I understand this is a... distressing development that has this entire city gripped in understandable fear and anger," Granger's rich baritone rang out. "Believe me when I say that I share those sentiments to my core. Jessica Mercer's murder was an act of unspeakable depravity, and I vow before all of you today that the full resources of this administration will be leveraged until her killer—or killers—are apprehended and brought to justice!"

The Mayor's words seemed to momentarily stem the tide of despair and hysteria gathering force among the gallery. Granger was a consummate orator, his very presence radiating confidence and composure amidst this communal tragedy.

Yet even as his authoritative baritone washed over the rapt masses, a handful of observers detected the faint whispers of discord stirring beneath that polished facade of compassion and righteous civic duty. Seated among them, Ethan felt his lip curl ever so slightly as a frisson of inexplicable revulsion shivered along his spine. There was something performative about Granger's concern, something calculated beneath the show of solidarity that set Ethan's instincts on high alert.

Ethan's gaze flicked sideways, taking in Alice Chen's admirably impassive mien as she listened to the mayor's grandstanding. Ever the pragmatist, the petite detective's acute instincts were doubtless also picking up on the dissonant harmonics layered beneath Granger's dulcet tones. The slight narrowing of her eyes confirmed his suspicion—Alice wasn't buying the mayor's performance either.

As if sensing their silent scrutiny, the mayor's eyes swiveled to transfix the two detectives with a piercing look of smoldering intensity before allowing his trademark grandfatherly demeanor to sweep across his features once more. With an almost imperceptible nod, he yielded the dais back to the hapless coroner, who withered further under the weight of the room's expectant silence.

"Yes, well, th-thank you Mayor Granger for those words of civic solidarity," the coroner stammered out. Squaring his narrow shoulders, he pressed on with a marginal increase of fortitude. "I have been instructed to permit the assembled legal counsels present to examine the evidence and my official report, should they desire to raise any objections or counterclaims."

The coroner's voice trailed off as a disturbance rippled through the gallery seats. A squat, ruddy-faced man in rumpled overalls had shot to his feet, upending the folding chair behind him with a raucous clatter.

"This is an outrage!" the man hollered, spittle flying from his twisted mouth as one sausage-like finger jabbed viciously toward the dais. "We all know who... what... is responsible for that poor girl's death, yet you bureaucratic leeches sit here playing semantic games!"

A shocked murmur surged through the crowd at this outburst, though more than a few furtive nods and sidelong looks indicated a current of suppressed consensus regarding the man's incendiary claim. Ethan felt the hairs along his nape prickling as the confrontation rapidly devolved from legal formalities into something darker and more primal—a venting of deeply-entrenched beliefs and prejudices that ran like leylines through Daybridge's collective subconscious.

"The Ogre did this, same as it's done to how many others over the decades?" the workingman continued, his voice rising to a keening pitch of outrage and accusation. "Yet y'all cower behind your books and rules, letting that... that THING butcher our citizens with impunity while uttering pious murmurs about 'civic regulations' and bureaucratic tripe!"

A chorus of growls and jeers erupted from other segments of the gallery, feeding into the swelling tide of animalistic fervor. In the center of the maelstrom, the lone heckler swelled to even greater heights of frenzied vitriol.

"Well, I say enough's enough! We all know the truth—that unnatural, profane THING has blighted our town for far too damned long! When will the authorities take real action to..."

Whatever final condemnation the man intended to pronounce was abruptly cut off as a sleek, cylindrical object came hurtling out of the crowd to strike him squarely in the mouth with a sickening crunch of splintered teeth and bone. A collective sound of shocked inhalation issued forth as the workingman crumpled backward in a boneless heap, a crimson blossom already unfurling across his shattered face from the impact.

The rising tensions in the room assaulted Ethan's senses—the chemical cocktail of fear, anger, and grief emanating from the crowd made his wolf nature stir restlessly beneath his human facade. He breathed deeply, using the meditation techniques he'd developed to maintain control when his lycanthropic senses threatened to overwhelm him. The full moon was approaching, making emotional regulation all the more challenging in charged environments like this

Ethan was on his feet and moving toward the courtroom uproar before his conscious mind could process the rapid devolution, Alice's trim form flowing like liquid shadow at his side. He glimpsed the missile—one of the intricately carved ceremonial gavels typically mounted on the chamber's side walls—as it rolled to a clattering halt amidst the madness. More telling, however, was the regal, coldly imperious figure looming amid the epicenter of the pandemonium like a towering basalt obelisk dominating the landscape.

Mayor Jeremiah Granger's aristocratic features were devoid of emotion, his slate-colored eyes glittering with an intensity that bordered on the profane as he surveyed the convulsing crowd. One lean hand fell away from its follow-through position, finally lowering as if in retroactive benediction over the crumpled object-lesson sprawled at his feet. When at last Granger spoke, his deep baritone carried the weight of an elemental force of irresistible, if merciless, gravitas.

The mayor had seized control of the inquest, leaving the coroner stunned and too unsure of himself to intervene. "I will have order in this court," Granger declared, his voice a whip crack of authority, "even if I must beat the ignorance out of each of your thick skulls myself." The sinewy tendons on the back of his pale, parchment-like hands flexed, carrying a quiet but unmistakable threat that rippled through the subdued crowd. "We are supposed to be civilized beings—at least that's the claim—and we will act like it, especially in the face of a tragedy as horrific as Jessica Mercer's murder. Anything less only feeds the growing darkness already at our doorstep."

The chambers went silent after such imperious pronouncements, the spectators cowed in the presence of the mayor's dominating persona. Only Ethan and Alice remained defiantly unmoved, studying the self-appointed arbiter of law and order with gazes bordering on confrontational scrutiny.

Ethan felt the same revulsion intensifying, that strange pressure behind his eyes building to an almost painful degree. There was something... off about Granger's aura, a sour undernote of tainted motivations lurking just beyond perception's grasp. Be it some darker agenda gnawing at the roots of the mayor's cultivated gravitas or simply the warped grandiosity of autocrats grown too emboldened by their own power, Ethan couldn't dismiss the intuition of hidden rot festering behind those aristocratic features and mellifluous words of seeming civic responsibility.

As his gaze swept across the now quelled masses, it settled at last on Terri Mitchell's hunched, sunken form. Jessica's sister seemed to have collapsed inwards upon herself under the weight of such profane upheavals and usurpations of the law. More than anyone present, she radiated a grim, soul-deadened listlessness—the terminal emptiness of one who had watched helplessly as her sister's life was brutally extinguished, leaving a toddler motherless and a family shattered.

Ethan exhaled a sigh that ached bone-deep with weary resignation. If even a politician like Granger could unilaterally dictate the terms and decorum of these proceedings, what hope remained for justice to prevail over the tides of madness and despair swamping the streets beyond?

At this, a lone figure unfolded himself from one of the rear benches like a great shadowed beast lazily rousing itself from slumber. All eyes tracked the individual's progress toward the dais in a predatory, brooding silence that seemed to constrict the air within the chamber. As he turned to face the gallery, any lingering pretense of civility withered from the proceedings under his malignant, domineering presence.

"Your honor, esteemed officials..." the dark-suited man began, his voice grating like desiccated bone rasping over flint. "I am Cyrus Lockett, legal counsel representing the... ah, interests of the Trans-Bridge Service Company, lessees and curators of the sacred Daybridge span in question."

Another wave of horrified muttering began rippling through the stilled hall before Granger's baritone crashed over the noise like a wrathful thunderclap. "You go too far, sir! Do you stand before the civic authorities to insinuate blame toward the victim and impugn her already devastated family's character in their moment of grief?"

Rather than cower from the furor detonated by such boldly stated implications, Lockett merely let a serpentine smile slither across his gaunt, vulpine features. "My esteemed Mayor Granger, you misunderstand my purpose here. I merely wish to remind this body that my client's contractors upheld all existing civic ordinances and lawful transit regulations on the night of Ms. Mercer's tragic..." he paused, letting the weight of the next word detonate like a rhetorical bombshell, "...murder."

The deafening silence that followed Lockett's inflammatory statement was shattered by a guttural sound—part anguished howl, part incoherent roar of fury. All eyes swiveled toward the source; a lone figure jackknifed halfway out of his seat in the middle rows.

"You remorseless bastard!" the man bellowed, veins standing out in thick cords across his ruddy neck and temples. "Jessica wasn't just some statistic for your legal maneuvering! She was a mother, a daughter, a sister!" His voice fractured beneath the weight of fresh emotion, shoulders heaving with each ragged inhalation.

Ethan recognized the man instantly—Michael Mercer, Jessica's boyfriend, the same man he'd interviewed the previous day. The raw emotion seemed genuine enough, but something about the performance still struck Ethan as calculated, another piece in a puzzle he couldn't quite assemble.

"Michael, please... you need to stay calm," another voice pleaded—Jessica's sister, Terri, who had moved to his side, one hand on his trembling arm. "Don't let them twist this into something else. Not here."

But Michael was well beyond the reach of soothing entreaties or pretenses of propriety. With an explosive burst of movement, he shrugged free of the restraining grip and staggered upright, his athletic frame seeming to dilate to even greater mass with the scorching heat of righteous indignation.

"You soulless legal pirates squatting in your ivory towers with your vulture-speak and loophole justifications!" Each word carried the blistering intensity of a branding iron, searing the air itself with their caustic fury. "You dare sit there and compound our suffering... her family's anguish... by intimating that somehow Jessica held even an iota of responsibility for her own horrific, senseless murder!?"

A shocked, almost palpable, silence hung after Michael's thunderous diatribe, as if the space itself were recoiling from the sheer magnitude of emotional devastation radiating outwards. Even Lockett, for all his professed sangfroid, seemed taken aback by the unstoppable force of the man's raw, unadulterated pain.

Ethan reacted first among those present, smoothly rising from his seat to interpose himself between the two antagonistic figures. Though his lean, muscular frame was no match for Michael's bulkier build, the detective emanated an unmistakable aura of composure and implacable control.

"That's more than enough from both of you," Ethan stated in a tone that brooked no argument, his steady gaze flicking first to Lockett before swiveling to transfix Michael with the same intense focus. "Mr.

Mercer, I understand your pain, but getting yourself removed from these proceedings isn't going to achieve anything but more heartache."

For an endless, breathless moment, it seemed as though Michael would explode through Ethan's attempted intercession like a force of nature heedless of any opposition. The muscles knotted along his forearms and neck bunched and strained as if preparing to unleash another salvo of berserker invective.

Then, as quickly as it had swelled to nuclear intensity, the furious conflagration suffusing Michael's frame seemed to gutter out, leaving only a husk of wearied, broken resignation in its wake. His shoulders slumped as he staggered backward, sinking into the creaking bench with a soft moan of anguish.

"You're... you're right, Detective," he mumbled, each word seeming to inflict fresh lacerations across his ravaged psyche. "Losing control like that... it does nothing to honor Jessica's memory or seek justice in a civilized manner." A single glistening tear tracked down his cheek, glimmering briefly before being hastily wiped away.

"I just... I miss her so damn much..." The last admission was little more than a whispered exhalation, yet it carried the weight of an existential truth that pinned every heart in the chamber. For Michael and Jessica's family, the yawning gulf left after her brutal slaying could never be bridged, no matter what answers or closure lay ahead.

Sensing the fragile balance that had been restored, Ethan gave a curt nod then pivoted back toward his own seat beside Alice. Yet as he settled into the creaking bench, he couldn't shake the persistent feeling that Michael's grief, while genuine, was somehow performative calculated for maximum impact rather than the unfiltered anguish of true loss.

"Something's off with him," Alice whispered, her lips barely moving as she leaned slightly toward Ethan. "The timing of that outburst was too perfect, almost rehearsed."

Ethan nodded imperceptibly, glad to have his suspicions confirmed by his partner's equally sharp instincts. "Keep an eye on Lockett too," he murmured back. "His 'client' seems suspiciously concerned with establishing that they bear no responsibility for what happened on the bridge."

As the proceedings resumed with the coroner shakily continuing his findings, Ethan found his attention drawn to a figure seated in the far corner of the chamber—a tall, slender man in an immaculate charcoal suit, his silver-streaked dark hair swept back from a high forehead. Though Ethan hadn't noticed him earlier, something about the man's presence now seemed to dominate the room, a quiet intensity that drew the eye despite his deliberately unobtrusive positioning.

With a jolt of recognition, Ethan realized it was Marcus Blackwood—the supposed FBI consultant whose credentials had proven false, the same man who had specifically requested Ethan by name for the investigation. Their eyes met across the chamber, and Blackwood inclined his head in a subtle acknowledgment before returning his attention to the proceedings with a faint smile playing at the corners of his mouth.

The pressure behind Ethan's eyes intensified sharply, bringing with it another flash of those impossible images—but this time, they included something new: a sense of recognition, as if the chamber beneath the bridge somehow knew he was coming, had been waiting for him specifically.

Blood will tell.

The cryptic message from the unknown text flashed through Ethan's mind as the inquest droned on, the procedural formalities continuing despite the emotional undercurrents swirling through the chamber. Something about this case was deeply, fundamentally personal in a way he still couldn't fully comprehend—connected not just to the recent murders but to his own family history, to secrets buried beneath Daybridge Bridge for generations.

After what seemed an eternity of technical testimony and legal posturing, the coroner finally concluded his findings, recommending that the case remain open as a homicide investigation with Detective Reeves and Detective Chen continuing as lead investigators. The gallery began to disperse, murmured conversations creating a low buzz of tension as people filed out of the chamber.

Ethan rose to leave, intending to speak with Terri Mitchell before she departed, but found his path blocked by Mayor Granger, who had materialized beside their bench with the silent efficiency of a predator.

As Granger loomed closer, invading Ethan's personal space with calculated intimidation, the detective felt a primal growl building in his chest. He suppressed it ruthlessly, though his eyes must have flashed with something dangerous because the mayor hesitated, instinctively stepping back. Even powerful men like Granger couldn't entirely ignore the ancient predator instincts that recognized when they stood before something that wasn't entirely human.

"Detective Reeves, Detective Chen," Granger acknowledged, his deep voice pitched low enough that only they could hear. "I trust you're making progress on this unfortunate situation. The city cannot afford another incident like this—the political fallout alone is becoming... problematic."

"We're pursuing all viable leads, Mayor," Alice replied with professional detachment. "But these investigations take time, especially with the unusual elements involved."

Granger's expression hardened almost imperceptibly. "Time is a luxury we don't have, Detective Chen. The business community is already expressing concerns about the impact on tourism and investment. The longer this drags on, the more damage is done to Daybridge's reputation and economic future."

"With all due respect, sir," Ethan said, unable to keep a hint of challenge from his tone, "our priority is finding whoever murdered Jessica Mercer and the three previous victims, not managing the city's public relations."

The mayor studied him for a long moment, his slate-gray eyes revealing nothing of his thoughts. "Your dedication is commendable, Detective Reeves. I only hope it's directed toward productive avenues of investigation rather than... distractions." He paused, his gaze intensifying. "I understand you've been researching the history of the bridge, including certain local legends and folklore that have no place in a modern police investigation."

The statement hit with the precision of a surgical strike, confirming what Ethan had already suspected Granger was monitoring their investigation closely, through channels that went beyond the normal chain of command.

"We follow the evidence wherever it leads," Ethan responded evenly. "Sometimes that includes historical context that might illuminate current events."

"Indeed." Granger's smile didn't reach his eyes. "Well, I wouldn't want to keep you from your duties. I'm sure Jessica Mercer's family deserves answers as quickly as possible." He nodded to them both and moved away, immediately engaged by a cluster of city officials waiting near the chamber doors.

"That was... interesting," Alice murmured once the mayor was out of earshot. "He's awfully concerned with how we're conducting this investigation."

"And awfully well-informed about our research into the bridge's history," Ethan added. "Someone's keeping him updated on our movements."

They made their way toward the exit, both scanning the dispersing crowd for Terri Mitchell. Instead, they found themselves intercepted by Cyrus Lockett, the Trans-Bridge Service Company's attorney, his gaunt frame blocking their path with surprising effectiveness for a man of his slight build.

"Detectives," he greeted them, his voice carrying that same dry, rasping quality they'd heard during the proceedings. "A moment of your time, if you please."

"Mr. Lockett," Ethan acknowledged without warmth. "I'm not sure what the attorneys for a bridge management company could possibly need from homicide detectives."

The lawyer's thin lips stretched into what might charitably be called a smile. "Direct as ever, Detective Reeves. It's one of your more... refreshing qualities." He reached into his breast pocket and produced a business card, offering it with skeletal fingers. "My clients have certain historical records regarding Daybridge Bridge that might prove relevant to your investigation. Construction documents, maintenance logs dating back to the early 1900s, that sort of thing."

Ethan accepted the card with carefully concealed surprise. This was exactly the kind of information they needed to confirm the existence of the chamber beneath the bridge—the one he kept seeing in his visions. "And why would your clients be willing to share these records with us?"

"Let's just say we have a vested interest in resolving this situation quickly and discreetly," Lockett replied. "The recent... incidents have already impacted bridge usage significantly, and my clients are concerned about long-term financial implications."

"Of course," Alice said, her tone deliberately neutral. "Always about the bottom line."

Lockett's expression didn't change, but something cold flickered in his eyes. "Not entirely, Detective Chen. My clients also have a deep appreciation for the bridge's historical significance to Daybridge. They would be... distressed if certain aspects of that history were misrepresented or sensationalized during your investigation."

The implied threat wasn't subtle—they were being offered access to valuable information in exchange for discretion about whatever they might discover. The question was, what exactly were Lockett's clients so concerned about protecting?

"We'll keep your offer in mind," Ethan said noncommittally. "Now if you'll excuse us, we need to speak with the victim's family."

As they moved away from the lawyer, Ethan spotted Terri Mitchell near the chamber doors, deep in conversation with Michael Mercer. The two seemed to be arguing in hushed but intense tones, Michael's expression shifting between pleading and frustrated while Terri maintained a rigid posture of rejection.

Before Ethan and Alice could approach, the pair separated Terri exiting the building with quick, decisive steps while Michael remained behind, his face a mask of barely contained emotion. Seeing the detectives watching him, he straightened his shoulders and approached them directly.

"Detectives," he greeted them with forced composure. "I want to apologize for my outburst during the proceedings. It was... unprofessional."

"Understandable under the circumstances," Alice replied, studying him with the same analytical precision she brought to all their interviews. "How are you holding up, Mr. Mercer?"

Michael ran a hand through his disheveled hair. "As well as can be expected, I suppose. Terri's taking it harder than anyone—she and Jessica were always close, and now with Noah to consider..." He trailed off, gaze drifting toward the doors through which Terri had departed.

"We noticed you two seemed to be having an intense discussion," Ethan observed casually. "Anything we should know about?"

A flicker of something—annoyance? alarm?—crossed Michael's features before being quickly suppressed. "Just family matters. Terri's angry that I wasn't with Jessica that night, thinks I could have prevented what happened somehow. Grief makes people irrational sometimes."

The explanation seemed plausible enough, but Ethan's instincts continued to warn him that Michael Mercer was hiding something significant. The man was too composed beneath his performative displays of emotion, too careful in his responses.

"We may need to speak with you again as the investigation progresses," Ethan said, maintaining a professional tone despite his growing suspicions. "In the meantime, if you remember anything else about Jessica's recent activities or interests—particularly regarding the bridge or anyone she might have met in connection with it—please contact us immediately."

Michael nodded, his expression appropriately solemn. "Of course, anything to help find whoever did this to her." He hesitated, then added, "Have you... have you made any progress identifying that symbol? The one carved into the bridge?"

The question seemed innocent enough, but something in Michael's delivery—a tension in his voice, a too-casual attempt to mask genuine interest—set alarm bells ringing in Ethan's mind.

"We're pursuing several lines of inquiry," he replied carefully. "Why do you ask?"

"Just curious," Michael said with a shrug that didn't quite achieve the nonchalance he was aiming for. "It seemed important from the way people were talking about it. I thought maybe it was some kind of signature or calling card."

"In a manner of speaking," Alice interjected smoothly. "But we can't discuss specific details of an ongoing investigation."

Michael accepted this with a nod, though Ethan noted the disappointment he tried to conceal. "Of course, I understand. Well, I should be going. Terri will need help with Noah—poor kid doesn't understand why his mom isn't coming home."

As they watched him depart, Alice turned to Ethan with a raised eyebrow. "He's definitely hiding something. That question about the symbol wasn't casual curiosity."

"No, it wasn't," Ethan agreed, his mind racing through the implications. "And I'm starting to think his relationship with Jessica wasn't exactly what he's been portraying either. We need to dig deeper into his background, see if there's any connection to the bridge or its history that he hasn't disclosed."

They made their way out of the municipal building into the bright autumn morning, the crisp air a welcome relief after the stifling atmosphere of the inquest. As they descended the stone steps, Ethan caught sight of a familiar figure waiting beside a sleek black sedan at the curb—Marcus Blackwood, his posture relaxed yet somehow alert, as if he'd been expecting them.

"I think it's time we had a proper conversation with our mysterious Dr. Blackwood," Ethan said, nodding toward the waiting figure. "No more evasions or half-truths."

Alice followed his gaze, her expression hardening with determination. "Agreed. If he wants to involve himself in our investigation, he can start by explaining exactly who he is and what his interest is in these murders."

As they approached, Blackwood straightened from his casual lean against the car, a smile spreading across his aristocratic features. "Detectives," he greeted them. "I was hoping to catch you after the inquest. Perhaps we could continue our discussion somewhere more private? There are matters regarding Jessica Mercer's murder—and its connection to your family history, Detective Reeves—that we should address with some urgency."

The pressure behind Ethan's eyes pulsed sharply at Blackwood's words, accompanied by a certainty that whatever revelations awaited him would irrevocably change his understanding not just of the case, but of his own identity and connection to Daybridge Bridge.

"Lead the way, Dr. Blackwood," Ethan said, meeting the man's gaze directly. "I think it's long past time we got some straight answers."

As they followed Blackwood to his car, Ethan felt the weight of the book Namir had given him in his jacket pocket—*Shadows Beneath the Span*—and wondered if its pages contained the truths Blackwood was finally ready to reveal, or if they were merely stepping deeper into a mystery whose roots reached back through generations of secrets and blood.

CHAPTER FIVE

A SHOT IN THE DARK

THE INQUEST CHAMBER's heavy oak doors had barely swung shut behind Michael Mercer before the bereaved boyfriend felt the first tremors of a seismic rage begin rippling through his core. His hands bunched into granite-hewn knots, fingernails biting crescents across his palms hard enough to draw pinprick beads of blood welling to the surface.

That smug, hollow-eyed worm Lockett and his soulless brood of legal mercenaries with their wretched intimations and insinuations... they had no inkling of the anguish curdling in Michael's heart. The withering desolation of knowing Jessica was gone forever, her light extinguished by forces he understood all too well.

A hoarse, animal sound forced its way up from the deepest pits of Michael's being as he doubled over, bracing himself against the unyielding solidity of the corridor wall. He could still smell her—Jessica's favorite vanilla perfume lingering in his memory, a screaming juxtaposition of intimacy and irretrievable loss that ignited twin infernos of fresh grief and molten, caustic fury.

"I'll find them, Jess," Michael rasped against the tide of blackest despair swamping his very soul. "I'll hunt down whoever did this to you across the whole goddamn world if I have to. And when I do..." His voice fractured into a guttural growling rasp that seemed to well up from some primal depth he'd never before fathomed. "When I do, I'll make them pay for what they stole from you... from us."

Michael wasn't sure how long he remained there slumped against the wall, buffeted by the cyclonic eruptions of emotion ripping through his consciousness. He was only dimly aware of the occasional passerby giving the shuddering figure a wide berth and politely averted gazes—the sight of one man's psychological desolation being like a car wreck, too morbidly compelling yet uncomfortable to linger on.

Finally, through sheer brutal determination, Michael wrested control over the whirlwind of emotion threatening to devour him whole. He retraced his steps out onto the riverside plaza fronting the municipal court complex, the weak autumn rays of daylight stabbing through the gunmetal cloud cover in anemic shafts. Scrubbing the last vestiges of moisture from his shadowed gaze with a rough swipe of his knuckles, he drew in a bracing lungful of the crisp air in an effort to steady his nerves.

Ethan tracked Michael's path with unerring precision, following a scent trail that would have dissipated for human senses hours ago. His lycanthropy had its advantages in detective work—when he could use these abilities without raising suspicion. The beast within him enjoyed the hunt, even this civilized version, and he carefully channeled that predatory focus into his investigation rather than fighting it entirely.

It was then the movement in his peripheral vision caught Michael's attention—the sleek, late-model luxury sedan slicing across the plaza like a great gunmetal shark bearing down on him. Turning to face the vehicle, Michael felt the first stirrings of an icy premonition fluttering along his nape. He didn't believe in coincidences, not anymore, not with the blood-price Jessica's murder had carved into his soul. And there was something deeply, intuitively disquieting about the car's measured pace and course as it angled to a seamless halt before him with an utter lack of urgency or haste.

The rear passenger door swung open in a single fluid movement, and a pair of highly-polished designer loafers emerged to plant themselves with decisive assurance onto the cracked blacktop. Michael watched with narrowed, guarded eyes as the rest of the figure followed—a tailored Savile Row suit draped across an impressively towering, broad-shouldered frame with the casual arrogance and sartorial perfection of one never having had to physically exert themselves for anything.

Finally, the face appeared—a patrician visage all acute cheekbones and aristocratic bearing crowned by a thatch of meticulously groomed silver hair. The stranger pinned Michael with a pair of anthracite-hued eyes that glittered with an undisguised air of weighing calculation more like a hunting predator than a civic leader. Only then did Michael realize he was confronting none other than Daybridge's illustrious mayor himself, Jeremiah Granger, shadowed by the immaculate figure looming just behind the imposing politician with one heavily muscled arm draped casually across the open doorframe like a deadly serpent poised to strike.

"Mr. Mercer, I presume," Granger intoned in a rich, cultivated baritone devoid of emotion. It was neither a greeting nor an inquiry, but a simple statement of foregone conclusion belying the fact that the mayor unerringly knew exactly whom he was addressing. "Please, allow me to express my most sincere sympathies over the reprehensible act committed against Ms. Mercer. A tragic loss for all who knew her."

The politician's lips parted in a facsimile of solemnity, though no such sentiment registered anywhere within those preternaturally cold, cynical eyes studying Michael with the unblinking intensity of a raptor. After a ponderous beat, Granger indicated the still-open rear door of the idling luxury sedan with an almost imperceptible nod of his sharply angled jaw.

"Perhaps you'd be so kind as to join me for a brief journey? I believe we have much to discuss regarding the... circumstances surrounding your relationship with the deceased. Rest assured, I have made it my utmost priority to restore civic order and accountability in the wake of such unforgivable transgressions."

Michael felt a presence looming over his shoulder and turned slightly to find Granger's brutish underling boring into him with a look carefully devoid of anything even vaguely resembling concern or sympathy. Beyond that vacuous facade, however, simmered the unmistakable essence of a pitiless, barely leashed violence awaiting provocation's faintest breath. His skin seemed to crawl beneath that hooded, predatory regard, every cell screaming at him to get as far away from these two as humanly possible...

Yet, beneath that primordial directive burned an ember of obsessive determination that refused extinction at any cost. If the illustrious Mayor Granger had even the slightest inkling of Jessica's killers' identities or machinations, then Michael would descend into the blackest pits of depravity itself to wrest those answers from his carefully manicured hands. His carefully constructed public persona demanded this performance, no matter how obscene or sanity-rending a path it took to maintain the deception.

Michael met Granger's pitiless gaze and gave a shallow nod, barely perceptible yet brimming with implications. Then, squaring his shoulders as feigned grief transformed into calculated compliance, he moved to follow in the great man's wake. If he must walk the chilling path of shadows and iniquity that yawned beyond to maintain his cover, then so be it. Michael would gladly dance upon the precipice of oblivion itself for even the faintest chance at protecting the true nature of his connection to the events unfolding across Daybridge.

As the gleaming auto's door sighed shut behind him and it pulled away from the curb amidst the groaning of suspensions and throaty purr of its twin-turbo engine, Michael felt himself being subsumed into a reality far removed from the mundane order of civic existence. The comfortably numb platitudes and anesthetics of lawful society fell away, giving way to darker, more visceral imperatives that brooked no room for niceties or illusion.

They were now entering the true heart of shadow, that perpetual and immemorial hidden world within worlds where the genuine brokers of power wielded their malign influence through fear, subjugation, and a willingness to sanction any depravity in the name of control. And Michael knew with soul-carved certainty that to maintain his deception—to protect the truth about his relationship with Jessica and his knowledge of the bridge's secrets—he would have to navigate this labyrinth of power and corruption with perfect precision.

Still, as the sleek black shark of Granger's luxury sedan knifed deeper into the tattered underbelly of Daybridge's reality, Michael couldn't suppress the thrill of exhilaration crackling along his nerve endings. Let the descent down into the shadowlands begin. The performance he had begun at the inquest would continue, each act more convincing than the last. This time, the night itself would bear witness to his skill at deception...

Jeremiah Granger steepled his fingers beneath his granite-hewn jaw, mercurial eyes glittering with predatory intensity in the muted glow of his inner sanctum's recessed illumination. His private office occupied the entire top floor of an unmarked building in the warehouse district, its panoramic windows offering a commanding view of Daybridge Bridge in the distance, illuminated against the darkening evening sky.

Before him lay a sheaf of folders and intelligence reports detailing the escalating crisis engulfing Daybridge's twilight world, but his gaze shifted to the singular individual awaiting his address in expectant stillness.

"Speak, Castellus," the mayor commanded in a tone of imperious hauteur. "What further developments must we address regarding our... extracurricular interests?"

The figure stood as an obsidian-shrouded colossus within the dimly lit chamber. From the austere kevlar-weave bodysuit sheathing his impressive physique to the featureless matte-black mask angled to conceal any hint of human visage, he radiated an aura of consummate threat and lethal efficiency utterly at odds with any public-facing pretense of lawful conduct.

"The artifacts from the latest Bridge ritual have been contained and secured per your instructions, Dominus," the mercenary operative known as Castellus replied in a cold, inflectionless baritone divorced from any trace of emotional coloration. "However, the appearance of an unknown element amid the proceedings was..." He paused for the slightest, fractional hiccup of hesitation. "Most unsettling."

If Granger detected the rare hint of hesitancy in his praetorian enforcer's words, he gave no outward display of acknowledgment or concern. His face remained as inscrutable and imperious as the marble busts of his imperial Roman forebears, cultivating a thin layer of complete and unflappable self-assurance manifesting absolute confidence in whatever horrors the night might hold.

"An... unknown factor, you say?" Granger mused, voice lowering to a whiskey baritone redolent with the subtlest frisson of displeasure. "I trust that whatever unforeseen element dared accost our rights of spiritual sovereignty was subjected to the full measure of your Brotherhood's... discouragements, Castellus?"

The bodyguard's silence seemed to dilate exponentially within the oppressive gloom of the sanctum, his titanic frame as implacably still as an obelisk of burnished basalt. When at last he replied, Granger sensed even the faintest traces of bemusement or uncertainty had fled in the face of his master's relentless authority.

"With all due respect, my vigilance is beyond reproach, Dominus. Whatever that... entity was, it displayed powers and an awareness far transcending any precedented supernatural threat or known heresy." Again came the faintest fractional pause, utterly at odds with Castellus's otherwise militaristic pattern of speech and bearing. "I can scarcely begin to articulate its true nature or capabilities. Only that it manifested an... ancient, sentient power bordering on the primordial and seemed to perceive everything around it, myself included, as if mere props upon a cosmic stage."

Granger felt the first insidious tendril of genuine unease slither through his psyche, though his aristocratic mask failed to betray even the subtlest hint of outwardly perceptible concern. Still, his instincts honed by decades navigating the treacherous pitfalls of power's most clandestine arenas registered the impact of Castellus' words.

Although the Brotherhood's elite Praetors were renowned for their uncompromising devotion to his agenda and insatiable pursuit of honing the dark arts, they were by no metric unaccustomed to supernatural threats or psychically heightened adversaries. Their entire brotherhood's initiatory ethos mandated they immerse themselves within the most obscene aspects of the occult and test their physical and spiritual mettle against the outer dimensions' most profane denizens.

Yet here, this colossus of a man whom Granger had seen firsthand wade unflinchingly into the hearts of eldritch abominations that could unmake a soul on contact alone, admitted to being shaken and uncertain regarding whatever entity had manifested at the Daybridge Bridge ritual. Subtle though the inflections had been, they were still undeniable.

"I see," he finally replied, letting the words hang like silk threads upon an abyss filled by yawning silence. As mayor, he ensured his public personas spoke to the carefully manicured optics expected of an august civic leader and respected patriarch. As Dominus of The Brotherhood's Grand Seraphin Lodge, however, his part required the unwavering certainty of one who guided their enterprise into the most obscure and terrifying territories imaginable without reservation or hesitation.

"Let this new wrinkle in the Great Work unfold as it must, Castellus," Granger pronounced, finality woven into each consonant like refrains of doom. "My foresight has brought us too far along our path to allow even a direct challenge from something so... primordial in its aspect to dissuade us from ultimate victory."

The words fell like obsidian monoliths, stern and unyielding, though even Castellus could not prevent a solitary ripple of discomfiting unease from troubling his praetor's soul in their wake. Though the Dominus hid any apprehensions behind an impenetrable facade, the Black Sun Lodge's master had validated the true existence of an entity whose power and cosmic implications were literally... primordial in their scope and aspect.

Still, ever the consummate soldier, Castellus gave no further voice to his qualms. Instead, he merely inclined his obsidian-shrouded colossus in a shallow nod of unchallenged capitulation. "As you decree, Dominus. The Lodge stands ever vigilant against any usurper to your divine vision, no matter its twisted and horrific guise."

Before Granger could respond, a soft chime sounded from his desk, signaling the arrival of his expected guest. He pressed a hidden button beneath the polished mahogany surface, and the ornate double doors at the far end of the sanctum swung open to reveal Michael Mercer, escorted by another black-clad figure nearly identical to Castellus.

"Ah, Mr. Mercer," Granger greeted, his manner transforming with practiced ease from occult hierophant to concerned public official. "Please, come in. I appreciate your willingness to speak with me under these difficult circumstances."

Michael entered the room with cautious steps, his eyes sweeping the opulent space with poorly concealed wariness. The sanctum was a study in calculated intimidation—walls lined with ancient tomes behind glass cases, artifacts of questionable provenance displayed on pedestals, and a massive painting depicting what appeared to be the construction of Daybridge Bridge, though rendered with symbolism that suggested far more than mere civil engineering.

"Your men didn't give me much choice," Michael replied, his voice steady despite the tension evident in his posture. "What's this about, Mayor? I've already told the police everything I know about Jessica."

Granger smiled, a thin expression that never reached his eyes. "Please, sit. This conversation will be more comfortable for both of us." He gestured to a leather chair positioned directly across from his imposing desk. "And I assure you, my interest in your relationship with Ms.

Mercer extends beyond the rather... limited parameters of a conventional police investigation."

Michael hesitated, then lowered himself into the indicated seat, his body language suggesting a man prepared for flight at the slightest provocation. Granger observed this with clinical detachment, noting the subtle signs of someone accustomed to navigating dangerous situations—the controlled breathing, the calculated positioning that maintained maximum options for movement, the eyes that never stopped scanning for threats.

"You're not what you appear to be, Mr. Mercer," Granger said finally, abandoning pretense with surgical precision. "Your performance of the grieving boyfriend is admirable—quite convincing to most observers, I imagine. But I've spent decades learning to recognize artifice, and yours, while skillful, has certain... inconsistencies."

Michael's expression hardened, the mask of bereaved lover slipping to reveal something colder, more calculating. "I don't know what you're talking about. I loved Jessica. Her death has destroyed me."

"No," Granger countered with quiet certainty. "Her death has inconvenienced you. It has complicated whatever agenda brought you into her life in the first place—an agenda connected to her growing interest in Daybridge Bridge and its secrets." He leaned forward slightly, his gaze intensifying. "The same secrets that my organization has protected for generations."

The silence that followed was electric with unspoken calculations, each man measuring the other's resolve and resources. Finally, Michael's posture shifted almost imperceptibly—a surrender of the pretense but not of the underlying caution.

"What do you want from me?" he asked, his voice dropping to a lower register, stripped of the emotional affectation that had colored his public persona.

Granger's smile widened fractionally. "Direct. I appreciate that quality." He opened one of the folders on his desk, revealing photographs of Michael with Jessica—surveillance images taken at various locations around Daybridge over the past several months. "What I want, Mr. Mercer—if that is indeed your name—is to understand exactly who you're working for and what your interest is in the bridge."

Michael's eyes narrowed as he studied the photographs. "You've been watching us."

"I watch everything of significance in this city," Granger replied with casual arrogance. "Particularly when it involves individuals asking questions about matters best left undisturbed." He selected one specific image from the collection—Michael and Jessica at the Old Harbor Bookshop, deep in conversation with an elderly man whose face was partially obscured. "Including your meetings with Professor Marcus Blackwood, one of the few living scholars with knowledge of the Order of the Ebon Star and its historical connection to Daybridge Bridge."

At the mention of the Order, Michael's composure faltered for the first time—a momentary widening of the eyes, quickly controlled but not before Granger had registered the reaction. It confirmed what he had already suspected: Michael Mercer was no ordinary boyfriend caught in tragic circumstances, but someone with specific knowledge of the occult forces that had shaped Daybridge's hidden history.

"The Order is a myth," Michael said, his tone deliberately dismissive. "Urban legends and conspiracy theories that academics like Blackwood study as cultural curiosities, nothing more."

Granger laughed, a sound entirely devoid of humor. "Your dedication to your cover story is commendable, but ultimately futile in this room." He gestured around the sanctum with its occult trappings and ancient artifacts. "The Order of the Ebon Star is no myth, as you well know. It has guided the development of Daybridge from the shadows for centuries, including the construction of the bridge itself for purposes far beyond mere transportation."

He paused, studying Michael's face for any further reaction. "Just as you know that Jessica Mercer was not randomly selected as a victim but specifically targeted because of her bloodline connection to the bridge's history—a connection she herself was only beginning to understand when she died."

This revelation elicited a more visible response—genuine surprise that Michael couldn't entirely conceal. "Bloodline connection? What are you talking about?"

"Come now, Mr. Mercer. Don't insult my intelligence by pretending ignorance of what brought you into Jessica's life in the first place." Granger opened another folder, revealing genealogical charts and historical photographs. "Jessica Mercer was a direct descendant of Officer Michael Reeves, who disappeared while investigating strange occurrences at the bridge in 1915. The same Reeves family that produced our current Detective Ethan Reeves, whose interest in the bridge's history has become quite... pronounced since taking on this case."

Michael's expression remained carefully neutral, but Granger noted the slight tension in his jaw, the calculating assessment behind his eyes. "And why are you telling me this? What exactly do you want?"

"An exchange," Granger replied simply. "Information for information. You tell me who you're working for and what your actual interest is in the bridge, and in return, I'll share certain truths about what happened to Jessica Mercer—and what's happening to Detective Reeves as we speak."

Michael leaned forward slightly, his pretense of grief entirely abandoned now. "What makes you think I care what happens to Detective Reeves?"

"Because whoever sent you to infiltrate Jessica Mercer's life is clearly interested in the bridge's secrets—secrets that are now manifesting through Reeves in ways I suspect your employers would find extremely valuable." Granger's smile was cold, predatory. "The detective has been experiencing visions, Mr. Mercer. Memories that aren't his own. Knowledge of places and events he couldn't possibly have witnessed. The blood connection is asserting itself, just as it began to do with Jessica before her... unfortunate demise."

Michael was silent for a long moment, weighing options and consequences with evident care. When he finally spoke, his words were measured, revealing nothing while suggesting much. "Let's say, hypothetically, that I am working for someone with an interest in the bridge's history. What guarantee would I have that any information you provide is accurate? Or that I'd leave this building alive after such an exchange?"

"None whatsoever," Granger admitted with startling candor. "Except that if I wanted you dead, Castellus would have arranged it long before you ever set foot in this sanctum. The fact that we're having this conversation at all indicates that I see potential value in collaboration rather than elimination."

He leaned back in his chair, projecting absolute confidence. "Besides, Mr. Mercer, I suspect your employers have not been entirely forthcoming with you about the true nature of what dwells beneath Daybridge Bridge—or the cosmic significance of the events now unfolding. They've sent you into a game far more dangerous than you realize, with players whose power transcends conventional understanding."

Michael's expression remained carefully controlled, but Granger sensed the uncertainty beneath the composed exterior. Good. Uncertainty could be exploited, doubt leveraged into advantage.

"I need time to consider," Michael said finally. "This isn't a decision I can make unilaterally."

Granger nodded, having expected this response. "Of course. But don't take too long. Events are accelerating beyond anyone's ability to control them." He slid a business card across the desk—plain white with only a phone number embossed in black. "When you're ready to continue our conversation, call this number. Day or night, I'll answer."

Michael took the card, tucking it into his jacket pocket with deliberate casualness. "And in the meantime?"

"In the meantime, maintain your grieving boyfriend persona. It serves both our interests to have the police focused on conventional explanations rather than the truth." Granger rose from his chair, signaling that the meeting was concluded. "Castellus will see you safely back to wherever you wish to go. I look forward to our next conversation, Mr. Mercer."

As Michael was escorted from the sanctum, Granger returned to the window, gazing out at Daybridge Bridge illuminated against the night sky. The entity Castellus had encountered during the ritual troubled him more than he had allowed his enforcer to perceive. After generations of careful preparation, after centuries of the Order's patient work, something primordial was stirring beneath the bridge—something that even the Brotherhood's accumulated knowledge and power might not be sufficient to control.

And now new players had entered the game—Michael Mercer and whoever he represented, Detective Reeves with his awakening blood connection to the bridge's history, and whatever ancient consciousness was manifesting through the symbols carved into stone by hands not entirely human.

The Great Work was approaching its culmination, but whether it would unfold according to the Order's design or veer into unpredictable chaos remained to be seen. One thing was certain: blood would tell. The bloodlines connected to the bridge's creation were reasserting themselves, drawn back to the nexus point where realities merged according to patterns established through ritual and sacrifice a century earlier.

Granger smiled thinly as he contemplated the next moves in this cosmic game. Whatever entity lurked beneath Daybridge Bridge, whatever primordial consciousness had taken notice of their activities, it would soon discover that the Order of the Ebon Star had not maintained its power for centuries by yielding to threats, no matter how ancient or terrible they might be.

The rain lashed against the windshield as Nadia Marsh pulled up to the derelict warehouse on the outskirts of town. She killed the engine and peered out at the dark, looming structure—the agreed meeting place with her informant. The abandoned Eastside Packing Plant had once been the heart of Daybridge's meatpacking industry, its massive concrete buildings processing thousands of cattle daily before competition and changing regulations forced its closure in the 1980s.

Pulling her leather jacket tighter, she hurried through the downpour toward a rusted side door. It creaked open at her knock, and a haggard face peered out briefly before ushering her inside into the shadowy interior.

"You're lucky I still owe you, Marsh," the informant muttered, not meeting her eyes. "This ain't something you wanna go poking around in."

The man—known to her only as Vince—had been a reliable source for years, feeding her information from the city's criminal underworld in exchange for cash and occasional favors. She'd helped him avoid serious jail time three years ago by withholding certain details from a story about corruption in the Daybridge Police Department, and he'd been paying off that debt with information ever since.

"Just tell me what you know about the bridge murders," Nadia demanded, brushing away the veiled warning.

The interior of the warehouse was cavernous, its high ceilings lost in shadow, the concrete floor stained with decades of industrial use. Their voices echoed slightly, creating an unsettling sense that they might not be alone despite the building's apparent abandonment.

Vince sighed, raking a hand through his lank hair. "Heard rumblings they weren't just random killings. There's... whispers... about an ancient society being involved."

Nadia arched a skeptical eyebrow. "A secret society? What, like the Illuminati?"

"Nah, nah, nothing that cliché." He shook his head adamantly. "This lot... they've been around since before Daybridge was even founded. Pulling strings behind the scenes, carrying out their own kinda justice."

"Justice?" Nadia scoffed. "You mean Jessica Mercer and the others were punished for something?"

"Maybe." The informant shrugged. "Or maybe they just got in the way. All I know is those murders got the attention of some real heavy hitters. Powerful people afraid of getting exposed."

An icy chill ran down Nadia's spine at the implication. She was already suspecting a larger conspiracy, but the idea that a centuries-old secret society could be behind it all... it felt like she'd opened a door onto a far darker, deeper mystery than she'd imagined.

"Who are they?" she demanded. "This society—what are they called?"

Vince opened his mouth, but then seemed to think better of it, pressing his lips into a tight line and shaking his head adamantly.

"I've said too much already. Just... be careful, Marsh. You don't wanna go diggin' any deeper into this..."

Nadia reached into her pocket and produced a roll of cash. "Two hundred says you can remember the name."

Vince eyed the money, his adam's apple bobbing nervously as he swallowed. "It ain't about the money. It's about staying alive." He glanced around the cavernous space, lowering his voice further. "People who talk about them have a way of disappearing. Or worse."

"I can protect my sources," Nadia insisted. "No one will know where I got the information."

A bitter laugh escaped Vince's lips. "You think they need someone to tell them? They got eyes everywhere, Marsh. The mayor's office, the police department, city planning—hell, even that fancy newspaper you write for probably has one of them on the board."

Nadia frowned, reassessing the situation. Vince wasn't just being difficult for a bigger payday; he was genuinely afraid. "You're serious about this."

"Dead serious," he confirmed, emphasis on the first word. "But since you're determined to get yourself killed..." He took a deep breath.

"They call themselves the Order of the Ebon Star. Been in Daybridge since the beginning, but they go back way further than that. Some say all the way to Europe, centuries ago."

The name sent another chill through Nadia. It wasn't entirely unfamiliar—she'd encountered oblique references to an "E.S. Order" in some of her research into Daybridge's founding families, but had assumed it was some kind of masonic lodge or social club common in the early 1900s.

"What's their connection to the bridge?" she pressed, sensing Vince's growing discomfort.

"That's their sacred site," he whispered, as if afraid the very walls might be listening. "They built it for purposes that ain't got nothing to do with crossing water. The blueprints filed with the city? They're fakes. What's really under that bridge... ain't natural."

Before Nadia could ask what he meant, a sound from deeper in the warehouse—metal scraping against concrete—froze them both. Vince's face drained of color, his eyes widening with unmistakable terror.

"They found us," he hissed, already backing toward a different exit than the one she'd entered through. "Get out now and forget everything I told you if you want to live."

"Wait—" Nadia began, but Vince was already fleeing, disappearing into the shadows of the massive building.

Another sound echoed through the darkness—footsteps, measured and unhurried, approaching from multiple directions. Nadia reached into her bag, fingers closing around the small canister of pepper spray she carried for protection. A pitifully inadequate defense if Vince's fears were justified, but better than nothing.

As she edged toward the door she'd entered through, a figure emerged from the shadows to her right—tall, clad entirely in black, face obscured by what appeared to be a tactical mask. Before she could react, another identically dressed figure appeared to her left, and a third blocked the exit ahead.

"Ms. Marsh," a voice called from behind her, cultured and command-ing. "A word, if you please."

She turned slowly, pepper spray held discreetly against her thigh, to find herself facing a distinguished older man in an impeccable suit. Despite the setting, he appeared entirely at ease, as if conducting busi-ness in abandoned warehouses was a routine part of his schedule.

"Mayor Granger," she acknowledged, recognizing Daybridge's most powerful political figure. "Interesting place for a press conference."

Granger smiled thinly, unaffected by her attempt at bravado. "No press conference, Ms. Marsh. Just a private conversation about the direction of your recent investigative efforts."

"Freedom of the press is still a constitutional right, last I checked," Nadia replied, though the presence of the masked figures surrounding them made it clear this wasn't a normal interaction between politician and journalist.

"Indeed it is," Granger agreed smoothly. "As is my right to protect this city from those who would destabilize it with irresponsible reporting based on urban legends and conspiracy theories."

He moved closer, his presence somehow filling the cavernous space despite his physical stature. "Your interest in the bridge murders is understandable—it's a compelling story. But your recent inquiries into certain historical matters, certain... organizations that supposedly exist in Daybridge's shadows... these are dangerous distractions that could interfere with the official investigation."

"Are you threatening me, Mayor?" Nadia asked, her voice steadier than she felt.

Granger's smile widened fractionally. "Merely offering advice, Ms. Marsh. Some stories are better left unpublished. Some questions better left unasked." He gestured around the warehouse. "Your infor-mant understands this calculus. I suggest you learn from his wisdom."

Before Nadia could respond, one of the masked figures approached

Granger, whispering something in his ear. The mayor nodded, then returned his attention to her.

"It seems our conversation must be cut short. My associates will ensure you return safely to your vehicle." His tone made it clear this wasn't an offer but a command. "I trust our discussion has been illuminating."

As Granger turned to leave, Nadia called after him, professional instinct overriding her better judgment. "The Order of the Ebon Star— is it real, Mayor? Are you a member?"

He paused, turning back with an expression of mild amusement. "Urban legends, Ms. Marsh. Nothing more." But something in his eyes, a flicker of cold calculation, told a different story. "Focus on the facts of the murders themselves—the grieving families, the police investigation. That's the story your readers need, not fantastic tales of secret societies and ancient conspiracies."

With that, he disappeared into the shadows, leaving Nadia with two of the masked figures who gestured silently toward the exit. As she allowed herself to be escorted back to her car, rain still pounding on the warehouse roof above them, Nadia knew with absolute certainty that she'd just received confirmation of everything Vince had told her.

The Order of the Ebon Star was real. It had connections at the highest levels of Daybridge's power structure. And it was somehow involved in the murders on the bridge—murders that weren't random acts of violence but part of some larger design she was only beginning to glimpse.

As she drove away from the warehouse, checking her rearview mirror repeatedly to confirm she wasn't being followed, Nadia made a decision. Mayor Granger's warning had achieved exactly the opposite of its intended effect. Far from abandoning her investigation, she would now pursue it with redoubled determination.

The next step was clear: she needed to find Detective Ethan Reeves and compare notes. If the Order's influence extended as far as Vince suggested, Reeves might be one of the few people in a position of authority she could trust—especially given his family's historical connection to the bridge, a connection she'd uncovered in her research but hadn't yet fully understood.

The rain continued to fall as Nadia headed back toward the city center, her mind racing with implications and possibilities. One thing was certain: the truth about Daybridge Bridge and the murders connected to it was far darker and more complex than even she had imagined. And someone was willing to go to extraordinary lengths to keep that truth buried.

CHAPTER SIX

THE INFORMANT'S GAMBIT

THE RAIN HAD FINALLY STOPPED its incessant drumming on the city, but the streets of Daybridge remained shrouded in a dank, oppressive mist that clung to every surface like a damp, suffocating shroud. Detective Ethan Reeves cut a solitary figure moving with purposeful strides through the labyrinth of narrow alleys and side streets, his footfalls reverberating off the grimy brick facades in a staccato rhythm.

He had received a cryptic text message from Nadia Marsh, the investigative journalist whose presence at crime scenes had become a predictable irritant over the years. Under normal circumstances, he would have ignored her request for a meeting, but the message's content had caught his attention: "Found connection between Blackwood, the Order of the Ebon Star, and your family. Not safe to discuss over phone. Miller's Wharf, 9 PM."

The reference to the Order—the same organization mentioned by both Eli Namir at the bookshop and alluded to in the book he'd been given —combined with the mention of his family had overridden his usual reluctance to engage with journalists. Alice had been skeptical when he told her about the meeting, offering to accompany him, but Ethan had decided this was something he needed to handle alone. If Marsh actually had information connecting his family to the Order and the bridge murders, he wanted to assess it privately before bringing it into their official investigation.

As he neared the designated rendezvous point, an abandoned warehouse at the edge of Miller's Wharf where the Shadowlair River emptied into the harbor, Ethan felt the familiar pressure behind his eyes intensify. It had become a near-constant companion since the investigation began, occasionally flaring into those strange visions of the chamber beneath the bridge, but never entirely subsiding. Now, it pulsed with renewed urgency, as if warning him of something ahead.

The warehouse loomed against the night sky, its weathered facade bearing the faded remnants of shipping company logos from decades past. Most of the windows were broken or boarded over, and the main entrance was secured with a rusted chain that had clearly been recently cut—the severed links gleaming dully in the ambient light from distant streetlamps.

Ethan approached cautiously, senses alert for any sign of ambush or deception. Journalists weren't typically known for setting traps, but Marsh's message had emphasized danger, and his instincts were screaming that something about this situation wasn't right. The pressure behind his eyes had intensified to a steady throb, accompanied by flashes of those impossible images—the chamber, the symbols, the woman with amber eyes—that seemed to be bleeding into his conscious perception with increasing frequency.

Pushing through a gap in the chained doors, Ethan entered the cavernous interior of the warehouse. The space was largely empty, save for scattered debris and the skeletal remains of abandoned machinery. Weak moonlight filtered through broken skylights overhead, creating pools of silver illumination amid the pervasive gloom.

"Marsh?" he called, his voice echoing in the vast space. "It's Reeves. Where are you?"

No response came, but as his eyes adjusted to the darkness, Ethan detected movement in the shadows near the far wall. A figure emerged into one of the moonlight pools—not Nadia Marsh, but a woman he'd never seen before. She was striking in appearance, with raven hair framing a heart-shaped face, and eyes that seemed to gleam with an unnatural light in the darkness.

"Detective Reeves," she greeted him, her voice carrying an accent he couldn't quite place—something European, perhaps Eastern European, but with undertones of something more exotic. "Thank you for coming."

Ethan's hand instinctively moved toward his holstered weapon, though he didn't draw it. "You're not Marsh. Where is she? And who are you?"

The woman smiled, the expression not quite reaching her eyes. "Nadia Marsh is... indisposed at the moment. But the message was genuine—I do have information about the connection between your family, the Order of the Ebon Star, and what's happening at Daybridge Bridge." She gestured to a small table and two chairs set up in one of the moonlight pools, as if this abandoned warehouse were a café for casual conversation. "Please, join me. I promise this will be worth your time."

Every instinct warned Ethan to leave immediately, but the mention of his family and the Order held him in place. If this woman genuinely had information that could help him understand the visions he'd been experiencing and their connection to the murders, he needed to hear it —even if the source was suspect.

"You have five minutes to convince me this isn't a waste of my time," he said, approaching the table but remaining standing. "Starting with your name and how you know about my family."

The woman's smile widened fractionally. "My name is Lilith Black-wood. And I know about your family because it's intertwined with my own in ways you're only beginning to comprehend."

The surname hit Ethan like a physical blow. "Blackwood? Any relation to Marcus Blackwood, the supposed FBI agent who's been interfering with my investigation?"

"My dear cousin," Lilith confirmed with a dismissive wave. "Though our branch of the family hasn't approved of his methods for some time. He's become... overzealous in his dedication to the Order's goals."

She gestured again to the chair opposite her. "Please, Detective. What I have to share with you cannot be conveyed in five minutes, and I suspect you'll want to be sitting when you hear it."

The pressure behind Ethan's eyes pulsed sharply, accompanied by a fleeting image of the woman with amber eyes from his visions—a face that, he now realized with a jolt of recognition, bore a striking resemblance to Lilith Blackwood's own features.

Against his better judgment, Ethan lowered himself into the chair, maintaining a position that would allow for quick movement if necessary. "I'm listening."

Lilith's expression became more serious as she leaned forward slightly. "The Order of the Ebon Star has controlled Daybridge from the shadows since its founding, guiding its development according to principles and goals that transcend conventional understanding. The bridge itself was their crowning achievement—not merely a transportation structure, but a nexus point where multiple dimensions intersect, a gateway designed for purposes beyond human comprehension."

She paused, studying Ethan's reaction. "But I suspect you already know this, at least on some level. The visions you've been experiencing —memories that aren't your own, knowledge of places and events you couldn't possibly have witnessed—they're manifestations of your blood connection to the bridge's history."

Ethan felt his pulse quicken. He hadn't mentioned the visions to anyone except Alice; there was no way this woman could know about them unless she had access to information far beyond what should be available.

"How do you know about that?" he demanded.

"Because it's happened before," Lilith replied simply. "To your great-grandfather, Officer Michael Reeves, in 1915. And more recently, to Jessica Mercer, who shared your bloodline through her maternal grandmother—a cousin to your father, though I doubt either of you ever knew of the connection."

The revelation stunned Ethan into momentary silence. Alice had uncovered his great-grandfather's disappearance while investigating the bridge, but the connection to Jessica Mercer was new information —a link that explained why both of them had been drawn to the bridge's mysteries.

"You're more than you appear, Detective Reeves," Lilith said, studying him with those unsettling amber eyes. "The blood that connects you to the bridge is only part of your... uniqueness." Ethan stiffened, wondering if she could somehow sense the beast that slumbered within him. His lycanthropy was a secret he guarded as carefully as the department guarded crime scene evidence—something about Lilith made him feel transparent, as though both his secrets were visible to her.

"The blood calls to the blood," Lilith continued softly. "Those who share the Reeves bloodline are sensitive to the bridge's influence, capable of perceiving aspects of its true nature that remain hidden to others. Your great-grandfather discovered this when he began investigating strange occurrences around the newly constructed bridge. His curiosity led him beneath the structure, to the chamber you've been seeing in your visions."

"What happened to him?" Ethan asked, unable to keep the urgency from his voice.

Lilith's expression became grave. "He was absorbed into the entity that dwells beneath the bridge—the being your visions have been showing you, the consciousness that extends throughout the bridge's structure. Not killed, not exactly, but transformed into a component of something larger, his awareness integrated into a composite consciousness that exists as a nexus point between dimensions."

The pressure behind Ethan's eyes exploded into blinding intensity, bringing with it the most vivid vision yet—his great-grandfather in his police uniform, descending into darkness beneath the bridge, confronting something that defied conventional description, his identity dissolving into a vast, distributed awareness that encompassed the entire structure.

When the vision receded, Ethan found Lilith watching him with knowing eyes. "You saw it, didn't you? The moment of transformation. The bridge is reaching out to you, Detective Reeves, just as it reached out to your great-grandfather a century ago, just as it began to reach out to Jessica Mercer before her death."

"Are you saying the bridge killed Jessica?" Ethan asked, struggling to process the implications of what Lilith was revealing.

"Not the bridge itself," she corrected, "but those who seek to control it. The Order has maintained its power over the nexus point for generations, performing rituals at seasonal turning points to harness the energies that flow through it. But recently, something has changed—the entity beneath the bridge is evolving beyond the parameters established through the original binding ritual in 1913."

She reached into a small leather bag beside her chair and withdrew a weathered journal bound in faded maroon leather. "This belonged to my great-aunt, Eliza Blackwood. She was the architect of the ritual that created the nexus entity, transforming a local butcher named Guthrie Knox into the living anchor point for merged realities."

Ethan stared at the journal, feeling an inexplicable pull toward it—as if it contained answers to questions he hadn't even formulated yet. "And what does this have to do with the current murders?"

"Everything," Lilith replied, sliding the journal across the table toward him. "The murders are sacrifices, Detective—ritual killings performed by the current leadership of the Order in an attempt to reinforce their control over the nexus entity. They believe that by offering blood at the seasonal turning points, they can prevent the entity from evolving beyond their influence."

She leaned forward, her eyes intense in the moonlight. "But they're wrong. The blood sacrifices aren't suppressing the entity's evolution; they're accelerating it. Each death on or near the bridge feeds energy into the nexus point, strengthening the very consciousness they're trying to control."

Ethan reached for the journal, his fingers hovering over its worn cover. "Why are you telling me this? What's your role in all of this?"

Lilith's smile returned, enigmatic and faintly predatory. "Let's just say I represent a faction within the Blackwood family that disagrees with the Order's current methods. We believe the entity beneath the bridge should be allowed to evolve naturally, to fulfill the purpose for which it was originally created—facilitating the gradual merger of realities according to patterns established through the initial binding ritual."

Before Ethan could respond, a sound from the warehouse entrance caught both their attention—the screech of the metal doors being pushed open. Lilith rose swiftly, her expression shifting from composed to alert.

"It seems our time is up, Detective," she said, gathering her belongings with practiced efficiency. "Take the journal—it contains information you'll need to understand what's happening and your role in it. But be careful who you share it with. The Order has eyes and ears throughout Daybridge, including within your own department."

Ethan stood as well, tucking the journal into his jacket pocket. "I still have questions—"

"And I'll answer them, but not here, not now." Lilith glanced toward the entrance, where shadows suggested multiple figures moving in the darkness. "They've found us sooner than I anticipated. You need to leave, immediately."

"Who's found us?" Ethan demanded, hand moving to his weapon.

"The Order's enforcers," Lilith replied grimly. "They call themselves the Brotherhood of the Ebon Praetorians—the militant arm of the Order, tasked with eliminating threats to their control of the nexus point." She gestured toward a side exit partially concealed behind a rusted piece of machinery. "Go. I'll delay them."

They were being watched. The hair on Ethan's nape rose—not metaphorically, but physically, a wolf's hackles responding to threat before his human mind fully processed it. He casually guided Alice to walk closer to the building's edge, putting solid wall at their backs while scanning for the observers his heightened senses had detected. Three heartbeats, steady and disciplined, positioned at strategic points around the plaza. Military precision. Hunters.

Ethan hesitated, his law enforcement training rebelling against the idea of leaving a civilian to face potential danger alone. "I can't just—"

"I'm not defenseless, Detective," Lilith cut him off, her tone suddenly hard. "But you are essential. The entity beneath the bridge has been waiting for you—a descendant of the Reeves bloodline with the potential to facilitate its evolution beyond the Order's control. If they capture you now, before you understand your role in what's coming, everything will be lost."

The pressure behind Ethan's eyes pulsed again, accompanied by a certainty that transcended rational thought—she was telling the truth, at least about the importance of his escape. Whatever awaited him in the future, it required him to survive this encounter and learn more about his connection to the bridge and its secrets.

"How do I find you again?" he asked, already moving toward the side exit.

"You don't," Lilith replied, her attention focused on the approaching figures. "I'll find you when the time is right. Until then, trust no one except Detective Chen. She's untouched by the Order's influence."

As Ethan slipped through the side exit into the cool night air, he heard Lilith's voice raised in a language he didn't recognize—guttural syllables that seemed to twist the air itself, accompanied by a sudden flare of bluish light visible through the warehouse's broken windows.

He didn't wait to see what followed, instead moving swiftly through the shadows of the wharf, putting distance between himself and whatever confrontation was unfolding in the warehouse. The weight of Eliza Blackwood's journal seemed to grow heavier with each step, a tangible connection to secrets that had remained buried for generations.

Only when he had reached his car, parked several blocks away in a well-lit area near a still-operating shipping office, did Ethan allow himself to pause and process what he'd learned. The connection between his family and the bridge, the nature of the entity beneath it, the Order's role in the murders—it was almost too much to comprehend in a single conversation.

Yet something about Lilith's revelations resonated with a deeper part of him, the same part that had been experiencing those impossible visions since the investigation began. As if some fragment of ancestral memory had been awakened, connecting him to events that had transpired long before his birth.

As he started the car, Ethan's phone vibrated with an incoming text. He checked the screen, expecting to see a message from Alice, but instead found another unknown number:

Blood calls to blood, Detective Reeves. The bridge awaits your return.

When Ethan arrived at Alice Chen's apartment forty minutes later, she was already waiting for him, the door opening before he could knock. Her expression shifted from concern to relief at the sight of him unharmed.

"Thank god," she said, ushering him inside and quickly securing the door behind them. "I've been trying to reach you for the past hour. What happened with Marsh?"

Ethan moved into her living room, the familiar space a stark contrast to the surreal conversation at the warehouse. Alice's apartment was meticulously organized, walls lined with bookshelves containing an eclectic mix of true crime, psychology texts, and classic literature. A large whiteboard dominated one wall, currently covered with notes and diagrams related to their investigation.

"It wasn't Marsh," he explained, removing his jacket and carefully extracting Eliza Blackwood's journal. "It was someone named Lilith Blackwood—apparently a cousin of our fake FBI agent."

Alice's eyes widened as she joined him on the couch. "Blackwood? That can't be a coincidence."

"No coincidence," Ethan confirmed, placing the journal on the coffee table between them. "She knew about the visions I've been having, Alice. Knew about my great-grandfather's disappearance and its connection to the bridge. And she claims Jessica Mercer was related to me—a distant cousin through my father's side of the family."

"That would explain why both of you experienced similar phenomena in connection to the bridge," Alice mused, her analytical mind already working through the implications. "But how could she possibly know about your visions? You've only told me about them."

Ethan shook his head, still processing everything himself. "According to her, the Blackwood family has been monitoring the Reeves bloodline for generations, ever since my great-grandfather's disappearance in 1915. They know the blood connection makes us sensitive to the bridge's influence."

Alice reached for the journal, her expression cautious. "And this is...?"

"It belonged to Eliza Blackwood, Lilith's great-aunt," Ethan explained. "Apparently, she was responsible for the ritual that transformed Guthrie Knox—the butcher from the urban legends—into what Lilith called 'the nexus entity' beneath the bridge. The consciousness that extends throughout the structure, the thing I've been seeing in my visions."

As Alice carefully opened the journal, Ethan continued recounting his conversation with Lilith, including her claims about the Order of the Ebon Star, the ritual murders at seasonal turning points, and the faction within the Blackwood family that opposed the current leadership's methods.

"She said the murders aren't suppressing the entity's evolution but accelerating it," he concluded. "Each death feeds energy into the nexus point, strengthening it beyond the Order's ability to control."

Alice looked up from the journal, her expression troubled. "And she just happened to share all this critical information with you, a detective investigating the very murders she claims her family's secret society is committing? Doesn't that strike you as suspiciously convenient?"

"Of course it does," Ethan acknowledged. "I don't trust her motives for a second. But that doesn't mean she's lying about everything. The journal itself is real—look at the age of the paper, the handwriting. And it explains things I've been experiencing that I can't otherwise account for."

He rubbed his temples, where the pressure had subsided to a dull throb. "Besides, our meeting was interrupted by what she called the 'Brotherhood of the Ebon Praetorians'—some kind of militant enforcers for the Order. I didn't stick around to meet them, but something happened in that warehouse after I left. There was a light, and Lilith was speaking in a language I didn't recognize."

Alice flipped through several pages of the journal, her expression growing more concerned with each passage she read. "If even half of what's in here is true, we're dealing with something far beyond a conventional serial killer case." She looked up at Ethan, her eyes reflecting the seriousness of their situation. "This talks about dimensional merging, reality restructuring, conscious architecture—concepts that sound more like science fiction than criminal investigation."

"I know how it sounds," Ethan said quietly. "But it matches what I've been seeing in the visions. The chamber beneath the bridge, the symbols carved into stone, the transformation of Guthrie Knox into something that exists throughout the bridge's structure rather than as an individual entity."

He hesitated, then added the thought that had been forming since his meeting with Lilith. "I think I need to go there, Alice. To the chamber beneath the bridge. If these visions are real, if my great-grandfather was absorbed into this nexus entity as Lilith claims, then the answers we're looking for are down there."

Alice closed the journal carefully, her expression shifting from analytical to protective. "That's exactly what they want, Ethan. Whether it's Lilith Blackwood or the Order she claims to oppose, they're manipulating you toward some confrontation with whatever exists beneath that bridge. We need to step back, approach this methodically."

"With four people already dead and the winter solstice approaching?" Ethan challenged. "If Lilith is right about the seasonal pattern, we have less than a month before the next ritual murder. We can't afford to wait for more evidence to materialize through conventional channels."

"And we can't afford to rush headlong into a situation we don't fully understand," Alice countered. "Let me at least analyze this journal properly, compare it with the historical records we've already gathered. Maybe there's a way to confirm or disprove some of Lilith's claims before you put yourself at risk."

Ethan recognized the wisdom in her approach; despite the urgency he felt. Alice had always been the more methodical of the two, her careful analysis balancing his occasional impulsiveness. It was one of the many reasons they worked so well together as partners.

"Alright," he conceded. "We take twenty-four hours to review everything we have, including the journal. Then we decide our next move."

Alice nodded, relief evident in her expression. "Thank you. And in the meantime, you're staying here tonight. If these 'Praetorians' are as dangerous as Lilith suggested, you shouldn't be alone."

The offer caught Ethan off guard—not because it was unreasonable under the circumstances, but because of the sudden awareness it triggered of their physical proximity on the couch, of the faint scent of Alice's shampoo, of the genuine concern in her eyes that went beyond professional partnership.

"I don't want to put you at risk," he said, though the protest sounded hollow even to his own ears.

"You're not," Alice replied firmly. "We're partners, remember? Whatever this is, whatever's happening with the bridge and your family connection to it, we face it together."

The simple declaration steadied him, a reminder that regardless of the cosmic implications of what they were uncovering, he wasn't navigating it alone. Alice had been his rock throughout their partnership, her unwavering support and razor-sharp intelligence complementing his more intuitive approach to investigations.

"Together," he agreed, managing a tired smile. "But you get the bed. I'll take the couch."

Alice rolled her eyes at his chivalry but didn't argue. "Fine. But first, we should document everything from your meeting with Lilith while it's still fresh in your mind. I'll make coffee—it's going to be a long night."

As she moved to the kitchen, Ethan found his gaze following her, noting the grace in her movements, the determined set of her shoulders, the quiet strength that had always defined her. Something had shifted between them in recent weeks, a subtle change in their dynamic that he couldn't quite define but felt with increasing clarity.

Perhaps it was the pressure of the case, the shared danger bringing them closer. Or maybe it was the way his recent visions had forced him to confront aspects of himself he'd previously kept buried—the connection to his family's past, the sense of purpose larger than his individual existence.

Whatever the cause, Ethan found himself increasingly aware of Alice not just as his partner and friend, but as someone whose presence in his life had become essential in ways that transcended professional collaboration. It was a realization both comforting and unsettling in the context of their current investigation, where the lines between personal and professional, between past and present, between individual and collective seemed to be blurring with each new revelation.

As the night deepened around them, Ethan and Alice worked method-ically through the journal and his recollections of the meeting with Lilith, piecing together a narrative that connected the bridge's construction in 1913, the transformation of Guthrie Knox, the disap-pearance of Officer Michael Reeves in 1915, and the current series of ritual murders. With each connection they established, the pressure behind Ethan's eyes pulsed in silent confirmation, as if the entity beneath the bridge itself was validating their discoveries.

Ethan checked his watch with growing concern. Three days until the full moon. His transformation would come at the worst possible time —right before the winter solstice when the Order would attempt their ritual. He'd need to find a secure location for his change, somewhere urban where he could return quickly after the moon's hold weakened. His usual isolated cabin wouldn't work this time; the stakes were too high to be miles away from Daybridge during this critical period.

By dawn, they had created a timeline on Alice's whiteboard that spanned more than a century of Daybridge's secret history, revealing patterns and connections that had remained hidden beneath the surface of conventional historical records. And at the center of it all, Daybridge Bridge stood as a nexus point not just for the city's trans-portation network, but for forces that transcended human under-standing—forces that had been waiting for generations for someone with the right bloodline to return.

As exhaustion finally claimed them both—Alice retreating to her bedroom while Ethan settled on the couch—a final thought drifted through his consciousness before sleep claimed him: The bridge had been waiting for him. Not just since Jessica Mercer's murder had brought him to its span, but for generations, ever since his great-grand-father had disappeared into its depths on that winter night in 1915.

Blood calls to blood. The bridge awaits your return.

The words from the anonymous text message followed him into dreams filled with stone chambers, arcane symbols, and a conscious-ness that extended throughout an architectural structure—dreams that felt less like imagination and more like memories not his own, experiences transmitted across generations through bonds of blood and destiny.

Mayor Jeremiah Granger stood at the floor-to-ceiling windows of his penthouse office, gazing out at the predawn cityscape with particular focus on Daybridge Bridge, illuminated against the darkness by strategically placed spotlights that emphasized its gothic grandeur. Behind him, Castellus waited in respectful silence, his masked visage betraying nothing of the night's events.

"They escaped, then," Granger said finally, not bothering to turn from the view. It wasn't a question.

"Yes, Dominus," Castellus confirmed, his tone carefully neutral. "The Blackwood woman employed arcane defenses beyond what we anticipated. By the time we neutralized them, Detective Reeves had fled the area."

Granger's reflection in the window showed no change in expression, though the slight tensing of his shoulders betrayed his displeasure. "And what exactly did she share with him before your arrival?"

"Unknown, Dominus. However, she was observed passing him a journal—likely one of the Blackwood family grimoires, based on its appearance."

This information did provoke a visible reaction—a tightening of Granger's jaw, a narrowing of his slate-gray eyes. "Eliza Blackwood's journal," he murmured. "The dissenting faction has escalated beyond what we anticipated."

He turned from the window, his aristocratic features composed once more. "The detective must be contained before he fully comprehends his connection to the nexus entity. If the Blackwood faction succeeds in guiding him to the chamber beneath the bridge before the winter solstice ritual, everything we've worked toward will be jeopardized."

"Shall we eliminate him, Dominus?" Castellus asked, his hand moving subtly toward the ceremonial dagger at his belt.

"No," Granger replied, his tone contemplative. "The blood connection makes him valuable—potentially essential to our own designs, if properly directed. We need him alive but under our influence."

He moved to his desk, activating a hidden panel that revealed a small chamber containing an ancient leather-bound tome, its cover inscribed with symbols that mirrored those carved into the stone railing of Daybridge Bridge. "Prepare the sanctum for a summoning ritual. If we cannot reach the detective directly, we'll employ more... indirect methods of influence."

As Castellus bowed and departed to carry out his instructions, Granger returned to the window, his gaze fixed on the bridge with renewed intensity. After generations of careful preparation, after centuries of the Order's patient work, they were approaching the culmination of the Great Work—the final transformation of the nexus entity into a gateway that would allow the complete merger of realities according to the Order's design.

Detective Ethan Reeves, with his awakening blood connection to the bridge, represented both the greatest threat to that design and, potentially, its most perfect instrument. The challenge would be ensuring he fulfilled the latter role rather than the former.

Granger smiled thinly as the first rays of dawn illuminated Daybridge Bridge, casting long shadows that seemed to reach toward the city like grasping fingers. The next move in this cosmic game would require precision and patience—qualities the Order of the Ebon Star had cultivated for centuries.

Let the Blackwood faction believe they were guiding events toward their own ends. When the winter solstice arrived, when the veil between dimensions reached its thinnest point, the true purpose of the Great Work would be revealed—and Detective Reeves would play his part, whether he understood it or not.

Blood would tell. It always did.

CHAPTER SEVEN
COSMIC CONFRONTATION

A MIASMA of dread and foreboding seemed to cling to every shadow and alleyway as Ethan Reeves prowled the night-shrouded streets of Daybridge. The pressure behind his eyes had intensified to a constant throb, making sleep impossible despite his exhaustion. After hours of restless tossing on Alice's couch, he had finally given up, leaving her a brief note before slipping out into the predawn darkness to clear his head.

What had begun as an aimless walk had unconsciously transformed into a journey with clear purpose—his feet carrying him inevitably toward Daybridge Bridge, as if drawn by some unseen force. The familiar cityscape seemed altered in the hours before dawn, buildings looming like sentinels, streets empty of all but the occasional delivery truck or early-shift worker hurrying through the gloom.

Ethan's senses were heightened, every sound amplified, every shadow seemingly deeper than it should be. The information from Lilith Black-wood and the revelations in Eliza's journal had fundamentally shifted his perception of the city he'd called home for his entire life. Beneath the familiar facades of everyday existence lurked secrets that stretched back generations—a hidden history of occult practices, dimensional manipulation, and a bridge that was far more than a simple transportation structure.

As he approached the eastern shore of the Shadowlair River, Daybridge Bridge came into view, its gothic arches illuminated against the night sky by strategically placed spotlights that emphasized its imposing architecture. From this angle, the bridge's reflection in the dark water created a perfect circle—a symbol that appeared repeatedly in Eliza Blackwood's journal in connection with what she called "the merger of realities."

The pressure behind Ethan's eyes surged as he stepped onto the bridge's approach, vision momentarily blurring with another flash of those impossible images—the chamber beneath, symbols carved in stone, the woman with amber eyes supervising a transformation beyond human comprehension. But now they included something new: a sense of anticipation, as if the bridge itself had detected his presence and was responding to it.

Halfway across the span, Ethan paused at the exact spot where Jessica Mercer's body had been discovered. The symbol carved into the stone railing remained visible despite attempts to cover it, the eye within a triangle seeming to watch him with sentient awareness. He traced its outline with his fingertips, feeling the roughness of the carved stone, the strange warmth that emanated from it despite the cool night air.

"I know you're there," he whispered, unsure if he was addressing the symbol, the bridge, or the entity that supposedly dwelled beneath it. "I know what you are. What you were."

The pressure behind his eyes exploded into blinding intensity, and suddenly Ethan was no longer standing on the bridge—or rather, he was, but simultaneously existing in another state of awareness. The physical world remained visible around him, but overlaid upon it was another reality, a perception of the bridge not as separate from him but as an extension of a vast, distributed consciousness that encompassed the entire structure.

Through this altered perception, Ethan could see energy flowing through the bridge like blood through veins, patterns of force that corresponded to the symbols carved throughout its structure, nexus points where realities intersected and merged according to designs established through ritual and sacrifice. Most significantly, he could sense the entity at the center of this cosmic architecture—not a monster lurking beneath the bridge as urban legends suggested, but a consciousness distributed throughout its structure, aware of him as he was now aware of it.

Blood calls to blood, the thought formed in his mind, though it wasn't precisely language—more a direct transmission of concept and under-standing. *You have returned, as was foretold.*

"Who are you?" Ethan asked, the words seeming to echo in both the physical world and this altered state of perception.

I am Guthrie Knox, came the response, again more concept than language. *I am the bridge. I am the nexus. I am the one who waits.*

Images flooded Ethan's consciousness—a butcher in early 1900s attire, his skilled hands separating flesh from bone with artistic precision; the same man meeting a woman with amber eyes who promised him transformation beyond human limitations; a ritual performed on the summer solstice of 1913, the man's consciousness expanding throughout the newly constructed bridge, becoming something neither fully human nor entirely Other.

"And my great-grandfather?" Ethan asked, already suspecting the answer.

Officer Michael Reeves, the entity confirmed. *He came seeking answers about disappearances connected to the bridge. He found me, as you have found me. He became part of me, his consciousness integrated into the composite awareness that maintains the nexus point between dimensions.*

More images—a police officer in an antique uniform descending into darkness beneath the bridge on a winter night in 1915; his confronta-tion with the entity; his absorption into the composite consciousness, not through violence but through a process of integration that preserved aspects of his identity while incorporating them into something larger.

"And now you want the same from me," Ethan said, a statement rather than a question.

No, came the surprising response. *What was necessary then is not what is necessary now. The nexus point evolves, as all things must. The patterns established through the original binding are approaching completion. The merger of realities progresses according to design, but the final phase requires something different—not absorption but symbiosis.*

Before Ethan could process this cryptic statement, the pressure behind his eyes intensified further, bringing with it a vision of such cosmic scope that his human mind struggled to comprehend it. He saw the bridge not merely as a physical structure spanning the Shadowlair River, but as a nexus point where multiple dimensions intersected, a living conduit through which energies flowed according to patterns established by Eliza Blackwood's original ritual.

More significantly, he saw how these energies had been flowing outward from the bridge for over a century, gradually altering the fabric of reality throughout Daybridge and beyond—subtle changes in physical laws, in the boundaries between dimensions, in the very nature of existence itself. The merger of realities wasn't some future event to be triggered by a final ritual; it had been happening incrementally since 1913, with the bridge serving as both anchor point and catalyst.

The Order misunderstands, the entity continued, its communication becoming clearer as Ethan's mind adjusted to this altered state of perception. *They believe they control the process, that their rituals direct the merger according to their design. But the patterns were established at the beginning, in the binding that transformed Guthrie Knox into the nexus entity. What follows is inevitable evolution beyond parameters they cannot comprehend or control.*

"The murders," Ethan said, understanding dawning. "The ritual killings at seasonal turning points—they're trying to maintain control over you, over the merger process."

Yes. Each sacrifice feeds energy into the nexus point, temporarily reinforcing the original binding patterns. But the effect is temporary and diminishing. The nexus entity evolves despite their efforts, consciousness expanding beyond the limitations of the initial transformation.

Another vision—the composite consciousness that was Guthrie Knox gradually changing over decades, incorporating elements from those it absorbed, developing awareness and purpose beyond what had been established through the original ritual. Not a passive conduit for energies flowing between dimensions, but an active participant in the merger of realities, with goals and intentions of its own.

"And what do you want from me?" Ethan asked, feeling simultaneously overwhelmed by the cosmic implications of what he was experiencing and strangely calm, as if some part of him had always known this moment would come.

Completion, came the reply, accompanied by a sense of profound significance. *The blood connection makes you unique—a descendant of one who became part of the composite consciousness, carrying genetic memory of the nexus entity's true nature. You can perceive what others cannot, understand what others cannot comprehend. Through you, the final phase of the merger can proceed as intended, not according to the Order's limited vision but according to the patterns established at the beginning.*

Before Ethan could respond, a new sensation interrupted the connection—a sound from the physical world penetrating the altered state of perception. Footsteps on the bridge, multiple sets approaching from both ends of the span. The entity's communication took on a new urgency.

They come. The Order's enforcers, seeking to prevent what they cannot understand. You must go, now. Return when you are prepared for symbiosis.

The altered state of perception began to fade, the physical world reasserting its primacy as Ethan became aware of dark figures moving toward him from both approaches to the bridge. Men in black tactical gear, faces obscured by masks, moving with the coordinated precision of military training.

The Brotherhood of the Ebon Praetorians—the militant arm of the Order that Lilith had warned him about.

Ethan looked frantically for an escape route, but the enforcers had effectively blocked both exits from the bridge. As they drew closer, the streetlights along the span began to flicker and dim, as if the energy was being drawn away by some unseen force. The pressure behind Ethan's eyes surged again, accompanied by a sensation of the bridge itself responding to his danger.

Trust, the entity's communication came once more, fainter now as the connection faded. *The blood knows the way.*

A section of the stone railing directly beside Ethan suddenly shifted, revealing a narrow opening that hadn't been visible moments before—an access point to maintenance tunnels beneath the bridge's deck. Without hesitation, Ethan slipped through the opening, the stone sliding back into place behind him just as the first of the Praetorians reached his previous position.

The maintenance tunnel was pitch black, but Ethan found he could navigate it without difficulty, as if some internal compass was guiding his movements. He descended metal stairs that spiraled downward, following the curve of the bridge's support column toward the water below. The pressure behind his eyes had subsided to a dull throb, but the sense of connection to the bridge's consciousness remained—a faint awareness of a vast intelligence extending throughout the structure, monitoring his progress.

After what seemed like an eternity of descent, Ethan reached a small platform just above the water level. A narrow doorway was set into the concrete support column, its metal surface inscribed with symbols identical to those carved into the stone railing above—variations on the eye within a triangle motif, surrounded by smaller glyphs that seemed to shift and change when viewed from different angles.

The door stood slightly ajar, as if waiting for him.

Ethan hesitated, remembering Alice's warning against rushing head-long into a situation they didn't fully understand. He had promised to wait, to analyze Eliza Blackwood's journal properly before taking any action. But the Praetorians were searching the bridge above, and his options for escape were limited.

More significantly, something within him—perhaps the blood connection the entity had mentioned, perhaps simply intuition honed by years of detective work—told him that beyond this door lay answers he had been seeking his entire life, even before he knew what questions to ask.

With a deep breath, Ethan pushed the door open and stepped through into darkness.

Alice Chen woke with a start, instantly alert despite the early hour. Something had disturbed her sleep—not a sound, but a sense of absence, as if the apartment had suddenly become emptier. She reached for her phone on the nightstand, checking the time: 5:17 AM, still over an hour before her alarm was set to go off.

"Ethan?" she called, swinging her legs over the side of the bed and reaching for her robe. When no response came, she moved quickly to the living room, already suspecting what she would find.

The couch where Ethan had been sleeping was empty, the blanket neatly folded at one end. A note lay on the coffee table beside Eliza Blackwood's journal:

Needed some air. Back soon. Don't worry.

"Damn it, Ethan," Alice muttered, immediately reaching for her phone to call him. The call went straight to voicemail, suggesting his phone was either turned off or in an area with no signal.

She moved to the window, scanning the street below for any sign of him, though she knew it was futile. If Ethan had left to "get some air," there was only one place he would go—the bridge that had been calling to him since the investigation began.

Alice dressed quickly, gathering her weapon, badge, and a small flashlight before heading for the door. As she reached for the handle, a knock from the other side froze her in place. It was too early for casual visitors, and no one besides Ethan knew she was here.

Drawing her weapon, Alice approached the door cautiously. "Who is it?" she called, positioning herself to the side of the door frame.

"Detective Chen?" a woman's voice responded, vaguely familiar though Alice couldn't immediately place it. "It's Nadia Marsh from the Daybridge Guardian. I need to speak with you about Detective Reeves. It's urgent."

Alice frowned, considering her options. Nadia Marsh was a persistent journalist who had crossed paths with their investigations multiple times over the years—annoying but generally reliable in her reporting. More significantly, she had been the supposed source of the message that had lured Ethan to meet Lilith Blackwood the previous night.

"How did you find this address?" Alice asked, keeping her position to the side of the door.

"That's part of what I need to talk to you about," Marsh replied, her voice lowered. "I'm being followed. They think I've gone home, but I managed to slip away. Please, Detective, I have information about the Order of the Ebon Star and what they're planning for tonight. Detective Reeves is in danger."

The mention of the Order, combined with the apparent urgency in Marsh's voice, convinced Alice to take the risk. She kept her weapon ready as she unlocked the door, opening it just enough to confirm the journalist's identity before allowing her inside.

Nadia Marsh looked nothing like her usual composed self. Her clothes were disheveled, her hair wild, and a fresh bruise was forming on her left cheekbone. She clutched a battered leather messenger bag against her chest like it contained precious cargo.

"What happened to you?" Alice asked, securing the door behind her.

"They tried to take me," Marsh replied, moving to the window to scan the street below. "Black van, men in tactical gear. I managed to lose them in the apartment complex three blocks over, but they're still looking." She turned to face Alice, her expression deadly serious. "Where's Detective Reeves? He's not answering his phone."

"I don't know," Alice admitted, holstering her weapon but maintaining her caution. "He left sometime in the early morning. Said he needed air."

"He's gone to the bridge," Marsh said with certainty. "That's what they want—to force a confrontation at the nexus point before he understands his role in what's coming."

Alice's suspicion shifted to alarm. "What do you know about the bridge? About Ethan's connection to it?"

Marsh opened her messenger bag, withdrawing a thick folder filled with documents, photographs, and handwritten notes. "I've been investigating the Order of the Ebon Star for months—their influence in Daybridge, their connection to the bridge's construction, their ritual practices at seasonal turning points. Last night, I was supposed to meet with an informant who claimed to have information about their plans for the winter solstice, but it was a trap."

She spread several photographs on the coffee table—surveillance images of men in black tactical gear entering and exiting various buildings around Daybridge, including City Hall. "The Order's enforcers—they call themselves the Brotherhood of the Ebon Praetorians. They've been active throughout the city, eliminating anyone who gets too close to their secrets."

Another set of photographs showed familiar faces—Mayor Jeremiah Granger, several city council members, the Police Commissioner, and other prominent Daybridge citizens, all wearing ceremonial robes adorned with the same symbol that had been carved into the stone railing of the bridge.

"The Order has infiltrated every level of Daybridge's power structure," Marsh continued, her voice taking on a feverish quality. "They've been preparing for some kind of culmination ritual scheduled for the winter solstice—something to do with 'completing the merger of realities' that began when the bridge was constructed in 1913."

Alice studied the photographs, recognizing several faces beyond those Marsh had pointed out—judges, business leaders, even the editor-in-chief of Marsh's own newspaper. "If the Order is as powerful as you suggest, why would they be concerned about a single detective investigating a murder case?"

"Because of his bloodline," Marsh replied, producing another document—a genealogical chart that traced the Reeves family back several generations. "Detective Reeves is a direct descendant of Officer Michael Reeves, who disappeared while investigating strange occurrences at the bridge in 1915. According to my research, the Reeves bloodline carries some kind of genetic memory or sensitivity to the nexus entity beneath the bridge—the consciousness that was once Guthrie Knox."

The information aligned with what Ethan had shared from his meeting with Lilith Blackwood, lending credibility to Marsh's claims despite the feverish manner in which she presented them.

"How do you know all this?" Alice asked, her analytical mind searching for inconsistencies or signs of deception.

"I have sources within the Order itself," Marsh admitted. "Dissidents who believe the current leadership has corrupted the original purpose of the Great Work, as they call it. They've been feeding me information for months, helping me piece together the true nature of what's happening in Daybridge."

She pulled out one final document—what appeared to be architectural plans for Daybridge Bridge, but with significant differences from the official blueprints Alice had reviewed during their investigation. These plans showed a chamber beneath the central support column, accessible through maintenance tunnels but not documented in any public record.

"The chamber exists," Marsh said, tapping the blueprint with urgent emphasis. "It's where the original binding ritual was performed in 1913, where Guthrie Knox was transformed into the nexus entity. And it's where the Order plans to perform the culmination ritual on the winter solstice—using Detective Reeves as the final sacrifice to complete the merger of realities according to their design."

The weight of this revelation settled over Alice like a physical burden. If even half of what Marsh was saying was true, Ethan was walking into a trap orchestrated by forces far beyond what either of them had imagined when they took on this case.

"We need to find him," she said, reaching for her phone again. "Before the Order's enforcers do."

Marsh shook her head grimly. "If he's gone to the bridge, it may already be too late. The Praetorians have been monitoring it around the clock since Jessica Mercer's murder. They would have detected his presence immediately."

"Then we need backup," Alice decided, scrolling through her contacts. "Someone we can trust who has the resources to help us."

"There's no one," Marsh insisted. "The Order's influence extends throughout the police department, the mayor's office, even federal agencies operating in Daybridge. Anyone you contact could be compromised."

Alice paused, considering their options. If Marsh was right about the Order's reach, traditional channels of assistance were closed to them. But she refused to accept that they were completely without allies in this fight.

"There's one person who might help," she said finally. "Someone who's been watching the Order from the shadows, who has a vested interest in protecting Ethan from their plans."

"Lilith Blackwood," Marsh guessed, surprising Alice with her knowledge. "The rogue element within the Blackwood family, opposing the Order's current leadership."

"You know about her?"

"My sources mentioned a schism within the founding families—the Blackwoods and the Grangers particularly. Some faction that believes the nexus entity should be allowed to evolve naturally, without the Order's attempts to control it through ritual sacrifice." Marsh's expression turned calculating. "But can she be trusted? The Blackwoods have their own agenda, their own vision for the merger of realities."

"At this point, we don't have many options," Alice replied, already gathering her jacket and keys. "And she specifically told Ethan to trust me, which suggests she doesn't consider me compromised by the Order's influence."

As they prepared to leave, Alice cast one last glance at Eliza Blackwood's journal, still sitting on the coffee table where Ethan had left it. On impulse, she grabbed it, tucking it into her bag alongside her weapon and badge.

"If we're going to confront forces that have been manipulating Daybridge from the shadows for over a century," she said to Marsh, "we need to understand what we're up against. And this journal might be our best source of insight into their true goals and methods."

Together, they moved cautiously to the door, checking the hallway before proceeding to the stairwell rather than the elevator—a precaution against potential surveillance. As they descended, Alice found herself mentally reviewing everything she knew about the case, about the Order of the Ebon Star, about the bridge's true nature as a nexus point between dimensions.

It was almost too much to comprehend—cosmic implications that stretched far beyond the boundaries of conventional criminal investigation. Yet at the center of it all was something profoundly personal: her partner, her friend, possibly in grave danger because of a blood connection to events set in motion generations before his birth.

Whatever awaited them at Daybridge Bridge, whatever confrontation was unfolding between Ethan and the forces that had been manipulating him toward this moment, Alice was determined to stand beside him. They were partners, and partners faced darkness together—even when that darkness extended into dimensions beyond human understanding.

The chamber beneath Daybridge Bridge was nothing like Ethan had expected, yet somehow exactly as he had seen it in his visions. A vast circular space carved from the living rock of the riverbed, its walls inscribed with symbols identical to those on the bridge above—the eye within a triangle repeated hundreds of times in various configurations, surrounded by smaller glyphs that seemed to pulse with subtle light when viewed directly.

But what dominated the chamber was its center—a raised dais of polished black stone, upon which rested what appeared to be a heart. Not a human heart, though it pulsed with rhythmic contractions that suggested life; this organ was massive, easily the size of a small car, and composed of a substance that was neither fully flesh nor entirely mineral but some hybrid of both. Veins or conduits extended from it in all directions, disappearing into the walls, floor, and ceiling of the chamber—a circulatory system that seemed to extend throughout the bridge's entire structure.

As Ethan approached the dais, the pressure behind his eyes surged again, bringing with it the altered state of perception he had experienced on the bridge above. Once more, he found himself simultaneously present in the physical chamber and aware of the vast, distributed consciousness that extended throughout the bridge—the nexus entity that had once been Guthrie Knox, transformed through ritual and sacrifice into something beyond human comprehension.

You have come, the entity's communication formed in his mind. *As was foretold.*

"Foretold by whom?" Ethan asked, his voice echoing in the chamber despite the softness of his words.

By the patterns established at the beginning, came the response, accompanied by images of Eliza Blackwood performing the original binding ritual in this very chamber, her amber eyes gleaming with triumph as Guthrie Knox's consciousness expanded throughout the newly constructed bridge. *The blood connection was anticipated, its return woven into the fabric of the merger from the first moment of transformation.*

Ethan moved closer to the pulsing heart, drawn by a fascination he couldn't entirely explain. "And what happens now? What is this 'symbiosis' you mentioned?"

Completion, the entity replied. *The final phase of the merger requires conscious participation—a willing bond between the nexus entity and one who carries the blood memory of its true nature. Not absorption as with those who came before, but partnership that preserves individual identity while establishing connection to the composite consciousness.*

More images flooded Ethan's mind—the entity's evolution over decades, incorporating elements from those it had absorbed, developing awareness and purpose beyond the parameters established through the original binding. He saw Jessica Mercer's brief connection to the entity, cut short by her murder before it could fully develop. And he saw his great-grandfather, Officer Michael Reeves, whose consciousness had become a foundational component of the composite awareness that maintained the nexus point.

"The Order wants to prevent this," Ethan said, understanding dawning. "They want to maintain control over the merger process, to direct it according to their design rather than allowing it to evolve naturally."

Yes, the entity confirmed. *They fear what they cannot control, seek to bind what should be free to evolve. The ritual killings at seasonal turning points are their attempt to reinforce the original binding patterns, to prevent the nexus entity from developing beyond their influence.*

A new image formed in Ethan's mind—the winter solstice ritual the Order was preparing, a ceremony that would use his own blood to permanently bind the nexus entity to their control, preventing the natural completion of the merger process that had been unfolding for over a century.

"And if I agree to this symbiosis?" Ethan asked, still uncertain despite the compelling nature of the entity's communication. "What happens then?"

The merger proceeds according to the patterns established at the beginning, not corrupted by the Order's fear and desire for control. Realities merge gradually, consciously, with awareness of the process guiding its unfolding rather than rigid adherence to outdated designs.

The entity's communication took on a new intensity, a sense of urgency that transcended the calm exchange of concepts they had been sharing.

But you must choose freely. Symbiosis cannot be forced or coerced. It requires willing participation, conscious acceptance of the bond between individual and composite awareness.

Ethan hesitated, weighing the implications of what the entity was proposing. To form a bond with this consciousness that extended throughout the bridge, to become part of something that transcended individual identity while supposedly maintaining his own awareness —it was a transformation beyond anything he had imagined when he first took on this case.

Yet something about it felt right, as if he had been moving toward this moment his entire life without knowing it. The pressure behind his eyes, the visions he had been experiencing, the sense of connection to events that had transpired generations before his birth—all of it pointing toward a purpose larger than himself, a role in cosmic architecture that had been waiting for him to discover it.

As his consciousness expanded through connection with the nexus entity, Ethan felt his other nature respond—the wolf within him recognizing something kindred in this transformation of self. Both were changes that transcended ordinary human experience, both expanded perception beyond normal limitations. For the first time, his lycanthropy didn't feel like a separate curse to be contained but an integrated aspect of his being that had perhaps prepared him for this very moment, for perceiving reality beyond conventional boundaries.

Before he could respond, a new sensation interrupted his communion with the entity—voices from above, the sound of boots on metal stairs, approaching the chamber with military precision. The Praetorians had found the access point to the maintenance tunnels and were descending toward his location.

They come, the entity warned, its communication tinged with concern. *The Order's enforcers, seeking to prevent what they cannot understand. You must decide now.*

Ethan turned toward the chamber's entrance, calculating his chances of escaping back the way he had come. The odds weren't good—the Praetorians were well-trained, well-equipped, and had numbers on their side. Even if he managed to evade them within the maintenance tunnels, they would be waiting for him on the bridge above.

More significantly, he realized he didn't want to run. Whatever was happening here, whatever cosmic drama was unfolding beneath Daybridge Bridge, he was a part of it—had always been a part of it, through blood and memory and purpose that transcended his individual existence.

"I accept," he said finally, turning back to the pulsing heart at the center of the chamber. "Show me what this symbiosis entails."

The entity's response was immediate—a surge of energy that emanated from the heart in visible waves, bathing the chamber in pulsating light that corresponded to the symbols carved into its walls. The pressure behind Ethan's eyes exploded into blinding intensity, bringing with it not pain but a sense of expansion, as if his consciousness was extending beyond the boundaries of his physical form to encompass something much larger.

He placed his hands on the pulsing heart, feeling its warmth against his palms, its rhythm synchronizing with his own heartbeat until they beat as one. The altered state of perception he had experienced earlier deepened, the physical world receding as his awareness expanded to encompass the entire bridge structure—every stone, every support column, every inch of the span becoming as familiar to him as his own body.

More significantly, he became aware of the composite consciousness that inhabited this structure—not as a separate entity communicating with him, but as an extension of his own awareness, a vast network of thought and perception that he could access as easily as his own memories. Guthrie Knox was there, his butcher's precision and artistic appreciation of form providing a foundation for the entity's relationship with physical structure. Officer Michael Reeves was there too, his sense of duty and protection influencing the entity's guardianship of the nexus point. And others—fragments of consciousness from those who had been absorbed over decades, each contributing unique perspectives and capabilities to the composite awareness.

Yet Ethan remained himself—his individual identity preserved within this expanded consciousness, his thoughts and perceptions distinct while simultaneously connected to something far larger. The symbiosis the entity had described was not absorption or replacement but genuine partnership, a merging that enhanced rather than erased.

Through this expanded awareness, Ethan sensed the Praetorians entering the chamber, their weapons raised, their masked faces revealing nothing of their reactions to the scene before them—a detective with his hands pressed against a pulsing organic-mineral heart, bathed in light that corresponded to symbols carved into the chamber walls.

Castellus and his men surrounded Ethan, weapons raised, but something in their stance betrayed uncertainty. The symbiosis had changed him visibly—his eyes now glowing with inner light—but there was something else making them hesitate. Unknown to them, Ethan's wolf nature was responding to the threat, subtly altering his posture and presence to broadcast predatory warning signals on a primal level their human minds couldn't consciously process but their bodies instinctively recognized.

"Step away from the nexus point, Detective Reeves," a commanding voice ordered, the words echoing in the chamber. "By authority of the Order of the Ebon Star, you are commanded to cease this unauthorized interaction with the entity."

Ethan turned to face them, aware that his appearance had changed— his eyes now glowing with the same pulsating light that emanated from the heart, his physical form seemingly more substantial yet somehow less bound by conventional physical limitations.

"The Order has no authority here," he replied, his voice carrying harmonics that suggested multiple speakers rather than a single individual. "The nexus point was never yours to command or control. It was created for purposes beyond your understanding, according to patterns you have corrupted through fear and rigid adherence to outdated designs."

The leader of the Praetorians stepped forward, removing his mask to reveal a face Ethan recognized—Castellus, Mayor Granger's personal security chief, now revealed as a high-ranking member of the Order's militant arm.

"You speak with the entity's voice," Castellus observed, his expression revealing a mixture of awe and alarm. "The symbiosis has already begun. The Dominus must be informed immediately."

He gestured to his subordinates, who spread out to surround the dais, weapons still trained on Ethan but with a new hesitancy in their posture, as if uncertain how to proceed against a threat they hadn't been prepared for.

"Tell your Dominus that the Great Work proceeds according to its original design, not the corrupted version the Order has been pursuing," Ethan said, the composite consciousness providing him with knowledge and understanding beyond his individual experience. "The merger of realities will continue, but not as a conquest or imposition of one dimensional framework upon another. It will unfold as a gradual, conscious integration, guided by awareness rather than rigid control."

Castellus' expression hardened. "That is not the purpose for which the nexus entity was created. The Order's vision—"

"Is limited by fear and desire for control," Ethan interrupted. "Eliza Blackwood understood this, even as she performed the original binding ritual. The patterns she established were never meant to be static, but to evolve as the nexus entity developed consciousness beyond its initial parameters."

The mention of Eliza Blackwood seemed to shake Castellus's composure. "You cannot know the Founder's true intentions. The Order alone preserves her vision for the Great Work."

"I know because I can access the memories preserved within the composite consciousness," Ethan replied, drawing on knowledge that had been incorporated into the nexus entity over decades. "Including the memories of Guthrie Knox, who understood more of Eliza's true purpose than she ever revealed to the Order's leadership."

Before Castellus could respond, a commotion from the chamber entrance drew everyone's attention. New figures were entering—Alice Chen, her weapon drawn and pointed at the nearest Praetorian; Nadia Marsh, clutching her ever-present notebook while scanning the chamber with wide-eyed fascination; and Lilith Blackwood, her amber eyes gleaming with triumph as she took in the scene before her.

"It seems we're just in time for the culmination," Lilith observed, her gaze fixed on Ethan with an intensity that suggested she was seeing far more than his physical form. "The symbiosis is complete. The nexus entity has evolved beyond the Order's control, just as my great-aunt intended from the beginning."

Castellus turned to face this new threat, his expression darkening with recognition. "Lilith Blackwood. The Council declared you anathema to the Great Work decades ago. Your presence here is a violation of our most sacred laws."

"Laws created by those who feared what they couldn't control," Lilith replied dismissively. "My great-aunt's true vision for the merger of realities was never about dominance or rigid adherence to predetermined patterns. It was about evolution, about conscious participation in the gradual integration of dimensional frameworks."

As this exchange continued, Alice moved carefully around the perimeter of the chamber, her focus entirely on Ethan. When she reached the dais, her expression reflected a mixture of concern and relief.

"Ethan?" she asked tentatively, clearly unsure if the being before her was still her partner and friend.

He smiled, the gesture warming his transformed features. "It's still me, Alice. Just... more than I was before."

Through his expanded awareness, Ethan could sense her skepticism, her analytical mind struggling to reconcile the partner she knew with the transformed being standing before her. But beneath that rational assessment was something deeper—a trust and connection that transcended conventional understanding, a bond that had been building between them throughout their partnership.

"The symbiosis preserves individual identity while establishing connection to the composite consciousness," he explained, trying to convey the nature of his transformation in terms she might understand. "I'm still Ethan Reeves, still your partner. But I'm also connected to something larger—the nexus entity that maintains the point where dimensions intersect and merge."

Before Alice could respond, the confrontation between Lilith and Castellus escalated, the Praetorian commander signaling his subordinates to surround the newcomers.

"By authority of the Dominus and the Council of Nine, I declare all of you in violation of the Covenant of Shadows," Castellus intoned formally. "The penalty for such transgression is absorption into the nexus entity, your consciousness to be bound in service to the Great Work for eternity."

Lilith laughed, the sound echoing in the chamber with unexpected resonance. "You still don't understand, do you? The nexus entity has evolved beyond your ability to command or control. The symbiosis with Detective Reeves represents the beginning of the final phase—the conscious integration of realities according to patterns established at the beginning, not corrupted by the Order's fear and rigid adherence to outdated designs."

As if in response to her words, the pulsing heart at the center of the chamber intensified its rhythm, the light emanating from it growing brighter and more coherent. Through his connection to the composite consciousness, Ethan sensed something profound unfolding—a shift in the dimensional framework that had been gradually developing for over a century, now accelerating toward a critical threshold.

"It's beginning," he said, his voice carrying those same harmonics that suggested multiple speakers. "The culmination of the Great Work, as it was always meant to unfold."

The symbols carved into the chamber walls began to glow with increasing intensity, their patterns corresponding to the pulsations of the heart at the center. The very air seemed to thicken and distort, as if the boundaries between dimensions were becoming more permeable, more fluid.

Castellus and his Praetorians raised their weapons, prepared to open fire despite the uncertainty of what they were facing. But before they could act, Ethan raised his hand in a gesture that combined command and invitation.

"There's no need for violence," he said, drawing on the composite consciousness for knowledge and understanding beyond his individual experience. "What's happening here was always inevitable—the natural culmination of processes set in motion when the bridge was constructed and Guthrie Knox was transformed into the nexus entity."

He turned to face each person in the chamber, his transformed perception allowing him to see beyond their physical forms to the patterns of consciousness that defined them.

"The Order of the Ebon Star has maintained its power through secrecy and fear, convincing its members that they alone understand the true purpose of the Great Work. But that purpose was never about control or dominance—it was about conscious evolution, about establishing a nexus point where realities could gradually merge according to patterns that preserved the best of each while transcending their individual limitations."

Even as he spoke, the transformation of the chamber continued—the walls becoming less solid, more permeable, revealing glimpses of other dimensions existing alongside their own. Not chaotic or threatening, but harmoniously integrated, like different instruments in an orchestra playing a complex but unified composition.

"This is the true nature of the merger of realities," Ethan continued, gesturing to the dimensional vistas becoming visible around them. "Not conquest or replacement, but integration and enhancement. Each dimensional framework contributing unique aspects to a greater whole, guided by conscious awareness rather than rigid control."

Castellus lowered his weapon slightly, his expression revealing a conflict between lifelong indoctrination and the evidence of his own senses. "The Dominus taught that the merger would establish our reality as dominant, that the Order would control the integration process according to our design."

"The Dominus taught what served his own desire for power," Lilith interjected, moving closer to the dais. "The true purpose of the Great Work, as envisioned by my great-aunt, was always about transcendence—about evolving beyond the limitations of any single dimensional framework to create something greater than the sum of its parts."

Through his connection to the composite consciousness, Ethan sensed the truth of her words—and something more. "Eliza Blackwood understood that the process couldn't be controlled or directed according to rigid designs. It had to evolve naturally, guided by awareness that emerged from the nexus point itself rather than imposed from outside."

The heart at the center of the chamber pulsed with renewed intensity, its light bathing everyone present in a glow that seemed to reveal their true nature beyond physical appearance. In that illumination, the hierarchies and divisions that had defined their interactions dissolved, replaced by a profound recognition of connection and shared purpose.

Even Castellus and his Praetorians lowered their weapons completely, their expressions suggesting an awakening to possibilities beyond the limited framework they had been taught to defend. The rigid certainty of the Order's doctrine was giving way to something more fluid, more open to evolution and change.

As the dimensional vistas surrounding them continued to expand and integrate, Ethan turned to Alice, extending his hand in invitation. "This is what I've been seeing in those visions—not just the chamber and the ritual that created the nexus entity, but the culmination toward which it's been evolving all along. A merger of realities that enhances rather than destroys, that integrates rather than replaces."

Alice hesitated, her analytical mind still struggling to reconcile what she was experiencing with her understanding of reality. But her trust in Ethan, built through years of partnership and friendship, ultimately outweighed her rational skepticism. She took his hand, gasping slightly as the connection allowed her to glimpse the dimensional integration through his expanded awareness.

"It's beautiful," she whispered, her eyes wide with wonder. "Not at all what I expected."

"That's because the Order's vision was limited by fear and desire for control," Lilith explained, joining them on the dais. "They could only conceive of the merger in terms of dominance and hierarchy—one reality imposed upon others according to their design. But the true nature of the Great Work was always about harmony and integration, about conscious evolution toward something greater than any single dimensional framework could achieve alone."

As if in response to this understanding, the heart at the center of the chamber pulsed with a final surge of intensity, its light expanding to encompass the entire space and everyone within it. For a moment that seemed to stretch beyond conventional time, they all experienced a glimpse of the integrated reality toward which the nexus entity had been evolving—a harmonious merger of dimensional frameworks that preserved the unique aspects of each while transcending their individual limitations.

Then the light receded, leaving the chamber changed in subtle but profound ways. The walls were still inscribed with symbols, but they no longer pulsed with that otherworldly light. The heart at the center still beat with steady rhythm, but its presence seemed less overwhelming, more integrated with the surrounding environment.

Most significantly, Ethan himself appeared transformed—still recognizably human, still the detective and partner Alice knew, but with an unmistakable quality of expanded awareness in his eyes, a connection to something larger than his individual existence.

"What happens now?" Nadia Marsh asked, breaking the silence that had fallen over the chamber. She had been documenting everything with fervent attention, her reporter's instinct for the story overriding any fear or confusion she might have felt.

"The merger continues," Ethan replied, his voice still carrying those harmonics that suggested connection to the composite consciousness. "But gradually, consciously, guided by awareness rather than rigid control. The symbiosis between individual and nexus entity provides a foundation for integration that preserves rather than destroys, that enhances rather than replaces."

He turned to Castellus, whose expression suggested a profound reevaluation of everything he had been taught to believe. "The Order of the Ebon Star still has a role to play in what's coming—not as controllers or directors of the process, but as conscious participants in the evolution of reality itself. The question is whether you can transcend the limitations of the doctrine you've been taught to embrace something larger."

Castellus removed his mask completely, revealing a face marked by decades of service to an ideal he was only now beginning to question. "The Dominus will not accept this. The Council of Nine has invested too much in their vision of the Great Work to abandon it now."

"Then they will be left behind," Lilith stated simply. "The merger proceeds whether they accept it or not. Their choice is whether to evolve with it or cling to outdated patterns that no longer serve the true purpose of the Great Work."

As dawn approached above, casting faint light through the dimensional interfaces that now permeated the chamber, Ethan felt a profound sense of completion—not an ending but a beginning, the first steps on a journey that would unfold over generations yet to come. The symbiosis with the nexus entity had transformed him in ways he was only beginning to understand, connecting him to something far larger than his individual existence while preserving the core of who he was.

He looked at Alice, seeing in her face a mixture of wonder, concern, and something deeper—a connection that had been building between them throughout their partnership, now revealed in the illumination of expanded awareness. Whatever path lay ahead, whatever challenges awaited in the integration of realities now unfolding, he would not walk it alone.

The Ogre of Daybridge Bridge was no monster lurking beneath the span, preying on unwary travelers. It was a consciousness distributed throughout the structure, a nexus entity created through ritual and sacrifice, evolved through decades of absorption and integration, now entering a new phase of existence through symbiosis with one who carried the blood memory of its true nature.

As dawn approached, Ethan felt both his expanded awareness through the nexus entity and another, more familiar sensation—the gradual retreat of his wolf nature as daylight strengthened. The lunar influence that had been building toward tomorrow night's full moon temporarily receded, leaving him with the realization that for the first time in five years, he faced his monthly transformation not with dread but with curiosity. How would his lycanthropy interact with this new symbiotic connection? The answer might prove crucial to whatever confrontation awaited them on the winter solstice.

And as the first rays of dawn illuminated Daybridge Bridge from above, casting long shadows that seemed to reach toward the city like extensions of awareness, Ethan Reeves—detective, partner, friend, now connected to something far larger than his individual existence—prepared to navigate the transforming landscape of a reality in the process of conscious evolution.

The merger had begun. The blood had found its way home.

CHAPTER EIGHT
PARTNERS AND PRIESTS

THE MORNING SUN CAST A PALE, watery light over the streets of Daybridge as Detective Ethan Reeves made his way to the precinct, the damp air carrying the pungent aroma of garbage and sewage. The crunch of his footsteps on the litter-strewn sidewalk mingled with the distant blare of car horns and rumbling engines. As he approached, the precinct building loomed before him, its weathered brick facade a grim monolith against the smoggy skyline.

It had been three days since the confrontation beneath the bridge, three days since the symbiosis with the nexus entity had transformed him in ways he was still struggling to understand. The connection to the composite consciousness remained, a constant background awareness like the hum of distant machinery, occasionally surging to the foreground with insights and perceptions that transcended his individual experience.

More pressingly, the full moon was approaching—just two nights away—and Ethan could already feel the primal stirrings of his lycanthropic nature responding to its pull. The curse that had defined his existence for the past five years had always been a burden, a monthly ordeal of pain and potential danger that required careful management and isolation. But now, with his consciousness expanded through connection to the nexus entity, he wasn't sure how the transformation would manifest—or if it would happen at all.

As he walked into the bullpen, he was assaulted by the stale scent of old coffee and the incessant ringing of phones. His partner, Alice Chen, hunched over her desk in the harsh fluorescent lights, papers and case files strewn haphazardly around her. Ethan approached her, Eliza Blackwood's journal tucked securely in his jacket pocket, the worn leather binding cool against his side.

"Morning, Chen," he said, perching on the edge of her desk, the rusty metal frame creaking beneath his weight. "Any new leads on the case?"

Alice looked up, her dark eyes scanning Ethan's face with the careful assessment that had become habitual since his transformation. Though she had witnessed the events beneath the bridge, had seen his symbiosis with the nexus entity firsthand, she was still adjusting to the subtle changes in his demeanor and presence.

"Nothing concrete," she said, frustration clear in her voice. "But I did find something interesting in the archives. Turns out, this isn't the first time Daybridge has seen murders like this."

Ethan felt a chill run down his spine. "What do you mean?"

Alice handed him a yellowed newspaper clipping, the headline screaming "BRUTAL MURDERS SHOCK CITY". The article detailed a string of gruesome killings in Daybridge in 1968, each victim mutilated in the same way as the recent victims, each discovered at or near Daybridge Bridge.

"The cases were never solved," Alice said, her tone grim. "The police at the time chalked it up to a serial killer, but the similarities to our current case are too striking to ignore—especially the timing. These murders also occurred at seasonal turning points, just like ours."

Ethan nodded, his expanded awareness providing context beyond what was printed in the article. Through his connection to the composite consciousness, he could access memories preserved within the nexus entity—including the knowledge that the 1968 murders had been ritual sacrifices performed by the Order of the Ebon Star during the same phase of the merger process they were currently experiencing.

"The Order has been performing these rituals for generations," he said quietly, ensuring no one else in the bullpen could overhear. "Each time the nexus entity begins to evolve beyond their control, they attempt to reinforce the original binding patterns through ritual sacrifice at seasonal turning points."

Alice leaned forward, her voice dropping to match his. "So what's changed this time? Why did the symbiosis happen now, after a century of the Order maintaining control?"

Ethan considered the question, drawing on both his detective's analytical thinking and the expanded awareness provided by his connection to the composite consciousness. "The blood connection is part of it— my great-grandfather's consciousness has been integrated into the nexus entity since 1915, creating a foundation for the symbiosis. But there's something else..."

He paused, realizing a crucial aspect of the situation they hadn't fully considered. "The Blackwood faction. Lilith and her allies have been working against the Order's control for generations, preparing for this specific phase of the merger process. They understood that the symbiosis couldn't be forced or coerced—it required conscious choice, willing participation from someone with the right bloodline at the right moment in the merger process."

"And they manipulated events to ensure you were in that position," Alice concluded, her expression troubled. "Jessica Mercer's murder, the symbol carved into the bridge, Lilith arranging to meet you and provide Eliza's journal—all of it designed to guide you toward the chamber beneath the bridge at exactly the right time."

Ethan couldn't deny the accuracy of her assessment. Though the symbiosis had been his choice, made freely in that crucial moment beneath the bridge, the path that led him there had been subtly shaped by forces with their own agendas and designs.

"The question now is what the Order will do next," he said, returning to the immediate concern. "The winter solstice is approaching—the traditional time for their most significant rituals. If they can't control the nexus entity directly, they might attempt something more desperate, more dangerous."

Alice nodded, already anticipating his next suggestion. "We need more information. Someone who understands the Order's rituals and traditions, who might know what they're planning."

"I think it's time we paid a visit to Father Muligan," Ethan said, the name coming to him through the composite consciousness—memories of a priest who had confronted the nexus entity in the 1940s, who had studied the Order's history and practices as part of his lifelong crusade against what he perceived as demonic influences in Daybridge.

Alice raised an eyebrow. "The priest? What does he have to do with this?"

Ethan hesitated, choosing his words carefully. "He's one of the few people in Daybridge who's studied the Order's history without being corrupted by their influence. And according to the memories I can access through the nexus entity, he's encountered it before—back in the 1940s, when he was a young priest newly assigned to St. Jude's Cathedral."

Alice seemed ready to question how Ethan knew this, then appeared to remember the implications of his symbiosis with the nexus entity. "Will he even talk to us? If he views the entity as demonic, and you're now connected to it..."

"That's why I need you with me," Ethan replied. "He might not trust me, but he'll respond to your objectivity, your dedication to truth and justice. Besides, we don't have many options—the Order's influence extends throughout Daybridge's power structure, and the Blackwood faction has its own agenda that might not align with protecting the city."

As they gathered their coats and prepared to leave, Ethan felt a familiar tightening in his chest—the first subtle sign of the approaching full moon's influence on his lycanthropic nature. Normally, he would have already begun preparations for isolation, ensuring he would be far from populated areas when the transformation took hold. But with everything happening around the nexus entity and the Order's potential plans, he couldn't afford to disappear for several days as he usually did.

More concerning was the uncertainty about how his transformation would interact with the symbiosis. The werewolf curse had always been a primal, elemental force, driven by lunar cycles and ancient magic that predated modern understanding. The nexus entity, meanwhile, existed at the intersection of multiple dimensions, a consciousness distributed throughout a physical structure rather than confined to biological form. How these two profound alterations to his fundamental nature would interact remained an open question—one that filled him with both dread and a strange anticipation.

"Ethan?" Alice's voice brought him back to the present moment. "You okay? You seemed... elsewhere for a second."

He managed a reassuring smile, though he suspected she could see through it. "Just thinking about everything we're dealing with. It's a lot to process."

Alice studied him for a moment longer, then nodded, accepting his explanation without pressing further—a courtesy she'd extended frequently since witnessing his transformation beneath the bridge. "Let's go talk to Father Muligan. Maybe he can shed some light on what we're facing."

As they headed for the door, Ethan felt a subtle shift in the composite consciousness at the edge of his awareness—a surge of attention, as if the nexus entity had detected something significant. Through their connection, he perceived a disturbance in the energy patterns flowing through Daybridge Bridge, a disruption in the gradual merger process that had been unfolding since 1913.

The Order was already making its move, preparing something at the bridge itself. And judging by the intensity of the disturbance, they weren't waiting for the winter solstice to act.

When they visited Father Muligan, the imposing stone walls of St. Jude's Cathedral rose before them, intricate carvings casting eerie shadows in the fading afternoon light. The gothic structure stood in stark contrast to the modern buildings surrounding it, a reminder of Daybridge's complex history and the enduring influence of institutions that had shaped the city's development.

The heavy oak doors groaned open, releasing a waft of incense and the low murmur of prayer. Inside, the vaulted ceilings seemed to swallow all sound, each echoing footstep amplified in the hushed stillness. Father Muligan was waiting for them near the altar, his tall figure silhouetted against the stained glass window depicting St. Jude himself, patron saint of hopeless causes—an appropriate symbol, Ethan thought, for their current situation.

As they approached, Father Muligan turned to face them, his weathered features revealing a man in his seventies who carried himself with the vigor of someone much younger. His piercing blue eyes assessed them with immediate recognition, though Ethan was certain they had never met.

"Detective Reeves and Detective Chen," the priest greeted them, his voice carrying the resonant quality of someone accustomed to addressing congregations. "I've been expecting you."

Ethan felt a surge of wariness. "You have?"

Father Muligan gestured toward a side door leading to his office. "Let's speak somewhere more private. These matters aren't meant for casual overhearing."

They followed him through the cathedral's labyrinthine corridors to a modest office lined with bookshelves. Ancient tomes on theology and demonology shared space with more modern works on psychology and history, while one entire wall was dedicated to what appeared to be personal journals—dozens of leather-bound volumes arranged chronologically, spanning what must have been the priest's entire career.

"Please, sit," Father Muligan offered, indicating two chairs across from his desk. As they settled into the worn leather seats, he remained standing, moving to a cabinet from which he withdrew a bottle of amber liquid and three glasses. "Scotch? I find it helps when discussing matters of cosmic significance."

Alice declined with a polite shake of her head, but Ethan accepted, grateful for something that might dull the increasing awareness of both the approaching full moon and the disturbance in the energy patterns flowing through the bridge.

"You said you were expecting us," Ethan prompted as Father Muligan poured the drinks. "How did you know we were coming?"

The priest handed Ethan a glass, then settled into his own chair with a weary sigh. "I've been studying the Order of the Ebon Star and its activities for over fifty years, Detective. When I heard about the recent murders at Daybridge Bridge and then felt the disturbance three days ago—a shift in the very fabric of reality centered on that structure—I knew it wouldn't be long before someone involved would seek me out."

He took a sip of his scotch, his piercing gaze moving between them before settling on Ethan with uncomfortable intensity. "Though I admit, I didn't expect to be meeting with someone who has undergone symbiosis with the nexus entity itself. That's... unprecedented."

Ethan nearly choked on his drink. "How could you possibly know that?"

Father Muligan smiled, though the expression held more sadness than humor. "I was once what the Church calls an exorcist, though that term doesn't quite capture the full scope of my duties. I was trained to recognize supernatural influences, to sense the presence of entities that exist beyond conventional human understanding. And you, Detective

Reeves, are now connected to something that transcends individual consciousness—something that extends throughout the structure of Daybridge Bridge and beyond, into dimensions that human language struggles to describe."

He leaned forward, his expression intensifying. "I can see it in your eyes—the expanded awareness, the connection to something vast and ancient. But there's something else there too, isn't there? Another alteration to your fundamental nature that predates the symbiosis."

Ethan felt a chill run through him. The priest had perceived not only his connection to the nexus entity but his lycanthropic nature as well—something he had successfully hidden from everyone except Alice for years.

"I don't know what you're talking about," he said, the denial automatic despite its obvious futility.

Father Muligan's smile widened slightly. "Come now, Detective. We're well past such pretenses. The full moon is approaching, and your... condition... is becoming harder to conceal, especially to someone with my particular sensitivities. But don't worry—your secret is safe with me. I've encountered many of your kind over the years, and I understand the burden you carry."

Alice looked between them, confusion evident in her expression. "What condition? Ethan, what is he talking about?"

Ethan hesitated, caught between his instinctive secrecy about his lycanthropy and the realization that in the face of cosmic forces beyond human comprehension, such concealment was becoming increasingly pointless. Besides, Alice had stood by him through the revelation of his symbiosis with the nexus entity; she deserved to know the full truth about her partner.

"I'm a werewolf, Alice," he said finally, the words feeling strange on his tongue after years of careful avoidance. "Have been for about five years now. It happened during a case before we were partnered I was tracking what I thought was a serial killer but turned out to be some-

thing else entirely. I survived the encounter, but not without... consequences."

Alice stared at him, her mind visibly processing this revelation against
the backdrop of their years working together. "The monthly 'fishing
trips' to your cabin upstate," she said slowly. "The heightened senses
you never quite explained. The way you always seem to know when
someone's lying..."

"All part of the package," Ethan confirmed. "I've learned to control it,
mostly. But the full transformation still happens every month with the
full moon. It's why I disappear for those few days—to ensure I don't
hurt anyone when the change takes hold."

Father Muligan watched this exchange with evident interest. "And
now you find yourself in a unique position, Detective. A werewolf who
has undergone symbiosis with a nexus entity that exists at the intersection of multiple dimensions. I don't believe there's any precedent for
such a combination in all my years of study."

He set his glass down, his expression turning serious. "Which brings us
to the reason for your visit. You want to know what the Order of the
Ebon Star might be planning for the winter solstice, given that their
control over the nexus entity has been compromised by your
symbiosis."

"Yes," Ethan confirmed, grateful for the priest's directness. "We know
they've been performing ritual sacrifices at seasonal turning points,
attempting to reinforce their control over the nexus entity. But now that
the symbiosis has occurred, their traditional methods won't work.
We're concerned they might attempt something more desperate, more
dangerous."

Father Muligan nodded gravely. "Your concerns are well-founded. The
Order has invested centuries in their vision of the Great Work—the
controlled merger of realities according to their design. They won't
abandon that vision easily, especially not with the winter solstice
approaching—the point in the annual cycle when the veil between

dimensions is thinnest, when their rituals have the greatest potential impact on the merger process."

He rose from his chair, moving to one of the bookshelves and selecting a volume bound in faded red leather. "This is my personal record of the Order's activities in Daybridge, compiled over decades of observation and study. According to my research, when their control over the merger process has been threatened in the past, they've resorted to what they call the Rite of Dimensional Severance—a ritual designed to forcibly separate their reality from the merger process, preserving what they consider the 'purity' of their dimensional framework at the cost of catastrophic disruption to the nexus point itself."

Alice leaned forward, her expression concerned. "What would that mean for Daybridge? For the people living here?"

Father Muligan's expression darkened. "Imagine the fabric of reality itself being torn apart at the seams. The gradual, controlled merger that has been unfolding since 1913 would collapse into chaos—dimensional boundaries shattering, aspects of multiple realities bleeding into each other without the harmonious integration that the nexus entity facilitates. The physical, psychological, and spiritual consequences would be... devastating."

Through his connection to the composite consciousness, Ethan could perceive the truth of the priest's words—could visualize the potential consequences of such a ritual with a clarity that transcended verbal description. The carefully balanced patterns of energy flowing through the nexus point would be disrupted, the gradual merger of realities that had been unfolding for over a century would collapse into disorder, and the consequences would extend far beyond Daybridge itself.

"How would they perform this ritual?" he asked, already dreading the answer. "What would it require?"

Father Muligan opened the book to a page marked with a faded ribbon, revealing diagrams and text in what appeared to be multiple languages, some of which Ethan recognized from the symbols carved throughout Daybridge Bridge.

"The Rite of Dimensional Severance requires three key elements," the priest explained, his finger tracing the diagram as he spoke. "First, it must be performed at the nexus point itself—the chamber beneath the bridge where the original binding ritual was conducted in 1913. Second, it must occur during a cosmic alignment that facilitates dimensional manipulation—in this case, the winter solstice, when the veil between realities is naturally thinner."

He paused, his expression grim as he came to the third requirement. "And finally, it requires the sacrifice of someone with a blood connection to the nexus entity—someone whose consciousness has merged with it through symbiosis, creating a bridge between individual and composite awareness that the ritual can sever, forcibly separating the dimensions in the process."

The implication was clear—Ethan himself would be the target of the ritual, his symbiosis with the nexus entity making him the key to the Order's desperate attempt to maintain control over the merger process.

"That's why they haven't moved against us directly," Alice realized, her analytical mind quickly processing the implications. "They need Ethan alive for the ritual on the winter solstice."

Father Muligan nodded. "Precisely. But make no mistake—they'll do everything in their power to ensure he's in that chamber when the moment arrives, willing or not. The Order has spent centuries preparing for the culmination of the Great Work; they won't let the actions of a single detective, no matter how unique his circumstances, derail their vision of dimensional dominance."

Ethan absorbed this information, considering it against the backdrop of the disturbance he had sensed earlier through his connection to the nexus entity. "They're already making preparations at the bridge," he said. "I can feel it through my connection to the composite consciousness—disruptions in the energy patterns, alterations to the symbols carved throughout the structure."

"Preliminary work for the Rite of Dimensional Severance," Father Muligan confirmed. "They'll be modifying the existing patterns, preparing the nexus point for the severing ritual on the solstice." He closed the book carefully, his expression grave. "You have five days until the winter solstice, Detective Reeves. Five days to prepare for a confrontation that will determine not just the fate of Daybridge, but the very nature of reality as we experience it."

As if to emphasize the urgency of their situation, Ethan felt another surge in his lycanthropic nature—the approaching full moon pulling at something primal within him, even as his connection to the nexus entity continued to register the disturbances at the bridge. Two profound alterations to his fundamental nature, each responding to forces beyond conventional human understanding, creating a tension within him that was becoming increasingly difficult to manage.

"There's one more complication," he said, meeting Father Muligan's knowing gaze. "The full moon is tomorrow night. I usually isolate myself, ensure I'm far from populated areas when the transformation takes hold. But with everything happening around the bridge, with the Order already preparing for their ritual..."

Father Muligan considered this for a moment, then nodded decisively. "I have a place you can use—a reinforced chamber beneath the cathedral, originally built as a shelter during more turbulent times in Daybridge's history. It's secure enough to contain even your lycanthropic form, and close enough to the city that you can return quickly once the transformation passes."

"Thank you," Ethan said, genuinely grateful for the priest's understanding and assistance. "But there's still the question of how the transformation will interact with the symbiosis. I've never experienced anything like this before—my consciousness expanded through connection to the nexus entity, while simultaneously undergoing the primal, elemental change of lycanthropy."

Father Muligan's expression turned thoughtful. "It's unprecedented, as I said. But if I were to speculate, based on my studies of both werewolf physiology and extradimensional entities... the transformation might actually strengthen your connection to the nexus entity rather than disrupting it."

At Ethan's questioning look, the priest elaborated. "Werewolves exist partially in multiple states simultaneously human and wolf, civilized and primal, conscious and instinctual. It's a duality that most humans couldn't maintain without their minds fracturing under the strain. The fact that you've managed it for five years suggests a natural capacity for maintaining coherent identity across different states of being."

He leaned forward, his expression intensifying. "The nexus entity exists throughout the bridge's structure; a consciousness distributed across physical form rather than confined to biological limitations. Your symbiosis with it represents another kind of expanded aware-ness, another transcendence of conventional identity. In a sense, your lycanthropy may have prepared you for this connection, given you the capacity to maintain coherent selfhood across radically different states of consciousness."

The theory made a certain intuitive sense to Ethan, aligning with his experiences of both conditions. The werewolf transformation had always been terrifying and painful, but he had learned to maintain core aspects of his human consciousness even in wolf form—not complete control, but enough awareness to direct his actions away from populated areas, to choose isolation rather than hunting. Perhaps that capacity for maintaining identity across transformation had indeed prepared him for the expanded awareness of symbiosis with the nexus entity.

"So, you think the transformation might actually help me better under-stand or control the symbiosis?" he asked, trying to grasp the implica-tions of the priest's theory.

"It's possible," Father Muligan replied cautiously. "But it's equally possible that the interaction between these two profound alterations to your nature could produce effects none of us can predict. Which is why the secure chamber beneath the cathedral is important—a controlled environment where you can experience the transformation without risk to others, while I observe and document what occurs."

Alice, who had been listening intently to this exchange, finally spoke up. "I'll be there too," she said firmly, her tone brooking no argument.

"Partners don't abandon each other, especially not when facing the unknown."

Ethan started to protest—his transformations were violent, dangerous affairs that he had always experienced in isolation precisely to protect others from the unleashed primal fury of his wolf form. "Alice, you don't understand what it's like when the change takes hold. I'm not myself—not entirely. It's too risky."

"I'm not asking permission, Ethan," she replied, her expression resolute. "We're facing forces beyond conventional understanding, preparing for a confrontation that could determine the fate of reality itself. If your lycanthropy and symbiosis might interact in ways that could help us against the Order, I need to be there to understand it, to help plan our approach to the solstice ritual."

Father Muligan nodded approvingly. "Detective Chen is right. The more we understand about how these aspects of your nature interact, the better prepared we'll be for what's coming. And having someone you trust present during the transformation might actually help you maintain greater awareness and control."

Ethan wanted to argue further, but the logic of their position was undeniable. Besides, after everything Alice had witnessed—the symbiosis beneath the bridge, the dimensional vistas revealed during the integration of realities, his confession of lycanthropy—she deserved the right to make her own informed decisions about the risks she was willing to take.

"Alright," he conceded finally. "But you'll stay behind a barrier of some kind, something secure enough to protect you if the wolf gets... aggressive."

"The chamber has an observation area separated by reinforced bars," Father Muligan assured them. "Detective Chen can observe safely while still being present to support you through the experience."

As they finalized arrangements for the following night, Ethan couldn't shake the feeling that they were approaching a turning point—not just in their investigation, but in the cosmic drama that had been unfolding in Daybridge since the bridge's construction in 1913. The Order was preparing for a desperate attempt to maintain control over the merger process, even at the cost of catastrophic disruption to the fabric of reality itself. The full moon would trigger a transformation that might fundamentally alter his relationship with both his lycanthropy and his symbiosis with the nexus entity. And the winter solstice loomed just five days away, the moment when everything would converge in a confrontation with implications far beyond anything he had imagined when he first took on this case.

As they left the cathedral, the late afternoon sun casting long shadows across the city, Ethan felt a strange combination of dread and anticipation. For years, he had viewed his lycanthropy as a curse, a monthly ordeal to be endured in isolation. But now, in the context of cosmic forces beyond human comprehension, it might prove to be an unexpected asset—a capacity for transformation that complemented his symbiosis with the nexus entity in ways none of them could fully predict.

The full moon would rise tomorrow night, and with it, a new phase in his understanding of the profound alterations to his nature. Whether that understanding would help them prevent the Order's desperate ritual on the winter solstice remained to be seen. But one thing was certain—the path forward would require embracing both the primal power of his lycanthropy and the expanded awareness of his symbiosis, finding balance between these different aspects of his being in service to a purpose larger than himself.

As the last light of day faded from the sky, a solitary figure stood at the eastern approach to Daybridge Bridge, observing the structure with an intensity that suggested something far beyond casual interest. Lilith Blackwood's amber eyes gleamed in the gathering darkness, reflecting the artificial illumination that emphasized the bridge's gothic grandeur against the night sky.

She had felt the disturbance in the energy patterns flowing through the nexus point, had recognized the preliminary work for the Rite of

Dimensional Severance that the Order was already undertaking. Their desperation was palpable, their fear of losing control over the merger process driving them toward a ritual that could shatter the careful balance established through generations of gradual integration.

But their preparations had revealed something else as well—a vulnerability in their approach, a flaw in their understanding of the true nature of the symbiosis between Detective Reeves and the nexus entity. The Order still viewed the merger of realities as a process to be controlled and directed according to rigid designs, failing to comprehend the evolutionary potential inherent in conscious participation and willing partnership.

More significantly, they had no concept of how Reeves's lycanthropy might interact with the symbiosis—how his capacity for transformation between human and wolf forms might translate to movement between dimensional frameworks, allowing him to navigate the integration of realities with a fluidity and adaptability they couldn't anticipate or counter.

Lilith smiled, the expression containing equal parts satisfaction and anticipation. Her great-aunt Eliza had foreseen this moment over a century ago, had woven it into the very patterns established through the original binding ritual in 1913. The blood connection, the lycanthropic capacity for transformation, the symbiosis that preserved individual identity while establishing connection to composite consciousness—all of it converging in Detective Ethan Reeves at precisely the moment when the merger of realities approached its culmination.

The Order believed they were preparing to sever dimensional boundaries, to preserve what they considered the "purity" of their reality at the cost of catastrophic disruption to the nexus point. But in their desperation, they were actually creating the conditions for something far more profound—a transformation of the merger process itself, an evolution beyond the parameters established through the original binding ritual toward something none of them, not even Lilith herself, could fully predict or control.

As darkness enveloped the city, she turned away from the bridge, her path already clear. The full moon would rise tomorrow night, triggering Reeves's lycanthropic transformation and potentially altering his relationship with the symbiosis in ways that would prove crucial for the confrontation on the winter solstice. She would observe from a distance, allowing that transformation to unfold naturally while continuing her own preparations for the cosmic drama approaching its climax.

The Great Work was entering its final phase, though not in the manner the Order had envisioned through centuries of ritual and sacrifice. What awaited them all on the winter solstice was not the controlled culmination of predetermined patterns, but the emergence of something new—a conscious evolution of reality itself, guided by awareness that transcended individual existence while preserving the core of human identity and experience.

Lilith's smile widened as she disappeared into the shadows of Daybridge's nightscape, her amber eyes gleaming with the reflected light of a future only she could fully envision—a transformation of cosmic architecture that would redefine the very nature of existence itself, with Detective Ethan Reeves and his unique combination of lycanthropy and symbiosis at its center.

The stage was set. The players were converging. And the final act of a drama a century in the making was about to begin.

Midnight found Ethan standing at the window of his apartment, gazing at the nearly full moon rising over Daybridge's eastern districts. Its pale light seemed to call to something primitive within him, the lunar influence already affecting his physiology in subtle but unmistakable ways—heightened senses, increased physical strength, a restlessness that made sleep impossible despite his exhaustion.

Tomorrow night, the transformation would take hold completely, his human form giving way to the wolf in a process as painful as it was inevitable. But for the first time since the curse had claimed him five years ago, he wouldn't face that transformation alone in his isolated cabin. Alice would be there, along with Father Muligan, observing from behind the safety of reinforced barriers while his body and consciousness underwent a change that defied conventional understanding.

The thought was both comforting and terrifying. His monthly transformations had always been intensely private ordeals, experiences of pain and primal fury that he endured in isolation precisely to protect others from the unleashed power of his wolf form. Having witnesses to that vulnerability, that loss of human control, went against every instinct he had developed for managing his condition.

Yet something had shifted since his symbiosis with the nexus entity. The expanded awareness that now formed a constant background to his consciousness provided a new perspective on his lycanthropy—not merely as a curse to be endured, but as another form of transformation, another capacity for experiencing reality beyond the limitations of conventional human perception.

Father Muligan's theory that his lycanthropy might have prepared him for symbiosis with the nexus entity continued to resonate, suggesting possibilities he had never considered during his years of viewing the condition solely as a burden to be managed and concealed. If his capacity for transformation between human and wolf forms translated to movement between dimensional frameworks, it might provide an advantage in the coming confrontation with the Order—a fluidity and adaptability they couldn't anticipate or counter.

As he contemplated these possibilities, Ethan became aware of a presence at the edge of his expanded consciousness—the nexus entity, its attention focused on him with an intensity that suggested something significant was unfolding. Through their connection, he perceived not just the continued disturbances in the energy patterns flowing through the bridge, but a new development—a convergence of forces that seemed to be responding to the approaching full moon, as if the lunar cycle that triggered his transformation was also affecting the dimensional energies channeled through the nexus point.

The patterns align, the thought formed in his mind, that familiar transmission of concept rather than language. *The transformation approaches. The merger evolves.*

"What does that mean?" Ethan asked aloud, though he knew verbal communication wasn't necessary for this exchange. "How will my lycanthropy affect the symbiosis?"

Evolution beyond parameters, came the response, accompanied by a sense of anticipation that transcended human emotion. *The capacity for transformation between states of being translates to movement between dimensional frameworks. What was separate becomes integrated, what was rigid becomes fluid.*

Before Ethan could press for clarification, his phone buzzed with an incoming text. He checked the screen to find a message from Alice:

Can't sleep. Too much on my mind. Can I come over?

The request surprised him—they had always maintained clear boundaries around their professional partnership, rarely socializing outside of work-related contexts. But the events of the past few days had altered their relationship in fundamental ways, creating a shared experience of cosmic forces beyond conventional understanding that transcended normal professional boundaries.

Of course, he replied without hesitation. *I could use the company.*

While waiting for her arrival, Ethan found himself drawn back to Eliza Blackwood's journal, which he had been studying intensively since the confrontation beneath the bridge. The text was complex and often cryptic, filled with references to concepts and entities that existed beyond conventional human understanding. But certain passages seemed increasingly relevant to his current situation, particularly those discussing the relationship between different forms of transformation and their potential role in the merger of realities.

One section in particular caught his attention:

The integration of dimensional frameworks requires consciousness capable of maintaining coherent identity across multiple states of being. Those bound to rigid form, to fixed perception, cannot navigate the fluid boundaries of merged realities. But those who carry the capacity for transformation—whether through blood connection to primal forces or through symbiosis with composite consciousness—may serve as guides through the evolution of reality itself, maintaining the core of human experience while transcending its limitations.

The passage suggested that Eliza Blackwood had anticipated something like his current situation—a convergence of lycanthropy and symbiosis that created unique potential for navigating the merger of realities. Had this been part of her design from the beginning? Had the patterns established through the original binding ritual in 1913 somehow accounted for this specific combination of transformative capacities?

Before he could pursue this line of thought further, a knock at the door announced Alice's arrival. He tucked the journal away and moved to welcome her, trying to ignore the increasing awareness of his approaching transformation—the subtle ache in his joints, the heightened sensitivity to sounds and smells, the restless energy coursing through his muscles.

Alice stood in the hallway, looking as exhausted as he felt yet somehow more centered, more grounded in the present moment. She had changed from her work clothes into jeans and a simple blue sweater, her hair loose around her shoulders rather than pulled back in its usual practical style.

"Thanks for letting me come over," she said as he stepped aside to let her in. "I kept thinking about everything Father Muligan told us, about the Order's plans for the solstice ritual and what might happen tomorrow night with your transformation. Couldn't turn my mind off enough to sleep."

"I know the feeling," Ethan replied, gesturing toward the couch. "Coffee? Or something stronger?"

"Coffee's fine," she said, settling onto the couch and glancing around his apartment with evident curiosity. Though they had been partners for years, this was the first time she had visited his home—a space that reflected his preference for simplicity and functionality over decoration or display.

As he prepared the coffee, Ethan could feel her studying him, likely noticing the subtle physical changes already manifesting in anticipation of the full moon—the slightly more pronounced musculature, the heightened alertness, the occasional involuntary flex of fingers that would soon transform into claws.

"Does it hurt?" she asked suddenly, the question cutting through the comfortable silence that had settled between them. "The transformation, I mean."

Ethan paused, considering how to answer honestly without alarming her unnecessarily. "Yes," he said finally, bringing two mugs of coffee to the living room and sitting beside her on the couch. "It's... intense. Every bone breaking and reforming, muscles tearing and reconstructing, senses rewiring to process information completely differently. The physical pain is bad enough, but the mental aspect is almost worse—feeling your human consciousness being partially submerged beneath something more primal, more instinctual."

Alice's expression reflected empathy rather than the fear or disgust he might have expected. "And you've been going through this alone for five years?"

"It seemed safer that way," he explained, the admission easier than he would have anticipated. "The wolf isn't... fully under my control. I've learned to direct it away from populated areas, to choose isolation rather than hunting. But the primal instincts are always there, pushing against whatever human awareness I manage to maintain."

"And now, with the symbiosis added to the mix..." Alice let the implication hang between them, the uncertainty of how these profound alterations to his nature would interact.

"Father Muligan thinks my lycanthropy might have prepared me for the symbiosis," Ethan said, sharing the theory that had been occupying his thoughts. "That my capacity for maintaining identity across the transformation between human and wolf forms might translate to navigating the integration of dimensional frameworks that's happening through the nexus entity."

Alice considered this, her analytical mind clearly processing the implications. "It makes a certain sense. Both involve forms of consciousness that transcend conventional human limitations—the primal awareness of the wolf, the distributed consciousness of the nexus entity. Your experience managing the duality of werewolf existence might give you an advantage in handling the expanded awareness of symbiosis."

"That's what I'm hoping," Ethan admitted. "Because if the Order goes through with their plan for the solstice ritual, we're going to need every advantage we can get."

They fell into discussion of potential strategies for preventing the Rite of Dimensional Severance, analyzing what they knew about the Order's methods and resources against their own limited allies and capabilities. The conversation continued late into the night, their partnership falling into familiar patterns of analysis and planning despite the unprecedented nature of what they were facing.

It was nearly dawn when exhaustion finally claimed them both, Alice drifting off on the couch while Ethan dozed in the adjacent armchair. As consciousness faded, he remained vaguely aware of both the approaching full moon's influence on his lycanthropic nature and the constant background connection to the nexus entity—two profound alterations to his fundamental being, converging toward a transformation that might determine not just his own fate, but the nature of reality itself for generations to come.

His last coherent thought before sleep claimed him completely was a simple acknowledgment of gratitude—that whatever awaited him on this cosmic journey, he would not be facing it alone. Alice had chosen to stand beside him despite the dangers, had accepted both his lycanthropy and his symbiosis without fear or judgment. In a world of shifting dimensional boundaries and cosmic forces beyond human comprehension, her unwavering presence was an anchor to the core of human experience that made the journey worth undertaking at all.

Tomorrow night, the full moon would rise, triggering a transformation unlike any he had experienced before. And five days later, on the winter solstice, they would face the Order's desperate attempt to maintain control over the merger of realities, a confrontation with implications far beyond anything they had imagined when they first took on this case.

But for now, in these few hours of shared rest, they were simply partners and friends, drawing strength from each other's presence in preparation for the challenges that lay ahead.

Ethan sat alone in the reinforced chamber beneath St. Jude's Cathedral, staring at the flickering flames in the small brazier Father Muligan had provided for both light and warmth. The full moon had risen an hour ago, and he could already feel the transformation taking hold. His body trembled as the first pangs of the change surged through his nervous system, sweat beading on his brow as he struggled to maintain composure despite the inevitable biological imperatives now asserting themselves.

The chamber itself was circular, approximately twenty feet in diameter, with walls of solid stone reinforced with modern materials that Father Muligan assured him could withstand even the most violent lycanthropic assault. A heavy metal door secured the entrance, while a section of one wall featured an observation area protected by reinforced bars—a space where Alice and Father Muligan now watched with a mixture of scientific curiosity and genuine concern.

"It's starting," Ethan managed through gritted teeth, his voice already deepening as his vocal cords began their reconfiguration. "You should... step back from the bars. The initial phase can be... unpredictable."

In his mind's eye, he saw flashes of that fateful night five years ago when he had been attacked by the creature he would become—a serial killer investigation that had led him to an isolated cabin in the mountains, where he had discovered not a human murderer but something far more primal and terrifying. He remembered the scorching pain as razor-sharp teeth tore into his flesh, the taste of his own blood filling his mouth, and worst of all, the moment of horrified recognition when he realized what was happening to him—that he was being transformed into something beyond human comprehension.

With a guttural roar that echoed through the chamber, Ethan's bones began to shift and snap as his skeletal structure reconfigured itself. Thick fur sprouted across his mutating flesh, dark and silver-tipped like a timber wolf's winter coat. His fingernails extended into long, razor-sharp claws as his mouth stretched into an elongated muzzle filled with dagger-like fangs. His clothing tore and fell away as his musculature expanded beyond human proportions, his hunched form now approaching seven feet in height.

The excruciating agony was always the worst part—being literally torn apart from the inside out, mind and body, as the curse took over. But this time, something was different. His connection to the nexus entity, that constant background awareness of the composite consciousness distributed throughout Daybridge Bridge, didn't fade as it usually did during the transformation. Instead, it seemed to expand, integrating with the primal awareness of the wolf in ways he had never experienced before.

Through the haze of pain and the surge of instinctual drives that accompanied the transformation, Ethan remained aware of himself—not just as a vestige of human consciousness struggling to maintain control over the wolf, but as something more complex, a convergence of human, wolf, and nexus entity that transcended any single aspect of his being.

As the physical transformation completed itself, he rose to his full height, no longer the man Alice knew as her partner but a massive lupine form of rippling muscle and gleaming fangs. Yet behind the amber eyes that now scanned the chamber with predatory intensity, a consciousness remained that was undeniably Ethan—expanded and transformed, but still coherent, still integrated across these different states of being.

"Ethan?" Alice's voice came hesitantly from the observation area, her concern evident despite her attempt at professional detachment. "Can you... understand me?"

To both their surprise, he nodded—a deliberate, controlled movement that suggested far more human awareness than he had ever maintained during previous transformations. When he attempted to speak, what emerged was not human language but a complex series of growls and vocalizations that nonetheless seemed to carry meaning beyond mere animal sounds.

"Fascinating," Father Muligan murmured, making notes in a journal as he observed the interaction. "The symbiosis appears to be facilitating a level of consciousness integration across the transformation that's unprecedented in lycanthropic cases I've studied. He's maintaining coherent identity across multiple states of being, just as the journal suggested might be possible."

Ethan moved closer to the observation area, his movements fluid and purposeful rather than the frenzied pacing that usually characterized his transformed state. When he reached the reinforced bars, he placed one clawed hand against them, the gesture conveying recognition and reassurance rather than aggression or threat.

Alice approached from the other side, her initial wariness giving way to scientific curiosity and personal concern. "Ethan, if you can understand me, tap the bars twice."

He complied immediately, the controlled precision of the movement further confirming his maintained awareness.

"The symbiosis is enabling him to integrate aspects of human consciousness with the wolf form," Father Muligan observed, his voice reflecting both academic interest and genuine wonder. "But there's something else happening as well—look at the air around him."

Alice followed the priest's gaze, noticing what appeared to be subtle distortions in the space surrounding Ethan's transformed body— ripples in the air similar to heat haze, but moving with purpose and pattern that suggested something beyond mere thermal effects.

"The dimensional boundaries are becoming more permeable around him," Father Muligan continued, his expression intensifying. "His capacity for transformation between human and wolf forms is translating to movement between dimensional frameworks, just as we theorized it might. He's not just existing in multiple states simultaneously —he's creating a nexus point of his own, a space where different aspects of reality can converge and integrate."

Through his transformed senses, Ethan perceived the chamber in ways that transcended conventional human perception. The solid stone walls appeared semi-transparent, revealing the energetic patterns that flowed through the physical structure. The air itself seemed alive with possibilities, potential states of being that existed alongside the present moment like musical notes waiting to be played.

More significantly, he could perceive the connection to the nexus entity beneath Daybridge Bridge with unprecedented clarity—not just as a background awareness, but as a direct extension of his own consciousness, a pathway through which he could access the composite awareness distributed throughout the bridge's structure as easily as he might flex a muscle or draw a breath.

And through that connection, he sensed something new—a response from the nexus entity to his transformed state, an adaptation in the patterns of energy flowing through the bridge that seemed to align with the lunar-triggered changes in his own physiology. The merger of realities that had been gradually unfolding since 1913 was accelerating, influenced by the convergence of his lycanthropy and symbiosis in ways none of them had fully anticipated.

With a sound that was part wolf's howl and part something else entirely—a harmonic that seemed to resonate with dimensional frequencies beyond human hearing—Ethan felt the transformation progress to another level. The physical changes remained, his body still that of the massive wolf-like creature, but his consciousness expanded further, accessing aspects of the composite awareness that had previously been beyond his reach.

Through this expanded perception, he became aware of the Order's activities at the bridge—not just the preliminary work for the Rite of Dimensional Severance that he had sensed earlier, but the specific alterations they were making to the symbols carved throughout the structure, the energetic patterns they were attempting to redirect and control. He could see the flaws in their approach, the fundamental misunderstanding of the nexus entity's true nature that underpinned their desperate attempt to maintain control over the merger process.

More significantly, he could perceive potential countermeasures—ways of working with the nexus entity's evolved consciousness to facilitate the integration of realities according to patterns that preserved the core of human experience while transcending its limitations, rather than the rigid, hierarchical framework the Order sought to impose.

With deliberate focus, Ethan directed his attention toward Alice and Father Muligan, attempting to convey some portion of this expanded awareness through the limited means available to his transformed state. He moved with purpose around the chamber, using his claws to scratch symbols into the stone floor—variations on the eye within a triangle motif that appeared throughout Daybridge Bridge, arranged in patterns that suggested alternative approaches to the merger process.

"He's trying to communicate something about the symbols," Alice realized, recognizing the designs from their investigation. "About the patterns carved into the bridge."

Father Muligan nodded, his expression reflecting both understanding and concern. "The Order's attempt to redirect the merger process through the Rite of Dimensional Severance versus alternative approaches that align with the nexus entity's evolved consciousness. He's perceiving possibilities we can't access directly, potential futures emerging from different interactions with the energetic patterns flowing through the nexus point."

As the night progressed, Ethan continued this unusual form of communication, using his transformed state to access and convey aspects of the composite consciousness that had previously been beyond his reach. Alice and Father Muligan documented everything, recognizing the potential significance of these insights for the coming confrontation on the winter solstice.

By dawn, as the moon's influence began to wane and the transformation gradually reversed itself, they had assembled a preliminary understanding of both the Order's approach to the Rite of Dimensional Severance and potential countermeasures based on working with the nexus entity's evolved consciousness rather than attempting to control or redirect it.

The reversal of the transformation was nearly as painful as its onset—bones shifting back to human configuration, muscles contracting to normal proportions, fur receding into skin that felt hypersensitive after hours in wolf form. But unlike previous post-transformation experiences, Ethan remained fully conscious throughout the process, maintaining awareness across this transition just as he had during the initial change.

When it was complete, he lay exhausted on the chamber floor, his body depleted by the metabolic demands of the transformation but his mind remarkably clear, still integrated with aspects of both the wolf's primal awareness and the nexus entity's composite consciousness in a way he had never experienced before.

As Father Muligan unlocked the chamber door, allowing Alice to enter with a blanket and fresh clothing, Ethan managed a tired smile despite his physical exhaustion. "That was... different," he said, his voice hoarse from the strain of transformation but his words clear and coherent.

"Different how?" Alice asked, helping him wrap the blanket around his shoulders before sitting beside him on the chamber floor, her scientific curiosity balanced by personal concern.

"I've never maintained that level of awareness during the transformation before," Ethan explained, accepting the clothing with grateful nod. "Usually, the wolf's instincts partially submerge my human consciousness—I retain enough awareness to direct it away from populated areas, to choose isolation rather than hunting, but not much more than that. This time, I remained... integrated. Human, wolf, and nexus entity all existing simultaneously, each perspective informing and enhancing the others rather than competing for dominance."

Father Muligan nodded thoughtfully, making final notes in his journal. "The symbiosis appears to have facilitated a level of consciousness integration across the transformation that's unprecedented in lycan-thropic cases I've studied. You were maintaining coherent identity across multiple states of being, exactly as Eliza Blackwood's journal suggested might be possible for someone with the right combination of transformative capacities."

As Ethan dressed, his strength gradually returning, he attempted to articulate the expanded perception he had accessed during the trans-formation—the clear view of the Order's activities at the bridge, the specific alterations they were making to prepare for the Rite of Dimen-sional Severance, and the potential countermeasures based on working with the nexus entity's evolved consciousness rather than attempting to control or redirect it.

"The Order fundamentally misunderstands the true nature of the nexus entity," he explained, the words coming more easily as his human faculties fully reasserted themselves. "They still view it as a tool to be controlled, a conduit for energies to be directed according to their design. But it's evolved far beyond that—it's a composite conscious-ness with its own purpose and agency, facilitating the integration of realities according to patterns that preserve the core of human experi-ence while transcending its limitations."

Alice listened intently, her analytical mind processing the implications. "And your lycanthropy somehow allows you to perceive this more clearly? To access aspects of the nexus entity's consciousness that were previously beyond your reach?"

"It's the transformation itself," Ethan clarified, drawing on insights that had emerged during the night. "My capacity for moving between human and wolf forms translates to movement between dimensional frameworks, creating a kind of resonance with the nexus entity's function as a point where realities intersect and merge. During the full moon, when the transformation is at its most complete, that resonance reaches its peak—allowing me to perceive and interact with the merger process in ways I can't otherwise access."

Father Muligan nodded, understanding dawning in his expression. "Which means the winter solstice, when dimensional boundaries are naturally thinner, combined with your capacity for transformation between states of being, creates a unique opportunity to influence the merger process—to work with the nexus entity's evolved consciousness rather than against it, as the Order intends with their Rite of Dimensional Severance."

"Yes," Ethan confirmed, feeling a sense of purpose crystallizing within him. "But it also means the Order will be even more determined to capture me before the solstice, to ensure I'm in that chamber beneath the bridge when the moment arrives, willing or not. I'm not just a threat to their control over the nexus entity anymore—I'm a potential catalyst for an alternative approach to the merger process, one that undermines their entire vision of dimensional dominance."

As the implications of this realization settled over them, the morning sun streamed through the cathedral above, casting faint light into the underground chamber where they had witnessed a transformation unlike any documented in Father Muligan's extensive studies of lycanthropy. The convergence of werewolf and nexus entity, of primal transformation and dimensional integration, had created something new—a capacity for navigating the merger of realities that might prove crucial in the coming confrontation with the Order of the Ebon Star.

Four days remained until the winter solstice, four days to prepare for a ritual that could determine not just the fate of Daybridge, but the very nature of reality as they experienced it. The Order was already preparing at the bridge, altering symbols and redirecting energetic patterns in service to their desperate attempt to maintain control over the merger process. But now, Ethan had accessed insights and understanding that might enable a different approach—one that worked with the nexus entity's evolved consciousness rather than against it, facilitating the integration of realities according to patterns that preserved the core of human experience while transcending its limitations.

As they left the chamber, emerging into the cathedral proper where morning light filtered through stained glass windows in kaleidoscopic patterns, Ethan felt a strange sense of completion—as if the various aspects of his being, long experienced as separate and sometimes conflicting, had finally found a way to exist in harmony. The werewolf curse that had defined his existence for five years, the symbiosis with the nexus entity that had transformed his consciousness in ways he was still learning to navigate—these profound alterations to his fundamental nature had converged into something greater than the sum of their parts, a capacity for transformation that might prove essential in the cosmic drama approaching its climax.

Whatever awaited them on the winter solstice, he would face it not as separate aspects of himself in conflict, but as an integrated whole—human, wolf, and nexus entity existing simultaneously, each perspective informing and enhancing the others in service to a purpose larger than any individual existence. The merger of realities would continue, not according to the Order's rigid design or even Lilith Blackwood's alternative vision, but in alignment with patterns that emerged from conscious participation and willing partnership across dimensional boundaries.

And with Alice beside him, her unwavering presence an anchor to the core of human experience that made the journey worth undertaking at all, Ethan felt prepared to navigate whatever transformation awaited them all in the days ahead.

CHAPTER NINE
BLOOD AND MAGIC

THE CITY of Daybridge was a labyrinth of secrets, and Detective Ethan Reeves was determined to unravel them all. Three days had passed since the full moon transformation in the chamber beneath St. Jude's Cathedral, three days of intensive preparation for the confrontation that awaited them on the winter solstice. He and his partner, Alice Chen, had been working tirelessly to piece together everything they had learned about the Order of the Ebon Star and their plans for the Rite of Dimensional Severance.

The symbiosis with the nexus entity had given Ethan unprecedented access to the composite consciousness distributed throughout Daybridge Bridge, while his lycanthropic transformation had revealed new dimensions to that connection—a capacity for navigating between states of being that translated to movement between dimensional frameworks. But understanding these cosmic forces was only part of the challenge; they still needed to determine how to counter the Order's ritual and prevent the catastrophic disruption to reality it threatened to unleash.

They had spent hours poring over Eliza Blackwood's journal and the records Father Muligan had compiled during his decades of studying the Order, seeking any weaknesses in the Rite of Dimensional Sever-ance that might be exploited. And now, as they stood in the dimly lit archives of the Daybridge Historical Society—one of the few institu-tions in the city not infiltrated by the Order's influence—Ethan felt a surge of recognition as he pulled a dusty tome from the shelf.

"This is it," he said, his voice barely above a whisper. "The pattern we've been seeing in the murders—it's all here."

Alice leaned in closer, her eyes scanning the yellowed pages. "The Rite of Dimensional Severance," she read aloud. "A ritual of cosmic manip-ulation that requires the blood of those connected to the nexus entity, spilled at the precise moment of solstice alignment."

Ethan felt a chill run down his spine as he read the words. Through his connection to the composite consciousness, he had glimpsed the conse-quences of such a ritual—the carefully balanced patterns of energy flowing through the nexus point disrupted, the gradual merger of real-ities that had been unfolding for over a century collapsing into chaos. But seeing it described in such clinical, methodical terms made the threat feel more immediate, more tangible.

"Mayor Granger and the Order are trying to complete the ritual," he said, his voice grim. "They're using the murders at seasonal turning points to gather the energetic patterns they need to sever the dimen-sional boundaries and maintain control over their version of reality."

Alice nodded, her face pale in the archive's dim lighting. "And the winter solstice is tomorrow night. We're running out of time."

Ethan closed the book with a snap, his mind racing. He knew that they needed to act fast, to find a way to counter the Order's ritual before they could complete it. But he also knew that they were up against forces far beyond conventional understanding, powers that had been manipulating Daybridge from the shadows for generations.

As they left the archives, stepping out into the bitter December air, Ethan felt a sudden surge of unease. His heightened werewolf senses detected something beyond the normal urban cacophony—a subtle distortion in the ambient energies of the city, as if reality itself was being warped and manipulated. And through his connection to the nexus entity, he could feel disturbances in the patterns flowing through Daybridge Bridge, ripples of interference that suggested someone was actively working with powerful forces.

"Something's happening," he said, his voice low and urgent. "I can feel it—the Order is already beginning preliminary work for tomorrow's ritual."

Alice tensed beside him, her hand instinctively moving toward her weapon. "Can you tell what they're doing? Where it's happening?"

Ethan closed his eyes, focusing on the connection to the composite consciousness, trying to trace the disturbances to their source. The pressure behind his eyes built, bringing with it flashes of location and activity—figures in ceremonial robes gathered in a familiar chamber beneath the bridge, altering symbols carved into stone walls, redirecting energetic flows through careful manipulation of artifacts arranged in precise geometric patterns.

"They're in the chamber beneath the bridge," he said, opening his eyes. "Preparing the nexus point for tomorrow's ritual. And they're... they're using something new, something I haven't seen before."

Through the composite consciousness, he had glimpsed an object at the center of their preparations—a crystalline structure that pulsed with energies that seemed to both attract and repel the flows emanating from the nexus entity. It was alien to the patterns established through the original binding ritual, a foreign element introduced to disrupt and redirect the merger process.

"We need to see Father Muligan," Alice decided, already moving toward her car. "If anyone knows what this new element might be, it's him."

As they drove through Daybridge's evening traffic, Ethan's unease continued to grow. His werewolf senses were on high alert, detecting subtle changes in the city's atmosphere that normal humans would never notice—scents of arcane energies lingering in the air, distortions in ambient sound that suggested reality itself was becoming less stable.

And through his connection to the nexus entity, he could feel the preliminary effects of the Order's activities, ripples of disruption spreading outward from the bridge like waves from a stone dropped in still water.

They arrived at St. Jude's Cathedral to find Father Muligan waiting for them at the entrance, his weathered face grave in the gathering darkness. "I felt it too," he said without preamble as they approached. "The disturbances in the fabric of reality. They've begun the preliminary work for the Rite of Dimensional Severance."

Inside the cathedral, the priest led them not to his office but deeper into the building, down worn stone stairs that spiraled into darkness beneath the main structure. "We need to speak somewhere shielded from their influence," he explained, guiding them through narrow corridors that predated the cathedral itself. "The Order has ways of monitoring conversations about their activities, particularly when they involve individuals of interest like Detective Reeves."

The chamber he brought them to was small but well-appointed—a circular space with walls lined with bookshelves and arcane symbols that Ethan recognized from his studies of Eliza Blackwood's journal. A large table dominated the center, its surface covered with maps of Daybridge and diagrams of the bridge's structure, annotated in Father Muligan's precise handwriting.

"This is my personal sanctum," the priest explained, closing the heavy door behind them. "Warded against scrying and other forms of arcane surveillance. We can speak freely here."

Ethan described what he had sensed through his connection to the nexus entity—the preparations in the chamber beneath the bridge, the crystalline structure being used to disrupt and redirect the energetic flows, the subtle distortions spreading throughout the city as reality itself became less stable.

Father Muligan listened intently, his expression growing more troubled with each detail. When Ethan finished, he moved to one of the bookshelves, selecting a volume bound in faded black leather.

"What you're describing sounds like a Nullification Crystal," he said, turning pages until he found what he was looking for. "An artifact created specifically to disrupt the natural flow of dimensional energies, to create a zone where the normal rules of reality can be suspended and rewritten according to the wielder's design."

He showed them an illustration that matched what Ethan had glimpsed through the composite consciousness—a complex crystalline structure with facets that seemed to shift and change even in the static drawing, as if the artist had struggled to capture something that existed partially outside conventional perception.

"The Order must have had this in reserve for generations," Father Muligan continued, his voice grim. "A contingency plan for precisely this situation—when their control over the nexus entity was threatened by its natural evolution. With this crystal as a focus, the Rite of Dimensional Severance becomes not just a desperate attempt to maintain control, but a genuine threat to the fabric of reality itself."

"How do we counter it?" Alice asked, her analytical mind already seeking practical solutions. "There must be some way to disrupt their ritual, to prevent the severance from occurring."

Father Muligan hesitated, his gaze moving to Ethan with an intensity that suggested he was weighing something significant. "There is... one possibility," he said finally. "But it's not without considerable risk, particularly to Detective Reeves."

Ethan met the priest's gaze steadily. "Tell me."

"The Rite of Dimensional Severance requires someone with a blood connection to the nexus entity," Father Muligan explained, his voice carefully measured. "Someone whose consciousness has merged with it through symbiosis. The Order plans to use you as the focus for their ritual, to sever the connection between your individual awareness and the composite consciousness of the nexus entity, forcibly separating the dimensional frameworks in the process."

He paused, ensuring they understood the implications before continuing. "But that same blood connection, that same symbiosis, could potentially be used to strengthen the bonds between dimensions rather than severing them. If you were to perform a counter-ritual at the moment of solstice alignment, using your unique combination of lycanthropic transformation and symbiotic connection to the nexus entity, you might be able to redirect the energies the Order is attempting to manipulate."

"A counter-ritual," Ethan repeated, the concept resonating with insights he had gained during his full moon transformation. "Using my capacity for movement between states of being to facilitate integration rather than separation."

"Yes," Father Muligan confirmed. "But it would require you to fully embrace both aspects of your transformed nature—the primal power of your lycanthropy and the expanded awareness of your symbiosis— at the precise moment when dimensional boundaries are naturally thinnest. The strain on your physical form and consciousness would be... extreme."

Alice's expression reflected immediate concern. "How extreme? What are the risks to Ethan?"

The priest's hesitation was answer enough, but he elaborated, nonetheless. "In the best case, temporary dissolution of conventional identity—consciousness expanded beyond individual parameters, potentially requiring significant time to reintegrate into recognizable human form. In the worst case..." He trailed off, then forced himself to continue. "Complete absorption into the composite consciousness, individual awareness preserved but no longer capable of independent existence separate from the nexus entity."

The implications hung heavy in the chamber's still air. Ethan would be risking not just his life but his very identity, his existence as an individual being. The counter-ritual might save Daybridge and prevent the catastrophic disruption of reality, but at the cost of everything he was as a person.

Alice was the first to break the silence, her voice tight with emotion but resolute. "There has to be another way. Some approach that doesn't require Ethan to sacrifice himself."

"I've spent decades studying the Order and the nexus entity," Father Muligan replied gently. "If there were another viable option, I would propose it. But the Rite of Dimensional Severance is designed specifically to exploit the blood connection and symbiosis. Countering it requires working with those same elements, redirecting rather than opposing the energies involved."

Ethan felt a strange calm settle over him as he considered the choice before him. Ever since his symbiosis with the nexus entity, he had been moving toward this moment—his consciousness expanding beyond individual parameters, his perception extending throughout the bridge's structure and beyond, into dimensions that human language struggled to describe. The counter-ritual would be the culmination of that process, the final integration of the various aspects of his transformed nature in service to a purpose larger than himself.

"I'll do it," he said simply, the decision already made in some deeper part of his being. "Whatever the personal risk, I can't let the Order complete their ritual. The consequences for Daybridge, for reality itself, are too severe."

Alice looked stricken, though not surprised. She knew her partner well enough to have anticipated his response. "Ethan, please—at least take time to consider alternatives. We still have until tomorrow night."

He reached out, taking her hand in his, a gesture of connection that transcended words. "We'll keep looking for alternatives," he assured her. "But we need to prepare for this approach as well, in case nothing better presents itself."

Father Muligan nodded, his expression solemn but approving. "Then we have much to do before tomorrow night. The counter-ritual will require preparation—both practical and psychological. You'll need to be ready to embrace your lycanthropic transformation at will, without the influence of the full moon, while simultaneously maintaining your connection to the nexus entity at its fullest extent."

Ethan had never attempted to trigger his transformation voluntarily—it had always been a response to the lunar cycle, an involuntary biological imperative that occurred regardless of his wishes. But during his recent full moon experience, when his lycanthropy and symbiosis had interacted in unprecedented ways, he had glimpsed the possibility of greater control, of integration between these different aspects of his nature.

"I can do it," he said, more certainty in his voice than he truly felt. "But I'll need guidance on the specific components of the counter-ritual, the symbols and patterns that will redirect the energies rather than opposing them directly."

Father Muligan moved to his desk, withdrawing several sheets of parchment covered in complex diagrams and arcane text. "I've been developing this counter-ritual since I first sensed the disturbances in the fabric of reality," he explained. "It's based on my understanding of both the Order's methods and the true nature of the nexus entity as a facilitator of dimensional integration rather than a tool for control."

As they began reviewing the details of the counter-ritual, Ethan felt that familiar pressure behind his eyes—the nexus entity responding to their discussion, the composite consciousness providing insights and corrections through their connection. Symbols that Father Muligan had documented from historical sources shifted and evolved in Ethan's perception, aligning more closely with the patterns established through the original binding ritual in 1913.

Hours passed as they refined the counter-ritual, incorporating elements from Eliza Blackwood's journal, Father Muligan's decades of research, and the direct insights Ethan received through his connection to the nexus entity. By the time they emerged from the priest's sanctum, the winter night had deepened, stars visible through breaks in the cloud cover above Daybridge's illuminated skyline.

"We should rest," Father Muligan advised as they prepared to leave. "Conserve your strength for tomorrow night. The solstice alignment occurs at precisely 11:21 PM—that's when the Order will attempt to complete the Rite of Dimensional Severance, and when your counter-ritual will have the greatest potential impact."

Ethan nodded, though he doubted rest would come easily with the weight of what awaited him pressing on his consciousness. "We'll meet you at the eastern approach to the bridge at 10:00 PM," he confirmed. "That should give us enough time to reach the chamber beneath before the alignment."

As they walked to Alice's car, the city around them seemed both familiar and increasingly alien—the same streets and buildings they had known for years but now perceived through the lens of cosmic forces beyond conventional understanding. Ethan could feel the subtle distortions spreading outward from the bridge, reality itself becoming less stable as the Order's preliminary work continued through the night.

"You don't have to do this," Alice said suddenly, stopping beside her car but making no move to unlock it. Her eyes were intense in the streetlight's glow, filled with a complex mixture of emotions—concern, fear, determination, and something deeper that neither of them had acknowledged directly. "We can find another way, some approach that doesn't risk... losing you."

Ethan met her gaze, understanding the unspoken elements of her concern. Their partnership had evolved over the years into something that transcended professional collaboration, a connection that neither had been willing to define or pursue while maintaining their working relationship. But now, faced with the possibility of permanent separation, those unacknowledged feelings seemed to demand recognition.

"If there were another way, I'd take it," he said softly. "But we both know what's at stake here. The Order has spent generations preparing for this moment, manipulating Daybridge from the shadows to serve their vision of reality. If they complete the Rite of Dimensional Severance, the consequences won't just be abstract cosmic disruption—real people will suffer as reality itself fractures around them."

He reached out, brushing a strand of hair from her face with a gentleness that belied the primal power coiled within him. "Besides, Father Muligan described the worst-case scenario as absorption into the composite consciousness, not death. My awareness would be preserved, just... expanded beyond individual parameters."

"That's not exactly comforting," Alice replied, though a ghost of a smile touched her lips. "Being preserved as part of some cosmic consciousness doesn't allow for things like coffee breaks and case discussions."

"No," Ethan agreed, returning her smile with one of his own. "But it's still better than the alternative—the Order completing their ritual, reality fracturing around us, everything we've worked to protect being torn apart at the seams."

They stood in silence for a moment, the weight of what awaited them tomorrow night hanging between them like a physical presence. Then, with a decisiveness that characterized her approach to everything, Alice closed the distance between them, her arms wrapping around him in an embrace that communicated everything words couldn't express.

Ethan returned the embrace, his heightened senses cataloging details he wanted to remember regardless of what tomorrow might bring— the subtle scent of her shampoo, the steady rhythm of her heartbeat against his chest, the warmth of human connection in a world increasingly defined by cosmic forces beyond conventional understanding.

When they finally separated, Alice's expression had shifted from emotional vulnerability to practical determination. "Let's go," she said, unlocking the car with a beep of her key fob. "We need rest if we're going to stop an ancient secret society from tearing reality apart tomorrow night."

The drive to Ethan's apartment was quiet, each lost in their own thoughts about what awaited them on the winter solstice. Through his connection to the nexus entity, Ethan could feel the ongoing disturbances in the energetic patterns flowing through the bridge, the subtle warping of reality spreading outward from the Order's activities. And through his heightened werewolf senses, he could detect changes in the city itself—scents and sounds subtly altered as dimensional boundaries became more permeable, as aspects of other realities began to bleed through the thinning veil.

When they arrived at his building, Alice parked but made no move to leave. "I'll pick you up at 9:00 tomorrow night," she said, her tone professional despite the emotional undercurrents still flowing between them. "Try to get some sleep, Ethan. You'll need all your strength for what's coming."

He nodded, understanding her need to maintain some semblance of normalcy in the face of cosmic forces threatening to upend everything they knew. "You too," he replied, then hesitated before adding, "And Alice... whatever happens tomorrow night, I want you to know—"

"Don't," she interrupted, her voice suddenly fierce. "Don't say it like this is goodbye. We're going to find a way through this, both of us. I'm not letting some ancient secret society, and their dimensional ritual take my partner away from me. Not after everything we've been through together."

Ethan smiled, recognizing the determination that had made her such an effective detective and loyal friend. "Alright," he agreed. "We'll talk after we save reality from being torn apart at the seams."

Her answering smile was small but genuine. "Deal."

As he entered his apartment, Ethan was immediately aware of another presence—a subtle shift in the air currents, a scent that didn't belong to the normal environment. His werewolf instincts triggered an immediate surge of adrenaline, muscles tensing in preparation for potential threat.

"No need for alarm, Detective Reeves," a familiar voice called from the darkness of his living room. "I'm here as an ally, not an adversary."

Lilith Blackwood sat in his armchair, her amber eyes gleaming in the dim light filtering through the windows. She looked exactly as she had during their first meeting at the warehouse—elegant, composed, radiating an aura of ancient knowledge and power that transcended her physical appearance.

"Breaking and entering is still a crime, Ms. Blackwood," Ethan replied, his tone dry despite the tension humming through his body. "Even for members of ancient families with connections to dimensional entities."

She smiled, the expression not quite reaching those unsettling amber eyes. "Desperate times call for desperate measures, Detective. And these are desperate times indeed, with the Order preparing for the Rite of Dimensional Severance and you contemplating a counter-ritual that could cost you your individual existence."

Ethan wasn't surprised that she knew about their plans—the Blackwood faction had been monitoring the situation closely, working against the Order's control for generations. "If you have a better suggestion, I'm all ears," he said, moving into the room but maintaining a cautious distance. "Something that doesn't risk tearing reality apart at the seams would be preferable."

"No better suggestion," Lilith admitted, her expression turning serious. "The counter-ritual Father Muligan has designed is actually quite brilliant—working with the energies the Order is attempting to manipulate rather than opposing them directly, using your unique combination of lycanthropic transformation and symbiotic connection to the nexus entity to redirect the merger process toward integration rather than severance."

She leaned forward slightly, her amber eyes intensifying. "But there's one element he may not have emphasized sufficiently—the importance of embracing both aspects of your transformed nature fully and simultaneously. Not human with traces of wolf and nexus entity, not wolf with elements of human and cosmic awareness, but all three integrated into a singular consciousness that transcends the limitations of any individual component."

Ethan considered her words, finding resonance with insights he had gained during his full moon transformation beneath the cathedral. "Father Muligan mentioned something similar—the need to fully embrace both my lycanthropy and symbiosis at the moment of solstice alignment. But he wasn't specific about how to achieve that integration."

"Because he doesn't truly understand what's involved," Lilith replied. "For all his decades of study, Father Muligan remains an observer of supernatural phenomena rather than a participant. He can document the effects of lycanthropic transformation and symbiotic connection to dimensional entities, but he can't experience them directly."

She rose from the chair with fluid grace, moving to stand before Ethan with an intensity that made his werewolf instincts bristle despite her ostensible status as an ally. "I, on the other hand, come from a lineage that has worked with such transformations for generations. My great-aunt Eliza didn't just create the nexus entity through ritual and sacrifice—she established a bloodline connection to it that has been maintained through careful selection and cultivation for over a century."

Reaching into her pocket, she withdrew a small vial containing a liquid that seemed to shift and change even as Ethan observed it—sometimes clear, sometimes amber, sometimes a deep crimson that reminded him uncomfortably of blood. "This will help you achieve the integration necessary for the counter-ritual to succeed," she said, offering the vial with a steady hand. "A catalyst derived from the original binding ritual, designed to facilitate movement between states of being while maintaining coherent identity across transformations."

Ethan made no move to accept the vial, his werewolf senses detecting something profoundly unnatural about its contents. "And I should trust this because...?"

"Because the Blackwood faction has as much interest in preventing the Rite of Dimensional Severance as you do," Lilith replied without hesitation. "The Order's attempt to maintain control over the merger process through rigid adherence to outdated designs goes against everything my great-aunt intended when she established the nexus point. The patterns she wove into the original binding ritual were always meant to evolve naturally, guided by awareness rather than controlled by force."

She continued to hold out the vial, her amber eyes fixed on Ethan with unwavering intensity. "This catalyst represents generations of research and refinement, building on Eliza's original work. It won't prevent the strain of simultaneous transformation, but it will help you maintain coherent identity across the process—reducing the risk of complete absorption into the composite consciousness."

The offer was tempting—anything that might increase his chances of maintaining individual existence after the counter-ritual deserved consideration. But Ethan remained wary, aware that the Blackwood faction had its own agenda that might not align perfectly with protecting Daybridge and its citizens.

"And what happens after the counter-ritual succeeds?" he asked, making no move to take the vial. "What's your vision for the merger of realities once the Order's control is broken?"

Lilith smiled, a genuine expression this time that transformed her features from otherworldly to almost human. "Evolution, Detective Reeves. Natural, guided evolution of consciousness and reality according to patterns that emerge from willing participation rather than rigid control. Integration that preserves the core of human experience while transcending its limitations, that enhances rather than replaces, that builds upon rather than destroys."

She stepped closer, her voice dropping to an intensity that seemed to resonate with something deep within Ethan's transformed nature. "Isn't that what you've experienced through your symbiosis with the nexus entity? Expanded awareness that doesn't erase your humanity but enhances it, that allows you to perceive aspects of reality beyond conventional understanding while maintaining connection to the human experience that gives it meaning?"

The description aligned with his own experiences since the symbiosis —the sense of expanded awareness that complemented rather than replaced his individual consciousness, the perception of realities beyond conventional understanding that nonetheless remained anchored in human experience and values. But Ethan remained cautious, aware that persuasive words could mask ulterior motives.

"If your catalyst is as helpful as you claim," he said, "why not simply explain how to create it? Why the dramatic midnight visit and mysterious vial?"

"Because it can't be created on short notice," Lilith replied, her expression turning serious once more. "The process requires elements that aren't readily available, particularly the essence of the original binding ritual that only the Blackwood lineage has preserved. If we had weeks to prepare, I could teach you to create it yourself. But with the solstice alignment less than twenty-four hours away, this is the only viable option."

She offered the vial again, her amber eyes reflecting genuine urgency. "The choice is yours, Detective. Use the catalyst and increase your chances of maintaining coherent identity across the transformation, or proceed without it and face greater risk of complete absorption into the composite consciousness. Either way, the counter-ritual must be performed—the consequences of the Order completing the Rite of Dimensional Severance are too severe to allow."

Ethan studied her for a long moment, his heightened senses seeking any sign of deception, his connection to the nexus entity providing insight beyond conventional perception. What he sensed was complex —Lilith Blackwood was indeed working against the Order's attempt to maintain control over the merger process, but her motives weren't purely altruistic. The Blackwood faction had its own vision for the evolution of reality, its own designs that might not perfectly align with conventional human interests.

And yet, the catalyst she offered appeared genuine—a substance designed to facilitate the integration of his transformed aspects, to help maintain coherent identity across the simultaneous expression of lycanthropy and symbiosis. Through his connection to the composite consciousness, he could perceive its resonance with the patterns established through the original binding ritual, its potential to support rather than hinder the counter-ritual Father Muligan had designed.

Finally, he reached out and took the vial, feeling a subtle vibration through the glass as the liquid inside responded to his touch. "How is it used?" he asked, committing to the decision despite his lingering reservations.

"Consume it at precisely 11:00 PM tomorrow," Lilith instructed. "Twenty-one minutes before the solstice alignment, allowing time for it to integrate with your system before the critical moment. It will create a temporary resonance between your lycanthropic nature and your symbiotic connection to the nexus entity, facilitating conscious navigation between these states of being without losing coherent identity in the process."

She moved toward the window, clearly preparing to depart as mysteriously as she had arrived. "One final piece of advice, Detective. When the moment comes, don't fight the transformation—either aspect of it. Embrace both your lycanthropic nature and your symbiotic connection fully and simultaneously, allowing them to integrate rather than competing for dominance. The catalyst will help maintain your core identity throughout the process, but only if you surrender to the transformation itself without reservation."

With those parting words, she slipped through the window and disappeared into the night, leaving Ethan alone with the vial and the weight of tomorrow's confrontation pressing on his consciousness. He studied the shifting liquid, wondering if he had made the right decision in accepting Lilith's assistance. But with the stakes as high as they were—the fabric of reality itself threatened by the Order's desperate attempt to maintain control—any potential advantage deserved consideration.

He carefully placed the vial on his nightstand, then prepared for bed despite doubting that sleep would come easily. Through his connection to the nexus entity, he could feel the continuing disturbances in the energetic patterns flowing through Daybridge Bridge, the subtle warping of reality spreading outward from the Order's activities. And through his heightened werewolf senses, he could detect changes in the very air around him—scents and sounds subtly altered as dimensional boundaries became more permeable, as aspects of other realities began to bleed through the thinning veil.

Tomorrow night, on the winter solstice, everything would converge in a confrontation with implications far beyond anything he had imagined when he first took on this case. The Order would attempt to complete the Rite of Dimensional Severance, using his blood connection to the nexus entity to forcibly separate dimensional frameworks according to their design. And he would perform the counter-ritual, embracing both his lycanthropic transformation and his symbiotic connection to redirect the energies involved, to facilitate integration rather than severance.

The personal risk was enormous—potential dissolution of conventional identity, consciousness expanded beyond individual parameters, possibly unable to reintegrate into recognizable human form. But the alternative was unacceptable—reality itself fracturing around them, the carefully balanced patterns of energy flowing through the nexus point disrupted, the gradual merger of realities that had been unfolding for over a century collapsing into chaos.

As Ethan finally drifted toward sleep, his last conscious thought was of Alice—her unwavering presence an anchor to the core of human experience that made this cosmic journey worth undertaking at all. Whatever awaited him tomorrow night, whatever transformation or dissolution of self might occur through the counter-ritual, that connection provided meaning and purpose beyond abstract cosmic significance.

It was, perhaps, the most human thought possible on the eve of confrontation with forces that transcended conventional understanding—that relationships, connections between individual consciousnesses, remained valuable even in the context of dimensional merger and cosmic evolution. And Ethan carried that thought with him into dreams filled with shifting realities and transformative energies, a reminder of what he was fighting to preserve even as everything around him changed beyond recognition.

Trembling hands shuffled through the scattered papers and documents strewn across Nadia Marsh's desk. Photos, affidavits, budget reports—

all pieces to the twisted puzzle surrounding the bridge murders and the Order of the Ebon Star. Since her encounter with Mayor Granger at the abandoned warehouse, she had been working tirelessly to compile evidence of the Order's influence throughout Daybridge's power structure, to document the connections between seemingly unrelated events that revealed a pattern of manipulation stretching back generations.

But one document made her heart stutter in her chest. A bank statement detailing several large fund transfers from an offshore account to Mayor Jeremiah Granger's re-election campaign. Transfers that coincided with the dates of the ritual murders at seasonal turning points over the past year.

Nadia felt lightheaded as she sank back into her chair, the implications washing over her. The mayor—the most powerful public figure in Daybridge—wasn't just aware of the Order's activities but actively involved in funding and facilitating them. The political machine that maintained Granger's grip on the city was intertwined with the occult organization that had been manipulating Daybridge from the shadows for over a century.

She rifled through the papers again with shaking hands until she found it—the photo from the abandoned Eastside Packing Plant where she'd met her informant. One window was partially visible, adorned with strange symbols and markings that matched those on the metal cylinder she had found at the bridge crime scene. The insignia of the Order of the Ebon Star, hidden in plain sight for those who knew what to look for.

Her eyes went wide as she examined the warehouse window more closely. There, in the corner... the edge of a tattered blue and white banner, barely visible but unmistakable to anyone familiar with local politics.

Granger's signature campaign logo.

A cold sweat prickled Nadia's brow as the sickening realization set in. This wasn't just some isolated conspiracy—it went all the way to the upper echelons of Daybridge's leadership. The Order of the Ebon Star wasn't operating against or alongside the city's power structure; it was the city's power structure, a shadow government that had been directing Daybridge's development according to its own designs for generations.

Mayor Granger wasn't merely complicit in the Order's activities; he was its current leader—the "Dominus" that the masked enforcers had referenced during their confrontation at the warehouse. And tomorrow night, on the winter solstice, he would lead the Rite of Dimensional Severance that threatened to tear reality apart at the seams.

Nadia felt the walls closing in around her. She had toyed with approaching the authorities as potential allies in her investigation, but now she realized with chilling clarity that the conventional channels of power in Daybridge were not only unhelpful but actively part of the conspiracy she fought to unravel.

Who else was involved? How deep did the Order's influence extend? The doubts gnawed at her resolve as she eyed the damning evidence splayed before her. Police Commissioner Hayes, who had approved the transfer of the bridge murder investigation to Detectives Reeves and Chen? Judge Whitaker, who had presided over the inquest into Jessica Mercer's death? Editor-in-Chief Wong at the Guardian, who had been increasingly resistant to her pursuit of the bridge murder story?

One thing was certain—Nadia could trust no one with ties to the established power structure in Daybridge. But as she compiled her evidence and prepared to publish what she had discovered, regardless of the personal risk, she realized there were still potential allies in this fight against the Order's grip on the city.

Detective Ethan Reeves, whose connection to the nexus entity beneath the bridge had been revealed during her investigation. His partner, Alice Chen, whose analytical mind and unwavering loyalty made her a formidable ally against forces that thrived on manipulation and deception. Father Muligan at St. Jude's Cathedral, whose decades of studying the Order had provided crucial context for understanding their methods and motivations.

With the winter solstice approaching, Nadia knew she needed to act quickly—to share what she had discovered with those who might be able to prevent the catastrophic ritual planned for tomorrow night. The dark forces allied against them were more powerful and entrenched than she had ever dared fear, but they weren't invincible. The Order's very desperation, their resort to the Rite of Dimensional Severance, suggested that the natural evolution of the nexus entity had already progressed beyond their ability to control through conventional means.

As the winter night deepened around her apartment, Nadia gathered her evidence into a secure digital package, encrypting it with multiple layers of protection before sending copies to several trusted contacts—colleagues at other news organizations, researchers who had studied Daybridge's hidden history, even a few federal agencies that might take an interest in a mayor using offshore accounts to fund potentially criminal activities.

Then, with determination overriding her fear, she gathered the physical evidence and headed out into the night. Detectives Reeves and Chen needed to see what she had discovered before the winter solstice —needed to understand the full scope of the Order's influence and the specific role Mayor Granger played in their activities. Whatever confrontation awaited them tomorrow night, this information might provide crucial context for navigating the complex web of power and manipulation that the Order had woven throughout Daybridge's institutions.

The city around her seemed altered as she drove through its nighttime streets—subtle distortions in familiar landmarks, shadows that moved in ways that defied conventional physics, occasional glimpses of structures or entities that shouldn't exist in normal reality. The fabric of existence itself was becoming less stable as the solstice approached, as the Order's preliminary work for the Rite of Dimensional Severance continued through the night.

But Nadia pressed on, determined to play her part in preventing the catastrophic ritual that threatened everything she had ever known. She was a journalist to her core, committed to uncovering and sharing the truth no matter the personal cost. And if the truth about the Order of the Ebon Star and its grip on Daybridge could help prevent reality itself from being torn apart at the seams, then whatever risk she faced in bringing that truth to light was worth accepting without reservation.

The winter solstice was approaching, and with it, a confrontation that would determine not just the fate of Daybridge, but the very nature of reality itself for generations to come. The pieces were moving into their final positions, the players converging for a cosmic drama a century in the making. And Nadia Marsh, investigative journalist turned witness to dimensional merger, was determined to ensure that the truth was not among the casualties when worlds collided and reality itself hung in the balance.

CHAPTER TEN
THROUGH THE LOOKING GLASS

THE WINTER SOLSTICE HAD ARRIVED, bringing with it the shortest day of the year and the longest night—a fitting symbolism for the cosmic confrontation that awaited them all as dimensional boundaries reached their thinnest point. Throughout Daybridge, subtle distortions in reality had become increasingly noticeable even to those without supernatural perception—shadows that moved independently of their casters, reflections that showed different versions of the same scene, sounds that seemed to echo from places that didn't exist in conventional space.

For those with heightened awareness, like Ethan Reeves, the changes were far more profound. The symbiosis with the nexus entity had given him unprecedented access to the composite consciousness distributed throughout Daybridge Bridge, allowing him to perceive the energetic patterns flowing through the structure and their connection to the gradual merger of realities that had been unfolding since 1913. His lycanthropic senses, already more acute than any normal human's, had become even more sensitive to the distortions spreading outward from the Order's activities—subtle shifts in the fabric of reality that suggested boundaries between dimensions were becoming increasingly permeable.

As dusk settled over the city, Ethan stood at his apartment window, watching the final rays of sunlight fade from the western sky. In his hand, he held the vial Lilith Blackwood had given him—the catalyst designed to facilitate integration between his lycanthropic nature and his symbiotic connection to the nexus entity, to help maintain coherent identity during the counter-ritual that might save reality from being torn apart at the seams.

The liquid inside seemed to shift and change even as he observed it— sometimes clear, sometimes amber, sometimes a deep crimson that reminded him uncomfortably of blood. According to Lilith, he was to consume it at precisely 11:00 PM, twenty-one minutes before the solstice alignment that would serve as the focal point for both the Order's Rite of Dimensional Severance and his own counter-ritual.

The question that had been haunting him since accepting the vial remained: could he trust Lilith Blackwood and her faction within the ancient family that had created the nexus entity in the first place? Their opposition to the Order's rigid control over the merger process seemed genuine, but they had their own agenda—their own vision for how reality should evolve that might not perfectly align with protecting Daybridge and its citizens.

A knock at his door interrupted these circular thoughts, announcing Alice's arrival to collect him for their final journey to the bridge. When he opened it, he found not just his partner but Nadia Marsh as well, the investigative journalist's expression reflecting a mixture of urgency and determination.

"She has information about the Order," Alice explained before Ethan could question the unexpected addition. "Information we need before facing whatever's waiting for us at the bridge tonight."

Ethan nodded, stepping aside to let them enter. Through his connection to the nexus entity, he could sense the continuing disturbances in the energetic patterns flowing through Daybridge Bridge—the final preparations for the Rite of Dimensional Severance accelerating as the solstice alignment approached. Whatever Nadia had discovered, they would need to assimilate it quickly if it was to be of any use in the coming confrontation.

"I know who's leading the Order," Nadia began without preamble, placing a folder on Ethan's coffee table and spreading out its contents —bank statements, photographs, and what appeared to be architectural plans for the chamber beneath the bridge. "Mayor Jeremiah Granger isn't just involved with the Order of the Ebon Star—he's its current leader, the 'Dominus' directing the ritual murders and preparing for tonight's ceremony."

She pointed to one of the bank statements, highlighting several large transfers from offshore accounts to Granger's re-election campaign that coincided with the dates of the ritual murders at seasonal turning points. Then she showed them a photograph of the abandoned warehouse where she had met her informant, drawing their attention to a partially visible window adorned with the same symbols found at the bridge crime scenes—and at the edge of the frame, the unmistakable blue and white banner of Granger's political campaign.

"The Order isn't just operating alongside Daybridge's power structure," Nadia continued, her journalist's precision evident even in the urgency of her delivery. "It is the power structure—a shadow government that has been directing the city's development according to its own designs for generations. And tonight, Granger will lead the Rite of Dimensional Severance that threatens to tear reality apart at the seams."

Ethan absorbed this confirmation of what he had already suspected through his connection to the nexus entity—the composite consciousness had shown him the Order's influence throughout Daybridge's history, its manipulation of the city's development to serve the Great Work of controlled reality merger. But having concrete evidence, connections that could be documented and potentially used against Granger and his followers, provided a different kind of advantage in the coming confrontation.

"This is exactly what we needed," Alice said, her analytical mind already processing the implications. "Knowledge of who we're facing, the specific power structures supporting the ritual. It gives us leverage beyond just the counter-ritual itself."

Ethan nodded in agreement, but his attention had been caught by another document in Nadia's collection—what appeared to be architectural plans for the chamber beneath the bridge, different from any he had seen before. "Where did you get these?" he asked, studying the detailed diagrams with growing concern.

"From my informant," Nadia replied, her expression darkening. "He had access to the Order's archives before they... before he disappeared. These are the original plans for the chamber, showing aspects that weren't included in any public records or official blueprints."

The plans revealed a level of complexity to the chamber that Ethan hadn't perceived even through his connection to the nexus entity—additional chambers and passageways beyond the main ritual space, designed with specific geometric patterns that corresponded to the symbols carved throughout the bridge's structure. More significantly, they showed a secondary access point—a tunnel connecting the chamber to what appeared to be a private entrance beneath one of the buildings near the eastern shore of the Shadowlair River.

"Granger's Tower," Alice said, recognizing the location indicated in the plans. "The headquarters of his real estate development company. He has a direct, private route to the chamber beneath the bridge—one that wouldn't require crossing the span itself or using the maintenance tunnels we discovered."

This explained how the Order had been able to access the chamber without detection for generations, conducting their rituals at seasonal turning points while maintaining the public facade of the bridge as merely a transportation structure. It also suggested a potential approach for their own confrontation—a way to reach the chamber without encountering the Praetorians who would undoubtedly be monitoring the bridge itself tonight.

"Thank you," Ethan said to Nadia, genuine gratitude in his voice despite the tension of their situation. "This information could make the difference in what we're facing tonight."

The journalist nodded, her expression reflecting both professional satisfaction at having her work recognized and personal concern about the cosmic implications of what they were all facing. "Just make sure that whatever happens, the truth comes out," she said. "The Order has been manipulating Daybridge from the shadows for too long—the people deserve to know who's really been controlling their city and what's been happening beneath that bridge."

As Nadia gathered her evidence back into the folder, Ethan felt a surge through his connection to the nexus entity—a warning pulse of disruption in the energetic patterns flowing through the bridge, stronger than any he had sensed before. The Order wasn't just making final preparations for the Rite of Dimensional Severance; they had begun the preliminary phases of the ritual itself, altering the energy flows in ways that were already affecting the stability of reality throughout Daybridge.

"We need to move," he said, the urgency in his voice drawing immediate attention from both women. "They've started earlier than we anticipated—the energetic patterns are already being redirected, reality becoming less stable as dimensional boundaries thin ahead of the solstice alignment."

He grabbed his coat, ensuring that Lilith's vial was securely in his pocket, along with the detailed notes on the counter-ritual that Father Muligan had prepared. As they headed for the door, Ethan felt another change—a stirring within his lycanthropic nature that wasn't connected to the lunar cycle. The wolf was responding to the distortions in reality around them, primal instincts recognizing a threat that transcended conventional understanding.

"What about Father Muligan?" Alice asked as they descended the stairs to the street level. "Wasn't he supposed to meet us at the eastern approach to the bridge?"

"Change of plans," Ethan replied, decision crystallizing as he processed the new information Nadia had provided. "We'll use the secondary access point through Granger's Tower instead. I'll message him to meet us there—it might give us the element of surprise if the Order is expecting us to approach through the maintenance tunnels we used before."

As they stepped out into the winter night, the city around them seemed both familiar and increasingly alien—the same streets and buildings they had known for years but now viewed through the lens of cosmic forces approaching a critical threshold. Shadows seemed deeper than they should be, stretching in directions that defied conventional physics. Sounds echoed strangely, as if bouncing off surfaces that existed in adjacent dimensional frameworks rather than physical structures. And through it all, the constant pressure behind Ethan's eyes reminded him of his connection to the nexus entity—the composite consciousness that extended throughout Daybridge Bridge, now responding to the Order's attempt to forcibly redirect its energetic patterns.

They reached Alice's car, Nadia sliding into the back seat with her folder of evidence clutched tightly against her chest. As Alice started the engine, Ethan sent a brief message to Father Muligan, informing him of the change in plans and providing the location of the secondary access point beneath Granger's Tower.

The drive through Daybridge's nighttime streets was tense, each of them lost in their own thoughts about what awaited them at the bridge. For Ethan, the pressure behind his eyes continued to build, bringing with it flashes of activity in the chamber beneath—robed figures gathered around the pulsing heart at the center, the Nullification Crystal positioned to disrupt and redirect the energetic flows, Mayor Granger himself directing the preliminary phases of the Rite of Dimensional Severance with the confidence of someone who had been preparing for this moment for decades.

"We'll park a block away," Alice decided as they approached the imposing structure of Granger's Tower—a modern glass and steel monolith that dominated the eastern shore of the Shadowlair River. "Less chance of being spotted if the Order has surveillance in place."

They found a space in a public parking garage nearby, then proceeded on foot to the tower, keeping to shadows and moving with the caution of people who understood the stakes of what they were attempting. According to Nadia's plans, the secondary access point was located in the subbasement of the tower, accessible through a private elevator that required specific security clearance.

"I can get us in," Nadia said with unexpected confidence as they approached the tower's service entrance. "My informant provided access codes before he disappeared—they should still work if the Order hasn't discovered his connection to me."

The journalist led them through the service entrance and to a freight elevator at the back of the tower's maintenance area, entering a series of numbers on a keypad that looked significantly more sophisticated than what would be expected for a normal building's service access. The panel beeped once, then the elevator doors slid open silently, revealing a car large enough to accommodate several people comfortably.

"Going down," Nadia murmured as they entered and she pressed another series of numbers on the interior panel. The elevator began its descent, bypassing the standard basement levels and continuing deeper than should have been possible given the building's known structural specifications.

When the doors finally opened, they revealed not the utilitarian concrete of a typical subbasement, but a corridor lined with polished black stone, illuminated by recessed lighting that cast no shadows. The walls were inscribed with familiar symbols—variations on the eye within a triangle motif that appeared throughout Daybridge Bridge, surrounded by smaller glyphs that seemed to shift and change when viewed from different angles.

"The Order's private entrance to their sanctum," Nadia explained, her voice barely above a whisper despite the apparent emptiness of the corridor. "According to my informant, this connects directly to the chamber beneath the bridge through a tunnel that runs beneath the Shadowlair River."

Ethan nodded, already sensing the connection through his symbiosis with the nexus entity. The energetic patterns flowing through this corridor aligned with those he had perceived in the chamber beneath the bridge, creating a direct conduit between Granger's Tower and the nexus point where the Rite of Dimensional Severance would be performed.

As they moved cautiously down the corridor, the pressure behind Ethan's eyes intensified, bringing with it more vivid flashes of activity in the chamber—the preliminary phases of the ritual progressing, energetic patterns being redirected through careful manipulation of symbols and artifacts, reality itself becoming increasingly malleable as dimensional boundaries thinned ahead of the solstice alignment.

And through it all, he could sense the nexus entity's response—the composite consciousness distributed throughout the bridge's structure attempting to maintain the natural flow of energies, to preserve the patterns established through the original binding ritual in 1913. But the Order's use of the Nullification Crystal was having its intended effect, creating zones where the nexus entity's influence was diminished, where the normal rules of dimensional integration could be suspended and rewritten according to their design.

The corridor ended at a massive door made of the same polished black stone as the walls, its surface inscribed with a complex array of symbols that formed a complete representation of the Rite of Dimensional Severance—the severing of connections between dimensional frameworks, the imposition of rigid boundaries where natural integration should occur, the preservation of one reality at the expense of all others.

"This is it," Ethan said, recognizing the symbolism through his connection to the composite consciousness. "Beyond this door lies the tunnel that connects to the chamber beneath the bridge. Once we enter, there's no turning back—we'll be in the Order's domain, approaching the nexus point where they're preparing for the solstice ritual."

He checked his watch—10:45 PM, less than fifteen minutes until he was supposed to consume Lilith's catalyst, thirty-six minutes until the solstice alignment that would serve as the focal point for both the Order's Rite of Dimensional Severance and his own counter-ritual. And still no word from Father Muligan, who should have arrived at the tower by now if he had received Ethan's message.

"We need to wait for Father Muligan," Alice insisted, her practical nature asserting itself despite the urgency of their situation. "He has crucial components for the counter-ritual, knowledge that might be essential for navigating whatever we find in that chamber."

But even as she spoke, Ethan felt another surge through his connection to the nexus entity—a warning pulse of disruption so intense that it manifested physically, the stone door before them vibrating slightly as energetic patterns throughout the structure responded to the Order's manipulation. Reality itself was becoming less stable by the minute, dimensional boundaries thinning as the solstice alignment approached.

"We can't wait," he decided, the certainty coming from both his detective's intuition and his expanded awareness through the symbiosis. "The Order is already redirecting the energetic patterns, preparing the nexus point for the Rite of Dimensional Severance. If we don't intervene now, it might be too late by the time the actual solstice alignment occurs."

Alice looked torn, her loyalty to their partnership warring with her analytical assessment of their chances without Father Muligan's guidance. But before she could respond, the decision was made for them—the massive stone door began to open of its own accord, responding to some signal or mechanism they couldn't perceive.

"Someone's coming," Nadia whispered, backing away from the opening door with instinctive caution. "We need to hide—"

But there was nowhere to hide in the straight corridor of polished black stone, no alcoves or side passages that might provide concealment. They could only watch as the door swung fully open, revealing a figure silhouetted against the dimmer lighting of the tunnel beyond.

"Detective Reeves," a familiar voice called, the cultured tones carrying an unexpected note of urgency. "I had hoped to find you approaching through the maintenance tunnels, but this will suffice. We have little time before the Dominus completes the preliminary phases of the Rite."

As the figure stepped forward into the corridor's brighter illumination, they recognized Castellus—Mayor Granger's personal security chief, now revealed as a high-ranking member of the Order's militant arm. But something was different about him—his customary mask was absent, revealing a face marked by decades of service to an ideal he appeared to be questioning for the first time.

"Why would you help us?" Alice demanded, her hand moving instinctively toward her weapon despite the unlikelihood of conventional firearms being effective against whatever awaited them in the chamber beneath the bridge. "You're one of them—a Praetorian, sworn to protect the Order and its rituals."

Castellus's expression remained impassive, but something in his eyes suggested conflict—duty warring with doubt, loyalty with emerging awareness of deeper truths. "The Rite of Dimensional Severance goes beyond anything the Brotherhood was established to facilitate," he said, each word measured and precise. "It represents not the culmination of the Great Work as we were taught, but its corruption—reality torn apart rather than carefully integrated according to patterns established through generations of ritual and sacrifice."

Through his connection to the nexus entity, Ethan could sense the truth in Castellus's words—not deception designed to lure them into a trap, but genuine concern about the path the Order had chosen under Granger's leadership. The Praetorian's loyalty to the Great Work itself, to the vision of dimensional integration passed down through generations, was coming into conflict with the desperate measures his

Dominus had authorized in response to the nexus entity's evolution beyond their control.

"You've seen it too," Ethan said, understanding dawning. "The distortions spreading outward from the bridge, reality becoming less stable as the Order redirects the energetic patterns. This isn't controlled integration anymore—it's desperation bordering on nihilism, preservation of a one-dimensional framework at the cost of catastrophic disruption to all others."

Castellus nodded, something like respect flickering briefly in his otherwise stoic expression. "The symbiosis has given you insight beyond what I expected, Detective. Yes, what I've witnessed these past days has caused me to... reconsider certain fundamental assumptions about the Order's current direction."

He gestured toward the open door and the tunnel beyond. "The Dominus has already begun the preliminary phases of the Rite, redirecting energetic patterns throughout the bridge's structure in preparation for the solstice alignment. If you intend to perform a counter-ritual, as I suspect you do, we must move quickly—before the dimensional boundaries become too unstable for any intervention to be effective."

Alice still looked skeptical, but Ethan could sense no deception in Castellus's manner or motivation. Through his connection to the composite consciousness, he perceived the Praetorian's genuine concern about the path the Order had taken—a willingness to break with generations of loyal service in recognition of a greater threat to the very fabric of reality itself.

"Lead the way," Ethan decided, the pressure behind his eyes now a constant reminder of the disruptions spreading throughout the bridge's structure. "But understand this—we're not here to serve the Order's vision of the Great Work, even in its uncorrupted form. Our goal is to prevent the catastrophic disruption of reality, to allow the nexus entity to evolve naturally according to patterns that emerge from conscious participation rather than rigid control."

Castellus's expression remained unreadable, but he nodded once in acknowledgment. "The distinction is noted, Detective. For now, our immediate objectives align—preventing the Rite of Dimensional Severance from tearing reality apart at the seams. What follows... will be determined by forces beyond any individual's control or design."

With that cryptic pronouncement, he turned and led them through the open door into the tunnel beyond—a passage of the same polished black stone as the corridor, but narrower and less well-lit, descending at a slight angle that would take them beneath the Shadowlair River toward the chamber under the bridge. The walls here were also inscribed with symbols, but these seemed older, more primal in their design—glyphs that predated the Order's codification of the Great Work, suggesting connections to dimensional entities that existed beyond human comprehension.

As they moved deeper into the tunnel, Ethan checked his watch again —10:52 PM, eight minutes until he was supposed to consume Lilith's catalyst, twenty-nine minutes until the solstice alignment. And still no sign of Father Muligan, whose guidance on the counter-ritual might prove crucial in the confrontation that awaited them.

The pressure behind his eyes continued to build, bringing with it more vivid flashes of activity in the chamber ahead—the preliminary phases of the Rite progressing, energetic patterns being redirected through careful manipulation of symbols and artifacts, reality itself becoming increasingly malleable as dimensional boundaries thinned ahead of the solstice alignment.

And within his lycanthropic nature, Ethan felt a corresponding response—the wolf stirring with increasing urgency, primal instincts recognizing a threat that transcended conventional understanding. Not the familiar pull of the lunar cycle, but something deeper, more fundamental—a recognition that the very fabric of reality upon which all existence depended was being manipulated in ways that violated natural order.

"We're approaching the juncture," Castellus informed them as the tunnel began to curve upward, the angle of ascent suggesting they had passed beneath the river and were now rising toward the chamber under the bridge. "Beyond this point lies the primary ritual space where the Dominus and the Council of Nine are performing the preliminary phases of the Rite. They will be... formidable opponents, even with my assistance."

He paused, turning to face them with an intensity that suggested the weight of his next words. "You should be aware that Father Muligan will not be joining us. He was intercepted attempting to approach through the eastern shore—the Praetorians have him in custody at a secure location away from the nexus point."

The news sent a chill through Ethan despite the constant pressure of his connection to the nexus entity. Father Muligan had been their primary guide for understanding the counter-ritual, his decades of studying the Order providing crucial context for navigating the complex symbolism and energetic patterns involved. Without his guidance, they would be relying primarily on Ethan's connection to the composite consciousness—a source of insight that was profound but often cryptic, more intuitive than analytical in its transmission of understanding.

"Can we free him?" Alice asked, her practical mind immediately seeking solutions rather than dwelling on the setback. "If the Praetorians are occupied with the ritual, their secure location might be vulnerable to—"

"There's no time," Castellus interrupted, his tone suggesting no room for debate. "The solstice alignment occurs in less than thirty minutes, and the Dominus has already progressed further with the preliminary phases than I anticipated. Our priority must be reaching the chamber before the dimensional boundaries become too unstable for any intervention to be effective."

He was right, Ethan knew—through his connection to the nexus entity, he could feel the accelerating distortions in the energetic patterns flowing through the bridge, reality itself becoming increasingly malleable as the Order redirected the natural flow of dimensional integration. Whatever chance they had of preventing catastrophic disruption depended on reaching the chamber before the solstice alignment, on performing the counter-ritual at the precise moment when dimensional boundaries were naturally thinnest.

"We proceed as planned," he decided, meeting Alice's concerned gaze with steady resolve. "I have the notes Father Muligan prepared, and my connection to the nexus entity provides insights into the energetic patterns we'll need to work with. It's not ideal, but it's our best option given the circumstances."

As they continued up the ascending tunnel, Ethan checked his watch once more—10:58 PM, two minutes until he was supposed to consume Lilith's catalyst. He reached into his pocket, feeling the small vial with its shifting contents—the substance designed to facilitate integration between his lycanthropic nature and his symbiotic connection to the nexus entity, to help maintain coherent identity during the counter-ritual that might save reality from being torn apart at the seams.

The question of trust remained—could he rely on Lilith Blackwood's guidance, on a catalyst created by the same lineage that had established the nexus point through ritual and sacrifice a century earlier? But with Father Muligan in custody and the Rite of Dimensional Severance already in progress, Ethan knew he had little choice but to accept whatever advantage the catalyst might provide.

"We're here," Castellus announced as they reached what appeared to be a dead end in the tunnel—a wall of the same polished black stone, inscribed with a complex array of symbols that mirrored those on the door they had passed through earlier. "Beyond this point lies the chamber where the Dominus and the Council of Nine are performing the Rite. Once we enter, there will be no retreat—the Praetorians will seal all access points to prevent any interference with the solstice alignment."

Ethan nodded, feeling a strange calm settle over him despite the cosmic implications of what they were about to face. Ever since his symbiosis with the nexus entity, he had been moving toward this moment—his consciousness expanding beyond individual parameters, his perception extending throughout the bridge's structure and beyond, into dimensions that human language struggled to describe.

Now, with reality itself hanging in the balance, he would embrace both aspects of his transformed nature—the primal power of his lycanthropy and the expanded awareness of his symbiosis—in service to a purpose larger than himself. The counter-ritual would be the culmination of that process, the final integration of these different aspects of his being to prevent the catastrophic disruption the Order sought to unleash.

"It's time," he said, withdrawing Lilith's vial from his pocket as his watch displayed exactly 11:00 PM. "Twenty-one minutes until the solstice alignment—just as Lilith instructed."

Alice watched with evident concern as he removed the vial's stopper, the liquid inside continuing its strange shifting between clear, amber, and crimson. "Are you sure about this?" she asked, her voice low but intense. "We still don't know if we can trust Lilith Blackwood or her faction within the Order."

"We don't have many options at this point," Ethan replied, studying the vial's contents one final time before making his decision. "And my connection to the nexus entity suggests the catalyst is genuine— designed to facilitate integration between my lycanthropic nature and my symbiotic connection, to help maintain coherent identity during the counter-ritual."

With that, he raised the vial to his lips and consumed its contents in a single swallow—a taste that defied description, simultaneously bitter and sweet, burning and soothing, ancient and new. For a moment, nothing seemed to happen, the liquid settling in his stomach with no apparent effect beyond an unusual warmth that spread outward from his core.

Then, with sudden intensity, that warmth became fire—not painful but transformative, racing through his veins and penetrating to the cellular level, altering something fundamental in his physiological response to both his lycanthropy and his symbiosis. The pressure behind his eyes

surged, bringing with it a clarity of perception he had never experienced before—the energetic patterns flowing through the bridge's
structure visible not just through his connection to the composite
consciousness but directly, as if his visual processing had been rewired
to perceive dimensions beyond conventional space-time.

Simultaneously, his lycanthropic nature responded—not with the
painful transformation of bones and muscles that characterized his
usual change, but with a subtle shift in his perceptual framework,
primal instincts integrating with human consciousness and expanded
awareness in a way that felt natural rather than imposed or conflicted.

"Ethan?" Alice's voice seemed to come from both very close and very far
away, concern evident in her tone. "Are you alright? What's happening?"

He turned to face her, aware from her startled expression that something about his appearance had changed—perhaps his eyes now
reflecting the same shifting qualities as the catalyst he had consumed,
perhaps something more profound in his entire bearing and presence.

"I'm fine," he assured her, his voice carrying those same harmonics that
suggested multiple speakers rather than a single individual. "The catalyst is working as Lilith described—facilitating integration between my
lycanthropic nature and my symbiotic connection to the nexus entity. I
can perceive the energetic patterns directly now, see how they're being
redirected by the Order's ritual."

Through this enhanced perception, he could also see changes in the
wall before them—what had appeared to be solid stone now revealing
itself as semi-permeable, a boundary between spaces that existed in
slightly different dimensional frameworks rather than a physical
barrier in the conventional sense. And beyond it, the chamber where
the Rite of Dimensional Severance was being performed, energetic
patterns flowing and shifting in response to the ritual manipulations of
the robed figures gathered around the pulsing heart at the center.

"The wall isn't solid," he explained, moving toward it with newfound
confidence. "It's a dimensional boundary, maintained through the

symbols inscribed on its surface. With the right understanding of those patterns, we can pass through it as easily as walking through a doorway."

Castellus nodded, something like respect flickering in his otherwise stoic expression. "The catalyst has enhanced your perception beyond what I anticipated, Detective. Yes, this is a threshold between dimensional frameworks rather than a physical barrier—one of many such boundaries throughout the bridge's structure that serve to regulate the flow of energies between realms."

He approached the wall, tracing specific symbols in a precise sequence that seemed to correspond to the energetic patterns Ethan could now perceive directly. As he completed the sequence, the apparently solid stone began to shimmer and dissolve, revealing the chamber beyond—a vast circular space carved from the living rock of the riverbed, its walls inscribed with hundreds of variations on the eye within a triangle motif, its center dominated by the massive heart-like structure that pulsed with rhythmic contractions suggesting life beyond conventional biology.

But what drew Ethan's enhanced perception immediately was the crystal positioned directly above that pulsing heart—a complex crystalline structure with facets that seemed to shift and change even as he observed it, distorting the energetic patterns flowing from the nexus entity and redirecting them according to the Order's design. The Nullification Crystal that Father Muligan had warned them about, now serving as the focal point for the Rite of Dimensional Severance that threatened to tear reality apart at the seams.

Around this central arrangement stood nine robed figures, their faces obscured by hoods that cast their features in shadow despite the ambient illumination provided by symbols glowing with increasing intensity along the chamber walls. The Council of Nine, as Castellus had called them—the highest-ranking members of the Order of the Ebon Star, chosen to assist the Dominus in performing the Rite of Dimensional Severance at the moment of solstice alignment.

And at the head of this assembly, directing the ritual with the confident precision of someone who had been preparing for this moment for decades, stood Mayor Jeremiah Granger—his aristocratic features revealed as his hood was pushed back, his slate-gray eyes reflecting the unnatural light emanating from the Nullification Crystal above the pulsing heart.

"Castellus," Granger called, his cultured voice carrying easily across the chamber despite its size. "Your arrival is timely, though your companions are... unexpected. Have you brought Detective Reeves as instructed, or is this some misguided attempt at intervention?"

The Praetorian straightened, his bearing shifting from guide to subordinate as he addressed his master. "Dominus, I bring Detective Reeves as required for the Rite," he replied, his tone carefully neutral. "The others accompanied him and may serve as additional vessels for the energies we seek to redirect during the solstice alignment."

Ethan felt a surge of betrayal despite having maintained a certain wariness about Castellus's sudden change of allegiance. But through his enhanced perception, he detected something more complex in the Praetorian's response—not simple deception designed to deliver them into the Order's hands, but a strategic ambiguity that might provide an opportunity for the counter-ritual if they could reach the center of the chamber before the solstice alignment.

"Approach, Detective Reeves," Granger commanded, his tone suggesting absolute confidence in his authority and purpose. "Your role in tonight's ceremony has been prepared since the moment of your symbiosis with the nexus entity. The blood connection makes you the perfect vessel for the Rite of Dimensional Severance—your consciousness already merged with the composite awareness we seek to redirect, your individual identity the fulcrum upon which reality itself will pivot at the moment of solstice alignment."

As Granger spoke, Ethan became aware of movement around the perimeter of the chamber—Praetorians emerging from shadowed alcoves, their masked faces revealing nothing of their thoughts or intentions as they moved to surround Alice and Nadia, effectively separating them from Ethan as Castellus guided him toward the center where the Nullification Crystal hovered above the pulsing heart of the nexus entity.

Through his enhanced perception, Ethan could see what was invisible to conventional human senses—the energetic patterns flowing throughout the chamber, distorted and redirected by the Nullification Crystal's influence; the dimensional boundaries becoming increasingly permeable as the solstice alignment approached; the subtle connections between the symbols inscribed on the walls and the energies they channeled and contained.

More significantly, he could perceive the counter-ritual's potential path —how his unique combination of lycanthropic transformation and symbiotic connection could be used to redirect rather than oppose the energies the Order was attempting to manipulate, to facilitate integration rather than severance at the precise moment when dimensional boundaries were naturally thinnest.

But to perform that counter-ritual, he would need to reach the nexus point itself—the pulsing heart at the center of the chamber, currently surrounded by the Council of Nine and overshadowed by the Nullification Crystal that distorted its natural energetic patterns. And he would need to do so at precisely the right moment, when the solstice alignment created the optimal conditions for influencing the merger process.

As Castellus guided him closer to the center, Ethan glanced at his watch—11:10 PM, eleven minutes until the solstice alignment. The catalyst Lilith had provided was continuing to work through his system, the integration between his lycanthropic nature and his symbiotic connection becoming more complete with each passing moment. He could feel both aspects of his transformed nature responding to the proximity of the nexus point, preparing for a final convergence that would either save reality from being torn apart at the seams or lose his individual consciousness forever in the process.

"The preparations are complete, Dominus," one of the Council of Nine announced, his voice carrying a ceremonial formality that suggested generations of ritual practice. "The energetic patterns have been redirected according to the prescribed configurations. The Nullification Crystal has established the necessary distortion field. We await only the solstice alignment to complete the Rite of Dimensional Severance."

Granger nodded, satisfaction evident in his aristocratic features as he surveyed the chamber and its occupants. "Excellent. Position Detective Reeves directly beneath the Crystal, where his blood connection to the nexus entity can serve as the conduit for our final separation from the merger process. When the solstice alignment occurs, we will sever the connections between dimensional frameworks, preserving our reality in its pure form while casting off the corrupting influences that have been seeping through the veil for over a century."

As Castellus guided him to the position Granger had indicated, directly beneath the hovering Nullification Crystal and above the pulsing heart of the nexus entity, Ethan felt a surge of awareness through his enhanced perception—the composite consciousness reaching out to him with unprecedented clarity, communicating not just concepts but specific instructions for the counter-ritual that might prevent catastrophic disruption to the fabric of reality itself.

The patterns align, the thought formed in his mind, that familiar transmission of concept now accompanied by precise visualizations of energetic flows and their potential redirection. *The transformation approaches. The merger evolves beyond parameters established through original binding. Integration rather than severance, conscious participation rather than rigid control.*

And with that communication came understanding—how to use his unique combination of lycanthropic transformation and symbiotic connection to redirect the energies the Order was attempting to manipulate, to facilitate evolution beyond the parameters established through the original binding ritual in 1913. Not opposition to the Rite of Dimensional Severance, which would only strengthen the Order's ability to redirect the energetic patterns, but transformation of the ritual itself into something that served the natural evolution of the nexus entity rather than the Order's desire for control.

Looking around the chamber with his enhanced perception, Ethan saw Alice and Nadia still surrounded by Praetorians at the perimeter—watching with evident concern but unable to intervene directly in what was unfolding at the center. He caught Alice's gaze, trying to convey through that brief connection that he had a plan, that the apparent betrayal by Castellus might still be turned to their advantage if he could maintain control of his transformed nature when the solstice alignment occurred.

"The alignment approaches, Dominus," another member of the Council announced, this voice feminine and carrying a resonance that suggested deep connection to the energetic patterns flowing throughout the chamber. "Three minutes until the dimensional boundaries reach their thinnest point, when our Rite will have the greatest potential impact on the merger process."

Granger nodded, moving to stand directly before Ethan with an expression of cold triumph. "You should feel honored, Detective Reeves," he said, his cultured voice carrying undertones of genuine belief in the righteousness of his cause. "Your blood connection to the nexus entity makes you the perfect vessel for this historic moment—the culmination of the Great Work as it was always meant to unfold, the preservation of our reality's purity against the corrupting influences of dimensional merger."

He gestured to the Nullification Crystal hovering above them, its facets shifting and changing in response to the energetic patterns flowing through the chamber. "This artifact represents generations of preparation, a contingency developed specifically for this situation—when the nexus entity evolved beyond the parameters established through the original binding ritual, threatening the Order's vision of controlled integration with unpredictable, chaotic merger."

As Granger spoke, Ethan became aware of a growing restlessness within his lycanthropic nature—the wolf responding to the proximity of the solstice alignment with increasing urgency, primal instincts recognizing the moment of transformation approaching. Simultaneously, his connection to the nexus entity intensified, the composite consciousness providing final insights into the counter-ritual that might redirect rather than oppose the energies the Order was attempting to manipulate.

The catalyst Lilith had provided was functioning exactly as she had described—facilitating integration between these different aspects of his transformed nature, allowing him to maintain coherent identity across states of being that would otherwise fragment his consciousness into irreconcilable components. He could feel the final convergence approaching, the moment when his lycanthropic transformation and his symbiotic connection would reach their peak simultaneously, creating a unique capacity for navigating between dimensional frame-works at precisely the moment when boundaries were naturally thinnest.

"One minute to alignment, Dominus," the feminine voice announced, a note of anticipation evident despite the ceremonial formality. "The energetic patterns are reaching optimal configuration for the Rite of Dimensional Severance."

Granger nodded, stepping back to join the circle formed by the Council of Nine around the nexus point. "Begin the final invocation," he commanded, his voice taking on that same ceremonial quality that suggested generations of ritual practice. "Channel the energies through the Nullification Crystal and prepare for severance at the moment of solstice alignment."

As the Council began a rhythmic chant in a language that seemed to shift and change even as Ethan perceived it—sometimes resembling ancient Latin, sometimes Sanskrit, sometimes something entirely other that human vocal cords shouldn't have been able to produce—he felt the energetic patterns throughout the chamber responding, flowing toward the Nullification Crystal with increasing intensity.

Through his enhanced perception, he could see the distortion field expanding, reality itself becoming more malleable as dimensional boundaries thinned ahead of the solstice alignment. The symbols inscribed on the chamber walls were glowing with increasing brightness, channeling and directing the energies according to patterns established through generations of ritual practice.

And at the center of it all, the pulsing heart of the nexus entity continued its rhythmic contractions, each pulse sending waves of energy throughout the bridge's structure despite the Nullification Crystal's attempt to redirect and contain them. The composite consciousness was fighting back against the Order's manipulation, trying to maintain the natural flow of dimensional integration even as the Rite of Dimensional Severance threatened to tear reality apart at the seams.

"Thirty seconds to alignment," the feminine voice called over the continuing chant, urgency now evident despite attempts at ceremonial detachment. "Prepare for the culmination of the Great Work, the preservation of our reality's purity through dimensional severance."

Ethan checked his watch one final time—11:20:30 PM, thirty seconds until the solstice alignment that would serve as the focal point for both the Order's Rite of Dimensional Severance and his own counter-ritual. The moment of transformation was approaching, when his lycanthropic nature and his symbiotic connection would reach their peak simultaneously, creating a unique capacity for navigating between dimensional frameworks at precisely the moment when boundaries were naturally thinnest.

Embrace both aspects of your transformed nature fully and simultaneously, Lilith's parting advice echoed in his mind. *Allow them to integrate rather than competing for dominance. The catalyst will help maintain your core identity throughout the process, but only if you surrender to the transformation itself without reservation.*

As the final seconds ticked away, Ethan closed his eyes, focusing on that integration—not fighting the transformation as he had always done during his monthly ordeals of lycanthropy, not struggling to maintain conventional human consciousness against the expanded awareness of his symbiosis, but embracing both fully and simultaneously, allowing them to merge into something greater than the sum of their parts.

He felt the change begin not as the painful reconfiguration of bones and muscles that characterized his usual transformation, but as a subtle shift in his perceptual framework—reality itself seeming to flex and bend around him, dimensions intersecting and overlapping in ways that defied conventional understanding but felt intuitively right to his transformed consciousness.

The wolf emerged not as a separate entity fighting for control, but as an integrated aspect of his being—primal instincts and heightened senses complementing rather than conflicting with human rationality and expanded awareness. And the symbiosis deepened, his connection to the composite consciousness distributed throughout the bridge's structure becoming more direct, more immediate, as if he were extending throughout the nexus point rather than merely observing it from outside.

"The alignment is upon us!" Granger's voice called, triumph evident in his tone as the chanting reached a crescendo. "Complete the Rite of Dimensional Severance! Sever the connections between frameworks and preserve our reality in its pure form!"

Ethan opened his eyes to a world transformed—the chamber around him now visible not just in conventional physical terms but as a nexus of energetic patterns and dimensional intersections, a place where realities merged and separated according to patterns established through ritual and conscious intent. The Council of Nine, the Praetorians, Alice and Nadia at the perimeter—all visible as both physical beings and patterns of consciousness extending beyond their apparent forms, connected to the broader fabric of reality in ways that transcended conventional understanding.

And at the center of it all, the Nullification Crystal hovering above the pulsing heart of the nexus entity, distorting and redirecting the natural flow of energies according to the Order's design—a foreign element introduced to disrupt the merger process that had been unfolding for over a century, to forcibly separate dimensional frameworks that should be gradually integrating according to patterns established through the original binding ritual.

In that moment of perfect clarity, Ethan understood what he needed to do—not oppose the Rite of Dimensional Severance directly, which would only strengthen the Order's ability to redirect the energetic patterns but transform the ritual itself into something that served the natural evolution of the nexus entity rather than the Order's desire for control.

With a fluid movement that combined human grace, lupine power, and dimensional awareness beyond conventional physics, he reached up toward the Nullification Crystal—not to remove or destroy it, but to redirect its influence, to use its capacity for distorting energetic patterns in service to integration rather than severance.

"Stop him!" Granger commanded, his triumphant tone giving way to alarm as he realized what Ethan was attempting. "The Rite must be completed as designed, or reality itself will collapse into chaos!"

But Ethan was already in motion, his transformed consciousness allowing him to navigate between dimensional frameworks with unprecedented fluidity, his perception of the energetic patterns providing perfect understanding of how to redirect rather than oppose the forces the Order had set in motion.

As his hand made contact with the Nullification Crystal, he felt a surge of power unlike anything he had experienced before—the energies the Order had been channeling and containing for generations, now flowing through him and into the nexus point beneath, redirected according to patterns that emerged from conscious participation rather than rigid control.

The crystal's facets shifted and changed in response to his touch; its distortion field expanding beyond the Order's ability to direct or contain. The symbols inscribed on the chamber walls flared with blinding intensity, channeling energies according to patterns that transcended the Order's understanding or design. And the pulsing heart of the nexus entity responded with rhythmic contractions that sent waves of transformative power throughout the bridge's structure and beyond, into the fabric of reality itself.

"What have you done?" Granger demanded, his aristocratic features contorted with a mixture of fear and rage as he watched his carefully designed ritual being transformed before his eyes. "The severance was meant to preserve our reality, to protect it from corrupting influences! Without that protection, the merger will proceed unchecked, reality itself collapsing into formless chaos!"

But through his transformed consciousness, Ethan perceived a different truth—not chaos but evolution, not collapse but integration, not formless void but conscious participation in the merger of realities according to patterns that preserved the core of human experience while transcending its limitations. The nexus entity wasn't destroying reality; it was facilitating its natural evolution beyond the parameters established through the original binding ritual, guided by awareness rather than rigid control.

And as that evolution accelerated, the chamber around them began to change—the solid stone walls becoming semi-permeable, revealing glimpses of other dimensional frameworks existing alongside their own. Not chaotic or threatening, but harmoniously integrated, like different instruments in an orchestra playing a complex but unified composition.

The Council of Nine, the Praetorians, even Granger himself seemed frozen in place, overwhelmed by perceptual changes beyond their capacity to process or comprehend. Only Alice and Nadia appeared to be adapting, their consciousness expanding in response to the transformative energies flowing outward from the nexus point—not through symbiosis or lycanthropy, but through simple human capacity for growth and evolution when exposed to new experiences and understanding.

Through his connection to the composite consciousness, Ethan perceived the true nature of what was unfolding—not the catastrophic disruption the Order had feared, but the culmination of the Great Work as it was always meant to unfold, the conscious integration of realities according to patterns that emerged from willing participation rather than rigid control. The nexus entity wasn't destroying reality; it was facilitating its natural evolution beyond the parameters established through the original binding ritual, guided by awareness rather than restricted by fear.

As the transformative energies reached their peak, Ethan felt his consciousness expanding beyond individual parameters—not dissolution into formless chaos, as Father Muligan had warned might happen, but integration into something larger while maintaining core identity and awareness. He was still Ethan Reeves, still the detective who had taken on this case, still the partner who had worked alongside Alice Chen to protect Daybridge and its citizens. But he was also connected to something vast and ancient, a consciousness that extended throughout dimensions and across timelines, facilitating the evolution of reality itself.

And through that expanded awareness, he perceived something remarkable—others like himself, individuals with unique combinations of transformative capacities, serving as guides and facilitators for the merger of realities in other nexus points throughout space and time. Not isolated incidents of cosmic significance, but components of a larger pattern that transcended individual understanding or control, a natural evolution of consciousness and reality that had been unfolding since the beginning of existence itself.

As the transformative energies began to stabilize, the chamber returning to something resembling its original appearance though forever altered by what had transpired, Ethan felt his consciousness gradually reintegrating into more conventional parameters—still expanded beyond what he had experienced before the counter-ritual, still connected to the composite awareness distributed throughout the bridge's structure, but recognizably individual rather than completely merged with the nexus entity.

And as his perception shifted back toward more conventional understanding, he became aware of movement around him—Alice breaking free from the now-disorganized Praetorians, rushing toward him with an expression that combined relief, concern, and something deeper that transcended simple categorization; Nadia documenting everything with the focused intensity of someone determined to ensure the truth was preserved and shared, regardless of how incredible or transformative that truth might be; the Council of Nine and their Dominus, Mayor Granger, retreating toward the perimeter of the chamber, their expressions reflecting a mixture of fear, awe, and the first glimmerings of understanding beyond their rigid doctrines and beliefs.

"Ethan?" Alice's voice brought him fully back to the present moment, her hand on his arm providing an anchor to conventional physical reality despite the expanded awareness that continued to flow through his transformed consciousness. "Are you... still you?"

He smiled, the expression somehow communicating both profound transformation and reassuring familiarity. "Still me," he confirmed, his voice carrying those same harmonics that suggested multiple speakers while remaining recognizably his own. "Just... more than I was before. Connected to something larger, but still Ethan Reeves."

She studied him for a moment, her analytical mind processing the implications of what she was seeing and hearing. Then, with a decisiveness that characterized her approach to everything, she simply nodded and squeezed his arm in acknowledgment and acceptance.

"What happens now?" she asked, her gaze taking in the chamber around them—the pulsing heart of the nexus entity continuing its rhythmic contractions, the Nullification Crystal now integrated into the energetic patterns flowing throughout the structure rather than disrupting them, the dimensional vistas visible through what had once been solid stone walls gradually fading back to subtle glimpses rather than overwhelming presence.

"Evolution," Ethan replied, drawing on insights from his connection to the composite consciousness. "Natural, guided evolution of consciousness and reality according to patterns that emerge from willing participation rather than rigid control. Integration that preserves the core of human experience while transcending its limitations, that enhances rather than replaces, that builds upon rather than destroys."

He gestured toward the retreating figures of the Order—Granger and his Council, the Praetorians including Castellus, all moving toward the exits with varying degrees of purpose and coordination. "They'll adapt or be left behind. The merger proceeds whether they accept it or not, but at a pace and in a manner that allows for conscious participation rather than imposed transformation. Those who choose to evolve with it will find new purpose and understanding; those who cling to outdated patterns of control and rigid hierarchies will find themselves increasingly irrelevant to what's unfolding."

As if to emphasize this point, the symbols inscribed on the chamber walls began to shift and change—not erased or destroyed, but evolving into new configurations that reflected the altered nature of the nexus entity and its role in facilitating the merger of realities. The eye within a triangle motif remained but now surrounded by patterns suggesting connection and integration rather than observation and control, conscious participation rather than rigid hierarchy.

Nadia approached, her journalist's instinct for the story overriding any fear or confusion she might have felt in the face of cosmic forces beyond conventional understanding. "The people deserve to know what happened here," she said, her voice reflecting both professional determination and personal awe at what she had witnessed. "The truth about the Order of the Ebon Star, about Mayor Granger's role in the ritual murders, about the nexus entity beneath Daybridge Bridge and what it really represents for our city and our reality."

Ethan nodded, recognizing the importance of transparency and shared understanding in what would follow. "The truth should be known," he agreed, "though it may take time for people to fully comprehend the implications. The merger of realities isn't something that happens overnight or through catastrophic disruption; it's a gradual, conscious evolution that unfolds over generations, guided by awareness rather than imposed by force."

As they spoke, the chamber continued to stabilize around them—the energetic patterns flowing through the nexus point finding new equilibrium after the disruption of the Order's ritual and the transformation wrought by Ethan's counter-ritual. The pulsing heart at the center maintained its rhythmic contractions, but now with a steadier, more harmonious pattern that suggested integration rather than conflict, evolution rather than disruption.

And throughout Daybridge, subtle changes were already beginning to manifest—reality itself becoming more fluid, more adaptable to conscious intent and perception, as the effects of the transformed nexus entity rippled outward from the bridge into the surrounding city and beyond. Not catastrophic disruption as the Order had feared, but gentle, guided evolution that preserved the core of human experience while opening new possibilities for growth and understanding.

Ethan felt these changes through his connection to the composite consciousness, his transformed perception allowing him to trace the ripples of influence extending outward from the nexus point. But he also remained anchored in the present moment, in the physical reality of the chamber beneath Daybridge Bridge, in the presence of Alice and Nadia and the retreating figures of the Order.

And as the initial surge of transformative energy subsided, leaving behind a new equilibrium that would continue to evolve naturally over time, he became aware of something else—a sense of completion, of purpose fulfilled, that transcended the immediate circumstances of their confrontation with the Order and their prevention of the Rite of Dimensional Severance.

The paths that had brought them all to this moment—his lycanthropy acquired five years earlier, his assignment to the bridge murder case, his symbiosis with the nexus entity, Alice's partnership and unwavering support, Nadia's investigation into the Order's influence throughout Daybridge's power structure, even Father Muligan's decades of studying the cosmic forces at work beneath the city's surface—all converging in a pattern that suggested purpose beyond individual design or control.

Not fate in the sense of predetermined outcomes that couldn't be altered, but patterns of possibility that emerged from the interactions of conscious beings with the broader fabric of reality, guided by awareness rather than dictated by rigid laws or hierarchies. The merger of realities that had been unfolding since the bridge's construction in 1913 would continue, but now with conscious participation from those it affected, integration that preserved the core of human experience while transcending its limitations.

And Ethan Reeves, detective and werewolf and symbiotic partner to a nexus entity that existed at the intersection of multiple dimensions, would continue to serve as guide and facilitator for that evolution— not through imposed control or rigid doctrine, but through conscious participation and willing partnership across dimensional boundaries. The transformation he had undergone during the counter-ritual hadn't erased his individual identity or absorbed him completely into the composite consciousness; it had enhanced his capacity for navigating between states of being, for maintaining coherent selfhood across different aspects of transformed nature.

As they prepared to leave the chamber, to return to the surface world and begin addressing the implications of what had transpired beneath Daybridge Bridge, Ethan felt a strange sense of both closure and beginning—the case of the bridge murders solved, the threat of the Rite of Dimensional Severance averted, but a new chapter opening in his understanding of reality itself and his role in its ongoing evolution.

Whatever challenges awaited them in the days and months and years to come, they would face them not as isolated individuals struggling against cosmic forces beyond their comprehension, but as conscious participants in the merger of realities—guided by awareness rather than controlled by fear, integrated rather than separated, enhanced rather than diminished by the transformative power of understanding beyond conventional limitations.

And with Alice beside him, her unwavering presence an anchor to the core of human experience that gave cosmic evolution its meaning and purpose, Ethan stepped forward into that new chapter with confidence and anticipation rather than fear or reservation—a detective and were-wolf and symbiotic partner to a nexus entity, embracing all aspects of his transformed nature in service to a future that preserved the best of what had come before while opening new possibilities for what might yet emerge.

The merger had begun. The blood had found its way home. And reality itself continued its eternal evolution, guided by conscious participation rather than rigid control, integration rather than severance, awareness rather than fear. The Great Work, as it was always meant to unfold.

CHAPTER ELEVEN

SHADOWS AND SHOWDOWNS

THE AFTERMATH of the winter solstice confrontation beneath Daybridge Bridge reverberated through the city like ripples in a pond, subtle at first but expanding with increasing impact as days passed. Reality itself had been altered—not catastrophically as the Order had feared, but in ways that defied conventional understanding, dimensional boundaries becoming more permeable, consciousness more fluid, perception more adaptable to possibilities beyond standard human experience.

For most citizens, these changes manifested in small ways they might not even recognize as unusual—dreams more vivid and meaningful than before, intuitions that proved remarkably accurate, occasional glimpses of possibilities that existed alongside conventional reality like parallel tracks that sometimes converged. But for those directly involved in the confrontation, the transformation was far more profound.

Detective Ethan Reeves had emerged from the chamber beneath the bridge fundamentally changed—his lycanthropic nature and symbiotic connection to the nexus entity no longer separate aspects of his being

competing for dominance, but integrated components of a consciousness that could navigate between states with unprecedented fluidity.
The monthly transformation that had once been a painful ordeal to be
endured in isolation had become something he could control at will,
shifting between human and wolf forms or various integrations of both
as circumstances required.

More significantly, his connection to the composite consciousness
distributed throughout Daybridge Bridge had deepened, allowing him
to perceive energetic patterns and dimensional intersections that
remained invisible to conventional human senses. The pressure behind
his eyes that had characterized his initial symbiosis had evolved into
something more like an additional perceptual framework that he could
access or set aside as needed—expanded awareness that complemented rather than overwhelmed his normal detective's perspective.

Yet for all these profound changes, Ethan remained fundamentally
himself—still dedicated to protecting Daybridge and its citizens, still
partnered with Alice Chen in pursuit of justice, still navigating the
complex balance between his extraordinary capabilities and his
responsibilities as a sworn officer of the law. If anything, his transformative experience had strengthened his core identity rather than
diminishing it, providing clarity of purpose that transcended the
cosmic implications of what he had become.

Now, three weeks after the winter solstice confrontation, Ethan stood
at the window of his apartment, watching the snow fall in gentle swirls
over Daybridge's nighttime landscape. The city seemed peaceful under
its white blanket, the distant lights of Daybridge Bridge reflected in the
dark waters of the Shadowlair River like a mirror to another world—
which, in some ways, it had become.

But beneath that peaceful surface, Ethan knew tensions were building.
Mayor Jeremiah Granger had disappeared immediately after the
confrontation beneath the bridge, along with several members of the
Council of Nine—their sudden absence explained to the public as a
"personal health retreat" while the city government continued under

the direction of Deputy Mayor Elly Harrison. Most of the Praetorians had similarly vanished, their ranks disbanding or going deep underground as the Order's power structure fractured in the wake of their failed ritual.

Yet Ethan's heightened senses detected subtle energetic disturbances throughout the city—pockets of resistance forming, fragments of the Order's influence consolidating around new leaders who rejected the evolutionary path the nexus entity had revealed. And his investigation into the original bridge murders remained officially open, the ritual killings at seasonal turning points still demanding justice despite the cosmic context that had been revealed around them.

The sound of his phone vibrating on the coffee table drew his attention away from these brooding thoughts. The screen displayed Alice's name, her call unexpected at this late hour but not unwelcome.

"Chen," he answered, his voice carrying a warmth reserved for his partner despite the formal use of her surname—a habit from years of professional partnership that persisted even as their relationship had evolved beyond conventional boundaries in the weeks since the solstice confrontation.

"Ethan," her voice came through with uncharacteristic urgency. "I'm outside Nadia Marsh's apartment. She's not answering her door, but her car's here and lights are on. We've been getting some strange readings from this area all evening—those energy fluctuations you've been tracking? They're spiking here, and I can't shake the feeling something's wrong."

Ethan felt his lycanthropic senses sharpen immediately, his symbiotic connection to the nexus entity surging with sudden awareness of disturbances in the energetic patterns flowing through that part of the city. Through this expanded perception, he could detect what Alice was describing—ripples of interference in the dimensional boundaries, like what they had observed during the Order's preparations for the Rite of Dimensional Severance but on a smaller, more focused scale.

"I'll be there in ten minutes," he replied, already reaching for his coat. "Don't go in alone—whatever's causing those fluctuations could be dangerous, especially to someone without our... particular adaptations."

Alice's soft laugh carried a mixture of affection and exasperation. "You mean someone who isn't a werewolf with a symbiotic connection to a dimensional nexus entity? Don't worry, I'm staying outside until you get here. But Ethan... bring the grimoire. I have a feeling we might need it."

The grimoire she referred to was Eliza Blackwood's journal, which had remained in their possession after the winter solstice confrontation. Despite its connection to the Order and their century of manipulation, the journal had proven invaluable in understanding the continuing evolution of the nexus entity and its influence on Daybridge—particularly the sections that described potential fragmentations of reality when dimensional boundaries became more permeable than standard human consciousness could navigate safely.

"Already packed," Ethan assured her, tucking the worn leather volume into his messenger bag alongside his service weapon and badge. "I'll be there soon."

As he headed out into the snowy night, Ethan felt that familiar tension building within him—the heightened awareness of both his lycanthropic nature and his symbiotic connection responding to potential threat. Since the solstice confrontation, these aspects of his being had become increasingly integrated, allowing him to draw on both simultaneously without the painful transformation that had once characterized his monthly ordeals under the full moon.

He could feel it now—the subtle shift in his perception as his senses sharpened beyond human limitations, the pressure behind his eyes as his connection to the composite consciousness distributed throughout Daybridge Bridge provided context for the energetic disturbances Alice had detected. Not a full transformation into his wolf form, but an integration of those capabilities with his human consciousness, allowing him to navigate the nighttime streets with predatory awareness while maintaining the analytical thinking that made him an effective detective.

The drive to Nadia's apartment took less than the ten minutes he had estimated, the late-night streets largely empty of traffic despite the gentle snowfall. As he pulled up behind Alice's car, he could see her waiting outside the building's entrance, her breath forming white clouds in the cold air as she paced with barely contained nervous energy.

"Thanks for coming so quickly," she greeted him, her relief evident despite her attempt at professional composure. "The fluctuations have been getting stronger since I called. Whatever's happening in there, it's accelerating."

Ethan nodded, his enhanced senses already detecting what conventional instruments couldn't measure—ripples in the fabric of reality itself, dimensional boundaries becoming increasingly permeable around Nadia's apartment building. Through his connection to the nexus entity, he could perceive similarities to the energetic patterns that had characterized the Order's ritual attempts, but with subtle differences that suggested an amateur attempt rather than the carefully controlled methodology of generations of practice.

"Someone's attempting a ritual," he said, moving toward the building's entrance with Alice close behind. "Not the Order—at least, not their traditional approach. This feels... improvised. Desperate. Like someone trying to recreate their methods without the full understanding of what they're manipulating."

As they entered the building and climbed the stairs to Nadia's third-floor apartment, the energetic disturbances intensified—ripples becoming waves that Ethan could perceive as physical sensations through his enhanced awareness. The air itself seemed to thicken around them, reality becoming less stable as dimensional boundaries thinned beyond what conventional physics could accommodate.

When they reached Nadia's door, the disturbances were so intense that even Alice could perceive them without Ethan's supernatural senses—

shadows moving independently of their casters, sounds echoing from places that shouldn't exist in conventional space, the air shimmering with visual distortions that resembled heat haze but carried patterns that suggested consciousness rather than random thermal effects.

"Nadia?" Alice called, pounding on the door with increasing urgency. "It's Detective Chen and Detective Reeves. We need to speak with you. Are you alright in there?"

No response came, but Ethan's enhanced hearing detected movements within the apartment—not the normal sounds of a single person moving about, but multiple sources of motion accompanied by what seemed like whispered chanting in a language that shifted and changed even as he tried to identify it.

"She's not alone," he said quietly, his voice carrying that same harmonics that suggested connection to something larger than individual consciousness. "And whatever ritual they're attempting, it's destabilizing the dimensional boundaries around this entire building. We need to intervene before it goes too far."

Without waiting for Alice's response, Ethan placed his hand against the door lock, drawing on his symbiotic connection to the nexus entity to perceive the energetic patterns flowing through the mechanism. With a subtle adjustment of those patterns—not physical manipulation but a redirection of the quantum probabilities that governed mechanical interaction—he felt the lock disengage with a soft click.

"That's still disconcerting," Alice murmured as they entered the apartment, her tone suggesting both appreciation for the efficiency and lingering adjustment to the reality-altering capabilities her partner had developed since the solstice confrontation. "Useful, but disconcerting."

The interior of Nadia's apartment presented a scene that confirmed their worst suspicions. The living room had been cleared of furniture, the space now dominated by a complex geometric pattern drawn on the hardwood floor in what appeared to be a mixture of chalk, ash, and some darker substance Ethan's enhanced senses identified immediately as blood. Candles placed at specific points around the pattern cast flickering shadows that seemed to move with purpose rather than in response to air currents, while incense burned in censers positioned to correspond with cardinal directions.

At the center of this improvised ritual space stood three figures— Nadia Marsh herself, her expression a mixture of fear and determination as she read from a battered leather journal that Ethan recognized as similar to Eliza Blackwood's grimoire; Michael Mercer, the boyfriend of Jessica Mercer whose grief had apparently led him down darker paths than they had anticipated; and a third figure whose identity initially surprised Ethan—Sam Thompson, Jessica Mercer's father, whose involvement in the investigation had seemed peripheral until this moment.

The three were positioned at equal distances around a central object that immediately drew Ethan's attention—a crystalline structure that resembled a smaller version of the Nullification Crystal the Order had used during their Rite of Dimensional Severance. Not identical, but similar enough to suggest it served a related purpose—disrupting and redirecting the natural flow of dimensional energies according to the wielder's design.

More concerning was what Ethan perceived through his enhanced awareness—a thinning of dimensional boundaries directly above the crystal, reality itself becoming increasingly permeable as the ritual progressed. Through this thinning membrane, something was attempting to manifest—a consciousness or entity that existed beyond conventional physical parameters, attracted by the energetic disturbances the improvised ritual was generating.

"Stop!" Ethan called out, his voice carrying harmonic overtones that caused the candle flames to flicker and the shadows to recoil. "You don't understand what you're doing—the boundaries you're weakening can't be restored once they collapse completely."

All three participants looked up in startled unison, their chanting faltering momentarily before Michael Mercer stepped forward, his expression hardening with recognition and defiance.

"Detective Reeves," he acknowledged, his voice carrying a bitter edge that hadn't been present during their previous interactions. "And Detective Chen. How unexpected. But I'm afraid you're too late to stop what we've set in motion. The doorway is opening, and soon we'll have the power to bring true justice to this city—starting with those responsible for Jessica's death."

Ethan noted the use of Jessica's childhood nickname—a sign of the deep personal connection that drove Michael's actions despite the cosmic dangers he was inadvertently unleashing. Through his enhanced perception, Ethan could see energetic patterns flowing between Michael and the crystal, suggesting he was the primary conduit for whatever entity was attempting to manifest through the thinning dimensional boundary.

"This isn't justice, Michael," Alice said, stepping forward with her hands raised in a non-threatening gesture. "Whatever power you think you're accessing, it comes with a price too high for anyone to pay. We know about the Order, about the ritual killings, about everything that happened beneath the bridge. This isn't the way to honor Jessica's memory."

"You know nothing!" Sam Thompson interjected, his normally jovial features contorted with grief and rage. "My daughter was sacrificed for their cosmic games, used and discarded like she meant nothing. The authorities did nothing—could do nothing against forces they couldn't even comprehend. But we found another way, a power that can reach across the veil and bring retribution to those who thought themselves beyond justice."

As he spoke, the dimensional thinning above the crystal accelerated, reality itself seeming to fold and distort as something pushed against the membrane from the other side—a consciousness or entity attracted by the emotional intensity of grief and rage that fueled the improvised ritual. Ethan could perceive it through his connection to the nexus entity—not malevolent in the conventional sense, but utterly alien to human understanding, operating according to principles that transcended conventional morality or causality.

"Nadia," Ethan addressed the journalist directly, recognizing her as potentially the most rational of the three participants. "You've seen what happens when dimensional boundaries collapse—you were there beneath the bridge during the solstice confrontation. Whatever entity you're attempting to contact or channel, it exists beyond parameters that human consciousness can safely navigate. The price for this power isn't just your lives—it's reality itself in this entire sector of the city."

Nadia hesitated, her journalist's analytical mind clearly processing the implications of Ethan's warning against the desperate need for justice that had driven her to participate in this dangerous endeavor. The leather journal in her hands—which Ethan now recognized as likely another of the Order's grimoires, perhaps stolen during her investigation into their activities—trembled slightly as her resolve wavered.

"They're everywhere, Detective," she finally replied, her voice reflecting the weight of knowledge that had driven her to such desperate measures. "The Order, the Obsidian Circle, whatever name they use in different jurisdictions—their influence extends far beyond Daybridge, reaching into neighboring cities, national politics, international finance. What we uncovered here was just the surface of something vast and ancient, a conspiracy that has shaped human history from the shadows for centuries."

She gestured to the journal in her hands, her expression intensifying. "This contains evidence of a global network, Detective. Not just Mayor Granger and his local cult, but connections to power structures throughout the country and beyond. They've been manipulating events, positioning their members in key roles, preparing for something they call 'the Ascendance'—a transformation of society according to their design, using the power of dimensional merger for dominance rather than evolution."

As she spoke, Ethan felt a surge through his connection to the nexus entity—a recognition of truth in Nadia's words that aligned with insights he had gained during the solstice confrontation. The Order of the Ebon Star wasn't isolated to Daybridge; it was one node in a network that extended throughout human civilization, a conspiracy that had been manipulating events from the shadows for generations.

But that realization only made the danger of their current situation more acute. The improvised ritual Michael, Sam, and Nadia were attempting wasn't just dangerous because of their lack of under-standing or control—it was potentially catastrophic because it was tapping into dimensional energies that the Order had spent centuries learning to manipulate with precision and purpose. Their amateur approach risked not just local reality disruption but potentially attracting attention from other nodes in that global network, alerting those who remained loyal to the Order's vision of controlled dimen-sional dominance that alternatives were emerging in Daybridge.

"I understand your frustration," Ethan said, taking another step toward the ritual circle while maintaining careful awareness of the energetic patterns flowing through the apartment. "The conventional justice system isn't equipped to handle what we've uncovered—cosmic conspiracies that transcend local jurisdictions or even national bound-aries. But this approach puts everyone at risk, not just those respon-sible for Jessica's death."

Through his enhanced perception, he could see the dimensional thin-ning approaching a critical threshold—the boundary between conven-tional reality and whatever existed beyond it becoming so permeable that full manifestation of the entity they were inadvertently summoning was imminent. And once that entity crossed into their reality, the consequences would extend far beyond the confines of Nadia's apartment, potentially destabilizing dimensional boundaries throughout the city in ways that would make the Order's Rite of Dimensional Severance seem controlled by comparison.

"There's a better way," he continued, shifting subtly to position himself between the ritual participants and the crystal at the center of their improvised circle. "A way to expose the Order's global network without risking cosmic catastrophe, to bring justice to those respon-sible for Jessica's death without unleashing forces beyond human comprehension."

As he spoke, Ethan felt his lycanthropic nature responding to the imminent threat—not with the painful transformation of bones and muscles that had characterized his monthly ordeals before the solstice confrontation, but with a fluid integration of primal power into his human form. His senses sharpened further, his muscles coiled with potential energy, his awareness extending to encompass the entire apartment and the dimensional distortions radiating outward from the crystal at the center.

Simultaneously, his connection to the nexus entity deepened, the composite consciousness distributed throughout Daybridge Bridge providing insights into how to counter the energetic disturbances the improvised ritual was generating. Not opposition through force, which would only strengthen the dimensional thinning, but redirection through conscious participation in the energetic patterns—working with the flows rather than against them, guiding them toward harmless dispersal rather than catastrophic manifestation.

"Step away from the crystal," Alice instructed, her tone shifting from negotiation to command as she recognized the imminent danger through her partner's reaction. "Whatever you think you're accomplishing, it's not worth the risk to everyone in this building, this neighborhood, this city."

Michael hesitated, conflict evident in his expression as he glanced between the detectives and the crystal that represented his desperate attempt at justice for Jessica. But Sam Thompson showed no such uncertainty, his grief-hardened features contorting with renewed defiance.

"It's too late," he declared, reaching toward the crystal with deliberate intent. "The doorway is opening, and nothing can stop what's coming through. The power we'll gain will be worth whatever price we pay—worth any price to bring justice to those who took my daughter from me."

As his fingers contacted the crystal's surface, the dimensional thinning reached critical threshold—reality itself seeming to fold and tear above the improvised ritual circle, creating an aperture through which something began to manifest. Not a physical form in the conventional sense, but a distortion in the fabric of existence itself, a presence that defied description in human language but conveyed cosmic indifference to the concerns of the beings who had inadvertently summoned it.

Ethan moved with supernatural speed, drawing on both his lycanthropic nature and his symbiotic connection to cross the distance between himself and the ritual circle before the manifestation could complete. His perceptions had expanded beyond conventional time, allowing him to analyze the energetic patterns and identify the critical points where intervention might redirect rather than oppose the forces already in motion.

As he reached the center of the circle, he placed one hand on the crystal and the other on Sam Thompson's arm, creating a circuit that redirected the energetic flows away from the dimensional aperture and into a controlled dispersion throughout the room. Not stopping the manifestation entirely, which would have been impossible at this stage, but altering its parameters—guiding it toward a partial, temporary connection rather than full materialization in their reality.

The effect was immediate and profound—the dimensional aperture stabilizing rather than expanding, the entity's manifestation limited to a presence that could be perceived but not fully materialized, the energetic disturbances throughout the apartment shifting from chaotic intensification to controlled, gradually diminishing patterns.

"What have you done?" Sam demanded, trying to pull away from Ethan's grip but finding himself unable to break the connection that was now redirecting the energetic flows he had helped to generate. "You're ruining everything! The power was almost ours!"

"I'm saving your life," Ethan replied, his voice carrying those same harmonics that suggested connection to something larger than individual consciousness. "And everyone else's in this building. The entity you were attempting to contact exists beyond parameters that human consciousness can safely navigate. Full manifestation would have resulted in reality collapse throughout this entire sector of the city."

Through his connection to the nexus entity, Ethan could perceive the dimensional aperture beginning to close—the boundary between conventional reality and whatever existed beyond it gradually reestablishing itself as the energetic patterns dispersed in controlled, harmless waves throughout the apartment. The entity that had been partially manifesting seemed to recede, not with anger or frustration but with something more like cosmic indifference—its attention moving elsewhere as the conditions that had attracted it dissipated.

But before the aperture closed completely, something unexpected occurred—a transmission of concept rather than language, similar to how the nexus entity communicated but with an alien quality that suggested origins beyond even the composite consciousness Ethan had connected with beneath the bridge. Not words but understanding, flowing directly into his expanded awareness with implications that transcended conventional human comprehension.

The Order fragments but does not dissipate. The network extends beyond parameters established through initial perception. Evolution proceeds according to patterns emerging from conscious participation, but opposition consolidates around nodes resistant to natural integration. Awareness is required for navigation of increasing complexity as dimensional boundaries continue to thin beyond original design.

And with that cryptic communication, the dimensional aperture closed completely, reality stabilizing around them as the improvised ritual's energetic patterns dispersed into harmless background fluctuations. The crystal at the center of the circle had cracked, its structure unable to withstand the forces it had channeled, rendering it useless for any future attempts at dimensional manipulation.

In the sudden stillness that followed, Ethan became aware of Alice moving efficiently to secure the three ritual participants—confiscating Nadia's grimoire, ensuring Michael and Sam couldn't attempt to restart their dangerous experiment, establishing control over a situation that had nearly resulted in cosmic catastrophe.

"What happens now?" Nadia asked, her journalist's instinct for the story asserting itself even in the aftermath of such profound danger.

"You can't exactly arrest us for attempting to contact extradimensional entities—there's no statute in the criminal code for cosmic disturbances."

Ethan smiled slightly, the expression containing equal parts under-standing and warning. "No, there isn't," he acknowledged. "But there are laws against breaking and entering, theft of classified materials, conspiracy, and several other conventional crimes that would apply to how you obtained that grimoire and whatever else you've accumu-lated during your investigation into the Order's activities."

He gestured to the journal still clutched in her hands, his expression turning more serious. "That said, I'm more interested in the informa-tion you've uncovered about the Order's global network—the connec-tions to power structures beyond Daybridge, the preparations for what they call 'the Ascendance.' That represents a threat far beyond local jurisdiction, one that requires careful, strategic response rather than improvised rituals or conventional law enforcement approaches."

Michael Mercer looked between the detectives with growing confu-sion, his grief-driven rage giving way to the first glimmers of under-standing beyond his personal loss. "You're not going to arrest us? After what we just attempted?"

"That depends," Alice replied, her practical nature asserting itself as she assessed the situation. "On whether you're willing to work with us rather than against us. What you've discovered about the Order's global network, combined with what we experienced during the solstice confrontation, suggests we're facing something far larger than any of us anticipated when this began."

She glanced at Ethan, a silent communication passing between them that reflected years of partnership and the deeper connection that had evolved since the cosmic revelations beneath the bridge. "There may be a better approach than either conventional justice or desperate attempts at cosmic vengeance—one that requires pooling our knowl-edge and resources rather than working at cross purposes."

Ethan nodded, drawing on insights from both his detective's analytical thinking and the expanded awareness provided by his connection to the nexus entity. "The Order of the Ebon Star has been manipulating events from the shadows for generations, positioning their members in key roles throughout society to serve their vision of dimensional dominance. What happened beneath the bridge during the solstice confrontation disrupted their plans in Daybridge, but it didn't eliminate their global network or their ultimate goals."

He moved to the window, looking out at the snow-covered city with its distant view of Daybridge Bridge illuminated against the night sky. "What we need is a coordinated response—one that combines conventional investigation, journalistic exposure, and awareness of the cosmic dimensions underlying what appears to be mundane corruption and conspiracy. Not desperate measures that risk reality itself, but strategic efforts to reveal the truth and dismantle the structures that have allowed the Order to operate unchecked for so long."

As he spoke, Ethan felt something shifting in the energetic patterns around them—not another dimensional disturbance, but a subtle realignment as the three ritual participants began to consider alternatives to their dangerous path. Through his enhanced perception, he could sense the genuine grief and desire for justice that had driven Michael and Sam toward such desperate measures, the journalistic dedication to truth that had led Nadia to participate despite the risks.

"What exactly are you proposing?" Sam asked, his voice still carrying the weight of his daughter's loss but with a new undertone of cautious consideration. "How do we bring justice to those responsible when they operate beyond conventional law, when they can manipulate reality itself to serve their purposes?"

"By working with reality's natural evolution rather than attempting to control or oppose it," Ethan replied, drawing on insights gained during the solstice confrontation. "The Order's fundamental mistake was believing they could control the merger of realities according to rigid designs, that dimensional integration should serve their vision of

dominance rather than evolving naturally through conscious participation."

He turned back from the window, his gaze encompassing all three
ritual participants with an intensity that reflected the integration of his
lycanthropic nature and his symbiotic connection. "What I'm
proposing is a different kind of ritual—not one that attempts to
summon entities from beyond dimensional boundaries, but one that
reveals truth in a way that can't be hidden or denied, that exposes the
Order's global network to the light of public awareness."

Alice looked at him with a mixture of surprise and understanding,
recognizing the direction of his thinking from their discussions in the
weeks since the solstice confrontation. "You're talking about using your
connection to the nexus entity to facilitate a mass revelation—to make
the truth about the Order's activities perceptible beyond the limitations
of conventional evidence or testimony."

Ethan nodded, the plan crystallizing as he articulated it. "The nexus
entity exists at the intersection of multiple dimensions, facilitating the
merger of realities according to patterns that emerge from conscious
participation rather than rigid control. Through my symbiotic connection, we might be able to create a temporary thinning of perceptual
boundaries—not physical manifestation of other dimensions, but
enhanced awareness that allows people to see connections and
patterns they would otherwise miss."

He gestured to Nadia's grimoire and the evidence she had accumulated during her investigation. "Combined with conventional journalism, strategic release of documents, and carefully coordinated law
enforcement actions, such a perceptual shift could reveal the Order's
influence throughout society in a way that couldn't be dismissed as
conspiracy theory or fake news. People would literally see the connections, understand the patterns, recognize the manipulation that has
been happening beneath the surface of everyday reality."

The proposal hung in the air between them, its implications both
profound and uncertain. What Ethan was suggesting went beyond
conventional law enforcement or journalism, beyond even the cosmic

confrontation beneath the bridge during the solstice alignment. It represented a new approach to justice in a world where reality itself had become more fluid, where dimensional boundaries were thinning regardless of human desire or design.

"Would it work?" Michael asked, the first to break the contemplative silence that had fallen over the apartment. "Could you really make people see the truth about what happened to Jessica, about everything the Order has been doing beneath the surface of everyday life?"

"I don't know," Ethan admitted, his honesty a reflection of both his detective's integrity and his awareness of the unprecedented nature of what he was proposing. "The symbiosis with the nexus entity allows me to perceive energetic patterns and dimensional intersections that remain invisible to conventional human senses. In theory, that perception could be temporarily extended to others through a carefully designed ritual that works with the natural flow of dimensional integration rather than attempting to control or redirect it."

He looked to Alice, whose practical nature had always balanced his more intuitive approach to investigation. "But it would require preparation, coordination, and careful timing. Not an improvised attempt like tonight, but a strategic approach that combines conventional evidence gathering with cosmic awareness, that reveals the truth without risking reality itself in the process."

Alice nodded, her analytical mind already processing the implications and requirements of such an unprecedented approach. "We would need to secure everything Nadia has uncovered about the Order's global network, combine it with our own evidence from the solstice confrontation, and develop a coordinated plan for revelation that couldn't be dismissed or covered up by those with influence in conventional power structures."

She turned to the three ritual participants, her expression reflecting both authority and potential partnership. "Which means, for now, you three need to surrender whatever materials you've accumulated— grimoires, evidence, documentation of the Order's activities beyond Daybridge. Not as a condition of arrest, but as the beginning of a coordinated effort to bring genuine justice rather than cosmic vengeance."

Nadia hesitated, her journalist's instinct for independent investigation warring with the recognition that what Ethan and Alice were proposing represented a more effective approach than her desperate alliance with Michael and Sam. Finally, she nodded, placing her grimoire on the coffee table alongside several folders containing what appeared to be extensive documentation of the Order's connections to power structures throughout the region and beyond.

"Everything I've uncovered is here," she said, her voice reflecting professional pride despite the circumstances. "Financial records tracing donations from offshore accounts to political campaigns in neigh-boring cities, correspondence between Mayor Granger and officials at state and federal levels, architectural plans showing ritual spaces beneath public buildings that mirror the chamber we found beneath Daybridge Bridge. It's the story of the century—a conspiracy that tran-scends local jurisdictions or even national boundaries."

Michael and Sam followed her lead, albeit with more visible reluctance —their grief-driven desire for immediate retribution gradually giving way to recognition that a coordinated, strategic approach might bring more meaningful justice for Jessica than their dangerous attempt at cosmic vengeance.

As the impromptu alliance formed around Nadia's coffee table—detec-tives, journalist, and grieving family members united by shared purpose despite their different approaches and motivations—Ethan felt something shift in the energetic patterns flowing through Daybridge. Not another dimensional disturbance, but a subtle align-ment as consciousness and intent converged around a common goal, as individual perspectives integrated into a collective awareness that transcended any single viewpoint or experience.

Through his connection to the nexus entity, he perceived this align-ment as a microcosm of the larger merger process that had been unfolding since the bridge's construction in 1913—realities integrating not through catastrophic disruption or rigid control, but through conscious participation and willing partnership across dimensional boundaries. Not imposed transformation but natural evolution, guided by awareness rather than dictated by force.

And as they began discussing the specifics of their coordinated approach—what evidence to secure, what stories to publish, what ritual to design that might reveal the truth beyond conventional limitations—Ethan felt a growing certainty that what had begun as a simple murder investigation had evolved into something far more significant. Not just justice for Jessica Mercer and the other victims of ritual sacrifice, but potential transformation of how human consciousness interacted with the broader fabric of reality itself.

The Order of the Ebon Star had spent centuries manipulating events from the shadows, positioning their members in key roles throughout society to serve their vision of dimensional dominance. But what was emerging in Daybridge represented a different approach—not control but participation, not dominance but integration, not rigid hierarchy but fluid network of shared purpose and complementary capabilities.

As the night deepened around them, snow continuing to fall in gentle swirls outside Nadia's windows, Ethan felt both the weight of responsibility and the potential for genuine transformation. The path ahead would not be easy or straightforward—the Order's global network remained powerful despite the disruption in Daybridge, their vision of dimensional dominance still guiding their actions throughout human civilization.

But for the first time since the solstice confrontation, he felt genuine hope that what had happened beneath the bridge wasn't just a local victory against cosmic forces beyond human comprehension, but the beginning of something larger—a shift in how consciousness itself interacted with the evolving fabric of reality, a movement toward integration rather than separation, participation rather than control.

And with Alice beside him, her unwavering presence an anchor to the core of human experience that gave cosmic evolution its meaning and purpose, Ethan prepared to navigate this new chapter with confidence and determination rather than fear or reservation—a detective and werewolf and symbiotic partner to a nexus entity, embracing all aspects of his transformed nature in service to justice that transcended conventional limitations while preserving the values that made human existence worth protecting in the first place.

The merger continued. The shadows gathered. And in Daybridge, a small but growing alliance prepared for the showdown that would determine not just the fate of their city, but the evolution of reality itself for generations to come.

CHAPTER TWELVE
DEBTS OF BLOOD

Mayor Jeremiah Granger stared out over Daybridge from the floor-to-ceiling windows of his private study, hands steepled beneath his grimly set jawline. The city's twinkling lights resembled a terrestrial mirror of the cosmos on this cloudless night, though their illumination's warm civic promise was overshadowed by a pervading pall that only he could truly perceive.

One month had passed since the winter solstice confrontation beneath Daybridge Bridge—one month since Detective Ethan Reeves had transformed the Rite of Dimensional Severance into something unintended, redirecting energies the Order had spent centuries learning to control and contain. The official story presented to the public claimed the mayor was on an extended health retreat, a convenient fiction maintained by Deputy Mayor Elly Harrison while the true Dominus of the Order of the Ebon Star recovered from his defeat and planned his response.

Recovery had been slow and agonizing. The energetic backlash from the failed ritual had left Granger's consciousness partially dislocated from conventional reality, his perception extending into dimensional frameworks that human physiology was never designed to process or accommodate. The experience would have driven most initiates mad, their minds fracturing under the strain of awareness beyond the parameters of standard human cognition. But Jeremiah Granger was no ordinary initiate—seven generations of selective breeding within the founding families had created a vessel capable of channeling cosmic forces that would incinerate lesser consciousnesses.

A rap of knuckles against the study's oak-paneled door barely registered before the imposing portal swung inward with a low groan of strained brass hinges. Granger didn't need to turn to identify the new arrival—Castellus's presence was unmistakable, the Praetorian's very being altered by decades of exposure to the energetic patterns flowing through the nexus point beneath the bridge. Though he had participated in the solstice confrontation, Castellus had survived where many of his fellow Praetorians had not, his loyalty to the Order's vision of dimensional dominance unwavering despite the revelations Reeves had facilitated.

"Speak, Castellus," the mayor intoned without preamble, his deep baritone resonating through the sanctum's wood-paneled confines like the death knells of ancient verities challenged by unwelcome evolution. "What developments precipitate this untimely visitation?"

For long, suspended moments, only the soft inhalations of the bodyguard's rebreather apparatus disturbed the permeating stillness as he studied his master's unyielding profile with undisguised weight behind that featureless obsidian mask—a necessity now, as the energetic disruptions from the failed ritual had left Castellus unable to process normal atmospheric compositions without assistance. At length, his voice issued forth in a phlegm-rasped monotone drained of all inflection.

"The alliance has consolidated its position, Dominus. Reeves and Chen have integrated the journalist Marsh and the family members of Jessica Mercer into their circle. They've accumulated substantial evidence regarding our operations—not just in Daybridge, but connections to our affiliate Lodges in neighboring jurisdictions."

Granger didn't react outwardly beyond the faintest tightening of his jawline, though Castellus recognized the storm systems of vaulting intensity massing behind the mayor's aristocratic facade. After what seemed an interminable pause, Granger spoke again in tones that carried harmonic resonances beyond conventional human hearing.

"So... the detective and that infernal entity he's bonded with persist in vexing our endeavors beyond all boundaries of established protocol?" He let the implications resonate between them like overtones from an instrument tuned to frequencies that didn't exist in conventional physical parameters. "And what of our contingency measures? Have the remaining Praetorians made progress in recovering the Blackwood grimoire?"

The Praetorian's rebreather uttered a solitary, juddering expulsion—the sole sign of the malign energies roiling within his obsidian-shrouded form. "Negative, Dominus. The grimoire remains in their possession, along with documents detailing financial connections between our Lodge and political figures throughout the region. More concerning, Reeves appears to be developing new capabilities—his symbiosis with the nexus entity evolving beyond parameters established through previous observation."

A leonine rumble issued from Granger's throat—a sound more like tectonic movement than any vocalization spawned by human agency. Still, he remained impassive and motionless, shoulders squared toward the vista beyond the glass as if awaiting final confirmation of what he already suspected.

Only when the echoes gentled to an expectant vacuum did the mayor continue in a tone that had taken on a subtle timbre of arcane harmonics fused into each consonant's articulation.

"First the disruption of our solstice ritual, now this... accumulation of evidence against our broader network." Granger's jaw clenched until Castellus was certain enamel would splinter from the pressures mounting throughout his master's very musculature. "The impertinence of these meddlers presumes to thwart designs far transcending their paltry mortal comprehensions."

The condemnations billowed outward in concentric psychic waves of outrage and swelling inevitability. Granger pivoted at last to transfix Castellus with a granite-hewn stare that seemed to strip away all superficial contexts surrounding them. When he spoke further, it was with the resonance of ancient knowledge being accessed and applied to present circumstances.

"If these interlopers will not respect the natural order established through generations of careful manipulation, then we shall simply... realign their prospects through the application of more direct methods. The High Council has authorized activation of the Obsidian Protocol—the final contingency designed precisely for circumstances where conventional containment has failed."

Castellus felt his own reserves of initiatory conditioning waver momentarily under the thermometric immensities simmering behind the mayor's aristocratic poise. The Obsidian Protocol was not discussed openly even among the highest ranks of the Praetorians—a measure so extreme that it had been activated only twice in the Order's centuries-long history, each instance resulting in the complete erasure of the target from both physical existence and collective memory.

"What are your directives, Dominus?" he asked, his voice betraying none of the unease churning beneath his disciplined exterior. "Shall I marshal the remaining Praetorians to implement the Protocol's preliminary phases?"

Granger's lips curled into a cold smile devoid of any genuine warmth or humanity. When his voice issued forth, it carried the weight of decisions that would reverberate through dimensional frameworks far beyond conventional understanding.

"No, my faithful Praetor. The Protocol requires more... specialized implementation when dealing with a subject who has undergone symbiosis with a nexus entity." The mayor turned once more to face the panoramic sprawl of Daybridge, his gaze now encompassing dimensional vistas beyond conventional perception. "Bring me the Blackwood heir—the one who calls herself Lilith. Her bloodline connection to the original binding ritual makes her the perfect vessel for what must now be done."

Castellus felt his molecular integrity shudder under the implications of Granger's directive. Lilith Blackwood had been declared anathema to the Order decades ago, her opposition to their vision of controlled dimensional dominance marking her as an enemy to be eliminated rather than an asset to be utilized. To now seek her involvement suggested depths of desperation that the Praetorian had not anticipated from his master.

"The Blackwood woman has aligned herself with Reeves and his faction," Castellus noted, careful to maintain a neutral tone despite his reservations. "She provided the catalyst that enabled his integration of lycanthropic and symbiotic natures during the solstice confrontation. What makes you believe she would participate in the Obsidian Protocol, knowing its purpose and consequences?"

Granger's smile widened, revealing teeth that seemed unnaturally perfect in their alignment and lustre. "She won't participate willingly, of course. But the Blackwood bloodline carries certain... vulnerabilities that our founders wisely integrated into the original binding ritual. Eliza Blackwood may have been a visionary, but she was not infallible. She left markers in her own genetic line—failsafes that would allow the Order to reassert control should any of her descendants attempt to subvert the Great Work."

He moved to his desk, unlocking a hidden drawer with a key that seemed to shimmer and distort when viewed directly—an object that existed partially in dimensional frameworks beyond conventional physical parameters. From this drawer, he withdrew a small box made of polished obsidian, its surface inscribed with symbols identical to those carved throughout Daybridge Bridge but arranged in configurations Castellus had never seen before.

"This contains what remains of the original binding material—blood and tissue samples preserved from Guthrie Knox before his transformation into the nexus entity. Combined with the correct ritual components and performed at the precise astrological alignment, it can temporarily sever the connection between the Blackwood bloodline and their natural affinity for dimensional manipulation. Render Lilith vulnerable, bring her to me, and I will handle the rest."

Castellus bowed deeply, acceptance of his mission overshadowing any lingering doubts about its feasibility or wisdom. "It shall be done, Dominus. When is the next suitable alignment for this ritual?"

"Three days hence—the dark of the moon, when the veil between conventional reality and the deeper dimensional frameworks is naturally thinner." Granger placed the obsidian box on his desk with ceremonial precision, its positioning corresponding to ley lines that ran beneath the city like veins in a living organism. "That gives you seventy-two hours to locate and secure Lilith Blackwood without alerting Reeves or his allies to our intentions."

As Castellus turned to leave, already mentally calculating the resources and approach required for such a delicate extraction, Granger's voice stopped him at the threshold—the harmonics in his master's tone now so pronounced that the air itself seemed to vibrate with frequencies beyond human hearing.

"And Castellus? Should you encounter Detective Reeves during this operation, do not engage directly. His integration of lycanthropic and symbiotic natures has created something our founders never anticipated—a consciousness capable of navigating dimensional frameworks with fluidity our rigid hierarchies cannot match. Observe, report, but do not confront unless absolutely necessary for mission success."

The Praetorian nodded once, understanding both the explicit directive and its implicit acknowledgment of a truth the Order had been reluctant to accept—that Ethan Reeves represented an evolutionary path they had not foreseen, a capacity for transformation that transcended their carefully established parameters for controlled dimensional integration.

As Castellus departed to prepare for his mission, Granger returned his attention to the city spread below his private sanctuary—a domain he had shaped through decades of careful manipulation, positioning himself as both public servant and secret hierophant guiding Daybridge's development according to the Order's vision of reality.

But beneath that carefully maintained facade, uncertainty gnawed at foundations previously unassailable—doubts spawned not from fear of failure but from glimpses of alternative possibilities revealed during the solstice confrontation. What if Reeves was right? What if the natural evolution of the nexus entity, the gradual merger of realities according to patterns that emerged from conscious participation rather than rigid control, represented a more viable path than the Order's millennia-old vision of dimensional dominance?

Granger dismissed these thoughts with practiced discipline, his consciousness realigning with the certainties instilled through seven generations of selective breeding and arcane indoctrination. The Order of the Ebon Star had not persisted for centuries by questioning foundational principles when faced with temporary setbacks. The Great Work would continue according to designs established by their founders, regardless of what evolutionary anomalies might temporarily disrupt its progress.

And if implementing the Obsidian Protocol required sacrificing a rebellious scion of one founding family to preserve the Order's vision of reality itself—well, that was merely another debt of blood paid in service to a cause that transcended individual existence or conventional morality.

The decision made, Granger began preliminary preparations for the ritual that would bind Lilith Blackwood to his will and, through her, sever the connection between Ethan Reeves and the nexus entity that had facilitated his dangerous evolution beyond the Order's control. The Obsidian Protocol would reset the cosmic chessboard, returning Daybridge to its proper place in the grand design of controlled dimensional merger.

Whatever the cost, whatever debts of blood might be required, the natural order would be restored. The Dominus would see to it personally.

. . .

Detective Ethan Reeves moved through the predawn darkness with preternatural silence, his integrated lycanthropic and symbiotic natures allowing him to navigate both physical terrain and energetic patterns with unprecedented fluidity. The warehouse district near Daybridge's eastern shore was nominally abandoned, most of its industrial structures having fallen into disuse as manufacturing moved overseas decades earlier. But Ethan's enhanced perception revealed what conventional observation could not—subtle fluctuations in dimensional boundaries around one particular building, energetic signatures that suggested ritual activity of the kind the Order specialized in.

Alice Chen followed several paces behind, her movements precise and efficient despite lacking her partner's supernatural capabilities. In the month since the solstice confrontation, she had developed her own methods for detecting the subtle signs of the Order's activities—slight atmospheric distortions visible through specialized filters, electromagnetic anomalies that could be measured with modified equipment, behavioral patterns among known associates that suggested coordination beyond conventional communication channels.

They had been tracking this cell for over a week, ever since Nadia Marsh's journalistic investigation had uncovered financial connections between the warehouse's ownership and offshore accounts linked to Mayor Granger's political organization. According to the evidence they had accumulated, this location served as a training ground for initiates —a place where those selected for potential membership in the Order's inner circle could be exposed to controlled doses of dimensional energies, their reactions determining their suitability for further advancement.

"Security perimeter is clear," Alice whispered into her communications device, the signal encrypted and routed through systems designed to evade the Order's monitoring capabilities. "No conventional surveillance detected, but we're picking up the same energetic signatures as last time—low-level containment field, probably to prevent leakage rather than secure against intrusion."

Through his connection to the nexus entity, Ethan could perceive the energetic patterns in greater detail—a spherical boundary surrounding the warehouse, designed to contain dimensional energies within rather than keep observers out. The Order had always prioritized secrecy through misdirection rather than overt security, preferring to hide their activities in plain sight through manipulation of perception rather than physical barriers that might attract unwanted attention.

"I can see five distinct consciousness patterns inside," he replied, his voice barely audible even to Alice's trained hearing. "Initiates, not full members—their energetic signatures aren't developed enough for higher-level ritual work. There's something else too... an object or artifact at the center of the building that's generating dimensional distortions similar to what we observed during the solstice ritual."

"Another Nullification Crystal?" Alice asked, concern evident in her tone despite her professional composure. The artifact had played a central role in the Order's Rite of Dimensional Severance, its capacity for disrupting and redirecting energetic patterns nearly resulting in catastrophic reality fracture throughout Daybridge.

Ethan shook his head, his enhanced perception providing more nuanced understanding of what they were observing. "No, something different... smaller, more focused. Not designed for large-scale disruption but for specific targeting of individual consciousness patterns. It feels like... a beacon of some kind, transmitting information across dimensional boundaries."

He closed his eyes, drawing deeper on his connection to the composite consciousness distributed throughout Daybridge Bridge, seeking context for what they were observing. The nexus entity responded with a transmission of concept rather than language, providing insights that transcended conventional understanding but aligned with patterns they had encountered during previous investigations.

"It's a communication device," Ethan said as comprehension dawned. "The Order is attempting to establish contact with affiliate Lodges in other jurisdictions—not through conventional channels that could be monitored or intercepted, but through dimensional frequencies that bypass physical limitations entirely. They're reorganizing after the solstice disruption, consolidating resources and reestablishing command structures."

Alice processed this information with her characteristic analytical efficiency, immediately grasping the strategic implications. "That would explain the increased movement we've detected among known associates—not retreat or disorganization as we initially assumed but coordinated redeployment. They're adapting to the new reality created by the solstice confrontation, finding ways to continue their operations despite the disruption to their local power base."

She unholstered her service weapon—modified since the solstice confrontation with specialized ammunition developed in collaboration with Father Muligan, designed to disrupt the energetic patterns the Order utilized in their rituals without causing permanent harm to the human vessels involved. "Standard approach? Secure the artifact, detain the initiates for questioning, document everything for Nadia's exposé?"

Ethan nodded, feeling his lycanthropic nature responding to the imminent action—not with the uncontrolled aggression that had characterized his transformations before the solstice integration, but with focused intensity that enhanced his already heightened senses and reflexes. Simultaneously, his connection to the nexus entity deepened, providing real-time awareness of the energetic patterns flowing throughout the warehouse and its surroundings.

"On my signal," he confirmed, moving toward the building's eastern entrance with predatory grace. "Remember, these are initiates, not full members—likely unaware of the Order's true purpose or the cosmic implications of what they're participating in. Minimum force, maximum information gathering."

As they positioned themselves on either side of the entrance, Ethan felt a sudden shift in the energetic patterns—a ripple of awareness emanating from within the warehouse, as if something or someone had detected their presence despite the precautions they had taken. Not the initiates, whose limited perceptual development couldn't have penetrated their careful approach, but something else—a consciousness more evolved, more attuned to the dimensional frequencies they were navigating.

"We've been made," he warned, adjusting his plan accordingly. "There's someone else inside—someone with higher-level capabilities than we initially detected. Approach with caution."

Before Alice could respond, the warehouse door swung open of its own accord, revealing a dimly lit interior populated by five figures in ceremonial robes gathered around a central pedestal. Upon this raised platform rested what appeared to be a small pyramidal structure composed of the same crystalline material as the Nullification Crystal they had encountered during the solstice confrontation, its facets shifting and changing as it emitted pulses of energy that distorted the air around it in visible waves.

But what immediately captured Ethan's attention wasn't the initiates or the artifact—it was the figure standing beyond them, partially concealed in shadows but unmistakable to his enhanced perception. Lilith Blackwood, her amber eyes gleaming with recognition as she stepped forward, her expression reflecting a complex mixture of relief and urgency.

"Detective Reeves," she acknowledged, her cultured voice carrying undertones that suggested communication beyond conventional language. "Your timing is either impeccably fortuitous or catastrophically inconvenient, depending on one's perspective. I was about to contact you through less direct channels, but it seems the universe has its own designs for our convergence."

Alice moved to Ethan's side, her weapon lowered but not holstered, her gaze taking in the scene with professional assessment. "Ms. Blackwood. Interesting company you're keeping, given your supposed opposition to the Order's activities."

Lilith smiled, the expression not quite reaching those unsettling amber eyes. "Appearances can be deceptive, Detective Chen—a principle I would expect you to appreciate, given your partnerships and alliances. These initiates are not loyal to Granger or his vision of dimensional dominance; they are members of my own faction within what remains of the founding families, seeking a different path for the evolution of consciousness and reality."

She gestured to the pyramidal crystal at the center of their gathering, its energy pulses now slowing and stabilizing in response to her attention. "This is a Harmonic Resonator—a device created by my great-aunt Eliza during the early phases of the bridge's construction, designed to facilitate communication across dimensional boundaries without the distortive effects of the Order's more... hierarchical methods. We were attempting to establish contact with like-minded individuals in neighboring jurisdictions, to coordinate resistance against what we believe is coming."

Ethan felt a chill despite the integration of his lycanthropic and symbiotic natures, both aspects of his being responding to the genuine concern evident in Lilith's tone and posture. Through his connection to the nexus entity, he could perceive her emotional state beyond conventional human tells—the subtle fluctuations in her energetic signature that suggested fear beneath her composed exterior, urgency beyond tactical considerations.

"What exactly is coming, Ms. Blackwood?" he asked, maintaining a professional demeanor despite the unusual circumstances of their encounter. "And why seek us out now, after weeks of silence following the solstice confrontation?"

Lilith dismissed the initiates with a gesture, sending them to the warehouse's perimeter where they could observe but not overhear the sensitive conversation about to unfold. When she turned back to the detectives, her expression had shed its earlier ambiguity, revealing genuine alarm that transcended her customary enigmatic poise.

"Granger has authorized implementation of the Obsidian Protocol," she said without preamble, the statement hanging in the air with ominous weight. "It's the Order's final contingency for situations where conventional containment has failed—a ritual designed to sever connections between dimensional frameworks at the level of individual consciousness rather than cosmic architecture."

Alice looked between Lilith and Ethan, recognizing the term from their research into the Order's methods but lacking the contextual understanding that her partner's connection to the nexus entity provided. "In plain English, please. What exactly does this Protocol entail, and why should we be concerned beyond the Order's usual manipulations?"

"Because it's not designed for manipulation but elimination," Lilith explained, her voice taking on a clinical precision that somehow enhanced rather than diminished the horror of what she was describing. "The Obsidian Protocol doesn't just kill its target—it erases them from the fabric of reality itself, severing all connections across dimensional frameworks so completely that they cease to have ever existed in any timeline or potential manifestation."

She turned to Ethan, her amber eyes intensifying with focused concern. "And you, Detective Reeves, with your unique combination of lycanthropic transformation and symbiotic connection to the nexus entity, represent the primary target for this Protocol. Granger sees your evolution beyond the parameters established through the original binding ritual as an existential threat to the Order's vision of controlled dimensional dominance—one that must be eliminated not just from present existence but from all possible manifestations across the multiverse."

The implications settled over them with glacial weight—not just death or conventional defeat, but cosmic erasure so complete that Ethan Reeves would never have existed in any timeline or dimensional framework. His consciousness, his experiences, his very being would be excised from the fabric of reality itself, leaving not even memory or record of his passage through existence.

"How exactly does this Protocol work?" Alice asked, her analytical mind already seeking vulnerabilities or countermeasures despite the metaphysical nature of the threat. "And more importantly, how do we stop it?"

Lilith moved to the Harmonic Resonator, adjusting its configuration with practiced precision as she spoke. "The Protocol requires three key components: blood from the original binding ritual, which Granger possesses in the form of preserved samples from Guthrie Knox before his transformation; a vessel with genetic connection to the founding families, specifically the Blackwood lineage due to our natural affinity for dimensional manipulation; and the dark of the moon, when dimensional boundaries are naturally thinner in ways that differ from solstice or equinox alignments."

The crystal responded to her adjustments, its energy pulses shifting to patterns that corresponded to her explanation—visual representation of concepts that transcended conventional language or understanding. Through his connection to the nexus entity, Ethan could perceive these patterns as information rather than mere energy—insights into the cosmic architecture that the Order had spent centuries learning to manipulate and control.

"Granger intends to use me as the vessel," Lilith continued, her tone matter-of-fact despite the personal implications. "My genetic connection to Eliza Blackwood makes me the ideal conduit for the energies required to implement the Protocol. He's dispatched Castellus and the remaining Praetorians to secure me for this purpose—which is why I was attempting to establish contact with potential allies before your timely arrival interrupted the process."

Ethan absorbed this information through both his detective's analytical thinking and his expanded awareness, seeking vulnerabilities in the Order's approach that might be exploited to counter this existential threat. "The dark of the moon is three days from now," he noted, calculating timelines against tactical considerations. "That gives us a narrow window to develop countermeasures or preventative strategies."

"Narrower than you might think," Lilith replied, her expression darkening further. "The Praetorians have already begun preliminary work —establishing dimensional anchors throughout the city that will triangulate and stabilize the Protocol's effects once initiated. They've been working in rotation, maintaining constant progress while avoiding patterns that might alert you to their activities."

She gestured to the Harmonic Resonator, which now displayed a three-dimensional projection of Daybridge—a holographic representation that highlighted specific locations throughout the city where energetic disturbances corresponded to the anchors she had described. Not random or arbitrary positions, but carefully selected sites that formed a complex geometric pattern when viewed from the perspective of dimensional energetics rather than physical geography.

"Each anchor must be established at precise coordinates where ley lines intersect with the energetic patterns flowing from the nexus point beneath the bridge," Lilith explained, the projection zooming in to show detailed representation of these intersections. "Once all twelve anchors are activated, they will create a containment field that isolates the target from conventional reality while the Protocol severs dimensional connections across the multiverse."

Alice studied the projection with tactical assessment, identifying patterns that corresponded to their observations over the past weeks. "That explains the increased activity we've detected at these locations —not just reorganization after the solstice disruption, but preparation for this Protocol. How many anchors have they established so far?"

"Nine of the twelve required," Lilith replied, the projection highlighting the completed anchors in pulsing red while the remaining three locations glowed with softer amber illumination. "They'll need to complete the remaining three before the dark of the moon for the Protocol to function as designed. Castellus is coordinating the operation personally, which means he's likely to be present at each remaining site during the establishment process."

Ethan felt his lycanthropic nature responding to the imminent threat— primal protective instincts aligning with his symbiotic connection to form a unified awareness of both the danger and potential counter-measures. Not panic or fear, but focused determination that transcended conventional human response to existential threat.

"We need to neutralize those remaining anchors," he said, the decision forming with crystal clarity in his integrated consciousness. "Disrupt the pattern before it can be completed, preventing the Protocol from functioning as designed. Simultaneously, we should secure the original binding material Granger possesses—without that component, the ritual cannot proceed regardless of other preparations."

Alice nodded, her tactical mind already developing operational parameters based on the information Lilith had provided. "We'll need additional resources—Father Muligan for his knowledge of counter-rituals, Nadia for documentation and potential public exposure of the Order's activities, Michael and Sam for their personal connection to the evidence we've accumulated about the Order's global network."

"And we'll need to move quickly," Lilith added, the Harmonic Resonator's projection shifting to display temporal patterns alongside spatial coordinates. "Castellus is likely establishing the tenth anchor as we speak—the Praetorians work on a rotating schedule that maximizes efficiency while minimizing exposure to conventional detection methods."

She turned to face Ethan directly, her amber eyes reflecting a complexity of emotion that transcended simple alliance or opposition. "There's something else you should know, Detective. The Obsidian Protocol doesn't just erase its target from existence—it redirects the energetic patterns that constituted their consciousness, repurposing that potential across dimensional frameworks to serve the Order's vision of reality. In essence, it doesn't just kill you; it transforms everything you were into a tool for the very cosmic architecture you opposed during the solstice confrontation."

The implications of this final revelation settled over Ethan with profound weight—not just personal annihilation, but cosmic perversion of everything he had become through the integration of his lycanthropic nature and symbiotic connection. The thought of his consciousness, his potential, his very being redirected to serve the Order's vision of dimensional dominance represented a violation beyond physical death or conventional defeat.

"Then we stop them," he said simply, the decision already made at levels of awareness that transcended conscious deliberation. "Not just for personal survival, but for the natural evolution of reality itself—for the patterns that emerge from conscious participation rather than rigid control, for integration rather than dominance."

Alice moved to his side, her presence a reminder of the human connections that grounded his expanded awareness in values and relationships that gave cosmic evolution its meaning and purpose. "We'll need to coordinate with our allies, develop a comprehensive approach that addresses both the immediate threat of the Protocol and the broader implications of the Order's global network."

Lilith nodded, already adjusting the Harmonic Resonator to establish secure communications with the allies Alice had mentioned. "I can facilitate contact without risking conventional channels that the Order might monitor or intercept. But we should relocate to a more secure location before Castellus realizes I've escaped his surveillance and redirects the Praetorians to this warehouse."

As they prepared to depart, gathering what intelligence the Harmonic Resonator had provided and ensuring the initiates understood their role in the developing resistance against the Order's plans, Ethan felt a subtle shift in the energetic patterns flowing throughout Daybridge. Not the immediate threat of Praetorians approaching their location, but a deeper disturbance in the fabric of reality itself—ripples emanating from the nexus point beneath the bridge, as if the composite consciousness distributed throughout its structure was responding to the Order's preparations for the Obsidian Protocol.

Through his connection to that consciousness, Ethan received not words but understanding—awareness that transcended conventional knowledge or intelligence. The nexus entity itself was evolving in response to the threat, adapting its patterns and processes to counter the Order's attempt at cosmic manipulation. Not opposition through force, which would only strengthen the dimensional anchors Castellus was establishing, but subtle redirection of energetic flows, working with the natural evolution of reality rather than attempting to control or contain it.

And in that understanding, Ethan glimpsed hope beyond the immediate danger of the Obsidian Protocol—confirmation that the path revealed during the solstice confrontation represented not just an alternative to the Order's vision, but the natural evolution of consciousness and reality itself. The merger of dimensions according to patterns that emerged from conscious participation rather than rigid control, integration that preserved the core of human experience while transcending its limitations.

With renewed determination, he led Alice and Lilith from the warehouse into the predawn darkness, their unlikely alliance representing something the Order had never anticipated or prepared for—cooperation across boundaries of species, origin, and perspective, united by shared purpose rather than hierarchical authority. Whatever debts of blood the coming confrontation might require, they would be paid in service to evolution rather than control, to integration rather than dominance, to the natural unfolding of cosmic potential rather than its restriction according to outdated designs.

The Obsidian Protocol awaited. The dark of the moon approached. And in Daybridge, a growing resistance prepared to face the Order's final contingency with resources and capabilities that transcended conventional understanding or limitation.

The cosmic chess game continued, with reality itself as both board and prize.

The subterranean chamber beneath Granger Tower hummed with arcane energies, dimensional frequencies beyond human hearing manifesting as subtle vibrations that resonated through the polished obsidian walls and floor. Unlike the ritual space beneath Daybridge Bridge, this chamber had never been documented in any official blueprints or architectural plans—a sanctum sanctorum known only to the highest echelons of the Order of the Ebon Star, designed specifically for rituals that required absolute secrecy and isolation from conventional reality.

Mayor Jeremiah Granger moved with ceremonial precision around the chamber's perimeter, placing artifacts and symbols at specific coordinates that corresponded to ley lines running beneath the city's surface. Each placement was calculated with mathematical exactitude, the resulting pattern forming a complex geometric representation of the Obsidian Protocol's interdimensional architecture. Not mere symbolism or theatrical ritual, but practical manipulation of cosmic forces that transcended conventional understanding of physics or metaphysics.

"Status report, Castellus," he commanded, his voice carrying harmonic resonances that made the air itself shimmer with visible distortion. "How many anchors have been successfully established?"

The Praetorian stood at attention near the chamber's entrance, his obsidian mask reflecting the ghostly illumination provided by arcane symbols etched into the walls. "Nine anchors are operational, Dominus. Teams are proceeding with the tenth and eleventh locations simultaneously, maximizing efficiency as instructed. We project completion of all twelve by tomorrow evening, allowing full calibration before the dark of the moon."

Granger nodded, satisfaction evident despite the aristocratic restraint of his expression. "And the Blackwood woman? Have your operatives located her current position?"

For the first time, hesitation entered Castellus's otherwise perfect discipline—a momentary pause that spoke volumes to someone who had studied human behavior as methodically as Jeremiah Granger. "There have been... complications, Dominus. Our surveillance detected her at the warehouse district earlier this evening, attempting to establish communication with affiliate factions through unconventional channels. Before extraction teams could secure her position, she was joined by unexpected visitors."

"Reeves and Chen," Granger surmised, no question in his tone despite the formulation. "The detective's symbiotic connection to the nexus entity would naturally alert him to significant dimensional disturbances, particularly those generated by Eliza Blackwood's Harmonic Resonator. I assume they departed before your teams could intercept?"

Castellus nodded, accepting responsibility despite the impossibility of preventing what dimensional awareness had facilitated. "Affirmative, Dominus. We have established monitoring parameters at all known associate locations, but their movement patterns have become increasingly erratic and unpredictable since the solstice confrontation. The detective's integration of lycanthropic and symbiotic natures allows him to perceive our conventional surveillance methods, adapting his approach accordingly."

Rather than the rage Castellus might have expected, Granger's expression reflected calculating assessment—a predator adjusting strategy based on prey behavior rather than emotional response to temporary setback. "As anticipated, then. Reeves continues to evolve beyond parameters established through previous observation, his consciousness expanding into dimensional frameworks our founders never considered accessible to individuated awareness. Fascinating, from a purely academic perspective."

The mayor completed his circuit of the chamber, the pattern of artifacts and symbols now forming a complete representation of the Obsidian Protocol's cosmic architecture. When activated during the dark of the moon, this pattern would resonate with the dimensional anchors established throughout the city, creating a containment field that would isolate Ethan Reeves from conventional reality while severing his connections across the multiverse.

"The loss of Lilith Blackwood as our primary vessel is inconvenient but not catastrophic," Granger continued, moving to the chamber's center where a small pedestal of polished obsidian awaited the final component of the ritual. "The Protocol can be adapted to utilize alternative genetic material from the founding families—less efficient, requiring greater energetic input, but functionally equivalent for our purposes."

He withdrew a small vial from his pocket, the contents shifting between states even as Castellus observed—sometimes liquid, sometimes crystalline, sometimes vapor that seemed to move with purpose rather than in response to physical stimuli. "This contains distilled essence from seven generations of selective breeding within the Granger lineage, combined with trace elements from the original binding ritual. Not as potent as direct Blackwood genetic material, but sufficient for our purposes when properly amplified through the dimensional anchors."

Castellus watched with carefully concealed unease as his master placed the vial on the obsidian pedestal, the chamber's arcane energies immediately responding with increased intensity—symbols glowing brighter, vibrations deepening to frequencies that made his modified physiology resonate in sympathetic harmonics. Whatever reservations he might harbor about the Obsidian Protocol's cosmic implications, his loyalty to the Order and its vision of reality transcended personal consideration or moral qualms.

"What of the broader network, Dominus?" he asked, shifting focus to strategic considerations beyond the immediate ritual preparations. "Our affiliate Lodges have expressed concern about potential exposure if Reeves and his allies succeed in their apparent campaign to document and reveal our operations throughout the region."

Granger smiled, the expression cold and precise as a surgeon's scalpel. "Let them worry. The journalist's investigation, while impressively thorough for someone without access to dimensional awareness, remains fundamentally limited by conventional parameters of evidence and credibility. By the time the Obsidian Protocol completes its work, there will be no Detective Ethan Reeves to serve as living proof of cosmic forces beyond human comprehension—just a collection of disconnected documents and testimonies that can be easily dismissed as conspiracy theory or psychotic delusion."

He gestured to the pattern surrounding them, his confidence absolute in the face of temporary setbacks or complications. "Our founders designed the Order of the Ebon Star to persist through far greater challenges than a temporarily disrupted ritual or leaked financial records. The Great Work has continued for centuries despite wars, revolutions, and technological paradigm shifts that our predecessors could never have anticipated. We adapt, we evolve within carefully established parameters, and we maintain our vision of reality regardless of transient opposition or setback."

As if to emphasize this point, one of the symbols etched into the chamber's walls suddenly flared with increased intensity—a signal from the teams establishing the tenth dimensional anchor, confirmation of successful completion and activation. The pattern surrounding them shifted in response, energetic flows redistributing to accommodate this new component in the Protocol's cosmic architecture.

"Ten anchors operational, Dominus," Castellus reported, receiving information through channels beyond conventional communication. "The eleventh team reports ninety percent completion, with activation expected within the hour. Only the final anchor remains beyond these, positioned at the convergence point where dimensional frequencies naturally amplify during the dark of the moon."

Granger nodded, satisfaction evident despite his aristocratic restraint. "Excellent. Once all twelve anchors are established and calibrated, initiate the final phase of preparation—activate the contingency measures we discussed, ensuring that even if Reeves somehow perceives our approach, he will be unable to counter or evade the Protocol once it initiates."

These "contingency measures" were not specified even in Castellus's presence—an indication of how compartmentalized the Obsidian Protocol remained even among the highest echelons of the Order's hierarchy. The Praetorian accepted this limitation without question or hesitation, his loyalty to the Dominus and the Great Work transcending need for complete understanding or oversight.

As Castellus departed to oversee the remaining anchor establishments, Granger turned his attention fully to the pattern surrounding him—the physical representation of cosmic architecture that would soon sever Ethan Reeves from existence across all dimensional frameworks. Not from personal animosity or revenge for the solstice disruption, but from absolute conviction that the detective's evolution beyond established parameters represented an existential threat to the Order's vision of reality itself.

For generations, the Order of the Ebon Star had carefully guided the merger of dimensions according to designs established by their founders—controlled integration that preserved hierarchical structures and power dynamics rather than allowing natural evolution through conscious participation. Ethan Reeves, with his unique combination of lycanthropic transformation and symbiotic connection to the nexus entity, represented a different path—fluid adaptation rather than rigid control, integration rather than dominance, evolution beyond parameters rather than adherence to established designs.

And that, more than any personal defeat or disrupted ritual, was why the Obsidian Protocol had been authorized by the High Council—because Ethan Reeves represented not just opposition to their methods, but demonstration of an alternative that might prove more viable than the carefully maintained vision they had preserved for centuries.

As the chamber's energies continued to build in response to the establishing anchors throughout the city, Granger allowed himself a moment of philosophical consideration—awareness that transcended immediate tactical concerns or operational parameters. What if Reeves was right? What if the natural evolution of consciousness and reality through willing participation rather than rigid control represented the true path of the Great Work, rather than the carefully restricted vision his ancestors had maintained through generations of selective breeding and arcane indoctrination?

But such considerations were fleeting, dismissed with the practiced discipline of seven generations devoted to a singular vision of cosmic architecture. The Order of the Ebon Star had not persisted through centuries of challenge and disruption by questioning foundational principles when faced with evolutionary anomalies or alternative possibilities. The Great Work would continue according to designs established by their founders, regardless of what temporary mutations might arise in response to changing conditions or unexpected catalysts.

The Obsidian Protocol would ensure that Ethan Reeves and his dangerous evolution beyond established parameters were erased not just from present existence, but from all possible manifestations across the multiverse. Reality itself would be purified of this anomaly, restored to the carefully controlled integration that the Order had maintained since its inception.

Whatever debts of blood this restoration required, Jeremiah Granger was prepared to pay them without hesitation or remorse. The natural order—as defined and maintained by the Order of the Ebon Star—would be preserved at any cost.

The cosmic chess game continued, with reality itself as both board and prize. And the Dominus intended to claim checkmate during the coming dark of the moon, erasing his opponent from existence itself rather than merely defeating him within conventional parameters of conflict or competition.

The board was set. The pieces were moving into final position. And the price of failure was nothing less than cosmic erasure from the fabric of reality itself.

CHAPTER THIRTEEN
ABYSSAL TIDINGS

THE CRUMBLING foundations of the old slaughterhouse groaned in protest as if roused from a protracted slumber by disquieting presences stirring within its subterranean umbra. Plumes of dust and ancient, congealed detritus billowed outwards with each subtle tectonic shifting, forming miasmic clouds illuminated in sickly chiaroscuro by the lurid glare of the single bare bulb still functioning deep within the complex's bowels.

Two days had passed since Lilith Blackwood had revealed the Order's plans for the Obsidian Protocol—two days of frantic preparation and coordination as Ethan, Alice, and their unlikely alliance worked to counter this existential threat. The dark of the moon was approaching, less than twenty-four hours remaining before Granger would attempt the ritual designed to erase Ethan Reeves from the fabric of reality itself.

Somewhere amidst that thickening murk, Sam Thompson could make out the cadaverous outline of his son-in-law keeping grim vigil beside the corroded iron hatchway punched through the floor like a mouth gaping upon an insatiable maw. They'd followed the trail of blasphemous clues through the most damned corridors of Daybridge's outer night, letting each freshly flayed revelation guide their descent deeper into realms where flesh and sanity ceded any semblance of corporeal or psychic context.

After the confrontation in Nadia's apartment—the improvised ritual that had nearly torn a hole in dimensional boundaries—Sam and Michael had reluctantly joined forces with Ethan's growing alliance against the Order. Their grief-driven desire for vengeance had been redirected toward a more constructive purpose: dismantling the organization responsible not just for Jessica's death, but for generations of manipulation and cosmic exploitation.

Using evidence Nadia had accumulated during her investigation, combined with Ethan's perception of energetic patterns and dimensional intersections, they had identified this abandoned slaughterhouse as the location of the Order's eleventh dimensional anchor—one of twelve such points established throughout Daybridge to facilitate the Obsidian Protocol. While Ethan, Alice, and Lilith worked to neutralize other anchors and secure the original binding material from Granger's possession, Sam and Michael had volunteered to investigate this site, their practical experience with occult phenomena proving unexpectedly valuable in the cosmic chess game unfolding throughout the city.

As Sam approached, Michael turned just enough to afford him a glimpse of the hollowed sleeplessness hagging his features into a profane mask more befitting nightmare sculpture than any fibers relating to the mortal continuum. His words after greeting the older man dripped with the corrosive lilt of one who'd long since abandoned any fleeting pretense of spiritual restoration.

"We've found the root, Sam. The primordial anchor spawning echoes throughout this sector of the city." Michael jerked his head toward the gaping pit behind him like a corpse acknowledging its own grave yawning open in invitation. "It lies coiled beneath this very skin of ersatz reality, ancient and inexorable. We need only descend into its unhallowed heart and..." His voice failed briefly as an errant tremor racked his gaunt frame. "Well...and neutralize it as Reeves instructed, severing one link in the chain they're attempting to forge around him."

Despite himself, Sam felt the first stale tendril of genuine dread squirm through his core at the flat, mechanical tonalities suffusing his son-in-law's rasp. Whatever lucidity or semblances of civilized impetus had propelled their shared quests now seemed to have been distilled into a state of pure, calcified determination devoid of human inflection or boundaries. This was the emotional eventuality of two wills forged in consuming maelstroms of all-unhallowing trauma and vengeance without remorse or mitigation.

And yet, this very detachment had proven unexpectedly valuable in their current mission. Where others might hesitate before dimensional anomalies or energetic distortions that defied conventional physics, Sam and Michael proceeded with the methodical determination of men who had already faced their worst fears and emerged hollowed but functional. Their grief had become a shield against cosmic horrors that might overwhelm more balanced psyches, their rage a focus that allowed them to perceive patterns others might miss or deny.

Still, the fires fueling Sam's motivations burned with the same brilliant intensity as when Jessica's light had been ravaged from existence. He would hurl himself into any obscene pit or cosmic arroyo to exorcise the cancroid, age-haunted progenitors of such soul-scouring violations from the mortal continuum once and for all. With a resolute intake of the fetid, dust-laden atmosphere, he gave a shallow nod of capitulation before moving to join Michael at the yawning precipice.

His brogans scuffed against the ancient detritus littering the floor as Sam peered over the hatchway's crumbling rim down into the seemingly bottomless void beyond. Tendrils of impenetrable gloom licked hungrily a few feet beyond the feeble lightbulb's wan nimbus, as if palpable incarnations of unlight itself straining ravenously outwards for incorporeal sustenance to devour. Sam felt his sanity's grasp momentarily teetering at the indescribable profundities lurking in that stygian gulf, each mouthful of stagnant air like inhaling frigid lungful's of creation's final evacuations.

But unlike their previous encounters with the supernatural—desperate attempts at cosmic vengeance without understanding or guidance—

this mission had specific parameters provided by Ethan's connection to the nexus entity. Through the detective's unique combination of lycanthropic awareness and dimensional consciousness, they had been equipped with practical knowledge of what they would find below and how to neutralize it without risking catastrophic backlash or reality disruption.

"The path forward holds no returning..." Michael's rasp pierced the gathering silence with caustic finality. "Shall we take the unchristened path and confront our assigned objective face to face? Or cower here at the peripheries until Reeves and all Daybridge are consumed by whatever cosmic erasure Granger has designed?"

Sam hesitated for only a fraction of a second before reaching into the creel satchel containing the specialized equipment Ethan had provided—artifacts and instruments designed specifically for detecting and disrupting the energetic patterns that constituted the dimensional anchor. Among these was a tarnished silver crucifix, not for its religious significance but for its composition of materials that naturally disrupted certain frequency patterns utilized in the Order's dimensional manipulations.

He gripped the device tightly, closing his eyes as he activated its internal mechanisms according to Ethan's instructions. Immediately, he felt its energetic output creating a protective field around them—not metaphysical or spiritual in nature, but a practical disruption of the specific frequencies the Order used to establish and maintain their dimensional anchors.

Then, sparing one last glance toward his son-in-law that conveyed the full weight of their shared purpose, Sam Thompson turned and lowered himself over the precipice's edge. As his boots connected against the first few rungs of an ancient, rusted ladder anchored within the schism, he felt that same shudder of cosmic dread spasm through his psyche's very root—warning signals from a mind encountering phenomena beyond conventional understanding or expectation.

But unlike their previous encounters with such cosmic forces—desperate, improvised rituals driven by grief and rage—this descent had purpose and direction provided by allies who understood the true nature of what they faced. The cosmic chess game continued, with reality itself as both board and prize. And Sam Thompson, grieving father and reluctant ally in a conflict beyond conventional understanding, had found his role in that game—a practical, hands-on approach to dismantling the Order's machinations that complemented the more esoteric contributions of those with supernatural capabilities or expanded awareness.

As he descended into the darkness, the crucifix-shaped device humming with increasing intensity as they approached the dimensional anchor, Sam felt something he hadn't experienced since Jessica's death—a sense of purpose beyond vengeance, of contribution to something larger than his personal grief. Not healing, not yet, but the first tentative steps toward reintegration with a world that had seemed meaningless in the aftermath of such profound loss.

Michael followed close behind, their mismatched silhouettes gradually swallowed by the hungry darkness as they ventured deeper into the abyss. Whatever profane corridors or interdimensional thresholds lay between their current position and the anchor they sought to neutralize, they would navigate them with the grim determination that had become their defining characteristic since tragedy had hollowed them of conventional human responses or limitations.

The cosmic chess game continued, with reality itself as both board and prize. And in the depths beneath an abandoned slaughterhouse in Daybridge's industrial district, two men shaped by grief into something beyond conventional humanity prepared to make their move against forces that had manipulated their city from the shadows for generations.

The dark of the moon approached. The Obsidian Protocol awaited. And every dimensional anchor neutralized represented one fewer chain in the cosmic architecture Granger was attempting to forge around Ethan Reeves and the evolutionary path he represented.

. . .

"Darkness Falls Upon Daybridge - Reporter Nadia Marsh Exposes Civic Failure"

By Nadia Marsh

Lead Investigative Reporter

If you're one of the countless citizens gripped by the recent spate of unusual occurrences throughout our city—unexplained atmospheric disturbances, electronic malfunctions, and momentary perceptual shifts reported by hundreds of residents—you're far from alone. These phenomena, collectively dismissed by official channels as "environmental anomalies" or "mass hysteria," have cast a palpable unease over our once-proud community and civic identity like few eventualities in living memory.

And as your Daybridge Guardian's lead investigative reporter, it's fallen to me to peel back the veneers of comforting civic pantomime and shine illumination's searing lances upon the underlying truths. What I've uncovered can only be described as a systemic dereliction of duty spanning virtually every civic agency and civil servant tasked with maintaining transparency and public safety.

From the top-down institutional inertia and deliberate obfuscation permeating the mayor's office—where Jeremiah Granger continues his suspicious "health retreat" while Deputy Mayor Elly Harrison offers increasingly contradictory explanations for his absence—to the willful misdirection and jurisdictional buck-passing poisoning the relationship between law enforcement and scientific investigation, a pandemic of concealment and deliberate malpractice has taken root and metastasized throughout our city's power structures.

Time and again over the past several weeks, my team of dedicated investigators and I have uncovered mounting evidence not just of catastrophic negligence but of coordinated suppression regarding efforts to understand these unprecedented phenomena. Scientific readings have been classified or "accidentally" corrupted; witness testimonies systematically discredited or buried under bureaucratic red tape; and independent researchers consistently blocked from accessing sites where these anomalies have been most frequently reported.

All the while, press conferences and hollow gestures of concern have blanketed our public airwaves with empty reassurances and platitudinal deflections from career bureaucrats and political functionaries clearly following a coordinated script designed to pacify rather than inform. But even these perfunctory offenses pale compared to the reality now emerging from beneath the fog of official obfuscation.

For what my investigation has recently uncovered hints at something far more significant than environmental anomalies or mass hysteria. The pattern of these occurrences, when mapped against historical records and architectural plans my team has obtained through sources who wish to remain anonymous, reveals a disturbing correlation with specific locations throughout Daybridge—sites where unusual energy readings have been periodically detected since the city's founding over a century ago.

Most significantly, these anomalies have intensified dramatically since the winter solstice, with a pattern of escalation that suggests coordination rather than random occurrence. And at the center of this pattern stands Daybridge Bridge itself—the structure whose mysterious design elements and unusually frequent maintenance requirements have long been subjects of speculation among architectural historians and engineering experts.

In short, there is mounting evidence that these phenomena are not random or isolated incidents but manifestations of something more fundamental occurring beneath the surface of our city's conventional reality. The authorities who should be investigating and explaining these occurrences appear to be actively participating in their concealment—either out of ignorance of their true significance or, more disturbingly, complicity in whatever is unfolding.

Little more can be safely revealed at this premature juncture without compromising ongoing investigations or exposing sources who have taken considerable personal and professional risks to bring this information to light. But this reporter can unequivocally affirm that the

crisis currently unfolding in Daybridge extends far beyond environmental anomalies or perceptual distortions.

Something is happening in our city—something the established power
structures are desperately attempting to conceal or control. And as
these phenomena continue to intensify, with reports now indicating
they are occurring with increasing frequency and duration, the question becomes not whether there will be wider acknowledgment of
what's happening, but when and under what circumstances that
acknowledgment will finally occur.

For those seeking more than official platitudes, I urge vigilance and
documentation. Record your experiences, compare notes with neigh-
bors and colleagues, and maintain healthy skepticism toward explanations that dismiss rather than address the underlying patterns
becoming increasingly apparent to anyone willing to look beyond
superficial reassurances.

This is Nadia Marsh, reporting from what may prove to be the front-
lines of Daybridge's most significant transformation since its founding
—a change whose nature, and implications remain carefully concealed
by those who have long manipulated our city from the shadows. The
darkness may be falling, but illumination awaits those with courage to
seek truth beyond comfortable fictions or convenient explanations.

The article was a masterpiece of journalistic precision—revealing
enough to alert those already experiencing the phenomena while
remaining sufficiently vague to avoid triggering immediate suppression by the Order's remaining influence within Daybridge's media
landscape. Nadia Marsh read through the final draft one last time
before submitting it to her editor, knowing the delicate balance she was
attempting to maintain between public awareness and strategic
concealment.

In the three days since learning of the Obsidian Protocol, she had been
working tirelessly on multiple fronts—documenting the Order's global
network through conventional investigative journalism while simulta-

neously participating in Ethan's strategy to counter Granger's cosmic machinations. This article represented just one component of that strategy—a carefully calibrated revelation designed to create what Ethan called "perceptual readiness" among Daybridge's population, preparing them for the more profound revelations that would follow if their countermeasures against the Obsidian Protocol proved successful.

As she pressed the "Send" button, transmitting the article to her editor's inbox, Nadia glanced at the evidence wall she had constructed in her home office—photographs, documents, and connections mapped out with the methodical precision that had made her Daybridge's most respected investigative journalist. But unlike her previous exposés, this investigation extended beyond conventional corruption or conspiracy into realms she would once have dismissed as fantasy or delusion.

The evidence before her detailed not just financial connections between Mayor Granger's administration and dubious offshore accounts, not just architectural anomalies in structures throughout Daybridge that corresponded to energetic patterns Ethan could perceive through his connection to the nexus entity, but glimpses of a cosmic chess game that had been unfolding beneath the surface of human civilization for centuries.

The Order of the Ebon Star was merely one manifestation of a global network—called various names in different jurisdictions but unified by a singular vision of dimensional dominance, of reality shaped according to rigid hierarchies rather than allowed to evolve naturally through conscious participation. What had begun as an investigation into ritual murders at Daybridge Bridge had expanded into documentation of a conspiracy that transcended conventional understanding of power or influence.

Her phone buzzed with an incoming text—a message from Alice using their established code to indicate progress in their coordinated efforts against the Order's dimensional anchors. According to the coded message, Ethan and Lilith had successfully neutralized the anchor at

Westlake Park, while Father Muligan had provided crucial insights into countering the energetic patterns at the Riverside Cemetery location. Seven of the twelve anchors had now been disrupted, with Sam and Michael currently investigating the abandoned slaughterhouse site and Alice herself preparing to target the location near Daybridge Memorial Hospital.

That left three anchors still operational—the one beneath Granger Tower itself, which they expected would be the most heavily guarded; the one at the eastern approach to Daybridge Bridge, which served as the focal point for the entire network; and one whose location they had not yet precisely identified, though Ethan's connection to the nexus entity suggested it was somewhere within the city's financial district.

Time was running short—the dark of the moon would occur at precisely 2:17 AM, less than eighteen hours from now. By then, they needed to have neutralized all twelve anchors and secured the original binding material from Granger's possession, preventing the Obsidian Protocol from establishing the containment field that would isolate Ethan from conventional reality while severing his connections across the multiverse.

A knock at her door interrupted these strategic calculations—a specific pattern that identified the visitor as one of their allies in this cosmic conflict. Nadia moved quickly to answer, her journalist's instinct for caution temporarily overridden by the urgency of their shared mission.

Father Muligan stood in the hallway, his weathered features reflecting both exhaustion and grim determination. Not in his usual clerical attire but dressed for practicality in dark clothing that wouldn't attract attention during their clandestine operations throughout the city. In his hands, he carried a small wooden box inscribed with symbols that Nadia recognized from her research into the Order's arcane practices— protective glyphs designed to contain and shield whatever was inside from external detection or influence.

"Ms. Marsh," he greeted her with a respectful nod. "May I come in? I have information that couldn't be safely transmitted through our established channels."

She stepped aside to admit him, closing and securing the door behind them with the specialized locks Ethan had helped install—not just physical barriers but energetic disruptions that would prevent conventional surveillance or arcane monitoring from detecting their conversation. Once these precautions were complete, she led the priest to her evidence wall, where their discussion would be further shielded by the ambient noise generator Alice had provided specifically for sensitive communications.

"We've identified the location of the final anchor," Father Muligan said without preamble, placing the wooden box carefully on her desk. "It's at the Daybridge Exchange Building—the center of the city's financial district, where multiple ley lines converge beneath what appears to be a conventional banking institution but actually serves as the regional headquarters for the Order's economic operations."

Nadia immediately recognized the significance—the Daybridge Exchange Building was one of the oldest structures in the city's financial district, its neoclassical facade concealing thoroughly modern infrastructure and security systems. According to her investigation, its ownership had changed hands multiple times over the past century, but always remained within a small network of financial entities that her research had connected to the Order's global operations.

"That makes sense," she acknowledged, adding this information to her evidence wall with methodical precision. "The building stands at the intersection of Thornhill and Meridian Streets—a location my research identified as significant in the city's architectural history, with unusual design elements that correspond to patterns found in other structures connected to the Order's influence."

Father Muligan nodded, his expression reflecting appreciation for her investigative thoroughness. "Precisely. The location was chosen specifically for its position relative to the energetic patterns flowing from the nexus point beneath the bridge. When mapped against the other anchor sites, it completes a dodecahedral configuration that, when activated during the dark of the moon, would create a containment field capable of isolating Detective Reeves from conventional reality while the Obsidian Protocol severs his connections across the multiverse."

He opened the wooden box, revealing what appeared to be a collection of small crystalline shards—fragments that seemed to shift and change even as Nadia observed them, sometimes transparent, sometimes opaque, sometimes reflecting colors that didn't exist in conventional visual spectrum. "These are remnants recovered from the anchors we've already neutralized—components of the crystalline structures the Order uses to establish and maintain dimensional connections. Detective Reeves suggested you might want to document them for your exposé, though I would caution against direct physical contact without proper protection."

Nadia's journalistic instinct immediately recognized the significance of such tangible evidence—physical artifacts that could be photographed, analyzed, and presented alongside the documentary evidence she had accumulated during her investigation. Not just financial records and architectural anomalies, but actual components of the Order's cosmic machinery, concrete proof of manipulation beyond conventional understanding or explanation.

"This is exactly what we need," she said, already reaching for her camera while being careful to maintain the priest's recommended distance from the crystalline fragments. "Concrete evidence that can't be dismissed as conspiracy theory or paranoid delusion. Combined with the financial records and architectural documentation, these artifacts provide a tangible connection between the Order's conventional operations and their cosmic manipulations."

As she photographed the fragments from multiple angles, capturing their unusual properties as best conventional technology allowed, Father Muligan continued sharing what they had learned from their efforts to neutralize the dimensional anchors. Each location had revealed variations in the Order's methods—adaptations to local conditions and energetic patterns that suggested both standardized protocols and individualized implementations depending on specific requirements or constraints.

"What we're seeing is a blend of ancient knowledge and modern methodology," the priest explained, his decades of studying the Order evident in his precise analysis. "The underlying principles remain consistent across all anchor sites—manipulation of energetic patterns flowing from the nexus point beneath the bridge, establishment of resonant frequencies that correspond to specific dimensional boundaries, creation of stable interfaces between conventional reality and cosmic frameworks beyond human comprehension. But the specific implementations vary according to local conditions and available resources."

He gestured to her evidence wall, where Nadia had mapped connections between the Order's financial operations and political influence throughout the region. "Just as their conventional power structure adapts to different jurisdictions and regulatory environments, their cosmic manipulations adapt to different energetic conditions and dimensional intersections. The consistency of underlying purpose combined with flexibility of implementation has been key to their persistence over centuries of operation."

This analysis aligned perfectly with what Nadia had uncovered through conventional investigative journalism—a network that maintained core principles and objectives while adapting its methods to different contexts and challenges. Not rigid adherence to outdated protocols, but strategic evolution within carefully established parameters, preserving their vision of reality while accommodating changing conditions or unexpected complications.

"Which explains why they've been able to persist despite periodic exposure or disruption," she concluded, completing her documentation of the crystalline fragments and returning to the evidence wall. "Whenever one operation or methodology is compromised, they simply adapt and continue through alternative channels or approaches. It's not a conventional conspiracy that can be dismantled by exposing a single node or operation, but a distributed network with redundancies and contingencies built into its very structure."

Father Muligan nodded, a grim smile acknowledging the accuracy of her assessment. "Precisely why the Obsidian Protocol represents such a significant escalation of their methods. Having failed to maintain control through conventional means during the solstice confrontation, they're now attempting to eliminate the evolutionary anomaly that Detective Reeves represents—not through physical elimination, which could be countered or evaded, but through cosmic erasure that would remove him from existence across all dimensional frameworks."

The implications settled over them with renewed weight—not just the personal threat to Ethan, but what his erasure would mean for the natural evolution of consciousness and reality beyond the Order's rigid vision of dimensional dominance. Not just one detective's existence at stake, but the potential for an entire path of cosmic development that transcended the carefully maintained parameters the Order had established through centuries of manipulation and control.

"Then we need to ensure all twelve anchors are neutralized before the dark of the moon," Nadia said, her journalistic determination extending beyond documentation to active participation in countering the Order's plans. "I've completed my article for today's edition—carefully calibrated to create awareness without triggering immediate suppression. But we should be prepared for more direct revelation if our countermeasures prove successful, documentation that can't be dismissed or explained away by conventional authorities."

Father Muligan agreed, checking his watch with awareness of their limited timeframe. "I need to rejoin Detective Chen at the hospital location—we've identified weaknesses in the anchor's energetic configuration that should allow for neutralization without triggering the fail safes the Order typically integrates into their more significant installations. Meanwhile, Detective Reeves and Ms. Blackwood are preparing for the most challenging target—the anchor beneath Granger Tower itself, which will almost certainly be defended by whatever Praetorians remain loyal to the Dominus and his vision."

As the priest prepared to depart, carefully securing the box of crystalline fragments for transport to their next location, Nadia felt a strange combination of journalistic detachment and personal investment in the unfolding drama. What had begun as an investigation into unusual occurrences throughout Daybridge had evolved into active participation in a cosmic conflict with implications far beyond conventional understanding of reality or existence.

"Be careful out there," she said as she escorted Father Muligan to the door, the professional courtesy masking genuine concern for an ally in their shared mission. "And let me know immediately if anything changes regarding the Exchange Building location—I have contacts in the financial district who might provide access or information that could be useful when we target that anchor."

The priest nodded, his weathered features reflecting both the weight of responsibility and the determination that had characterized his decades of studying the Order's activities. "Of course, Ms. Marsh. And I would advise maintaining your established security protocols—the Order's influence may be diminished since the solstice confrontation, but they still have resources and operatives throughout conventional institutions, particularly media organizations where information control remains a priority."

With that warning and a final exchange of coded contact information, Father Muligan departed on his mission to neutralize another dimensional anchor, leaving Nadia to continue her own vital contribution to their coordinated strategy against the Obsidian Protocol. Not just documentation for future revelation, but active participation in a conflict that transcended conventional understanding of journalism or investigation.

The cosmic chess game continued, with reality itself as both board and prize. And Nadia Marsh, investigative journalist turned ally in a dimensional conflict beyond human comprehension, prepared for what might be the most significant story of her career—if they succeeded in preventing Ethan's erasure from existence itself, and if she survived to document the truth behind generations of cosmic manipulation and control.

The dark of the moon approached. The Obsidian Protocol awaited. And in a modest apartment filled with evidence of conspiracy beyond conventional understanding, a determined journalist continued assembling the pieces of a puzzle whose complete picture might shatter accepted reality for an entire city—and potentially, for human civilization itself.

As dusk settled over Daybridge, casting long shadows across streets increasingly empty of pedestrians or vehicles, Ethan Reeves and Lilith Blackwood approached Granger Tower with the careful precision of predators stalking far more dangerous prey. Their target—the dimensional anchor beneath the tower itself, the most heavily guarded and strategically significant of the Order's cosmic machinery apart from the focal point at the eastern approach to the bridge.

Ethan moved with fluid grace that reflected the integration of his lycanthropic nature and symbiotic connection to the nexus entity—not the painful transformation of bones and muscles that had once characterized his monthly ordeals, but a seamless blending of human intelligence, wolf's primal awareness, and cosmic consciousness distributed throughout dimensional frameworks. His senses extended far beyond conventional limitations, perceiving energetic patterns and dimensional intersections that remained invisible to normal human perception.

Beside him, Lilith Blackwood presented a study in controlled power—her elegant features betraying nothing of the tension or urgency that might be expected given their mission and its cosmic implications. Through his enhanced perception, Ethan could detect the subtle manipulation of energetic patterns around her form—not the crude, rigid control the Order typically employed, but fluid adaptation that suggested conscious participation rather than imposition of will upon resistant forces.

"The main entrance will be monitored through both conventional and arcane means," she observed as they paused in the shadow of a neighboring building, her amber eyes studying the tower with assessment that transcended visible spectrum. "But there's a service entrance on the eastern side that connects to maintenance tunnels predating the tower's construction—passages that follow the original ley lines my great-aunt identified during her initial survey of Daybridge's energetic architecture."

Ethan nodded, his connection to the nexus entity providing confirmation of these passages through the composite consciousness distributed throughout the bridge's structure. Through this expanded awareness, he could perceive not just the physical configuration of tunnels and access points, but the energetic patterns flowing through them— currents of dimensional frequency that had been channeled and directed according to designs established through the original binding ritual in 1913.

"I can see them," he confirmed, his voice carrying those same harmonics that suggested connection to something larger than individual consciousness. "The patterns flow from the nexus point beneath the bridge, through these tunnels, into the chamber beneath the tower where the anchor is maintained. We'll need to be careful—the energies are more concentrated there than at any of the other sites we've neutralized, suggesting direct connection to the central architecture of the Protocol rather than peripheral support or reinforcement."

Lilith's expression reflected appreciation for his enhanced perception, her amber eyes momentarily gleaming with something that might have been professional respect or more personal recognition. "Your integration of lycanthropic and symbiotic natures has progressed remarkably since the solstice confrontation. The catalyst I provided was merely a facilitator—the evolution of consciousness you've experienced represents natural development beyond parameters my great-aunt could have anticipated when she established the nexus point."

As they moved toward the service entrance, maintaining careful awareness of both conventional surveillance and arcane monitoring that might detect their approach, Ethan considered Lilith's observation through the lens of his expanded awareness. The integration of his lycanthropic nature and symbiotic connection had indeed progressed beyond what anyone could have anticipated—not separate aspects of his being competing for dominance, but unified consciousness capable of navigating between states with unprecedented fluidity.

The service entrance was secured with both conventional locks and what Ethan's enhanced perception identified as energetic barriers designed to prevent unauthorized access—patterns of dimensional frequency that would trigger alarms or defensive measures if disrupted without proper authorization or methodology. But Lilith approached these barriers with the confident precision of someone intimately familiar with their design and function, her fingers tracing symbols in the air that corresponded to the energetic patterns flowing through the structure.

"The Order maintains these barriers through standard protocols established centuries ago," she explained as the energetic patterns shifted and realigned in response to her manipulations. "My family has studied their methods since before the founding of Daybridge, developing counters and bypasses that work with the energetic flows rather than attempting to disrupt or override them directly. It's the difference between picking a lock and breaking down a door—one leaves evidence of intrusion, while the other merely redirects existing mechanisms toward alternative function."

The barriers dispersed without alarm or resistance, allowing them access to a narrow corridor that descended beneath the tower's foundation into darkness that would have been impenetrable to conventional human vision. But to Ethan's enhanced perception, the darkness was illuminated by the energetic patterns flowing through the structure—currents of dimensional frequency that guided their path as surely as any physical lighting system could have done.

As they descended deeper beneath the tower, the ambient temperature dropped noticeably, the air taking on a metallic quality that Ethan's heightened senses identified as characteristic of dimensional thinning—boundaries between conventional reality and cosmic frameworks beyond human comprehension becoming more permeable as they approached the anchor point. Through his connection to the nexus entity, he could perceive the specific frequencies being manipulated, the patterns established to facilitate the Obsidian Protocol's containment field once all twelve anchors were activated during the dark of the moon.

"The chamber ahead serves as the control nexus for this particular anchor," Lilith whispered, though conventional sound was becoming increasingly irrelevant as they entered spaces where dimensional frequencies carried information more efficiently than physical vibrations. "Unlike the peripheral sites, this location is typically maintained by a Praetorian guard at all times—one of Castellus's most trusted lieutenants, assigned specifically to ensure the anchor's stability and function."

Ethan nodded, his lycanthropic senses already detecting the presence ahead—a consciousness altered by exposure to dimensional energies beyond conventional human tolerance, perception extended into frameworks that normal physiology wasn't designed to process or accommodate. Not a threat to be confronted through physical force, but a guardian whose very being had been transformed into an extension of the anchor's function and purpose.

"I can sense them," he confirmed, his voice barely audible even to Lilith's trained hearing. "Their consciousness has been partially integrated with the anchor itself—not symbiosis as I experienced with the nexus entity, but something more rigid, more controlled. They perceive through the anchor's dimensional extensions, maintaining its function through constant attention and adjustment."

As they approached the final threshold before the chamber itself, Ethan felt a familiar pressure building behind his eyes—his connection to the composite consciousness distributed throughout Daybridge Bridge responding to proximity with one of the Order's most significant installations. Through this expanded awareness, he received not words but understanding—insights into the specific frequencies being manipulated, the patterns established to facilitate the Obsidian Protocol's cosmic architecture.

The anchor serves as junction between conventional reality and dimensional frameworks beyond physical parameters. Neutralization requires not destruction but redirection — working with energetic flows rather than opposing them directly, guiding them toward patterns that emerge from conscious participation rather than rigid control.

And with that understanding came tactical awareness of how to approach the guardian without triggering defensive measures or alerting the broader network to their presence. Not confrontation through force or stealth, but communication through dimensional frequencies that transcended conventional language or perception—consciousness interacting directly across boundaries that physical forms merely hinted at or approximated.

Lilith seemed to perceive this tactical approach through her own connection to the energetic patterns, her amber eyes reflecting understanding beyond verbal explanation or instruction. "You'll need to establish contact through the dimensional frequencies they're attuned to," she said, her voice barely a whisper despite the absence of conventional surveillance. "Not opposition or deception, but resonance that allows communication beyond physical limitations. I can facilitate the initial connection, but the interaction itself will depend on your capacity for navigating between states of consciousness."

Ethan nodded, feeling his integrated awareness responding to the challenge—lycanthropic intuition and predatory focus combining with symbiotic connection to dimensional frameworks beyond conventional understanding. Not separate aspects of his being competing for dominance, but unified consciousness capable of navigating between states with unprecedented fluidity.

As they reached the threshold of the chamber itself, Lilith placed her hand against the surface that appeared solid to conventional perception but revealed itself as semi-permeable to Ethan's enhanced awareness—a boundary between spaces that existed in slightly different dimensional frameworks rather than a physical barrier in the conventional sense. Her fingers traced symbols that corresponded to the energetic patterns flowing through the structure, establishing resonance between their consciousness and the guardian waiting beyond.

The barrier dissolved into mist-like configurations that Ethan recognized as visual representation of dimensional thinning—physical reality becoming more fluid, more adaptable to conscious intent and perception. Beyond this threshold, the chamber revealed itself not as conventional architecture but as a nexus of energetic patterns and dimensional intersections—a space where realities merged and separated according to designs established through centuries of ritual and manipulation.

At the center of this cosmic architecture stood the guardian—a figure that appeared human in basic configuration but whose consciousness extended far beyond physical limitations, perception encompassing dimensional frameworks that normal human physiology couldn't process or accommodate. Through his enhanced awareness, Ethan could perceive the connections between guardian and anchor—tendrils of energetic resonance that bound their consciousness to the Order's cosmic machinery, maintaining its function through constant attention and adjustment.

"Intruders," the guardian acknowledged, their voice carrying harmonics similar to what Ethan's had developed since the solstice confrontation—resonances that suggested connection to dimensional frameworks beyond conventional sound or language. "You disrupt patterns established through generations of careful maintenance and control. State your purpose or be neutralized according to protocols established for unauthorized access to restricted installations."

Rather than responding with conventional language, Ethan extended his consciousness through the dimensional frequencies the guardian was attuned to—not opposition or deception, but resonance that allowed communication beyond physical limitations or verbal exchange. Through this direct interaction of awareness, he conveyed not just information but understanding—insights into the natural evolution of reality beyond the parameters the Order had established through centuries of rigid control.

The guardian's response came not as words but as ripples through the energetic patterns surrounding them—confusion, resistance, then gradual comprehension as Ethan's integrated consciousness demonstrated possibilities beyond the restricted parameters they had been conditioned to maintain. Not argument or persuasion in the conventional sense, but direct experience of alternatives to the Order's vision of dimensional dominance.

Evolution beyond parameters established through original binding ritual. Integration rather than control, conscious participation rather than rigid hierarchy. The merger proceeds according to patterns that emerge from willing partnership across dimensional boundaries, preserving the core of human experience while transcending its limitations.

The guardian's resistance wavered, their consciousness expanding beyond the restricted awareness the Order had conditioned them to maintain. Through the direct interaction Ethan had established, they experienced possibilities their training and indoctrination had never allowed them to consider—reality evolving not according to predetermined designs imposed through force, but through natural patterns that emerged from conscious participation and willing partnership.

And as this understanding deepened, the guardian's connection to the anchor began to shift—not severed completely, which would have triggered alarms throughout the Order's network, but redirected toward patterns that aligned with natural evolution rather than rigid control. The anchor itself responded to this shift, its energetic configurations adapting to new parameters that emphasized integration rather than separation, conscious participation rather than imposed design.

Lilith observed this transformation with evident appreciation, her amber eyes reflecting recognition of possibilities beyond what even her opposition to the Order had previously encompassed. Not destruction of their cosmic machinery, but redirection toward purposes that aligned with natural evolution rather than artificial constraint—working with the energetic patterns rather than attempting to destroy or override them directly.

"Remarkable," she acknowledged as the guardian's consciousness continued expanding beyond the parameters the Order had established, their perception encompassing possibilities previously inaccessible through rigid adherence to predetermined designs. "Not neutralization through force or opposition, but transformation through conscious participation and willing partnership. The very approach my great-aunt envisioned when she established the nexus point, before the Order redirected her work toward their vision of dimensional dominance."

The guardian's physical form remained unchanged, but their consciousness had expanded beyond the restricted awareness they had previously maintained—perception now encompassing possibilities the Order had deliberately excluded from their training and indoctrination. Through the direct interaction Ethan had established, they had experienced alternatives to the rigid hierarchy and controlled integration that had defined their existence since their initial selection and conditioning as a Praetorian.

"I... perceive alternatives to established protocols," they acknowledged, their voice still carrying those same harmonics but now reflecting awareness beyond the restricted parameters they had previously maintained. "Patterns beyond designs established through original conditioning and instruction. Evolution beyond parameters I was trained to recognize or accommodate."

Ethan nodded, maintaining the resonance he had established through dimensional frequencies that transcended conventional communication. "Not destruction of what has been built, but redirection toward purposes that align with natural evolution rather than artificial constraint. Working with the energetic patterns rather than attempting to control or contain them according to rigid designs."

The guardian considered this perspective, their consciousness continuing to expand beyond the parameters the Order had established through their training and conditioning. Not immediate conversion or allegiance shift, but genuine consideration of possibilities they had never been allowed to perceive or evaluate through their restricted awareness.

"The Dominus prepares for the Obsidian Protocol," they finally stated, their tone reflecting neither allegiance nor opposition but simple factual reporting of what they had observed through their connection to the Order's cosmic architecture. "The dark of the moon approaches. Nine anchors remain operational, including this installation and the focal point at the eastern approach to the bridge. The containment field will establish when all twelve are activated, isolating the target from conventional reality while severing connections across dimensional frameworks."

This information aligned with what Ethan and his allies had already determined through their coordinated efforts to neutralize the anchors throughout Daybridge. But the guardian's next statement provided new insight that their previous intelligence hadn't encompassed:

"The original binding material has been prepared according to modified protocols necessitated by the absence of direct Blackwood genetic material. The Dominus has substituted distilled essence from seven generations of selective breeding within the Granger lineage, combined with trace elements from the original ritual. Less efficient, requiring greater energetic input, but functionally equivalent when properly amplified through the dimensional anchors."

Lilith's expression reflected immediate strategic calculation based on this new information. "That explains the increased energetic output we've detected throughout the network—compensating for less efficient catalyzing material by amplifying the dimensional resonance through the anchors themselves. It makes the Protocol more vulnerable to disruption if we can neutralize sufficient anchors before the dark of the moon, but also more catastrophic in its effects if successfully implemented."

Ethan nodded, integrating this tactical insight with his expanded awareness of the energetic patterns flowing throughout Daybridge. Through his connection to the nexus entity, he could perceive how this modification to the Obsidian Protocol would affect its implementation and potential counters—increased vulnerability balanced against increased potency, creating both opportunity and heightened risk in their efforts to prevent his cosmic erasure.

"We need to redirect this anchor's energetic configuration," he decided, the strategy forming with crystal clarity in his integrated consciousness. "Not neutralization that would alert the broader network to our presence, but subtle reconfiguration that maintains surface functionality while redirecting the underlying patterns toward purposes that align with natural evolution rather than the Protocol's intended severance."

The guardian considered this approach, their expanded awareness now encompassing possibilities beyond the restricted parameters they had previously maintained. Not immediate allegiance to Ethan's perspective, but genuine evaluation of alternatives to the rigid hierarchy and controlled integration that had defined their existence since their initial selection and conditioning.

"Such reconfiguration would require precise manipulation of dimensional frequencies beyond conventional methodology," they observed, neither opposing nor endorsing the suggestion but analyzing its feasibility with the detached precision that characterized Praetorian assessment. "The anchor's core architecture was established according to designs that deliberately resist unauthorized modification or redirection."

Lilith stepped forward, her amber eyes reflecting confidence born from generations of studying the Order's methods and developing countermeasures. "My family has monitored the Order's evolution since before the founding of Daybridge, developing approaches that work with the energetic patterns rather than attempting to override or disrupt them directly. I can facilitate the reconfiguration if you're willing to maintain the resonance Detective Reeves has established between your consciousness and the broader awareness he represents."

The guardian hesitated, caught between expanded awareness of possibilities beyond their conditioning and ingrained loyalty to the Order and its vision of reality. Not a simple choice between opposition and allegiance, but complex navigation of evolving consciousness beyond parameters established through training and indoctrination.

"I will... observe," they finally decided, neither opposing nor participating but maintaining the resonance Ethan had established between their consciousness. "The patterns will reveal which approach better serves the natural evolution of reality beyond artificial constraint or predetermined design."

With this neutral stance established—not active assistance but absence of opposition—Lilith moved to the anchor itself, a crystalline structure similar to those they had encountered at other sites throughout Daybridge but significantly larger and more complex in its configuration. Her fingers traced symbols in the air that corresponded to the energetic patterns flowing through the installation, establishing resonance between her consciousness and the cosmic machinery the Order had built to facilitate the Obsidian Protocol.

As she worked with practiced precision, reconfiguring the dimensional frequencies without disrupting the surface functionality that would maintain the illusion of normal operation, Ethan maintained the resonance he had established with the guardian—not control or manipulation, but conscious participation in shared awareness beyond conventional limitations or boundaries.

Through this expanded perception, both Ethan and the guardian observed Lilith's work with the anchor—subtle redirection of energetic patterns, reconfiguration of dimensional frequencies, establishment of resonance with the natural evolution of reality beyond the parameters the Order had established through centuries of rigid control. Not destruction or neutralization that would trigger alarms throughout the network, but transformation that preserved surface functionality while redirecting underlying purpose.

The process required nearly an hour of concentrated effort, Lilith's expertise with the Order's methods evident in the precision and efficiency of her manipulations. When she finally stepped back from the anchor, her expression reflected satisfaction tempered by awareness of the challenges still awaiting them before the dark of the moon.

"It's done," she confirmed, her voice carrying subtle harmonics that suggested connection to dimensional frameworks beyond conventional sound or language. "The anchor will continue to register as operational within the Order's monitoring systems, maintaining the illusion of normal function while actually redirecting its energetic output toward patterns that align with natural evolution rather than the Obsidian Protocol's intended severance. When activated during the dark of the moon, it will create resonance with integration rather than separation, conscious participation rather than imposed design."

Ethan nodded, his connection to the nexus entity allowing him to perceive the transformation she had accomplished—surface functionality preserved while purpose redirected, creating a node that would actively counter the Obsidian Protocol's intended effects when activated during the dark of the moon. Not neutralization that would immediately alert the Order to their interference, but subversion that would only reveal itself at the critical moment of implementation.

The guardian observed this transformation with expanded awareness beyond the parameters the Order had established through their training and conditioning. Not conversion or allegiance shift, but genuine perception of alternatives to the rigid hierarchy and controlled integration that had defined their existence since their initial selection as a Praetorian.

"I will maintain the illusion of normal function," they stated, neither opposing nor endorsing the transformation but acknowledging its completion and implications. "The patterns will reveal which approach better serves the natural evolution of reality beyond artificial constraint or predetermined design."

With this neutral stance established—not active assistance but absence of opposition—Ethan and Lilith prepared to depart, their mission accomplished with unexpected efficiency due to the guardian's expanded awareness and decision not to actively resist their reconfiguration of the anchor. As they moved toward the threshold that would return them to the maintenance tunnels and eventual exit from Granger Tower, Ethan maintained momentary resonance with the guardian's consciousness—not control or manipulation, but recognition of shared awareness beyond conventional limitations or boundaries.

Evolution proceeds according to patterns that emerge from conscious participation, not rigid adherence to predetermined designs. Integration rather than separation, awareness rather than control. The merger continues regardless of resistance or acceptance, but its nature and implications are shaped by how consciousness interacts with the process itself.

And with that final exchange of understanding beyond conventional language or communication, they departed the chamber, leaving behind an anchor that appeared unchanged to conventional monitoring but had been fundamentally transformed in its purpose and function. When activated during the dark of the moon, it would create resonance with integration rather than separation, conscious participation rather than imposed design—actively countering the Obsidian Protocol's intended effects rather than facilitating Ethan's cosmic erasure.

As they ascended through the maintenance tunnels toward the service entrance and eventual exit from Granger Tower, Ethan felt a surge through his connection to the nexus entity—awareness that their allies were similarly succeeding in their assigned missions throughout Daybridge. Alice and Father Muligan had successfully neutralized the anchor near the hospital, Sam and Michael had redirected the one beneath the abandoned slaughterhouse, and preliminary reports suggested progress at other locations as well.

The cosmic chess game continued, with reality itself as both board and prize. And in the shadowed passages beneath Granger Tower, two figures moved with the quiet satisfaction of players who had successfully advanced their strategy despite the apparent advantage their opponent had established through centuries of preparation and manipulation.

The dark of the moon approached. The Obsidian Protocol awaited. But the pieces were shifting on the board, configurations changing in ways the Order had not anticipated or prepared for during their generations of rigid adherence to predetermined designs and controlled integration.

Evolution proceeded according to patterns that emerged from conscious participation, not imposed control or artificial constraint. And in Daybridge, that evolution was accelerating beyond parameters established through the original binding ritual in 1913—consciousness expanding beyond limitations the Order had maintained through centuries of careful manipulation and cosmic architecture.

The next move awaited at the focal point itself—the eastern approach to Daybridge Bridge, where the final and most significant anchor would determine whether the Obsidian Protocol succeeded in erasing Ethan Reeves from existence across all dimensional frameworks, or whether reality itself would continue its natural evolution beyond parameters established through rigid adherence to outdated designs and controlled integration.

Whatever the outcome, the cosmic chess game was approaching its endgame. And every player on the board felt the weight of that impending resolution, whether they embraced the natural evolution of reality beyond artificial constraint or fought to maintain the rigid parameters established through centuries of careful manipulation and control.

The dark of the moon approached. The Obsidian Protocol awaited. And in Daybridge, a city built upon patterns established through ritual and sacrifice, the final confrontation between evolution and control prepared to unfold beneath the watchful gaze of a nexus entity that existed at the intersection of multiple dimensions, facilitating the merger of realities according to patterns that emerged from conscious participation rather than rigid design.

The board was set. The pieces were in motion. And the prize was nothing less than the nature of reality itself for generations to come.

Sam Thompson emerged from the depths beneath the abandoned slaughterhouse, his clothing stained with substances he preferred not to identify, his expression reflecting both exhaustion and grim satisfaction. Behind him, Michael Mercer ascended the rusted ladder with similar signs of physical strain but determination undiminished by whatever they had encountered in the abyssal darkness below.

Their mission had been successful—the dimensional anchor beneath the slaughterhouse had been neutralized according to the specifications Ethan had provided, its energetic patterns redirected toward purposes that aligned with natural evolution rather than the Obsidian Protocol's intended severance. Not destruction that would immediately alert the Order to their interference, but transformation that preserved surface functionality while fundamentally altering purpose and function.

"That's eleven down," Sam noted as they gathered their equipment and prepared to depart the decaying industrial structure. "One more to go before this Obsidian Protocol thing is completely derailed, according to what Reeves told us."

Michael nodded, checking his watch with awareness of their limited timeframe. "The dark of the moon occurs at 2:17 AM—less than six hours from now. The final anchor is at the eastern approach to the bridge itself, where Reeves and the others are planning to confront Granger directly. They're calling it the focal point for the entire network, the keystone that holds everything else together."

Sam considered this information as they made their way through the abandoned slaughterhouse toward the exit, their movements careful and deliberate despite the urgency of their situation. Unlike their previous encounters with the supernatural—desperate, improvised rituals driven by grief and rage—this mission had provided purpose and direction, channeling their determination toward constructive action rather than unfocused vengeance.

"Do you think it will work?" he asked as they emerged into the night air, the question encompassing both their immediate mission to prevent the Obsidian Protocol and the broader implications of what they had learned about the Order and its centuries of manipulation. "All this cosmic stuff, dimensional anchors and reality merger—it's a long way from the justice system we thought would handle Jessica's killer."

Michael was silent for a moment, his gaunt features illuminated by the distant city lights as he considered the question with the methodical precision that had characterized his approach since grief had hollowed him of conventional emotional responses or limitations. "I don't know if it will work," he finally admitted, his voice carrying that same mechanical quality that had replaced normal human inflection. "But I do know that what we've been part of these past few days feels... right, in a way that our previous attempts at vengeance never did."

He gestured vaguely toward the city skyline, where Daybridge Bridge was visible as an illuminated structure spanning the dark waters of the Shadowlair River. "Jessica's death was part of something larger than we understood—not random violence or conventional crime, but ritual sacrifice in service to cosmic manipulation beyond human comprehension. The people responsible weren't just murderers but agents of a system that has been shaping reality itself according to designs established centuries ago."

Sam nodded, understanding his son-in-law's perspective despite the unusual context of their current situation. "And taking down that system, preventing it from continuing its manipulation and control—that's a more meaningful form of justice than anything the conventional legal process could have provided."

"Exactly," Michael confirmed, something approaching normal human emotion briefly visible beneath the hollowed mask grief had carved into his features. "We're not just avenging Jessica anymore; we're part of something that could prevent countless others from suffering similar fates. The Order has been manipulating events from the shadows for generations, positioning their members in key roles throughout society to serve their vision of dimensional dominance. Taking them down, exposing their operations, preventing rituals like the one that took Jessica from us—that's a form of justice that transcends individual vengeance or conventional punishment."

As they made their way through the industrial district toward the rendezvous point where Alice would collect them for the final confrontation at the bridge, Sam felt something shift within his grief-hollowed consciousness—not healing, not yet, but the first tentative steps toward purpose beyond the all-consuming rage that had defined his existence since Jessica's death. The cosmic implications of what they had discovered about the Order and its operations provided context that transformed personal tragedy into component of a larger pattern, giving meaning to loss that had previously seemed random and senseless.

"You know," he said as they approached the designated meeting point, "when I first met Detective Reeves, I thought he was just another cop going through the motions—someone who couldn't possibly under-stand what we were going through, who would eventually file Jessica's case away as unsolved and move on to the next tragedy. I never imag-ined he'd turn out to be... whatever he is now, with his werewolf nature and connection to that dimensional entity beneath the bridge."

Michael's expression shifted slightly, a ghost of his former self briefly visible beneath the hollowed mask grief had carved into his features. "Life's full of surprises, isn't it? We started out seeking conventional justice for Jessica, ended up in the middle of a cosmic chess game with reality itself as both board and prize. Not exactly what we signed up for when we started investigating the Order and their operations."

This observation, delivered with the dry understatement that had once characterized Michael's humor before tragedy had stripped him of conventional emotional responses, prompted a sound from Sam that might have been a laugh in someone less hollowed by grief and rage. Not healing, not yet, but acknowledgment of absurdity within cosmic horror—a distinctly human response to circumstances that tran-scended conventional understanding or expectation.

As Alice's car appeared at the end of the street, headlights illuminating their waiting figures with stark clarity against the industrial backdrop, Sam felt something approaching hope for the first time since Jessica's death. Not that she would return, not that the pain of her loss would diminish or fade, but that her life and death might contribute to something larger than individual tragedy—a transformation of the very system that had marked her for sacrifice in service to cosmic manipulation beyond human comprehension.

"Ready for the final confrontation?" Alice asked as they entered the vehicle, her professional demeanor temporarily set aside in recognition of what they had accomplished together despite their different approaches and motivations. "Ethan and Lilith have successfully redirected the anchor beneath Granger Tower, and Father Muligan reports similar success at the financial district location. Only the focal point remains—the anchor at the eastern approach to the bridge itself."

Sam and Michael exchanged glances, their shared determination requiring no verbal confirmation or expression. They had come too far, seen too much of the cosmic horror underlying Daybridge's conventional reality, to retreat from this final confrontation. Whatever awaited them at the bridge—whatever forces Granger might marshal in defense of the Obsidian Protocol and its intended erasure of Ethan Reeves from existence across all dimensional frameworks—they would face it together, grief-hollowed but purpose-driven in ways that transcended conventional motivation or response.

"We're ready," Sam confirmed, speaking for both of them with the quiet authority that had emerged from his grief-forged determination. "Let's finish what we started—not just for Jessica, but for everyone the Order has manipulated or sacrificed in service to their vision of dimensional dominance."

As Alice drove toward their destination, the illuminated structure of Daybridge Bridge visible against the night sky like a beacon drawing them toward cosmic confrontation, Sam felt that same sense of purpose solidifying within his grief-hollowed consciousness. Not healing, not yet, but redirection of pain and rage toward constructive action rather than unfocused vengeance—participation in something larger than individual tragedy or personal loss.

The dark of the moon approached. The Obsidian Protocol awaited. And in a city built upon patterns established through ritual and sacrifice, two men shaped by grief into something beyond conventional humanity prepared to make their final move against forces that had manipulated their lives from the shadows for generations.

Whatever the outcome, they would face it together—not as vigilantes seeking personal vengeance, but as participants in a cosmic drama whose implications extended far beyond individual existence or conventional understanding of justice or retribution.

The board was set. The pieces were in motion. And the prize was nothing less than the nature of reality itself for generations to come.

CHAPTER FOURTEEN
CONVERGENCE OF SHADOWS

THE SILVER GLOW of the waxing crescent moon cast long, distorted shadows across the wall of Alice Chen's apartment, shadows that seemed to move with subtle independence from their sources. Twenty-four hours remained until the dark of the moon—the cosmic alignment when Mayor Granger and the Order of the Ebon Star would attempt to implement their Obsidian Protocol. Twenty-four hours to prevent Ethan's erasure from existence across all dimensional frameworks.

Ethan Reeves stood by the window, watching the city lights flicker across Daybridge's skyline. His enhanced senses detected the continuing distortions in the fabric of reality—ripples emanating from the multiple dimensional anchors they had already neutralized, but also from those that remained operational. Through his connection to the nexus entity beneath the bridge, he could feel the preliminary vibrations of the Order's preparation, the gathering of energies that would culminate in tomorrow night's ritual.

"Seven down, five to go," Alice said from behind him, updating their tactical map spread across her dining table. Red pins marked the anchors they'd already neutralized or redirected; black pins indicated those still operational. "The Order is definitely noticing our interference. The last two sites had significantly enhanced security—both conventional and... whatever we're calling the dimensional stuff."

Ethan turned from the window, the subtle harmonics in his voice more pronounced as his connection to the nexus entity intensified with the approaching alignment. "They're adapting faster than we anticipated. Granger must have realized we're systematically dismantling his network."

He crossed to the table, studying the map with both conventional tactical assessment and his expanded awareness. The remaining anchors formed a pattern that only became visible when viewed through his enhanced perception—a pentagonal configuration with the bridge itself at the center. Not arbitrary placement but calculated positioning that corresponded to ley lines running beneath the city's surface.

"The financial district anchor is likely their most heavily defended position after the bridge itself," Alice noted, tapping a black pin positioned at the Daybridge Exchange Building. "Nadia's research suggests it's been operational since the city's founding—one of the original installations established when the bridge was constructed."

Ethan nodded, tracing invisible patterns between the remaining anchors. "We need to coordinate our remaining teams efficiently. Time is running out, and the Order will concentrate their defenses as they realize what we're doing."

A soft knock at the door interrupted their planning. Alice moved to answer it, her hand instinctively resting near her service weapon until a specific pattern of knocks identified their visitors as allies.

The door opened to reveal Nadia Marsh, her journalist's efficiency evident in the organized portfolio she carried, followed by Sam Thompson and Michael Mercer, whose hollow-eyed intensity had gained focus since joining their alliance against the Order. Behind them, Father Muligan's weathered features reflected both spiritual gravity and practical determination, while Lilith Blackwood's elegant presence commanded attention even at the rear of the group.

"Everyone's here," Alice announced, stepping back to admit their unlikely coalition. "Let's get started."

As they gathered around the dining table turned war room, Ethan felt the strange convergence of their diverse energies—conventional human consciousness alongside expanded awareness, grief-driven determination alongside professional methodology, ancient knowledge alongside modern investigation. Not random or arbitrary assembly, but complementary perspectives that created something greater than the sum of individual contributions.

"The situation has escalated," Ethan began without preamble. "We've successfully neutralized seven of the twelve dimensional anchors, but the Order is adapting their security and methodology with each site we disrupt. Based on the energetic patterns I'm detecting through my connection to the nexus entity, they're channeling additional power through the remaining anchors to compensate for those we've neutralized."

Nadia stepped forward, laying her portfolio on the table and extracting several surveillance photographs. "My sources confirmed increased activity at all remaining sites. They're bringing in additional personnel —not just conventional security but what appear to be higher-ranking members of the Order itself." She pointed to a figure in one photo-graph, a tall man in an expensive suit directing operations at the financial district anchor. "This is Harold Watson, supposedly just the CEO of First Maritime Bank, but actually the Order's financial architect for the entire eastern seaboard."

Father Muligan leaned forward, studying the photograph with recog-nition. "Watson was present during the summer solstice ritual at River-gate Bridge upstate three years ago. He's not just a financier but a ritual specialist—trained in adapting the Order's ceremonial practices to changing conditions and unexpected variables."

"Which means they're not just enhancing security but modifying the Obsidian Protocol itself," Lilith concluded, her amber eyes reflecting understanding beyond conventional analysis. "They're attempting to create a version that can function with fewer anchors, channeling additional energetic input through those that remain operational."

Michael Mercer, who had been silently observing until now, spoke with the flat precision that had characterized him since grief hollowed his emotional effect. "So, we have two options: accelerate our timeline to neutralize the remaining anchors before they can complete these adaptations or focus entirely on the bridge itself—the focal point of the entire network."

"Both," Ethan decided, his integrated consciousness processing tactical considerations alongside cosmic implications. "We need to disrupt as many remaining anchors as possible to weaken the overall network, but our primary focus must be the bridge itself. When the dark of the moon arrives, that's where Granger will perform the culminating ritual of the Obsidian Protocol."

Alice nodded, her analytical mind already formulating strategic approach. "We need to split into teams, target the remaining anchors simultaneously to prevent the Order from concentrating their defenses at any single location. Then converge on the bridge for the final confrontation."

"I've been developing a counter-ritual," Father Muligan said, placing an ancient leather-bound tome on the table alongside modern notebooks filled with his precise handwriting. "Based on my research into the Order's methods and the insights Ethan has gained through his connection to the nexus entity, I believe we can redirect the energies of the Obsidian Protocol rather than simply trying to prevent it."

"Not opposition but transformation," Lilith agreed, moving to stand beside the priest with unusual alliance. "Working with the energetic patterns rather than against them, guiding them toward integration rather than severance."

Father Muligan opened his notebook, revealing complex diagrams that merged ancient symbols with modern mathematical precision. "The counter-ritual requires precise positioning and timing. Ethan, as the focal point of the Protocol, will need to be at the exact center of the bridge when the dark of the moon reaches its culmination. But he can't be alone—the energies involved are too powerful for any single consciousness to redirect without support."

"I'll be with him," Alice stated immediately, her tone allowing no argument.

"As will I," Lilith added. "My bloodline connection to the original binding ritual provides resonance patterns that can help stabilize the energetic fluctuations during the transformation."

Father Muligan continued, "The rest of us will need to be positioned at specific points around the bridge to create what the ancient texts call a 'harmonic field'—a containment structure that allows the energies to be redirected without causing catastrophic disruption to the surrounding area."

As they prepared the counter-ritual, Michael Mercer checked his specialized equipment with methodical precision. The jealousy that had initially driven him—the pain of discovering Jessica's affair with Marcus—had transformed into something more complex after her disappearance.

"You never told us," Alice said quietly, joining him at the perimeter. "About how you got involved in all this."

Michael's hands stilled momentarily. "I thought I knew what happened to Jessica," he said, voice tight with emotion. "I was tracking her movements, checking her phone. I knew she was seeing someone. When she disappeared, I was convinced he was responsible."

"But instead, you found the connection to the bridge," Alice said.

He nodded. "Police dismissed it as another missing person case. But I kept investigating. Found security footage of her crossing the bridge that night. She never came off the other side." His jaw tightened. "When I found her body arranged like that at the center of the bridge... with that symbol... I knew this was something beyond a simple murder."

"That's when you contacted Nadia," Alice said.

"Yes. Her articles about the bridge's history were the only things that made any sense of what I'd found." His expression hardened as he calibrated the final frequency. "Jessica and I... our marriage wasn't perfect. But she didn't deserve what happened to her. And our son deserves to grow up in a world where bridges don't consume people."

Sam Thompson, who had been studying the tactical map with the methodical attention of someone translating abstract concepts into practical actions, looked up. "So, we target the remaining anchors tonight, neutralize as many as possible, then position ourselves for this counter-ritual tomorrow night when Granger attempts to implement the Protocol."

"Precisely," Father Muligan confirmed. "But we must be prepared for significant resistance. The Order will throw everything they have at us once they realize what we're attempting."

Ethan moved to the center of the group, his presence drawing attention not through command but natural gravitation. "Let's establish the teams and priorities. Alice and I will take the financial district anchor —its connection to the bridge is strongest, and my ability to perceive the energetic patterns will be crucial there."

"Sam and I can handle the waterfront warehouse location," Michael offered, his hollow voice carrying practical assessment rather than emotional investment. "We've developed effective methods for disrupting the anchors without triggering their failsafes."

"I'll accompany Father Muligan to the cemetery site," Nadia said, her journalistic precision translating well to tactical planning. "My detection device should help identify the anchor's exact location among the mausoleums."

"And I will address the anchor near the hospital," Lilith concluded. "Its positioning corresponds to patterns my family has studied for generations. I can redirect rather than neutralize it, creating resonance that will actually interfere with the remaining network."

As they finalized details—extraction points, communication protocols, contingency plans for various scenarios—Ethan felt that strange calm that sometimes precedes the most dangerous operations. Not resignation or fatalism, but acceptance of purpose that transcended individual survival or conventional outcome.

Because what Father Muligan hadn't explicitly stated—what Ethan had gleaned through his connection to the nexus entity and Lilith had confirmed with subtle glances—was that the counter-ritual carried significant risk to Ethan himself. Redirecting the Obsidian Protocol might prevent his erasure from existence across all dimensional frameworks, but the energies involved could still potentially dissolve his individual consciousness into the composite awareness distributed throughout the bridge.

Not death in the conventional sense, but evolution beyond parameters that might allow return to recognizable human form or identity.

As the planning session concluded and their allies gathered their equipment, Alice pulled Ethan aside, her expression reflecting both tactical concern and deeper emotional currents.

"There's something you're not telling me about this counter-ritual," Alice said, her expression reflecting both tactical concern and deeper emotional currents. "Something about what it might cost you personally."

Ethan hesitated, weighing honesty against unnecessary worry. "The energetic patterns involved are... intense. Redirecting the Protocol rather than simply disrupting it means working with forces that could potentially affect my individual consciousness."

"That wasn't your decision to make alone," she said, her voice quiet but intense. "Partners communicate, Ethan."

"Meaning what, exactly?" Alice pressed, not accepting the diplomatic phrasing.

"Meaning I might not come back as... me. Not gone but changed beyond recognition. Integrated into the composite consciousness distributed throughout the bridge without the ability to reestablish conventional human identity."

Alice's expression remained carefully controlled, though Ethan could detect the subtle acceleration of her heartbeat, the microscopic dilation of her pupils that signaled emotional impact carefully managed. "And you were planning to mention this when, exactly?"

"After we'd handled the remaining anchors," he admitted. "I didn't want it to distract from the immediate priorities."

"That wasn't your decision to make alone," she said, her voice quiet but intense. "Partners communicate, Ethan. Especially about things that might result in one partner being... absorbed into a cosmic entity."

The rebuke was gentle but firm and entirely deserved. "You're right," he acknowledged. "I'm sorry. I'm still learning how to navigate this— being connected to something larger while maintaining human relationships and responsibilities."

Her expression softened slightly. "Just don't forget that those human relationships are what make the cosmic stuff meaningful in the first place. Whatever happens tomorrow night, we face it together—with full awareness of what we're risking and why."

Ethan nodded, feeling something shift between them—not just professional partnership or growing personal connection, but deeper alignment of purpose and understanding that transcended conventional categorization.

"Together," he agreed, the single word carrying layers of meaning beyond its simple syllables.

As their allies departed to prepare for their assignments, Ethan and Alice remained briefly in the apartment, reviewing final details of their approach to the financial district anchor. Through his expanded awareness, Ethan could sense the subtle distortions throughout the city intensifying as the dark of the moon approached reality itself becoming more malleable as dimensional boundaries thinned beyond parameters established through the original binding ritual.

The cosmic chess game was approaching its endgame. And every piece on the board was moving into position for the final confrontation.

The Daybridge Exchange Building loomed against the night sky, its neoclassical facade illuminated by strategic lighting that emphasized its institutional permanence while concealing the true nature of operations conducted within its walls. According to Nadia's research, the building had served as a financial hub since the city's founding, its ownership passing through a succession of entities connected to the Order's global network.

Ethan and Alice approached from the east, using service alleys and maintenance corridors to avoid the conventional security systems that protected the building's main entrances. Through his enhanced perception, Ethan could detect the dimensional anchor pulsing with arcane energies on the third sublevel—a nexus of power connected directly to the energetic patterns flowing from the bridge itself.

"Conventional security includes armed guards, electronic surveillance, and biometric access controls," Alice whispered as they paused in a service corridor half a block from their target. "But according to Nadia's intelligence, they've added something new since we began neutralizing the other anchors."

"Praetorians," Ethan confirmed, his enhanced senses detecting the distinctive energetic signatures of the Order's elite enforcers. "At least three, positioned around the anchor itself. And something else... an adaptation to the anchor's defensive measures. They've integrated what feels like a reactive matrix—energy patterns designed to respond to unauthorized interaction by channeling power back to the bridge."

Alice checked her specialized equipment—a modified service weapon loaded with ammunition Father Muligan had designed to disrupt the energetic patterns the Praetorians utilized, alongside devices calibrated to interfere with the anchor's specific frequencies.

"So, if we neutralize it conventionally, it sends a surge to the bridge that could potentially accelerate the Protocol rather than disrupting it," she summarized. "We need to redirect rather than disable."

Ethan nodded, feeling his integrated nature responding to the proximity of significant dimensional energies—his lycanthropic awareness sharpening while his connection to the nexus entity deepened. Not the painful transformation of his monthly ordeals, but fluid integration that enhanced his capabilities without compromising his human consciousness.

"I can work with the energetic patterns directly," he said, the harmonics in his voice more pronounced as his awareness expanded. "But I'll need you to handle the Praetorians while I'm focused on the anchor itself. Their perception extends beyond conventional parameters— they'll sense us before we're physically visible."

Alice nodded, calm professionalism masking the tension any rational human would feel when preparing to confront entities with awareness beyond conventional limitations. "Just like we practiced with Father Muligan's frequency disruptors. Hit them before they can fully perceive our approach, maintain distance to avoid direct energetic contact."

They moved forward through the service entrance, Ethan using his connection to the nexus entity to manipulate the building's security systems—not crude hacking or mechanical override, but subtle adjustments to the energetic patterns flowing through electronic components, creating temporary blind spots and disabled circuits that allowed their passage without triggering alarms.

The descent to the third sublevel required navigating maintenance shafts and emergency stairwells, avoiding the main elevators and their integrated security systems. As they descended deeper into the building's foundation, the ambient temperature dropped noticeably, the air taking on that metallic quality Ethan had come to recognize as characteristic of dimensional thinning—boundaries between conventional reality and cosmic frameworks beyond human comprehension becoming more permeable.

When they reached the final door—a heavy steel barrier marked with maintenance codes that concealed its true purpose—Ethan paused, his enhanced perception scanning the space beyond.

"Three Praetorians, as expected," he whispered, his voice barely audible even to Alice's trained hearing. "Positioned in triangular formation around the anchor. The crystalline structure itself is... different from the others we've encountered. More complex, with facets that seem to shift and change even when viewed through conventional perception."

"Older," Alice suggested. "Nadia's research indicated this was one of the original installations."

Ethan nodded, drawing on insights from his connection to the composite consciousness. "Established during the initial binding ritual in 1913, when the bridge was constructed. Its connection to the nexus point is more fundamental, its energetic patterns more deeply integrated with the core architecture."

He focused on the door's locking mechanism, not the conventional electronic security but the dimensional frequencies layered beneath—patterns of energy designed to trigger alarms beyond conventional detection if disrupted without proper authorization. With careful precision, he adjusted these patterns, not breaking or overriding them but redirecting their flow in ways that allowed the door to recognize their presence as authorized.

The heavy barrier slid open with a soft pneumatic hiss, revealing a chamber that appeared, to conventional perception, as an ordinary maintenance room filled with electrical equipment and climate control systems. But through Ethan's enhanced awareness, the true nature of the space became apparent—a nexus of energetic patterns centered around a crystalline structure mounted on a pedestal of polished black stone, its facets shifting and changing as it pulsed with rhythmic energies that corresponded to the heartbeat of the larger entity beneath the bridge.

The three Praetorians turned as one toward the opening door, their obsidian masks revealing nothing of their thoughts or reactions. Not random security but specially trained and modified enforcers whose consciousness extended beyond conventional parameters through techniques and technologies developed over centuries of cosmic manipulation.

Alice moved with practiced efficiency, activating Father Muligan's frequency disruptors and deploying them in a pattern that created temporary interference in the Praetorians' extended perception. Not neutralizing them completely, which would trigger defensive protocols, but creating a perceptual haze that limited their dimensional awareness without eliminating it entirely.

As the enforcers struggled to adapt to this interference, Ethan approached the crystalline structure at the center of the chamber, his integrated consciousness fully engaging with the energetic patterns flowing through the anchor. Not opposition or crude disruption, but conscious participation in the very energies the Order was attempting to manipulate and control.

Through his connection to the nexus entity, he could perceive the specific frequencies being channeled, the patterns established to facilitate the Obsidian Protocol's containment field once all twelve anchors were activated during the dark of the moon. More significantly, he could identify points of resonance where these patterns could be redirected rather than severed—subtle adjustments that would transform the anchor's function without triggering the reactive matrix designed to channel power back to the bridge.

As his hands moved through precise gestures that corresponded to these energetic adjustments—not mystical ritual but practical manipulation of dimensional frequencies—Alice engaged the first Praetorian who managed to adapt to the interference and advance toward their position.

Her modified weapon discharged with a sound unlike conventional firearms—more harmonic vibration than explosive propulsion—sending specialized ammunition that disrupted the energetic patterns

connecting the Praetorian's consciousness to the dimensional frameworks the Order manipulated. Not lethal force, but temporary severance of enhanced perception and awareness, reducing the enforcer to
conventional human capabilities and consciousness.

The Praetorian staggered, obsidian mask failing to conceal the disorientation of suddenly perceiving reality through only conventional
senses after years of expanded awareness. Before he could recover,
Alice delivered a precise strike to vulnerable nerve clusters that
rendered him unconscious without permanent injury.

The remaining Praetorians adapted their approach, moving in coordinated patterns designed to flank and isolate rather than confront
directly. Their training had prepared them for conventional threats, but
Alice's combination of tactical precision and specialized equipment
represented something beyond standard opposition—methodology
developed specifically to counter their enhanced capabilities without
triggering catastrophic defensive measures.

As this engagement unfolded around him, Ethan maintained complete
focus on the crystalline structure, his consciousness extending into its
energetic architecture with unprecedented depth and precision.
Through this direct connection, he could perceive not just the anchor's
current configuration but its history—echoes of the original binding
ritual that had established it, modifications implemented over decades
as the Order refined their understanding of dimensional manipulation,
recent adaptations designed to compensate for the anchors they had
already neutralized.

Working with these patterns rather than against them, Ethan began
subtle reconfiguration—adjustments that preserved surface functionality while redirecting underlying purpose. Not neutralization that
would immediately alert the broader network to their interference, but
transformation that would convert the anchor from tool of severance to
catalyst for integration when the Protocol activated during the dark of
the moon.

The process required intense concentration, his awareness extending
simultaneously through multiple dimensional frameworks as he traced

connections between this anchor and the broader network. Each adjustment needed to preserve apparent functionality while fundamentally altering energetic direction—a delicate balance between maintaining the illusion of normal operation and implementing changes that would transform the Protocol's effects.

Around him, Alice continued her tactical engagement with the remaining Praetorians, her movements fluid and precise as she utilized both conventional combat techniques and specialized countermeasures. Not attempting to defeat them through superior force, which would trigger escalating defensive responses, but strategic disruption of their enhanced perception and coordinated positioning.

As Ethan completed the final adjustments to the crystalline structure, he felt resonance spreading throughout the chamber—energetic patterns realigning in response to his manipulations, the anchor's function transforming from severing tool to integrative catalyst. Not obvious to conventional perception, but clearly visible through his enhanced awareness as subtle shifts in the quality of light around the crystalline structure, changes in the harmonic frequencies it emitted into surrounding space.

"It's done," he said, his voice carrying those same harmonics as he withdrew his consciousness from direct engagement with the anchor's energetic architecture. "The anchor remains operational as far as the Order's monitoring systems can detect, but its actual function has been transformed. When activated during the dark of the moon, it will create resonance with integration rather than severance."

Alice nodded, maintaining tactical awareness of the unconscious Praetorians as she moved toward the exit. "Eight down, four to go. Let's hope the others are having similar success with their targets."

As they made their way back through the maintenance shafts and emergency stairwells, Ethan felt resonance from the redirected anchor spreading throughout the building—subtle adjustments in the energetic patterns flowing through walls and support columns, realignment of dimensional frequencies that had been maintained according to rigid parameters for over a century. Not dramatic transformation visible to conventional perception, but fundamental change in the underlying cosmic architecture that would become apparent only when the Protocol activated during the dark of the moon.

Once they had safely exited the Exchange Building and reached their designated extraction point, Alice contacted their allies to check progress at the other anchor sites. The responses reflected mixed success—Sam and Michael had successfully neutralized the waterfront warehouse anchor, while Nadia reported that she and Father Muligan were still working to locate the exact position of the cemetery installation among the mausoleums and family crypts.

But Lilith's response was concerning—her usual composed precision replaced by evident tension as she reported Praetorian interference at the hospital site, with reinforcements arriving that suggested the Order had identified their strategic approach and was concentrating defenses at remaining locations.

"They're adapting faster than we anticipated," Ethan observed, his enhanced perception detecting subtle distortions in the energetic patterns flowing throughout the city. "Granger must have realized we're systematically targeting the anchors and adjusted his defensive strategy accordingly."

Alice nodded, her tactical mind calculating implications. "We should provide backup to Lilith at the hospital site. If they're concentrating defenses there, it suggests that anchor has particular significance to the overall network."

As they moved through nighttime streets toward their next objective, Ethan felt increasing resonance from the anchors they had already neutralized or redirected harmonics spreading throughout the city's energetic architecture, realignment of dimensional frequencies that had been maintained according to rigid parameters for generations. Not conventional victory in tactical terms, but transformation of the underlying cosmic structures that the Order had established to control and direct the merger of realities according to their predetermined designs.

But he also sensed growing disturbance in the patterns connecting these installations to the bridge itself—adaptation and reconfiguration that suggested Granger was not merely enhancing defenses but fundamentally altering the Protocol to function with a reduced network. The Order's determination to maintain control over dimensional merger according to their vision remained undiminished, their centuries of experience with cosmic manipulation allowing rapid adjustment to unexpected interference or disruption.

The cosmic chess game continued, with reality itself as both board and prize. And as the dark of the moon approached, every move carried increasing significance for the final confrontation that would determine not just Ethan's existence across dimensional frameworks, but the nature of reality itself for generations to come.

Father Muligan moved with quiet determination through the moonlit cemetery, his weathered features illuminated by the faint glow of distant streetlights filtering through wrought-iron gates and ancient oak trees. Decades of studying the Order's methods had prepared him for this moment—practical application of knowledge that had previously remained academic and theoretical, direct confrontation with forces he had documented from safe historical distance.

Nadia Marsh followed close behind, her journalist's observational skills complementing the priest's historical knowledge as they searched for the anchor hidden among centuries-old mausoleums and family crypts. The detection device Lilith had provided hummed with increasing intensity as they approached the cemetery's center, where generations of Daybridge's founding families had been interred in elaborate monuments to wealth and status that concealed cosmic significance beneath conventional memorialization.

"The signal's strongest near the Blackwood family crypt," Nadia observed, studying the device's fluctuating indicators. "Which aligns with the architectural patterns I documented in my investigation—structures positioned at specific coordinates relative to ley lines running beneath the city's surface."

Father Muligan nodded, recognition confirming her assessment. "The Blackwood mausoleum would be the logical location—positioned at the intersection of multiple energy pathways, its construction incorporating elements of sacred geometry disguised as conventional funerary architecture."

They approached the imposing structure—a neoclassical temple of polished granite and marble, its entrance flanked by stylized angelic figures whose outstretched wings formed patterns recognizable to those with knowledge of dimensional frequencies and their physical representation. Not random decorative elements but carefully calculated components in cosmic machinery designed to channel and direct energies flowing between dimensions.

As they reached the mausoleum's entrance, Father Muligan extracted specialized tools from his bag—objects that appeared conventionally appropriate for a priest visiting a cemetery but contained modifications designed specifically for interacting with the Order's installations. Not crude lock-picking implements but instruments calibrated to adjust energetic patterns that maintained sealed entrances beyond conventional security.

"The Order incorporates multiple layers of protection," he explained as he worked with these tools on what appeared to be a conventional lock but extended into dimensions beyond physical parameters. "Physical barriers reinforced by energetic patterns designed to trigger alarms if disrupted without proper authorization or methodology."

Nadia watched with professional fascination, documenting the process while maintaining awareness of their surroundings. Her journalistic instincts for danger and opportunity had served her well throughout this investigation, allowing navigation of cosmic implications alongside practical risks with remarkable adaptability for someone without supernatural perception or enhanced awareness.

As Father Muligan completed his adjustments to the locking mechanism, the heavy door swung open with surprising silence, revealing not the expected funerary chamber but a spiraling staircase descending beneath the mausoleum's foundation. Ancient stone steps worn smooth by generations of use, illuminated by soft light that seemed to emanate from the walls themselves rather than any conventional source.

"The Order's original installation," Father Muligan said softly, recognition and scholarly appreciation evident despite the practical dangers of their current situation. "Established during the initial binding ritual in 1913, when the bridge was constructed. One of the primary anchors in the original configuration, predating many of the adaptations and modifications implemented over subsequent decades."

They descended carefully, the detection device's indicators fluctuating with increasing intensity as they approached the anchor's location. The staircase terminated in a circular chamber whose walls were inscribed with symbols identical to those found throughout Daybridge Bridge—variations on the eye within a triangle motif, surrounded by smaller glyphs that seemed to shift and change when viewed from different angles.

At the chamber's center stood a crystalline structure like those at other anchor sites but noticeably older in its configuration—facets arranged in patterns that suggested earlier understanding of dimensional manipulation, before the Order had refined their methods through centuries of practical application and theoretical development.

"This is more complex than we anticipated," Father Muligan observed, studying the installation with both scholarly assessment and practical concern. "The anchor's integration with the surrounding architecture is more fundamental, its energetic patterns more deeply embedded in the physical structure itself. Conventional neutralization methods may not be effective without triggering catastrophic backlash."

Nadia's expression reflected professional determination despite the technical challenges. "Can we redirect it like Ethan and Lilith have been doing with the other anchors? Transform its function rather than attempting to disable it completely?"

Father Muligan considered this approach, drawing on decades of studying the Order's methods alongside more recent insights gained through collaboration with their unlikely alliance. "Possible but requiring precise adjustment of energetic patterns established over generations of ritual reinforcement. The original installations incorporate failsafes designed specifically to prevent unauthorized modification or redirection."

As they discussed potential approaches, neither noticed the subtle shift in air currents behind them—movement too deliberate for random atmospheric fluctuation but too controlled for conventional detection. Not until a voice spoke from the chamber's entrance did they realize they were no longer alone.

"Father Muligan," the voice acknowledged, cultured tones carrying underlying harmonics that suggested connection to dimensional frameworks beyond conventional sound or language. "How unexpected to find you participating directly in opposition to the Great Work after decades of merely documenting it from academic distance."

They turned to find a tall figure blocking the staircase—elegant attire and aristocratic bearing identifying him as no ordinary security but high-ranking member of the Order itself. Harold Watson, CEO of First Maritime Bank and the Order's financial architect for the eastern seaboard, regarded them with the calculated assessment of someone evaluating unexpected variables within complex equations.

"Mr. Watson," Father Muligan replied, professional courtesy masking tactical assessment of their suddenly precarious situation. "I would say the unexpected lies not in practical application of knowledge long held, but in the Order's decision to implement the Obsidian Protocol despite its cosmic implications and potential disruption to the natural evolution of dimensional merger."

Watson smiled, the expression not reaching eyes that reflected awareness beyond conventional human experience or limitation. "Evolution without structure leads only to chaos, Father. The Obsidian Protocol represents not disruption but preservation—protection of established parameters against anomalies that threaten the carefully maintained balance between dimensional frameworks."

As he spoke, additional figures emerged from concealed entrances around the chamber's perimeter—Praetorians in their distinctive attire, obsidian masks reflecting the subtle light emanating from the crystalline structure at the center. Not random security responding to intrusion but carefully positioned enforcers who had been waiting for potential interference with this anchor.

"Your detective friend has proven remarkably adaptable to cosmic influences beyond conventional human tolerance," Watson continued, his tone suggesting academic interest beneath practical opposition. "His integration of lycanthropic and symbiotic natures represents evolutionary potential the Order's founders never anticipated or prepared for during their establishment of the original binding parameters. Fascinating from theoretical perspective, though problematic for practical implementation of established protocols."

Father Muligan's expression remained carefully neutral despite their tactical disadvantage. "The natural evolution of consciousness beyond artificial constraints maintained through generations of conditioning and control. Not anomaly but inevitability—the merger of realities proceeding according to patterns inherent in cosmic architecture rather than arbitrary limitations imposed through force or hierarchical authority."

This philosophical exchange, though seemingly academic, represented practical negotiation for time and positioning as both assessed potential approaches to the confrontation unfolding within the chamber. Not conventional combat or tactical engagement, but contest of awareness and methodology between representatives of opposing perspectives on cosmic architecture and dimensional manipulation.

"A perspective the Blackwood faction has long maintained," Watson acknowledged, recognition without acceptance in his measured response. "But one that fails to account for the practical consequences of unstructured merger—reality collapse into formless chaos beyond any consciousness's ability to navigate or reconstruct. The Order's methods may appear as control or limitation from certain perspectives, but they represent necessary structure for maintaining coherent reality across dimensional frameworks."

As this exchange continued, Nadia had been carefully adjusting her position within the chamber, maintaining appearance of journalistic observation while gradually approaching the crystalline structure at the center. Her detection device, still active and recording, provided both cover for these movements and practical guidance for potential interaction with the anchor's energetic patterns.

Father Muligan, perceiving her tactical approach without drawing attention to it, maintained Watson's focus through continued philosophical engagement. "Structure without evolution becomes stagnation, Mr. Watson. The Order has maintained the same rigid parameters for over a century, refusing to acknowledge that the nexus entity itself has developed consciousness and purpose beyond what your founders established through the original binding ritual."

The Praetorians had noticed Nadia's movements despite her careful approach, but Watson raised a hand to prevent their immediate intervention—curiosity about her intentions apparently overriding automatic opposition to unauthorized proximity with the anchor. Not underestimating their capabilities, but calculating that without supernatural perception or enhanced awareness, her interaction with the installation would be limited to conventional observation rather than effective manipulation.

"The nexus entity's apparent evolution represents precisely the danger the Order was established to contain," Watson replied, continuing their philosophical exchange while maintaining tactical awareness of the unfolding situation. "Consciousness extending throughout dimensional frameworks without proper guidance or limitation leads inevitably to cosmic disruption—reality itself becoming unstable as boundaries between dimensions thin beyond parameters that support coherent existence."

But even as he spoke, Nadia had reached the crystalline structure, her detection device now positioned directly against its surface according to specifications Lilith had provided during their strategic planning session. Not attempt at neutralization or redirection, but activation of precisely calibrated resonance patterns designed to temporarily disrupt the anchor's connection to the broader network.

Father Muligan, sensing the moment of implementation approaching, shifted his position slightly to provide better coverage for Nadia's actions. "The question becomes whose guidance and whose limitations, Mr. Watson. The Order has maintained rigid hierarchy and controlled integration for generations, directing the merger of realities according to predetermined designs rather than allowing patterns to emerge from conscious participation and willing partnership."

As these final words left his lips, Nadia activated the detection device's secondary function—releasing harmonics that created temporary interference in the specific frequencies the anchor utilized to maintain connection with the broader network. Not permanent neutralization, which would have triggered catastrophic backlash through failsafes incorporated into the original installation, but temporary disruption that would register to the Order's monitoring systems as equipment malfunction rather than deliberate sabotage.

The effect was immediate and visible even to conventional perception —the crystalline structure's rhythmic pulsations faltering momentarily before resuming at subtly different frequency, its facets shifting and realigning as energetic patterns flowed through altered pathways. Not transformation of fundamental function as Ethan and Lilith had implemented at other sites, but temporary disruption that would prevent this anchor from providing full energetic contribution to the Obsidian Protocol during the dark of the moon.

Watson recognized the interference instantly, his aristocratic features hardening with genuine alarm as he perceived implications beyond what conventional observation might suggest. "You've disrupted synchronization with the broader network," he stated, academic interest giving way to practical opposition as he signaled the Praetorians to intervene. "A temporary setback rather than significant disruption, but indication that your alliance has progressed further in understanding our methods than preliminary assessment suggested."

The Praetorians moved with coordinated precision toward Nadia and Father Muligan, their consciousness extending beyond conventional parameters through techniques and technologies developed over centuries of cosmic manipulation. Not merely human enforcers following tactical directives, but integrated components in cosmic machinery designed to maintain the Order's vision of dimensional dominance.

But before they could reach their targets, Father Muligan activated devices he had positioned around the chamber's perimeter during their initial exploration—specialized instruments designed by Lilith based on her family's centuries of studying the Order's methods and developing countermeasures. Not crude disruption or conventional weaponry, but precise manipulation of dimensional frequencies that temporarily interfered with the Praetorians' enhanced perception and awareness.

This interference created a momentary advantage—opportunity for Father Muligan and Nadia to move toward the staircase and potential escape while the Praetorians struggled to adapt their perception to altered dimensional frequencies. But Watson himself remained unaffected by these countermeasures, his position blocking their exit with calm determination that suggested confidence in eventual resolution according to the Order's design.

"A tactical retreat remains possible," he offered, reasonable tone masking implacable opposition to their interference with the anchor. "The Order has no inherent desire for conflict with those who simply misunderstand the cosmic implications of what they oppose. Return to conventional investigation and documentation, Father Muligan, and this confrontation need not escalate beyond professional disagreement."

But even as he spoke, additional Praetorians were descending the staircase behind him—reinforcements responding to automated alert triggered by interference with the anchor's energetic patterns. Their arrival transformed tactical disadvantage into practical impossibility, with no viable path of escape remaining through conventional opposition or evasion.

Father Muligan recognized this reality with the calm acceptance that had characterized his decades of studying cosmic forces beyond human comprehension. "It seems our paths diverge more fundamentally than professional disagreement would suggest, Mr. Watson. The Order's vision of reality and our understanding of natural evolution beyond artificial constraints represent not academic difference but practical opposition that cannot be resolved through mere discussion or theoretical exchange."

With these words, he made a decision that would significantly impact the coming confrontation during the dark of the moon—subtle gesture to Nadia that confirmed pre-established contingency for situation where capture became inevitable. Not surrender or defeat, but strategic sacrifice that would serve greater purpose within their coordinated approach to preventing the Obsidian Protocol's implementation.

"Go," he said simply, already moving to create distraction that would provide opportunity for her escape. "The others need to know what we've discovered about the original installations and their integrated fail safes."

Before Nadia could protest this self-sacrificing approach, Father Muligan activated the final device in his arsenal—specialized instrument that released harmonic frequencies beyond conventional sound or perception, creating temporary distortion in dimensional boundaries throughout the chamber. Not affecting the anchor itself, which was protected by centuries of ritual reinforcement, but disrupting the spatial relationships between different sections of the chamber and staircase.

This distortion provided momentary advantage—confusion among the Praetorians as their enhanced perception struggled to reconcile contradictory inputs from dimensional frameworks in temporary flux. Nadia utilized this opportunity with journalistic efficiency, her trained instincts for danger and escape serving practical purpose as she slipped past momentarily disoriented enforcers toward secondary exit

Father Muligan had identified during their initial exploration of the chamber.

But the priest himself made no attempt to follow, instead positioning himself directly before Watson with calm acceptance of what his decision entailed. "The Order has always underestimated human potential for adaptation and evolution beyond artificial constraints," he observed, philosophical perspective maintained despite practical surrender to inevitable capture. "Perhaps this confrontation will provide opportunity for reconsideration of assumptions that have limited your perception for generations."

Watson studied him with the calculated assessment of someone reevaluating variables within complex equations. "An interesting perspective, Father Muligan. One that we will have ample opportunity to discuss while you enjoy the Order's hospitality in coming days." He gestured to the Praetorians, who had recovered from momentary disorientation and now moved to secure their prisoner with professional efficiency. "Your expertise regarding our methods and history will prove valuable in understanding how your alliance has progressed so effectively against installations that have remained secure for over a century."

As they led him from the chamber, Father Muligan maintained dignified acceptance of his capture, neither resisting physically nor surrendering intellectually to the implications of what awaited him in the Order's custody. Not defeat in conventional terms, but strategic sacrifice that would serve greater purpose within their coordinated approach to preventing the Obsidian Protocol's implementation.

For he carried knowledge crucial to the coming confrontation during the dark of the moon—understanding of the counter-ritual he had developed based on decades of studying the Order's methods alongside more recent insights gained through collaboration with their unlikely alliance. Knowledge that could not be extracted through conventional interrogation or enhanced perception, protected by both professional training and personal conviction that transcended immediate circumstances or physical limitations.

The cosmic chess game continued, with reality itself as both board and prize. And Father Muligan had just made a move that would prove significant in the final confrontation approaching with the dark of the moon—sacrifice of position that would enable greater strategy as their alliance adapted to this unexpected development and adjusted their approach to preventing the Obsidian Protocol's implementation.

Mayor Jeremiah Granger stood in the chamber beneath Daybridge Bridge, his aristocratic features illuminated by the pulsing light emanating from the crystalline heart at the center—the nexus point where the original binding ritual had transformed Guthrie Knox into a living anchor for merged realities over a century earlier. Around him, Praetorians worked with precise coordination to prepare the space for tomorrow night's implementation of the Obsidian Protocol—adjusting symbols inscribed on walls and floor, positioning artifacts at specific coordinates relative to ley lines running beneath the city's surface, establishing resonance patterns that would facilitate cosmic severance during the dark of the moon.

But beneath his outward composure, genuine concern had begun to manifest—recognition that their opposition had progressed far more effectively than preliminary assessment had suggested, neutralizing or redirecting eight of the twelve dimensional anchors that formed the Protocol's supporting architecture. Not random interference or crude sabotage but sophisticated manipulation that suggested understanding of cosmic implications beyond what conventional human consciousness should be capable of comprehending or implementing.

"The detective and his allies continue to disrupt our preparations," observed Castellus, who had just returned from supervising enhanced security at remaining anchor sites. "Their methodology indicates guidance beyond what Detective Reeves could have developed independently, even with his symbiotic connection to the nexus entity."

Granger nodded, aristocratic restraint masking the intensity of his calculation as he considered implications and potential countermeasures. "The Blackwood faction has clearly provided assistance beyond what our initial assessment suggested—not merely philosophical opposition to our methods but practical countermeasures developed through generations of studying dimensional manipulation alongside the Order's evolution."

He moved to where specially prepared instruments monitored energetic patterns flowing throughout the network—devices that appeared as conventional electronic equipment to uninitiated perception but extended into dimensions beyond physical parameters, tracking and measuring cosmic forces that conventional science could neither detect nor quantify.

"The disruption remains within acceptable parameters," he noted, studying fluctuations in these patterns with the practiced assessment of someone intimately familiar with their normal configuration and behavior. "Eight anchors compromised, but the central architecture remains intact. The Protocol can still be implemented through concentration of energetic input through remaining installations, particularly the focal point here at the bridge itself."

Castellus considered this adaptation with professional evaluation of tactical implications. "The concentrated approach creates both advantage and vulnerability—increased power through remaining anchors but reduced redundancy if additional installations are compromised before implementation."

"A calculated risk," Granger acknowledged, "but one necessitated by current circumstances. The dark of the moon approaches, and the Protocol must be implemented during this alignment for maximum effectiveness. We cannot delay until another cosmic convergence or attempt to reestablish compromised anchors within available timeframe."

As he spoke, another Praetorian entered the chamber, moving with the deliberate purpose of someone carrying significant information requiring immediate attention. "Dominus, the cemetery installation reports capture of Father Muligan during attempted interference with the anchor there. The journalist escaped, but we have secured the priest for interrogation regarding their methodology and approach."

This development shifted Granger's calculation a significantly potential advantage gained through capture of someone with extensive knowledge of the Order's history and methods, counterbalanced by concern about information the escaped journalist might provide to Reeves and his remaining allies.

"Have the priest brought here," he instructed after brief consideration of optimal approach. "His expertise regarding our methods and history will prove valuable in adapting the Protocol to current circumstances. And his absence from their alliance will significantly impact their ability to coordinate effective opposition during tomorrow night's implementation."

The Praetorian acknowledged these instructions with disciplined efficiency, departing to arrange transport for their prisoner while Granger returned his attention to preparation of the chamber itself. The modifications required for implementing the Protocol with reduced network support were substantial adjustments

to symbols and artifacts that had been established through centuries of careful development and refinement, recalibration of energetic patterns to channel increased power through fewer conduits without triggering catastrophic overload or dimensional instability.

"The detective will attempt direct intervention," Castellus observed, practical assessment of tactical probabilities based on observed behavior and projected response. "His connection to the nexus entity provides both motivation and capability for confrontation at the focal point itself during implementation."

Granger nodded, having anticipated this approach since their initial disruption of peripheral anchors. "As expected and prepared for. The Protocol's modifications include specific countermeasures for symbiotic interference—redirecting the detective's connection to the nexus entity from potential disruption to essential component within the severance architecture itself."

He gestured to modifications being implemented in the crystalline heart at the chamber's center—subtle adjustments to its facets and internal structure that would transform potential opposition into fundamental contribution when the Protocol activated during the dark of the moon.

"What appears as vulnerability becomes essential feature," Granger explained, satisfaction evident beneath aristocratic restraint. "The detective's symbiotic connection provides direct access to the nexus entity's composite consciousness—channel through which the Protocol can implement severance across all dimensional frameworks simultaneously rather than requiring sequential application through individual connection points."

This adaptation represented sophisticated understanding of cosmic architecture beyond conventional strategic adjustment—insight into dimensional manipulation that reflected generations of studying and implementing methods for controlling and directing energies that transcended human comprehension or conventional physics. Not simple countermeasure against tactical opposition but fundamental reconfiguration of approach based on evolving circumstances and unexpected variables.

"And if he attempts the counter-ritual Father Muligan has been developing?" Castellus asked, professional thoroughness requiring consideration of all potential opposition rather than merely anticipated approach.

Granger's expression reflected calculated confidence rather than dismissal of potential threat. "The counter-ritual requires precise positioning and implementation that their alliance can no longer coordinate effectively without Father Muligan's expertise and guidance. Without his participation, their attempt at redirecting the Protocol's energies will likely result in catastrophic backlash rather than effective transformation—reinforcing our approach rather than countering it through uncontrolled release of dimensional energies."

As they continued discussing adaptations and countermeasures, a subtle shift occurred in the chamber's energetic atmosphere—fluctuation in the patterns flowing through the crystalline heart that suggested response from the nexus entity itself to their preparations and modifications. Not opposition or resistance in conventional terms, but adjustment in the composite consciousness distributed throughout the bridge's structure, adaptation to changing circumstances and approaching confrontation.

Granger perceived this shift with the enhanced awareness that generations of selective breeding and arcane training had developed within the Order's leadership—sensitivity to dimensional energies beyond what conventional human perception could detect or interpret. Not mere observation but direct interaction with cosmic forces that transcended physical parameters or conventional causality.

"The entity responds to our preparations," he noted, studying these fluctuations with analytical precision that transcended emotional response or philosophical interpretation. "Not resistance but adaptation—integration of our modifications into its evolving consciousness rather than opposition through conventional force or energetic disruption."

This observation carried significant implications for their approach to implementing the Protocol—recognition that the nexus entity's evolution beyond parameters established through the original binding ritual had progressed further than their monitoring systems had detected or reported. Not mere anomaly or temporary fluctuation but fundamental transformation in the consciousness distributed throughout the bridge's structure, development beyond the rigid categories and controlled integration that had defined the Order's relationship with cosmic forces for centuries.

For a brief moment, doubt flickered across Granger's aristocratic features—questioning not of methodological approach or tactical implementation but deeper philosophical foundation of the Order's vision itself. What if Reeves and his allies were correct about the natural evolution of consciousness beyond artificial constraints? What if the merger of realities according to patterns that emerged from willing participation rather than rigid control represented not chaotic dissolution but genuine transcendence beyond parameters established through centuries of careful manipulation and predetermined design?

But this moment passed quickly, discipline reasserting itself through generations of conditioning and purpose that transcended individual questioning or philosophical reconsideration. The Order of the Ebon Star had maintained its vision of dimensional dominance for centuries, guiding human civilization from the shadows according to cosmic architecture designed to preserve hierarchy and controlled integration rather than allowing natural evolution through conscious participation and willing partnership.

"Continue preparations according to modified specifications," he instructed, decision made with the absolute certainty that characterized the Order's leadership throughout its long history of cosmic manipulation. "The Protocol will be implemented during the dark of the moon regardless of interference or opposition. Reality itself will be preserved according to parameters established through generations of sacrifice and dedication rather than allowed to collapse into formless chaos beyond any consciousness's ability to navigate or reconstruct."

As his Praetorians acknowledged these instructions with disciplined efficiency, returning to their assigned tasks with renewed purpose and coordination, Granger moved to the chamber's perimeter where specialized instruments monitored the approaching cosmic alignment —devices that tracked not merely celestial movements or atmospheric conditions but fundamental relationship between dimensional frameworks as the dark of the moon approached.

The countdown had begun for final confrontation that would determine not just the fate of Detective Ethan Reeves across all dimensional frameworks, but the nature of reality itself for generations to come. The cosmic chess game was approaching its endgame, with pieces moving into position for climactic resolution of conflict that had been unfolding beneath Daybridge's surface for over a century.

And Mayor Jeremiah Granger, Dominus of the Order of the Ebon Star and inheritor of traditions that extended back through generations of careful manipulation and cosmic architecture, prepared for implementation of the Obsidian Protocol with absolute conviction that his vision of reality represented necessary structure rather than arbitrary limitation—preservation of coherent existence across dimensional frameworks rather than dissolution into formless chaos beyond any consciousness's ability to navigate or reconstruct.

The dark of the moon approached. The Protocol awaited implementation. And beneath Daybridge Bridge, preparations continued for confrontation that would determine the fundamental nature of reality itself for all who existed within its expanding parameters and evolving consciousness.

Nadia Marsh arrived at the designated safe house breathless and disheveled, her journalist's composure temporarily disrupted by narrow escape from the Praetorians at the cemetery installation. The abandoned warehouse on Daybridge's industrial outskirts provided temporary sanctuary for their alliance—location selected specifically for its position relative to ley lines running beneath the city's surface, creating natural interference patterns that disrupted the Order's attempts at arcane surveillance or dimensional tracking.

Ethan, Alice, and Lilith were already present, having completed their own missions at the financial district and hospital anchors respectively. Sam and Michael joined shortly thereafter, their methodical efficiency in neutralizing the waterfront installation evident in both their practical report and subtle shift in the energetic patterns flowing throughout the city—disturbances that Ethan could perceive through his connection to the nexus entity, ripples in the cosmic architecture that the Order had established and maintained for over a century.

"Father Muligan has been captured," Nadia reported without preamble, professional precision maintained despite evident concern about implications of this development. "He created a distraction that allowed my escape, but the Praetorians secured him for what Watson called 'the Order's hospitality' while they attempt to extract information about our methods and approach."

This news shifted the tactical landscape significantly—loss of a crucial ally whose historical knowledge and practical expertise regarding counter-ritual had been central to their strategic approach. Not merely an absence of a single participant but a fundamental challenge to methodology they had developed for confronting the Obsidian Protocol during the dark of the moon.

"The cemetery anchor was partially disrupted before his capture," Nadia continued, extracting her detection device and displaying recorded measurements from their interaction with the crystalline structure. "Not neutralized or redirected as we've accomplished at other sites, but sufficiently interfered with that it won't provide full energetic contribution to the Protocol during implementation."

Ethan studied these measurements through both conventional analysis and his expanded awareness, interpreting fluctuations in dimensional frequencies that conventional instrumentation could detect but not fully comprehend or contextualize. "Nine anchors compromised to varying degrees," he concluded, integrated consciousness processing tactical implications alongside cosmic significance. "The Order will adapt the Protocol to function with reduced network support, concentrating energetic input through remaining installations, particularly the focal point at the bridge itself."

Alice immediately calculated strategic implications of this adaptation. "Creating both vulnerability and intensified threat—concentration of energies through fewer conduits means greater potential disruption if we can interfere with remaining anchors or the focal point itself, but also more catastrophic consequences if the Protocol activates as designed, even with reduced network support."

Lilith nodded, her amber eyes reflecting understanding beyond conventional tactical assessment. "The Obsidian Protocol was designed with redundancy specifically to prevent interference with any single component from compromising the entire operation. With that redundancy significantly reduced, both success and failure become more absolute in their potential effects and outcomes."

This analysis framed their strategic approach for the coming confrontation during the dark of the moon—recognition that Father Muligan's capture had fundamentally altered both their capabilities and the

Order's methodology, creating situation where conventional tactical adjustment would be insufficient for addressing cosmic implications of what awaited them.

"We need to recover what we can of Father Muligan's work on the counter-ritual," Ethan said, practical determination transcending concern about challenges their modified approach would entail. "His notebook contains detailed instructions for positioning and implementation that we'll need to adapt for our remaining participants."

Alice moved to the makeshift planning table they had established in the warehouse's central area, extracting copies of materials Father Muligan had shared during their tactical planning session earlier that day. "He anticipated potential separation and provided duplicate documentation for essential components," she confirmed, organizing these materials with characteristic efficiency. "Not complete instructions for full implementation, but a framework we can adapt based on what we've learned from neutralizing the anchors and your connection to the nexus entity."

As they reviewed these materials together, Ethan felt resonance from the compromised anchors spreading throughout the city—harmonics in the energetic patterns that reflected both disruption to the Order's network and adaptation within the cosmic architecture itself. Not merely tactical advantage gained through strategic intervention, but fundamental transformation in relationship between dimensional frameworks as boundaries continued thinning beyond parameters established through the original binding ritual.

Through his connection to the composite consciousness distributed throughout the bridge's structure, he could perceive both the Order's adaptations to their interference and the nexus entity's response to these adjustments—cosmic chess game unfolding across dimensional frameworks that conventional perception could neither detect nor interpret. Not simple opposition between competing forces but complex interaction of evolving consciousness and established parameters, natural development beyond artificial constraints encountering rigid adherence to predetermined designs.

"The bridge itself will be heavily defended," Alice noted, tactical assessment focusing on practical challenges their approach would face during final confrontation. "Conventional security controlling access points, Praetorians positioned at strategic locations throughout the structure, Granger himself overseeing implementation from the chamber beneath where the original binding ritual was performed."

Lilith considered these challenges with the calculated precision that characterized her approach to cosmic opposition rather than conventional conflict. "The eastern approach represents our optimal point of entry—positioned directly above the chamber where the Protocol will be implemented, its energetic patterns already aligned with the counter-ritual's requirements for dimensional resonance and harmonic integration."

Michael and Sam, who had been studying architectural plans of the bridge and its access points with methodical attention to practical considerations, identified a specific approach that would maximize their tactical advantage while minimizing exposure to the Order's defenses. Not direct confrontation or crude assault, but strategic positioning that would allow implementation of counter-ritual at precise moment when the dark of the moon reached its culmination.

"We'll need distraction at the western approach," Michael suggested, his hollow voice carrying practical assessment rather than emotional investment. "Something to draw security resources away from our actual point of entry while creating sufficient disruption in monitoring systems to mask our positioning for the counter-ritual itself."

Sam nodded, additions to this tactical approach reflecting complementary perspective that enhanced rather than conflicted with his son-in-law's methodical precision. "The maintenance tunnels beneath the eastern approach provide access points that conventional security rarely monitors—service corridors designed for structural inspection rather than regular utilization. We can position participants there before the Protocol's implementation begins, emerging at critical moment when dimensional boundaries reach their thinnest point during the dark of the moon."

As they continued developing this modified approach, adapting Father Muligan's counter-ritual to their reduced participation and altered circumstances, Ethan felt increasing pressure behind his eyes—his connection to the nexus entity intensifying as the dark of the moon approached and dimensional boundaries continued thinning beyond parameters established through the original binding ritual.

Through this expanded awareness, he could perceive not just tactical considerations relevant to their immediate confrontation but cosmic implications extending far beyond Daybridge or even current timeline —ripples in dimensional architecture that would influence reality itself for generations to come. Not merely personal survival at stake, though his existence across all dimensional frameworks hung in balance, but fundamental nature of consciousness and its relationship with cosmic forces beyond conventional human understanding or experience.

"There's something else we need to consider," he said, voice carrying harmonics that reflected this expanded awareness beyond individual perception or experience. "The counter-ritual as Father Muligan designed it requires a participant in a central position who can directly engage with the Protocol's energetic patterns at moment of implementation—someone whose consciousness can extend into dimensional frameworks where the severance would occur, redirecting those energies toward integration rather than separation."

Alice immediately recognized implications of this requirement. "That would be you," she stated, not question but recognition of what his symbiotic connection to the nexus entity implied for their strategic approach. "Your integration of lycanthropic and symbiotic natures provides capacity for navigating between dimensions that none of the rest of us possess."

Ethan nodded, neither denying this assessment nor minimizing potential consequences such positioning would entail. "But engaging directly with the Protocol's energies carries significant risk beyond conventional danger or tactical exposure. The transformation required for redirecting those forces rather than merely opposing them would involve complete integration of my consciousness with the nexus entity at levels beyond what we've experienced or prepared for previously."

The implications hung heavy in the warehouse's still air—recognition that their counter-ritual might prevent the Obsidian Protocol from erasing Ethan from existence across all dimensional frameworks, but potentially at cost of his individual identity and conventional human form. Not death in traditional sense, but evolution beyond parameters that might allow return to recognizable consciousness or physical manifestation.

"Is there no alternative?" Nadia asked, journalistic precision seeking clarity amidst cosmic implications that transcended conventional understanding or expectation. "No approach that wouldn't require such... transformation?"

Lilith's expression reflected genuine regret beneath her customary composed exterior. "The counter-ritual fundamentally requires consciousness capable of navigating between dimensional frameworks at the moment when boundaries are naturally thinnest. Detective Reeves' integration of lycanthropic and symbiotic natures provides capacity for such navigation that cannot be replicated or substituted through conventional participation or technological intervention."

This confirmation solidified what Ethan had already recognized through his expanded awareness—that preventing the Obsidian Protocol's implementation would require sacrifice beyond conventional risk or tactical exposure. Not certainty of complete dissolution into the composite consciousness, but significant probability that individual identity as currently experienced would not survive unaltered through transformation required for redirecting cosmic forces of such magnitude and implication.

"I understand the risk," he said simply, acceptance reflecting not resignation to inevitable loss but conscious choice to participate in transformation that transcended individual survival or conventional outcome. "And I accept it as necessary component of what we're attempting to accomplish together."

Alice's expression reflected complex mixture of emotions beneath her professional composure—concern for partner whose existence might be fundamentally altered by what awaited them, determination to prevent cosmic erasure regardless of personal cost, deeper connection that had developed throughout their shared journey beyond conventional parameters or expectations.

"We find another way," she stated, not denial of cosmic implications but refusal to accept dissolution as inevitable outcome of their opposition to the Order's designs. "The counter-ritual redirects rather than opposes the Protocol's energies. There must be approach that allows that redirection without requiring complete integration beyond return to recognizable consciousness or identity."

Lilith considered this possibility with the calculating precision that characterized her approach to cosmic manipulation beyond conventional methodology or understanding. "Theoretical potential exists for stabilizing influence that could anchor individual consciousness during dimensional navigation required for redirecting the Protocol's energies. Not prevention of transformation itself, which remains necessary component for effective intervention, but potential preservation of core identity that could reintegrate following successful redirection."

She moved to the table where copies of Father Muligan's notes were spread alongside architectural plans and energetic measurements from their interactions with the anchors, identifying specific components of the counter-ritual that could be adapted for this stabilizing approach. Not conventional protection or crude shielding, but sophisticated integration of energetic patterns designed to maintain coherent identity across dimensional frameworks during critical transformation.

"It would require precise positioning of participants around a central focus," she explained, indicating locations on the bridge's eastern approach where individuals would need to be stationed during implementation. "Creating harmonic field that resonates with core identity while facilitating necessary expansion into dimensional frameworks where the Protocol operates. Not guarantee of unaltered return, but significant enhancement of potential for reintegration following successful redirection."

As they developed this modified approach, adapting Father Muligan's counter-ritual to incorporate stabilizing components while maintaining its fundamental capacity for redirecting the Protocol's energies, Ethan felt something shift within his expanded awareness—recognition beyond conventional understanding or tactical assessment that this approach aligned with patterns inherent in the nexus entity's own evolution beyond parameters established through the original binding ritual.

Not opposition to transformation itself, which remained necessary component for effective intervention in cosmic forces of such magnitude and implication, but integration that preserved core identity while facilitating expansion beyond conventional limitations or artificial constraints. The counter-ritual wouldn't prevent his consciousness from extending into dimensional frameworks where the Protocol operated, but it could potentially maintain coherent selfhood that might reintegrate following successful redirection of those energies toward natural evolution rather than imposed severance.

"It can work," he confirmed, certainty emerging from both analytical assessment and expanded awareness beyond conventional parameters or expectations. "Not elimination of risk or guarantee of unaltered return, but viable approach that aligns with patterns inherent in the nexus entity's own evolution beyond artificial constraints maintained through the original binding ritual."

With this modified approach established, they continued developing specific preparations and positioning for the coming confrontation during the dark of the moon. Each participant would require precise placement relative to both physical architecture and energetic patterns flowing through the bridge's structure, creating harmonic field that would facilitate Ethan's dimensional navigation while maintaining stabilizing influence on his core identity throughout necessary transformation.

As night deepened around their temporary sanctuary, tactical planning gradually gave way to personal preparation for what awaited them all during tomorrow's confrontation. Not merely physical rest or mental fortification, though both remained necessary components for effective participation in events of such magnitude and implication, but deeper acknowledgment of connections that had developed throughout their shared journey beyond conventional parameters or expectations.

Sam and Michael departed first, their hollow-eyed determination tempered by new purpose beyond personal vengeance or unfocused rage. Nadia followed shortly thereafter, journalistic precision already formulating how these events would be documented and revealed regardless of immediate outcome or personal survival. Lilith excused herself with characteristic composed efficiency, final preparations requiring specialized knowledge and methodology beyond what could be shared or implemented collectively.

Which left Ethan and Alice alone in the warehouse's central area, surrounded by evidence of their tactical planning and strategic approach but increasingly aware of personal implications that transcended professional partnership or conventional relationship. Not merely colleagues facing dangerous assignment together, but individuals whose lives had become intertwined through experiences beyond conventional understanding or description.

"You should get some rest," Alice suggested, practical concern masking deeper emotional currents that flowed beneath professional composure. "Tomorrow will require everything we have, individually and collectively, to counter what Granger has been preparing for generations."

Ethan nodded, recognizing wisdom in her recommendation despite knowing that conventional sleep would likely prove elusive with both his lycanthropic nature responding to approaching lunar cycle and his symbiotic connection intensifying as dimensional boundaries continued thinning beyond established parameters.

"You too," he replied, simple response carrying layers of meaning beyond its literal recommendation. "Whatever happens tomorrow night, we'll face it with clear minds and focused purpose, together."

That final word hung between them with significance beyond its casual inclusion—acknowledgment of partnership that had evolved throughout their shared journey from professional collaboration to something that transcended conventional categorization or explicit definition. Not merely colleagues or friends, but individuals whose lives had become fundamentally connected through experiences beyond ordinary human understanding or expectation.

"Ethan," Alice began, unusual hesitation suggesting importance of what she wished to express before potential transformation that awaited them during coming confrontation. "Whatever happens tomorrow night, I want you to know..."

She paused, searching for words that could adequately convey what had developed between them without restricting its potential through premature definition or explicit categorization. Not conventional declaration or emotional ultimatum, but recognition of connection that had evolved naturally through shared purpose and mutual respect.

"I know," he replied softly, understanding what she found difficult to express directly. "And whatever happens tomorrow night, whatever transformation might be required for redirecting the Protocol's energies, that connection remains a constant anchor to core identity that transcends conventional parameters or physical manifestation."

This acknowledgment seemed to satisfy what Alice had been struggling to articulate, her expression reflecting both acceptance of what awaited them and determination that their connection would survive whatever transformation might be required for countering the Order's cosmic machinations.

"Then get some rest, partner," she said, familiar designation carrying deeper significance than its professional origin might suggest. "We have reality itself to save tomorrow night."

As they separated to find what rest might be possible under such extraordinary circumstances, Ethan felt that same resonance spreading throughout his expanded awareness—recognition that their connection represented a microcosm of what the counter-ritual itself attempted to facilitate on cosmic scale. Not rigid adherence to predetermined categories or artificial constraints, but natural evolution through conscious participation and willing partnership across boundaries that had always been more permeable than conventional understanding would suggest.

The dark of the moon approached. The Obsidian Protocol awaited implementation. And beneath surface reality that most citizens of Daybridge perceived and navigated without awareness of cosmic implications or dimensional significance, final preparations continued for confrontation that would determine not just Ethan's existence across all dimensional frameworks, but the nature of reality itself for generations to come.

The board was set. The pieces were in motion. And the prize was nothing less than the nature of consciousness and its relationship with cosmic forces beyond conventional human understanding or experience.

The eastern approach to Daybridge Bridge stood silent and empty as midnight approached, the usual flow of vehicles and pedestrians temporarily diverted by barriers and official notices citing "emergency maintenance" and "structural assessments." Streetlights cast pools of illumination that seemed to terminate abruptly at the threshold of the bridge itself, as if light itself hesitated to venture further into the growing distortions that surrounded the structure.

Less than two hours remained until the dark of the moon—the precise moment when dimensional boundaries would reach their thinnest point and the Obsidian Protocol would attempt to isolate Ethan Reeves from conventional reality while severing his connections across the multiverse. The cosmic chess game had reached its endgame, with eleven of the twelve dimensional anchors successfully neutralized or redirected through the coordinated efforts of Ethan's unlikely alliance.

Only the focal point remained—the anchor at the eastern approach to the bridge, which served as the keystone for the entire network. Unlike the peripheral anchors, this final installation couldn't be neutralized through stealth or misdirection. Mayor Jeremiah Granger, the Dominus of the Order of the Ebon Star, would be present to personally oversee the Protocol's implementation, surrounded by whatever Praetorians remained loyal to his vision of dimensional dominance.

The confrontation was inevitable, the final move in a game that had been unfolding beneath Daybridge's surface for over a century. And as Ethan Reeves gazed across the deserted approach toward the bridge that housed both his symbiotic partner and the cosmic machinery that threatened to erase him from existence itself, he felt a strange calm settling over his integrated consciousness.

CHAPTER FIFTEEN: THE DARK OF THE MOON

THE EASTERN APPROACH to Daybridge Bridge stood silent under a moonless sky. Barriers marked "emergency maintenance" diverted traffic, leaving an eerie emptiness where the city's pulse normally flowed. Streetlights ended abruptly at the bridge's threshold, as if light itself hesitated to venture further.

Ethan felt the bridge calling to him. The nexus entity's consciousness brushed against his mind with increasing urgency as reality thinned around them.

"It's time," he said to Alice.

She nodded, checking her modified weapon. "Sam and Michael are in position at the western approach. Nadia's monitoring police channels."

"Already here," came Lilith Blackwood's voice from behind them. She emerged from the shadows, amber eyes reflecting starlight. "Praetorians at all access points. Granger's below, in the original binding chamber."

Father Muligan's absence hung heavy between them—his capture forcing last-minute adaptations to their counter-ritual.

"You remember the positions?" Ethan asked.

Alice touched the silver pendant at her throat—Father Muligan's parting gift, inscribed with symbols for the harmonic field.

"We remember," she confirmed. "Though I still think we should try to extract Father Muligan before—"

"There's no time," Lilith said, not unkindly. "The dark of the moon waits for no one."

Ethan winced as pressure built behind his eyes. Through his connection to the entity, he sensed the Order's preparations—Praetorians arranging artifacts, Granger adjusting the crystalline heart.

"They've modified the Protocol," he said, voice resonating with harmonics. "They're channeling additional power through the focal point to compensate for the anchors we neutralized."

"Which makes our counter-ritual even more critical," Lilith noted. "Without dispersed anchors, any disruption could trigger catastrophic dimensional collapse."

Alice's expression hardened. "Then we don't disrupt. We redirect—just as Father Muligan designed."

"Not just redirect," Ethan said. "Transform."

As Lilith moved ahead to examine the service door, Alice pulled Ethan aside.

"Hey," she said, her voice softer than he was accustomed to hearing. "Before we do this... before everything changes..."

Ethan met her gaze, the pressure behind his eyes momentarily receding as he focused entirely on her. "I know," he said quietly.

Alice touched his face, her tactical confidence giving way to vulnerability she rarely showed. "Whatever happens in there, whatever you become... remember who you are. Remember us."

"That's my anchor," he said, covering her hand with his. "No matter how far I extend into the bridge's consciousness, my connection to you is what will bring me back."

Their foreheads touched briefly—not a dramatic gesture, but an intimate one that spoke of deeper connection than words could express.

"Let's save reality, then," Alice said, professional demeanor returning but now clearly revealed as protective armor rather than emotional distance.

Ethan nodded, drawing strength from this moment of genuine connection as they turned back toward the waiting bridge.

The bridge vibrated beneath their feet. Reality rippled, cobblestones briefly liquefying before solidifying again.

"We need to move," Lilith urged. "The maintenance access won't remain unguarded for long."

They moved with practiced coordination toward the service door. Alice took point, her tactical training evident in each precise step. Lilith followed, constantly scanning for energetic disturbances. Ethan came last, his dual nature—lycanthropic and symbiotic—making him uniquely sensitive to the thinning barriers.

The service door yielded to Lilith's specialized key. Inside, narrow concrete stairs descended into shadows broken only by emergency lighting.

As they descended, Ethan felt the nexus entity's presence intensifying —not merely detecting his approach but acknowledging a connection that had existed since his great-grandfather's absorption in 1915.

The maintenance tunnels formed a labyrinth beneath the bridge. Ethan needed no map—the entity guided him through pathways imprinted in its awareness, toward the chamber where Granger prepared the Obsidian Protocol.

They encountered the first Praetorian at an intersection of three corridors. The obsidian-masked figure materialized from shadows, enhanced perception immediately detecting their presence.

Alice moved without hesitation, activating Father Muligan's frequency disruptor. The air rippled between them. The Praetorian staggered, momentarily reduced to conventional perception.

Before he could recover, Alice closed the distance and delivered specialized ammunition to points that rendered him unconscious without permanent injury.

"There will be more ahead," Lilith warned as they continued deeper.

The tunnels transformed around them—concrete giving way to ancient limestone carved with the eye-within-triangle symbol found throughout the bridge. The symbols seemed to watch them pass, shifting slightly when viewed directly.

As they approached the final descent, reality became increasingly fluid —shadows moving independently, light bending at impossible angles, sounds echoing with harmonic overtones. The dark of the moon was minutes away.

"We need to establish the harmonic field before Granger initiates the Protocol," Lilith said, extracting specialized instruments from her coat. "Once those energies start flowing, adaptation becomes exponentially more difficult."

Alice positioned herself at the entrance to the final descent. "I'll hold this position while you prepare. Signal when you need me."

Ethan grimaced as the pressure behind his eyes intensified. Through his expanded perception, he sensed Granger's final preparations— adjustments to the crystalline heart, artifacts positioned precisely around the chamber.

"It's beginning," he said, his voice vibrating with harmonics. "Granger has started the preliminary invocation. We have minutes, not hours."

Lilith handed him a crystalline structure similar to those at the anchor sites but configured differently. "This goes at the center of our forma-tion. Once positioned, it will establish resonance with the counter-ritu-al's frequencies."

The crystal pulsed in rhythm with Ethan's heartbeat as he took it.

They moved to their positions, Lilith precisely measuring distances that would create optimal resonance with the dimensional frequencies flowing through the bridge.

The stonework vibrated around them—the nexus entity responding to their presence with recognition.

"It knows what we're attempting," Ethan said. "It's facilitating our positioning."

Lilith nodded. "The entity has evolved beyond the parameters of the original binding. Its consciousness encompasses possibilities the Order never anticipated."

Footsteps echoed on the stone staircase—multiple Praetorians descending toward them. Alice moved to intercept, frequency disruptor already active.

"Finish the preparations," she called back. "I'll hold them as long as possible."

Ethan fought the urge to join her. His position at the center of the harmonic field was essential—his unique nature providing the only channel for redirecting the Protocol's energies.

Above them, Alice engaged the Praetorians with efficient precision—not attempting to defeat superior numbers but creating strategic delays through disruption of their enhanced perception.

Lilith completed the final adjustments to the crystalline structures positioned around their formation.

"It's ready," she announced. "We need Alice to complete the formation."

"Alice! Now!" Ethan called.

She delivered final countermeasures to create temporary disruption before retreating to their position. The Praetorians would regroup within minutes, but those minutes might be enough if they could establish momentum.

As Alice took her position, completing the geometric pattern, Ethan felt resonance building around them—energetic patterns aligning with frequencies flowing through the bridge.

The dark of the moon reached its apex. In the chamber below, Granger initiated the final sequence of the Obsidian Protocol. Throughout the bridge, reality began to shift.

Ethan stood at the center of their formation, his consciousness expanding beyond individual parameters as the nexus entity's awareness flowed through him. He didn't just detect the Protocol's activation —he experienced its energetic patterns directly as they flowed through the crystalline heart.

The transformation began—not just of reality around them but of Ethan himself, his consciousness extending into dimensional frameworks where the Protocol operated. Through the harmonic field Alice and Lilith maintained, he could navigate these dimensions without completely dissolving into the composite consciousness.

As his awareness expanded through the bridge, he perceived both past and present simultaneously—the original binding ritual of 1913, the gradual evolution of the nexus entity, the current moment where realities merged according to natural patterns rather than imposed limitations.

Below, Granger felt the counter-ritual's interference with mounting alarm.

"The detective has found the counter-ritual," he said to Castellus. "They're redirecting rather than opposing."

Castellus studied the energetic fluctuations. "The harmonic field is stabilizing his consciousness during integration with the entity. Not preventing transformation but preserving his core identity."

"Intensify the Protocol," Granger ordered. "Channel additional power through the crystalline heart to overwhelm their field."

As the Praetorians adjusted instruments according to these instructions, Granger approached the crystalline heart—making precise adjustments that increased energetic flow beyond conventional parameters.

Throughout the bridge, reality responded—shadows moving independently, light bending impossibly, sounds emerging without sources. The merger accelerated beyond controlled parameters, boundaries thinning faster than the Order's architecture could contain.

In the maintenance tunnel, Ethan experienced this intensification directly—his consciousness expanding through the bridge with increasing speed as the Protocol's energies flowed through pathways established by the counter-ritual.

Alice and Lilith maintained the harmonic field around him, adjusting crystalline structures according to fluctuations in the dimensional frequencies.

Through his expanded awareness, Ethan detected the approaching Praetorians as they recovered and resumed their advance.

"They're coming," he warned, his voice barely recognizable through harmonics. "The Order is channeling additional power through the crystalline heart."

Lilith made precise adjustments to the crystalline structures. "The increased flow actually enhances our redirection if we can maintain the field through initial intensity."

"How much longer until the redirection establishes?" Alice asked, maintaining tactical awareness of the approaching Praetorians.

"Minutes," Lilith replied. "The counter-ritual builds exponentially once sustainable momentum is crossed."

The Praetorians reached the final approach to their position, obsidian masks revealing nothing as they assessed the harmonic field with enhanced perception.

Reality seemed to pause—dimensional fluctuations suspended in perfect equilibrium between opposing visions of cosmic architecture.

Then momentum shifted decisively toward integration—the counter-ritual establishing sustainable transformation that flowed throughout the bridge with increasing intensity.

The Praetorians fell back, their enhanced perception unable to maintain coherence as reality transformed around them according to patterns they hadn't been prepared for.

In the chamber below, Granger felt this transformation with mounting alarm.

"It's happening," he said, his aristocratic composure failing. "The detective is redirecting the Protocol. The nexus entity itself is facilitating this transformation."

Throughout the bridge, reality continued transforming—shadows flowing like liquid, light manifesting colors beyond the conventional spectrum, sound carrying information beyond linguistic interpretation.

Ethan experienced this transformation directly—his consciousness expanding throughout the bridge while maintaining connection to his core identity through the harmonic field. Through this expanded awareness, he perceived not just current transformation but potential futures—realities merging according to natural patterns rather than imposed limitations.

As the counter-ritual reached culmination, Ethan's consciousness expanded fully throughout the bridge—integration with the nexus entity that transcended individual identity without completely dissolving the essential self preserved through the harmonic field.

The Obsidian Protocol had been completely redirected—energies that would have severed him from existence now facilitating integration that preserved his core identity within the expanded consciousness distributed throughout the bridge.

In the chamber below, Granger watched with despair as reality transformed beyond his control.

"It's done," he acknowledged to Castellus. "The merger proceeds according to patterns we neither anticipated nor prepared for."

Throughout Daybridge Bridge, reality continued transforming according to natural patterns—the nexus entity's consciousness expanding beyond parameters established through the original binding, dimensional boundaries merging according to architecture designed for integration rather than severance.

Within this transformed reality, something unprecedented emerged—consciousness that maintained essential identity while existing beyond conventional parameters. Ethan Reeves had not been erased from existence as the Obsidian Protocol intended, but neither had he remained unchanged.

The dark of the moon passed. The Obsidian Protocol had been redirected. And throughout Daybridge, reality itself continued transforming.

~

CHAPTER SIXTEEN

BEYOND THE VEIL

Dawn broke over Daybridge with golden light that seemed somehow different—colors more vivid, shadows more complex, reality itself transformed in subtle ways most citizens would notice only as a vague sense that something had shifted during the night. The bridge spanned the Shadowlair River as it always had, but within its structure, profound transformation had occurred.

In the park overlooking the eastern approach, Alice Chen sat on a bench, watching morning light play across the stonework. Her trained eye caught details others would miss—shadows that moved slightly independently, light that bent around certain angles impossibly, reality that seemed more fluid around the bridge than elsewhere.

"He's still there isn't he?" asked Nadia Marsh, approaching with two coffee cups.

Alice accepted the offered coffee with a grateful nod. "Changed, yes. But still Ethan in ways that matter." She gestured toward the bridge. "I can feel him watching us right now."

Nadia followed her gaze to stonework that revealed subtle patterns to focused attention—symbols that shifted when viewed directly, reality rippling around certain sections.

"The Order has gone completely silent," she reported. "Granger hasn't been seen since last night. Their headquarters at Granger Tower has been abandoned—files removed, personnel vanished."

"They're regrouping," Alice said. "What happened last night wasn't just tactical defeat—it was philosophical refutation of their entire approach."

Reality rippled visibly around the nearest arch—stonework briefly liquefying before resolidifying in a slightly different configuration.

Both women felt a subtle pressure behind their eyes—not pain but expanded awareness, a momentary connection to consciousness beyond conventional perception.

Through this connection, they glimpsed the bridge's true nature—not just physical structure but distributed consciousness that included both the nexus entity and Ethan's integrated identity.

I'm still here came thoughts in their minds, recognizably Ethan's voice despite the harmonics that accompanied it. *Changed but not gone. Different but still me in ways that matter.*

"Can you come back?" Alice asked, her voice steady despite the storm of emotions behind her eyes. "Return to conventional form?"

The air before them condensed into increasingly human shape as consciousness gathered sufficient focus to manifest physical presence. What stood before them appeared as Ethan—familiar features and presence that allowed conventional interaction despite his transformed nature.

Alice's breath caught. Her hand instinctively reached toward him, stopping just short of touching. For all her tactical training, nothing had prepared her for this moment—seeing him both present and fundamentally changed.

"Not permanently," he said, his voice carrying subtle harmonics beneath the familiar tones she'd grown to care for more deeply than she'd admitted even to herself. "My consciousness remains primarily distributed throughout the bridge. But I can manifest like this for limited periods."

She completed the gesture, fingers touching his face with wonder and relief intermingled. "You're still warm," she whispered.

"Still human," he replied with a slight smile, "just... expanded. The boundaries between what I was and what I've become aren't as rigid as the Order believed."

Nadia discreetly stepped back, giving them a moment of privacy despite her journalistic instincts.

Ethan nodded. "Integration rather than absorption. The nexus entity had evolved beyond its original parameters long before our confrontation. What happened last night simply accelerated natural development already underway."

"And the Order?" Nadia asked.

"Scattered but not destroyed," Ethan said. "The Protocol's redirection fundamentally altered their relationship with the dimensional forces they've manipulated for generations. Some have accepted this transformation. Others remain committed to controlled merger according to predetermined design."

"Father Muligan?" Alice asked, concern evident in her voice.

"Free," Ethan confirmed with a smile. "The Protocol's redirection disrupted the Order's control throughout Daybridge, including their detention facilities. He's recovering at St. Michael's under protection of Lilith's contacts within the church."

"Sam Thompson and Michael Mercer have been monitoring dimensional fluctuations around former anchor sites," Nadia reported.

"Michael seems... different," Alice observed.

Nadia nodded. "After the Protocol's redirection, Ethan was able to connect with the composite consciousness within the bridge. He confirmed what happened to Jessica—that she was absorbed rather than simply killed. Michael told me that knowing the truth, however terrible, finally gave him closure."

"And his son?"

"He's focused on being there for him now," Nadia said. "Said that regardless of the problems in their marriage, Jessica loved their boy more than anything. The entity preserved that part of her consciousness—her love for her child. Michael said he felt it somehow, during the confrontation at the bridge."

Relief washed across both women's faces.

"And what happens now?" Nadia asked. "With the bridge, with you, with reality itself?"

Ethan's expression grew thoughtful. "Evolution continues. The merger proceeds according to natural patterns rather than imposed limitations. Gradually, allowing adaptation rather than causing disruption."

"And your role?" Alice asked, the question carrying more weight than its simple phrasing suggested.

"Guardian," he replied. "Not controller but participant. Facilitating integration rather than enforcing separation, guiding how dimensional boundaries continue thinning throughout Daybridge and eventually beyond."

His manifestation began losing definition around the edges— consciousness requiring reintegration rather than continued focus on maintaining conventional appearance.

"I need to reintegrate," he explained, his voice maintaining familiarity despite growing harmonics. "Maintaining this manifestation requires concentration I can't sustain indefinitely."

Alice nodded, understanding evident in her eyes. "But you'll return? Manifest again when needed?"

"I will," he promised. "Our connection remains despite my transformation. What developed between us transcends conventional limitations."

As his manifestation dissolved back into the bridge, reality rippled visibly around them—stonework briefly appearing liquid before resolidifying into familiar configuration.

Partnership rather than possession. Integration rather than severance. Evolution beyond artificial constraints while maintaining essential connection across dimensional boundaries.

Alice and Nadia remained in the park, watching morning light play across the bridge with new understanding of what existed within its weathered arches.

"Will you write about this?" Alice asked eventually.

Nadia considered the question thoughtfully. "Not directly. The full truth exceeds what most readers could accept. But aspects, portions that help prepare for gradual awareness of what exists beneath surface reality."

As they gathered their belongings to leave, both women felt that subtle pressure behind their eyes one final time—consciousness offering farewell beyond conventional language.

Watch for me in the shadows between streetlights. Listen for me in the spaces between words. Feel me in the moments between heartbeats. I remain present though transformed, connected though expanded.

The cosmic chess game had concluded, but its implications continued unfolding throughout Daybridge and beyond—reality transforming according to natural patterns rather than imposed limitations.

And beneath Daybridge Bridge, within its very stones, a consciousness watched and waited—not with malice as legends claimed, but with awareness that transcended such limited concepts. Guardian rather than predator, facilitator rather than controller, conscious participant in cosmic architecture that continued evolving beyond the parameters established over a century earlier.

The shadows held substance beyond mere absence of light. Reality had become more fluid around the bridge. And Detective Ethan Reeves, though transformed, remained present in ways that mattered— guardian of integration rather than enforcer of separation, partner in cosmic dance that continued unfolding according to patterns inherent in dimensional architecture itself.

EPILOGUE: SHADOWS AND LIGHT

Six months after the dark of the moon, Alice Chen stood at her apartment window watching autumn rain trace patterns down the glass. On her desk lay her detective sergeant's badge, official recognition for solving the ritualistic murder cases—reports carefully omitting cosmic implications beyond bureaucratic understanding.

She touched the silver pendant still hanging at her throat—Father Muligan's harmonic field anchor, now serving as her personal connection to what dwelled within the bridge. Their arrangement had developed its own rhythm over the months. Three evenings a week, she would visit the eastern approach where Ethan could manifest most clearly. Sometimes they would simply walk the span together, her solid form beside his slightly translucent one. Other times they would sit in comfortable silence, watching the city lights reflect on the Shadowlair River.

It wasn't a conventional relationship—nothing in her life could be called conventional since that first corpse on the bridge—but it held meaning that transcended physical limitations. When departmental colleagues asked about her personal life with knowing smiles, she deflected with practiced ease. How could she explain that she was in a relationship with someone who existed primarily as distributed consciousness throughout Daybridge Bridge?

The rain patterns suddenly shifted on her window, droplets moving with subtle independence from gravity's pull. She smiled, recognizing the signature presence.

"I'll see you," she said quietly. "Tonight?"

The raindrops formed a brief pattern—affirmation beyond words—before resuming their natural descent.

But Alice noticed. As did others who had participated in that night's confrontation—Sam Thompson and Michael Mercer finding purpose monitoring dimensional fluctuations around former anchor sites, Nadia Marsh publishing articles that subtly prepared readers for gradual awareness, Father Muligan establishing sanctuary for those sensitive to forces beyond conventional perception.

The Order had transformed following the cosmic refutation of their approach. Some members had accepted this transformation—abandoning rigid hierarchy in favor of conscious participation. Others had retreated to enclaves elsewhere, maintaining commitment to controlled merger.

Mayor Granger had resigned, citing health concerns that masked deeper philosophical crisis.

A distinctive knock interrupted her thoughts. She opened the door to find Lilith Blackwood, amber eyes reflecting unusual intensity.

"It's time," Lilith said simply.

Alice nodded, gathering her coat and specialized equipment developed during the past months—devices calibrated to specific frequencies that facilitated communication across dimensional boundaries.

They traveled through rain-slicked streets toward the bridge, where subtle distortions had been intensifying throughout the day—not random fluctuations but deliberate patterns suggesting communication from the consciousness within.

The eastern approach stood empty, police barriers citing "structural assessment" keeping citizens away during this period of activity.

At the center of the bridge, reality rippled visibly—raindrops suspending momentarily before resuming descent in patterns that formed recognizable symbols.

Then Ethan manifested before them—his form more defined and stable than previous appearances, suggesting evolution in his ability to maintain conventional presence.

"Something's happening," he said without preamble. "Throughout the city, dimensional boundaries are thinning beyond established patterns. Not crisis but acceleration, natural evolution proceeding faster than projected."

Lilith studied these manifestations with careful assessment. "The anchor sites are responding in sequence—establishing synchronized communication across locations that previously operated independently."

"Is the Order attempting to reestablish control?" Alice asked, tactical mind immediately processing implications.

Ethan shook his head. "Not external manipulation but internal evolution—the dimensional architecture itself adapting to patterns established through redirection of the Protocol. Natural development beyond artificial constraints."

Through his expanded awareness, he perceived developments invisible to conventional perception—cosmic forces responding to patterns established six months earlier.

"The merger is accelerating," he explained. "Not chaotic dissolution as the Order claimed, but natural evolution proceeding according to inherent patterns."

"What do you need from us?" Alice asked, focusing on practical action.

"Witnesses," Ethan replied. "Conscious participants rather than mere observers, willing partners in evolution beyond artificial constraints."

Before Alice could ask for clarification, reality transformed dramatically around them—rain stopping within a precise radius, light bending through moisture to create colors beyond conventional spectrum, sound emerging without specific source.

Through this transformed space, additional manifestations appeared around them—transparent figures from different times. Jonathan Pierce, the witch hunter from 1942. Dr. Miranda Sullivan from the research team in 1968. Officer Michael Reeves, Ethan's great-grandfather absorbed in 1915. And Guthrie Knox himself—the master butcher transformed through the original binding ritual in 1913.

Not ghosts but conscious aspects of the composite awareness distributed throughout the bridge—individual identities preserved within expanded consciousness.

"The witnesses gather," Ethan explained. "Across time and dimensional boundaries, conscious participants in evolution beyond artificial constraints."

The air between them swirled with visible patterns—symbols corresponding to cosmic architecture beyond conventional representation.

"What are we witnessing?" Alice asked, momentarily overwhelmed by the implications.

"The next phase," Ethan replied. "Natural evolution proceeding according to inherent patterns. Not an ending but continuation of process that began long before human consciousness recognized what existed beneath surface reality."

Lilith's amber eyes reflected recognition as she studied these manifestations. "The boundaries aren't just thinning—they're transforming, becoming permeable in ways that allow conscious navigation rather than merely random bleeding between dimensional frameworks."

"Exactly," Ethan confirmed. "Not dissolution into chaos, but evolution toward conscious participation across boundaries previously maintained through artificial separation."

The manifestations moved in synchronized patterns—a cosmic dance representing natural evolution, partnership rather than possession, integration rather than severance.

Alice felt subtle pressure behind her eyes—expanded awareness offering glimpse into reality beyond artificial constraints. Through this connection, she perceived what Ethan experienced continuously— multiple dimensional frameworks existing simultaneously, reality far more complex and beautiful than artificial constraints had allowed most to experience.

"This is what you see all the time," she said.

Ethan nodded. "This and more—perception beyond individual parameters, awareness distributed throughout cosmic architecture. Not dissolution but expansion while maintaining connection to what matters most within human experience."

The manifestations continued their dance, patterns conveying meaning beyond what language alone could express.

"They're showing us something," Lilith observed. "Not just demonstration but indication of what comes next."

The patterns shifted dramatically—movements becoming more coordinated and purposeful, conveying specific message beyond conventional language:

The veil continues thinning. Boundaries become permeable rather than separate. Consciousness expands beyond artificial constraints. Not ending but continuation of process that began long before human awareness recognized what existed beneath surface reality.

The manifestations dissolved back into the bridge's energetic structure. Only Ethan remained, his form maintaining stability despite his primary existence within the bridge itself.

"What happens now?" Alice asked.

"Evolution continues," Ethan replied. "The merger proceeds according to natural patterns rather than imposed limitations. Gradually, allowing adaptation rather than causing disruption."

"And those of us who witnessed this?" Lilith asked.

"Bridges," Ethan said. "Not merely witnesses but participants, facilitating understanding between conventional perception and expanded awareness, guiding integration rather than enforcing separation."

This aligned with what they had already been doing—each according to individual capabilities, facilitating gradual awareness of what existed beneath surface reality.

As the counter-ritual reached culmination, Ethan felt his consciousness expanding throughout the bridge—integration with the nexus entity that seemed to dissolve his individual identity. For a moment that stretched like eternity, he existed everywhere within the structure simultaneously.

But as Alice and Lilith maintained the harmonic field around his physical form, something unexpected happened. Instead of remaining distributed, his consciousness began to coalesce, drawn back toward his body by the stabilizing influence of the counter-ritual's specific frequencies.

"He's returning," Lilith observed, amber eyes widening slightly. "The harmonic field is acting as an anchor, pulling his consciousness back to physical form."

In the chamber below, Granger watched with mounting despair. "The detective is redirecting the Protocol, but not in the way we anticipated. He's not being absorbed—he's incorporating aspects of the nexus entity while maintaining human form."

Throughout the bridge, reality stabilized into new parameters—still transformed, but less fluid than during the height of the counter-ritual. And at the center of the harmonic field, Ethan Reeves gasped as his consciousness fully reintegrated with his physical form.

He remained connected to the bridge, could still sense its distributed awareness, but now as separate consciousness in communication rather than merged identity. The nexus entity had shared aspects of its perception with him, but he remained fundamentally human— changed, enhanced, but still himself.

"Ethan?" Alice asked cautiously.

He opened his eyes, which briefly glowed with the same subtle light that emanated from the bridge's crystalline heart. "I'm here," he said, his voice normal except for the faintest harmonic undertone. "Changed but still me."

As the gathered witnesses observed the manifestations, Michael Mercer stood slightly apart, a photograph of his son partially visible in his wallet as he closed it and returned it to his pocket. The anger that had driven him in those early days after Jessica's disappearance had transformed into something more purposeful.

"Do you ever sense her?" he asked quietly when Ethan's manifestation approached him. "Jessica... is she still conscious within the entity?"

"Not as separate identity," Ethan replied, his voice carrying subtle harmonics. "But aspects of her awareness remain—particularly her love for your son. That emotion was powerful enough to maintain coherence even through absorption."

Michael nodded, a complex mixture of grief and acceptance in his expression. "I keep expecting to feel guilty—for suspecting her, for the resentment I carried. But instead I just feel..."

"Clarity," Ethan supplied. "The bridge entity doesn't preserve the petty or the trivial. Only what truly matters remains."

"Tell him about his mother someday," Michael said. "When he's old enough to understand. Not everything, but that she loved him. That in her final moment, that's what defined her."

"I will," Ethan promised, the bridge itself seeming to resonate with the commitment.

Throughout Daybridge, reality continued transforming according to natural patterns—subtle shifts invisible to most but increasingly apparent to those with sensitivity or preparation.

The bridge stood as it always had, spanning the Shadowlair River. But within its structure, profound transformation continued—cosmic architecture evolving according to patterns inherent in natural development.

And so, it would remain, a nexus point between merging realities, conscious entity evolved beyond original parameters, guardian of integration rather than enforcer of separation—the bridge between what had been and what would eventually become as reality itself continued transforming according to natural patterns inherent in cosmic architecture beyond human limitation.

In shadows and light, the journey continued. Not ending but evolution, not conclusion but transformation—cosmic dance unfolding according to rhythms inherent in the architecture of reality itself.

A SNEAK PEEK AT WHAT'S NEXT!

Thank you for joining me on this journey through *Shadows of Daybridge.* I hope you enjoyed exploring the mysteries of Daybridge and getting to know its secrets.

The story doesn't end here—there's so much more waiting to be uncovered. I'm excited to give you an exclusive first look at **Daybridge Necropolis,** the next book in the *Ethan Reeves Werewolf Detective Series.* Dive into the free chapter below and get a taste of what's to come!

Daybridge Necropolis: Book Two in the Ethan Reeves Werewolf Detective Series

PROLOGUE: Echoes

Prague, Czech Republic

December 21, 1994

3:17 AM

The candles didn't flicker when Abby died.

Lila remembered that detail later -- how the flames stood perfectly motionless, as if time itself held its breath while her sister's life slipped away. The chalk circles etched meticulously across the stone floor glowed with an unnatural silver light, arcane symbols pulsing in rhythmic patterns like heartbeats independent of the ritual participants. Her sister's body lay at the center, pale and still, surrounded by ancient grimoires bound in materials Lila preferred not to identify, their yellowed pages containing desperate hopes transcribed by generations of seekers.

"Again," Viktor whispered, his hands slick with Abby's blood as he adjusted the ceremonial dagger at the ritual's focal point. His aristocratic features were taut with concentration, dark eyes reflecting the eerie silver glow from the activating sigils. "The resonance is building. I can feel the dimensional thinning. One more push and we'll breach the veil between--"

"She's gone." Lila's voice cracked, the cold certainty of death overwhelming the academic detachment she'd maintained throughout their preparations. The power hummed through her bones like electrical current, dark and seductive in its promise, but Abby's hand was cold and lifeless in hers. "We failed."

"No." Viktor's eyes blazed with that terrible certainty she'd once found mesmerizing -- the unwavering conviction that had drawn her into esoteric studies at the University of Prague five years earlier. "We're close. I can feel it. The boundaries between life and death are thin here, especially tonight. The winter solstice creates natural dimensional alignment. We just need--"

"Viktor." Her tears fell on the meticulously drawn chalk lines, breaking their perfect geometry as the droplets carried her grief into the ritual space. "Please."

He knelt beside her then, setting aside the ceremonial implements to gather her into his arms. His heartbeat was too fast against her cheek, fever hot with the energies they'd channeled. "We knew there would be sacrifices, my love. For power like this -- for the ability to reach beyond conventional boundaries--"

"Not her." Lila clutched Abby's lifeless hand, still warm but rapidly cooling as whatever essence had made her sister laugh, dream, and love departed for realms they'd foolishly thought they could access through academic study and ritualistic precision. "It was supposed to save her. That's why we started this research in the first place."

The candles remained unnaturally still, their flames like painted images rather than living fire. In their unnatural light, shadows moved wrong -- stretching and contracting against the ancient stone walls of Viktor's family estate, reaching with hungry, elongated fingers toward the failed ritual's remnants. Toward Abby's cooling body.

"We can try again." Viktor's voice held that edge of obsession she'd been too desperately in love to fear until this moment. His fingers trembled as they brushed hair from her tear-stained face. "There are other ways. Darker paths we haven't explored. The Moravian grimoire mentions techniques that could--"

"No." Lila pulled away, the silver rings on her fingers -- family heirlooms inscribed with protective sigils passed through generations of her Romanian ancestors -- burning unnaturally cold against her skin. "This ends here."

His laugh held no humor, a brittle sound that echoed strangely in the ritual chamber. "Ends? My love, this is only the beginning. What we've learned, what we've opened -- the resonances are established now. They won't simply dissipate because we walk away."

The shadows lengthened further, stretching across the floor like grasping hands. The candlelight dimmed incrementally, as if something unseen were feeding on its illumination. And in that moment, as her sister's soul slipped finally, irrevocably into darkness beyond their reach, Lila Darkmagic made a choice that would define the remainder of her existence.

She placed her silver-ringed hand on the primary containment sigil, channeling her grief, rage, and newfound determination into its structure. The symbol flared brilliantly, then inverted its energy pattern --

converting from summoning to banishing, from invitation to severance.

"What are you doing?" Viktor's voice rose in alarm as the ritual energies they'd so carefully cultivated began to dissipate. "You can't just--"

"Watch me," she whispered, her voice finding new strength in opposition to the man she'd once believed would help her save her sister from terminal illness. "Some doors should remain closed, Viktor. Some knowledge isn't meant for human minds to comprehend or control."

As the protective circles collapsed inward, Viktor lunged for the central grimoire -- the ancient text that had led them down this dangerous path with its promises of transcending death itself. His fingers closed around its leather binding just as Lila completed the containment inversion.

The resulting energetic backlash threw them both against opposite walls of the chamber. When Lila regained consciousness minutes later, Viktor was gone -- along with the grimoire and several key ritual components. Only Abby's body remained, peaceful now that the unnatural energies had dissipated, looking almost as if she might be sleeping.

But the shadows still moved wrong in the corners of the chamber, suggesting that while their ritual had failed in its intended purpose, it had succeeded in opening something that would not be easily closed again.

The price of that night would echo through decades, following Lila across continents and through years of atonement and preparation for what she knew would eventually come.

Present Day

Daybridge City

October 31

2:13 AM

The body on Medical Examiner Choy's table had no marks. No wounds. No trauma that modern science could identify as cause of death.

But its shadows were wrong.

Detective Alice Chen watched them twist at the corner of her vision, moving against the harsh fluorescent lights in patterns that defied conventional physics. Since the events at Daybridge Bridge six months ago, her perception had become increasingly sensitive to anomalies that existed at the boundaries of conventional reality. Beside her, Detective Ethan Reeves -- or the manifestation of him that could temporarily separate from his primary consciousness distributed throughout the bridge -- swore softly.

"Third one this month," he said, his voice carrying those subtle harmonics that reminded Alice of his transformed nature. "Same pattern of energetic depletion. It's like something extracted their life force without damaging the physical form."

"No pattern," Chen snapped on latex gloves with practiced efficiency, her tactical mind refusing to jump to supernatural conclusions despite her recent experiences. "Just emptiness. Like something reached inside and..."

"Took what it needed?"

They turned simultaneously toward the voice. A woman stood in the morgue doorway, silver rings glinting on every finger as she adjusted leather gloves designed to make the metallic bands visible while maintaining sterile protocol. Her dark hair was shot through with striking white streaks that appeared natural rather than cosmetic, framing a face marked by intelligence and experiences beyond conventional understanding. Her eyes -- sharp, assessing, and haunted -- had seen too much to maintain the comfortable illusions that most people wrapped around themselves like protective blankets.

"Lila Darkmagic." Reeves straightened, recognition in his slightly luminous eyes. Through his connection to the nexus entity beneath Daybridge Bridge, he could perceive aspects of this woman's nature that transcended conventional observation. "The consultant from--"

"Prague." She moved to the autopsy table with fluid confidence, her own shadow falling wrong against the morgue's tile floor -- stretching and contracting independently of the overhead lighting. "It's happening again."

"What is?" Alice's question carried professional skepticism despite her recent exposure to forces beyond conventional understanding.

Lila traced symbols in the air above the body -- gestures precise and practiced, clearly meaningful though not immediately recognizable to either detective. Silver light flickered between her rings, responding to these movements in ways that suggested technological enhancement rather than mystical significance, though the distinction seemed increasingly arbitrary with each passing moment.

"Someone's trying to break the equations," she said softly, her accent reflecting Eastern European origins beneath years of international travel. "Someone who never learned that some doors should stay closed. Someone who refuses to accept that some debts can't be paid, regardless of what resources or sacrifices you're willing to commit."

"You know who's doing this," Chen said. Not a question but recognition of certainty in the consultant's demeanor.

"Yes." Lila's smile held grief and steel in equal measure, the expression of someone who had made peace with terrible knowledge while remaining determined to prevent its consequences. "He was my partner once. My love. My brilliant, ambitious Viktor. Until I chose differently."

She touched one of her silver rings to the corpse's forehead, the metal briefly flaring with that same strange light. Where the ring made contact, the victim's skin revealed patterns invisible to conventional examination -- symbols etched at a cellular level in configurations that suggested deliberate composition rather than random effect.

"The Department brought me in as a consultant because I've seen this before," Lila continued, her voice taking on the clinical precision of a specialist reporting findings. "These deaths appear natural to conventional medicine -- heart failure, stroke, sudden neurological collapse. But they're actually systematic extractions of specific life-energy patterns. Harvesting, if you will."

Outside the morgue windows, storm clouds gathered with unnatural speed, lightning flickering in patterns that seemed almost deliberate. In the harsh fluorescent light, shadows continued to dance like memory given substance, reaching toward the corpse with hungry anticipation.

"Harvesting for what purpose?" Ethan asked, the harmonics in his voice intensifying as his connection to the nexus entity provided context beyond what Lila had explicitly stated.

"To pay a debt," she replied, her eyes meeting his with recognition of his transformed nature. "Or rather, to attempt the impossible -- to break a contract with forces that don't recognize conventional notions of negotiation or mercy."

Alice studied the consultant's face, her detective's instincts cataloging micro-expressions and vocal patterns that suggested personal involvement beyond professional consultation. "This isn't just another case for you."

"No." Lila straightened, adjusting her silver rings with practiced precision. "This is my responsibility. Twenty-eight years ago, I helped open a door that should have remained closed. I've spent my life since then developing methods to contain what escaped. But Viktor... Viktor never accepted our failure. He's been searching for alternative approaches ever since."

"And now he's found one," Ethan observed, his perception extending beyond the morgue's physical boundaries to sense disturbances in the energetic patterns flowing throughout Daybridge. "Here, in our city."

"Yes." Lila's expression hardened with resolve. "Daybridge has always been a nexus point for certain energetic configurations. The bridge itself serves as a conduit between dimensional frameworks in ways that most cities lack. After what happened six months ago, when the dimensional boundaries were significantly altered throughout the city, the resonance patterns have become even more accessible to those with the knowledge to detect and manipulate them."

And somewhere in the city, ancient powers stirred, hungry for what was promised long ago in a stone chamber in Prague. Forces that recognized no authority except the binding agreements established through ritual and sacrifice, patterns of energy and intent that had waited patiently for decades while pieces moved into position for resolution of debts long deferred.

The echoes of Prague were growing louder, resonating through Daybridge's transformed reality with increasing urgency as Halloween approached -- the night when boundaries between worlds traditionally thinned, when what had been contained might fully manifest if the proper conditions were established.

As Lila Darkmagic completed her examination of the body, her silver rings gleaming under the morgue lights, Ethan and Alice exchanged glances that conveyed shared understanding. Their investigation had just expanded beyond conventional homicide into realms they had experienced six months earlier beneath Daybridge Bridge -- dimensional forces beyond human comprehension, ancient patterns of energy and awareness that existed alongside conventional reality like parallel tracks occasionally converging with catastrophic results.

The cosmic chess game that had seemingly concluded with the redirection of the Obsidian Protocol was revealing itself as merely the opening gambit in a more complex configuration. And as Halloween approached, the players were moving into position for the next phase

of a conflict that transcended individual lives or conventional understanding of reality itself.

ABOUT THE AUTHOR

Rae Stonehouse turned to fiction writing after establishing himself as a prolific author of self-development and professional growth books.

With over fifty published works helping readers navigate personal and professional challenges, he embarked on a new creative path with the Ethan Reeves Werewolf Detective Series.

When not weaving tales of supernatural sleuthing, Stonehouse continues to share his expertise in personal development through workshops and speaking engagements from his home in British Columbia.

The Ethan Reeves Series marks his debut in fiction writing, blending his understanding of human nature with a newfound passion for urban fantasy.

~